The Deepest Sin

The Deepest Sin

CAROLINE RICHARDS

BRAVA

KENSINGTON PUBLISHING CORP.
www.kensingtonbooks.com

BRAVA BOOKS are published by

Kensington Publishing Corp.
119 West 40th Street
New York, NY 10018

All Kensington titles, imprints and distributed lines are available at special quantity discounts for bulk purchases for sales promotion, premiums, fund-raising, educational or institutional use.

Special book excerpts or customized printings can also be created to fit specific needs. For details, write or phone the office of the Kensington Special Sales Manager: Kensington Publishing Corp., 119 West 40th Street, New York, NY 10018. Attn. Special Sales Department. Phone: 1-800-221-2647.

Brava and the B logo are Reg. U.S. Pat. & TM Off.

ISBN-13: 978-0-7582-4279-2
ISBN-10: 0-7582-4279-4

First Kensington Trade Paperback Printing: January 2012

10 9 8 7 6 5 4 3 2 1

Printed in the United States of America

Chapter 1

"Hold the lantern higher, if you will," Lady Meredith Woolcott commanded.

Murad complied, moving into the cooler shadows, his eyes narrowing with mounting disapproval. When he had first accepted the assignment from the British foreign office to accompany an Englishwoman around the sites of Cairo, he had anticipated the usual widow wreathed in black bombazine. Instead, and far worse where he was concerned, he'd been saddled with this tall red-haired female, her long legs encased in wide trousers, now clambering about the remains of an old Napoleonic fort in the village of Rashid. It was not seemly, he thought, even for an Englishwoman. Against his better instincts, he held the lantern higher.

Lady Woolcott murmured something under her breath, and Murad was certain it was ancient Greek words he'd heard. The woman squinted at what appeared to be faint inscriptions on the wall, heedless of the dust that hardly dulled the brightness of her hair. She had abandoned her serviceable bonnet hours earlier, tying it to the saddle of the horse she'd ridden alongside his from the port to Rashid, located a few miles from the sea in the western delta of the Nile.

Satisfied, she turned to face Murad directly. Her expression was unabashedly bold and his disapproval notched higher. "I do believe we established earlier that we share a common interest and educational background, Mr. Murad," she said in her low melodious voice, alluding to their initial meeting at the home of the British consulate in Cairo. "And so it should be of no surprise to you that these inscriptions, faint thought they are, appear in two languages, Greek and Egyptian." She paused. "But also in three scripts." Retreating from the tumble of rocks, she extracted a small notebook and pen from the pockets of her voluminous trousers.

Murad had indeed noticed.

Scribbling quickly, her full lips pursed, Lady Woolcott then snapped the notebook shut in one slender hand. She stepped away from the comparative coolness of the shadowed wall, seemingly impervious to the late-afternoon sun that blazed mercilessly in the rubble of the ruins of the former Napoleonic fort of St. Julien, abandoned fifty years ago when the French were chased out of Egypt by the British fleet. A few low walls, like jagged teeth, were all that remained. Tasting sand and guilt at the back of his throat, Murad wished that he could conclude his assignment and deposit Lady Woolcott back at her rooms at the Shepheard Hotel in Cairo. Long the haunt of foreign aristocrats, it was where she clearly belonged amid the opulent furnishings and private terraces.

As though divining his thoughts, Lady Woolcott leveled her gaze directly at his. "Mr. Murad," she said, tapping one dusty booted foot, and not looking in the least as though she was ready to return to Cairo or even the village, "are we certain that this is the old wall that was ordered demolished by French soldiers in order to extend the fort?"

"My Lady Woolcott," he said, with a faint bow of his head, "I'm certain you know that the claim is supported by the institute's Egyptian map, which indicates the fort was on the west bank of the Nile in the area of Rosetta—or Rashid, as we know it."

She nodded. "I am not doubting your qualifications, not at all. The consulate assured me of your credentials, Mr. Murad. I simply wished to see the site myself."

The Egyptian took a deep breath, the heaviness of his conscience lightening momentarily. "But of course. I am here to serve, my lady." It was hard for him to reconcile that this unusual creature was not only an expert horsewoman, having survived a four-hour trek in pitiless heat, but also fluent in several ancient languages. "As I advised earlier, there is not much here to see, rather a disappointment to you, I should imagine." He gripped the lantern more securely. "Nothing much remains other than these random inscriptions, barely visible, and indecipherable given their advanced age. And nothing that would link them directly to the Rosetta stone. There are other places to visit and slake your curiosity, Lady Woolcott. I'm certain you already know Napoleon brought two printing presses along with his expedition. The results of the discovery of the Rosetta stone were documented in a twenty-four-volume work, *Description de l'Egypte*, published between 1809 and 1828."

"Which resides in the British Museum at present."

"Indeed." First the French and then the British had ransacked his country. Lady Meredith Woolcott should have remained at home, he thought darkly. It was better that he did not know what she was seeking here in this abandoned fort, other than an escape from the ennui that seemed to afflict Western women of a certain age. That was a perception he could live with and from which he'd preferred not to deviate. He glanced over her shoulder to the horses waiting for them by the south entrance of the fort.

Lady Woolcott shaded her eyes against the sun, her ivory complexion having taken on a rosy hue. For at least the third time since meeting the Englishwoman, Murad speculated as to her years. She moved like a young girl and yet the fine lines around her eyes told a different story.

"We do know," she said, taking a look around the deserted site, which was no larger than an English cricket field, "that the circumstances of the stone's discovery are unclear. Some say it was found just lying on the ground."

"Yet others," Murad said smoothly in his perfect English, honed by a sojourn at Oxford, "claim that it was part of an old wall which was ordered demolished by French soldiers to extend the fort." The sky above them was a hard blue and the air preternaturally silent for late afternoon. They were alone amid the ruins and, although he carried a rifle, he felt the sudden urge to return to their mounts. Without glancing at his pocket watch, he knew it was time. "If you have seen enough, perhaps we can begin our return journey toward the village."

Detecting his unease, she stepped back into a shaft of sunlight, which glinted off the ebony fastenings of her linen riding jacket. "This area is quite deserted," she said to no one in particular. "Of interest only to very few, I should imagine."

Stubborn woman. The rendezvous time was fixed. And his honor was at stake. Murad cleared his throat to make the import of his words clear. "I should have preferred we take several guards with us when we left the barque." Not that the guards he'd intended to hire would have made a whit of difference. Regardless, Lady Woolcott had been adamant that they proceed alone, heedless of the dangers that resided in a country filled with antiquities, poverty and desperation.

Lady Woolcott lifted her chin. "I refuse to cower, Mr. Murad. I have had enough of hiding in my life." She did not elaborate further.

"Then if you have seen your fill," Murad repeated, ignoring her words and gesturing to the small copse of gnarled sycamore trees where their mounts waited.

Her wide mouth parted in a rueful smile and then she laughed, a curiously bitter sound. "I am a scholar, Mr. Murad, and for many years I was unable to fully indulge my pursuits. As my circumstances have changed, I am now free to travel at will, and I have taken the journey to see firsthand where this important stone was discovered. This journey is fundamental to the paper I am writing and will deliver several weeks hence at Burlington House in London. As you well understand, upon the stone's discovery, scholars immediately recognized that it contained the key to deciphering the ancient Egyptian language. As a result, interest in the Rosetta has not ceased in the ensuing fifty years."

"I understand completely, Lady Woolcott, but I apologize that there is nothing here that could possibly add to your scholarship," he said, gesturing to the wall with its faded inscriptions.

"Never fear," she said brightly. "Coming to Rashid is by far enough. And I've had weeks to sate myself on the cultural riches offered by your country, Mr. Murad, for which I thank you." She gestured to the lantern that swung by his side. "I believe we can dispense with the light at the moment. I have seen what I have come to see. Perhaps you are correct and it is time for us to return to the village."

Where he had secured them two rooms at the only lodgings available. He refused to think of the reality, that Lady Woolcott would never arrive at the humble inn. He felt another twinge of conscience. His honor was at stake. He had given his word. Whatever happened to Lady Woolcott was not his concern. Besides which, her learning, her athleticism and her confident regard were unsettling, an affront to the natural order, so different from the women of his country, who were kept from public view by impenetrable veils and high walls.

Lady Woolcott had already turned her back to him, balancing herself perfectly on a low wall before jumping, without his help, to the scrabbled path leading from the ruins.

She had a face and form that could haunt a man for years. As for Lord Richard Buckingham Archer, the Earl of Covington, it had only been two months since he'd been plagued by images of Lady Meredith Woolcott.

He was adept at staying in the shadows, his surveillance as invisible as the heavy air that had settled in like a suffocating mantle. He ignored the heat and kept his sights trained on the man and woman only twenty yards away. Her hair was unmistakable, despite its disciplined knot, a blaze of glory, and even from this distance, he remembered that singularly tempting mouth and the deep gray of her eyes, holding a cool disregard. For him.

He smiled inwardly, the sting of rejection a novel experience, the memory of her face a minor inconvenience. He never looked back, did not believe in introspection, never concerned himself with anything more than cold, hard contingencies, particularly if he found them reasonably diverting. He could kill a man, lie and cheat for all the right reasons, and turn his back on a personal fortune bequeathed to him by birth alone. An abbreviated encounter with Lady Woolcott should have been entirely forgettable. Except that it wasn't.

The jagged edge of a stone dug into the small of his back, reminding him of his reasons for following Lady Woolcott from England to Egypt. Yet watching her now, here in the sun-bleached outposts of a desert, had taken on the semblance of a dream. It was as though he had somehow conjured her from that stronghold in the north of England that she had called home to this parched piece of earth on the other side of the world.

She turned and said something to the man beside her, the column of her neck elegantly pale above the crisp linen of her riding jacket. Then she smiled and Archer swore he could hear her low laugh carry over the expanse of parched earth separating them. It reached inside him until he could hardly draw breath. He could not have wrenched his gaze away if he'd tried. Instead, he took a drink of tepid water from the silver flask in his hand.

The Arab by her side watched over her with a proprietary

air, stiff in the garb of an Englishman manqué, his hat set at an awkward angle. Lady Woolcott responded to him with none of the usual feminine affectations. Her movements were more familiar to Archer than they should be, the tilt of her head, the loose elegance of her limbs, a dangerous collision of subtle curves and taut litheness.

Archer studied the two figures and then she glanced across the rubble, her eyes meeting his for the briefest moment. But of course he knew that she only saw centuries-old rock and not the man who had come to hunt her down. He wanted to shut his eyes, resisting the urge to shift from behind the crumbling wall and move towards her. The voice of Sir Hubert Spencer rang in his ears.

"This shouldn't prove too difficult for you, Archer," he'd said a fortnight earlier, shoving a sheaf of documents across his desk with an ingratiating smile. "Although, truth be told, nothing ever is for you. Bloody irritating, that." The man sitting across from Spencer was the only son of an earl long dead and a wildly indifferent mother, and from his early dismissal from Eton due to his high spirits and blithe disregard for tradition to his years in the Royal Navy, he always seemed to have the wind at his back. Perhaps life had come too easily to the man, thought Spencer darkly, and at too low a price.

"Careful that I don't disappoint you one day."

"You've returned from the dead so many times, I shan't worry."

"Most kind of you," Archer said, crossing one booted foot over the other. "So what shall it be? Another last-minute rendezvous with one of your underworld brethren? Infiltration to the highest levels of the Admiralcy? Tempt me with something, Spencer. I am bored. And you know how much I dislike the condition."

"That's the cross you must bear," Spencer said dryly, "although I should have thought your last imbroglio involving the Rosetta stone and Lord Rushford would have sufficed for a while." Despite the declaration, Spencer knew otherwise.

"Seems like decades ago," Archer said, but without his usual good humor. He was thinking of Lord Rushford and Rowena Woolcott's wedding, which he'd attended in the immediate aftermath of the Rosetta stone debacle. The very idea of nuptials set his teeth on edge, but he'd put in an appearance in honor of his old friend. The two-day affair did not disappoint, made all the more intolerable by his introduction to Lady Meredith Woolcott, Rowena's guardian. Hellishly irksome woman. He much preferred the purely decorative sort when it came to female companionship, beauty without the thorns. The Countess Blenheim came readily to mind. Camille had been the perfect mistress these past two years.

Spencer lifted the corner of the dossier before dropping it again, intruding upon Archer's rambling thoughts. "This situation happens to concern Lord Rushford, peripherally." Rushford was on his wedding trip in Europe and would be joining Rowena's sister, Julia, and her husband, Lord Strathmore, in subsequent weeks. "More directly, it has to do with Lady Meredith Woolcott."

Archer's head shot up.

"I have your full attention, I can see. What a novelty! So I suppose I should make the most of the situation," Spencer said drolly. "Bluntly put, I am asking you to follow Lady Meredith Woolcott wherever she goes, to the ends of the earth if you must."

"And why would I wish to do that?" Archer asked.

"Because she *will* bring us to the Comte, Montagu Faron, if he is indeed still alive, as we suspect." The diplomat's smile broadened. "You have had a passing acquaintance with the lady, so we hear at Whitehall. Should pave the way somewhat."

Archer had indeed. The dimness of Spencer's Whitehall offices, the windows heavily draped to keep out prying eyes, and the dampness of autumnal London had a sobering effect. He needed a drink. A very large one. Instead, he settled more deeply into his chair, his interest in Lady Meredith Woolcott exerting a discomfiting draw that he had no desire to examine closely.

"By this time, I realize you know the details of her rather colorful past: the death of her father; the two girls she was left to raise at a young age," Spencer continued with a dismissive glance at the sheaf of papers on the desk. "Lady Meredith Woolcott also happens to be one of those troublesome bluestockings who dabbles in academics."

Troublesome didn't begin to describe the woman. "I shouldn't have thought her pastimes would be of particular interest to you," Archer said.

"They aren't. Except that they connect her to Faron," Spencer supplied smoothly, "the Frenchman who has been a thorn in our sides these past ten years." They both knew of the man, the scourge of the Continent and beyond, whose acolytes killed and lied on his behalf, single-mindedly intent upon the collection of ancient relics, scientific spoils and new lands. Much to Whitehall's vexation. "The last insult was Faron's attempt to steal the Rosetta stone from the British Museum, as you well know, an attempt just barely foiled. Thanks to you and Rushford."

"You're not convinced he's dead. Is that the crux of the matter?" Archer stared moodily over Spencer's head to the portrait of Queen Victoria in its gilt frame.

"I prefer to have hard evidence, this time," Spencer said, alluding to Faron's uncanny ability to escape death, once by fire and now, possibly, by drowning. "It is rumored," he continued, "that Woolcott and Faron were lovers."

Archer looked away from the portrait and swallowed hard, dismayed at the blood hammering in his ears. *Lovers.* That single word reverberated through his body, echoing like a stone dropped into a dark hole.

"Yes, lovers," Spencer repeated absently. "And the affaire did not end well. Likely the cause of the continued enmity between the two of them, as well as the reason for the Frenchman's designs on Lady Woolcott's wards—"

Archer interrupted. "Both of whom are now safe."

"Or so it seems," said Spencer. "In any case, Lady Woolcott feels she is no longer in danger, freed from the cloud that had her confined to that heap in the north of England with her two charges for so many years. Now she will indulge in her unorthodox interests, which, we're told, will involve travel to support her rather bizarre intellectual interests." He added ominously, "Who knows what may transpire? If he's still alive, Faron will wish nothing more than to see her gone."

Archer glanced briefly at the dossier lying between them, its pages containing the story, however incomplete, of Lady Woolcott and her youthful indiscretion with one of the Continent's most dangerous men. Whom they all hoped was dead.

However, past experience demonstrated that Spencer was nothing if not a practical man. "It is not her continued well-being that concerns us, Archer. Let me make that plain." He was not sending in a knight errant to protect a woman in distress. "Faron is obsessed with Lady Woolcott, a situation which presents us with an opportunity I should not like to miss. We would like nothing more than to flush the Frenchman out. If he is still alive."

"He's dead," Archer said flatly. "Lord Rushford made sure of it and witnessed his drowning in the Channel off the coast of France."

Spencer arched his brows. "So your old friend and colleague maintains. However, no one need tell you of Rushford's uneven history and divided loyalties."

Archer said softly, "I would suggest that you not cast aspersion on Lord Rushford, who has served the Crown admirably for most of his life. And certainly more consistently than I have. If you do not agree"—he flicked a glance at the dossier on the desk—"I shall like nothing more than to take my leave."

The mastermind who had catapulted his way to the upper echelons of Whitehall with little more than razor intellect to recommend him wisely changed tactics. "Let's set aside the subject of Rushford for the moment, then," Spencer said, all too aware that Archer would leave him in the dust if the mood struck him. As an agent to the Crown, the man sitting across from him was highly effective, if entirely uncontrollable. A ridiculously large fortune, coupled with peripatetic leanings, allowed Archer any number of options. He'd been known to disappear for months sailing into uncharted waters in his sloop, *The Brigand*. As well as appearing out of thin air to rescue agents of the Crown, including his friend Rushford, from the tightest of spots. His was a daredevil's temperament that had been effectively, if inconsistently, leveraged on Whitehall's behalf.

"Also be aware of Giles Lowther, whom we suspect is still lurking about." Faron's shadow was known to execute his master's wishes to the letter and to a fault. "He's gone to ground since the Frenchman's alleged death."

"Strange. An Englishman in league with a French peer."

"Nothing more than a guttersnipe and petty thief, we're told, saved from the gallows by Faron himself. And eternally grateful as a result."

"A dangerous combination, unthinking loyalty."

"Indeed. He was behind most of Faron's maniacal assignments, the Rosetta stone only one of many."

"All very interesting, Spencer, but I don't recall agreeing to take this on."

"We are simply asking you to keep Lady Woolcott well within your sights."

Archer asked abruptly, "Why me?"

Spencer shrugged. "You met at her ward's marriage to Rushford. So it would not appear suspicious to her or anyone else if you were to seek her company from time to time in the more exotic climes you seem to favor."

"To what end?" he asked abruptly, chiding himself for asking when the answer was obvious.

"No need to be disingenuous, Archer." Spencer folded his hands on the top of the highly polished desk. "We use Lady Woolcott as the draw. To get to Faron, if he still lives."

"Even if he gets to Lady Woolcott first," Archer said, suddenly uncomfortable. He rose from the chair.

Spencer's smile was serene. "Precisely."

Now in the cooling heat of the desert air, Archer watched the retreating figure of Lady Woolcott, her long strides outstripping the pace of her Arab guide. He stared hard, taking in her bright hair and supple figure before he glanced down, realizing that he was still holding the silver flask. He tossed back more of the water, the taste metallic.

Despite his height and muscled breadth, he had learned to move silently as a shadow. He edged out from behind the low wall to follow the two figures approaching the mounts waiting for them under the sycamore trees to the south of the fortress. Lady Woolcott untied a bonnet from her saddle, along with a leather flagon. Filling a cupped hand with water, she offered both horses a drink, her movements graceful and assured.

Once again he found it difficult to drag his eyes away. *He was getting too old for this.* A sudden rush of air announced the flight of a dark raven and broke his focus. The glistening black wings streaked against the sky, but Archer was already searching the horizon, every instinct on the alert. He took the pistol from his belt, the barrel glinting as the sun caught it and danced along its polished surface.

The Egyptian guide swung up on his mount just as Archer heard the clattering of hooves pounding in the dust.

* * *

Meredith stared wide-eyed at the three robed men looking down at her from horseback. Hawks looking for carrion. Her breath caught in her throat, her lips trying to form Murad's name. But her guide had disappeared, along with his horse, in a cloud of dust. One of the men urged his mount forward, close enough that she could see the curve of a pistol gripped in his right hand. As long as she held his gaze, he wouldn't shoot, she thought illogically. He was savoring the moment, looking down upon her.

The afternoon sun threw a strange light over the trio, casting shadows in odd places, making it impossible to see beyond the slits in the fabric over their heads that revealed obsidian eyes and little else. The customary fear that had been her companion for too long seized her chest like an old familiar. Despite the dry heat, she felt suddenly damp inside her clothes, the voluminous fabric of her trousers clinging to her legs, a trickle of sweat meandering down the length of her spine.

The man with the pistol barked a word in Arabic that she couldn't understand, intended for the men at his side. Meredith thought she detected a smile beneath the fabric that obscured his lips and chin. "You are not afraid?" His voice was heavy with sarcasm as his tongue wrapped around the English words.

"Afraid?" Meredith felt the warmth of her mount at her back, giving her false courage.

He didn't respond except to indicate with the pistol that she should move. When she failed to comply, she watched as one of the men maneuvered behind her, tethering her horse to his own saddle.

Even if she managed to escape, where could she go on foot? Meredith felt the fear in her chest harden as she willed the world around her to return to normal. But what was normal? The few months that had seemed to her a liberation already felt like a dream. She lifted her head higher, willing that world to continue. Her hands clenched at her sides and her breath clawed at her throat. Where was Murad? He'd been right beside her . . . but here she was now alone. Her heart hardened.

"You clearly have the wrong woman, sir. But if it is money you wish—" She gestured to the horse's saddle with an arm that already felt like someone else's.

He shook his head and motioned again with the pistol, urging his horse closer, a dull anger radiating from him like a banked fire.

Meredith placed one hand on her waist, as though to steady herself. It was not impossible to reach into her trousers, down in the pocket that rode against her hip. Her own pistol waited there, loaded, ready to use. She was not a novice, her aim practiced from skeet shooting on the grounds of Montfort under Mclean's watchful eye. "If you would give me a moment, I may actually have some sterling at hand."

He slid from his horse and closed the space between them with one stride, lowering his pistol as he took hold of her arm with his free hand. The men behind him moved their mounts closer until they surrounded her, all but blocking out the late-afternoon sunlight, the heavy air redolent of sweat and exotic oils.

"If it's not money that you want—" she tried again. His grip tightened, fingers digging into her, pressing down on the bone. She held her breath, refusing to wince.

He shook his head. "No, madam. It is not money that we want."

Meredith went cold. This was not happenstance, that they had come upon a lone woman in an abandoned fort, deserted by her guide. She did not believe in coincidence, never had. These three men surrounded her with intent. Montagu Faron. The name pulsed in time with her heart. Why did everything in her life coil back to that man who was now dead, carried away by the Channel's currents months ago?

"See here," she said, her voice deliberately low. Immediately, he dropped her arm and pushed against her, hard enough to send her to the ground. Her head cracked against an unforgiving knot of rock, her vision blurring and then swimming as the sunlight danced overhead. She was in a sprawl on her back, her hair tumbling around her shoulders.

Her face was hot, inflamed beyond the heat of the day. Digging her nails into the sand, she tried to ignore the coppery taste of blood filling her mouth. Struggling to rise, she slid her hand under her leg and close to the pocket of her trousers. Her assailant bent over her again, the cotton of his robes fluttering before her vision. Meredith scuttled backwards like a crab, lashing out with one foot, missing her target entirely. The man seized her ankle, his hard fingers like manacles against her skin and bone.

Her head hit the stone again. Her vision melted away just as her ankle was released and she heard the staccato shots of gunfire.

Chapter 2

Meredith Woolcott lay still on the ground, enveloped by a screen of dust left in the wake of horses' hooves. Two of the assailants galloped away from the fort and Archer wagered he'd clipped at least one of them. He could have killed both, but that was not his intent, despite the fact he hated loose ends unless they could be tied up in an eventual knot. The men were more useful to him alive, and he would get to them eventually, he thought idly.

He did not feel particularly generous toward the bastard releasing his hold on Meredith Woolcott's slender ankle. In a blur of movement, Archer grabbed the man from behind, neatly wrenching the pistol from his grasp before hurling him to the other side of the sycamores, where he landed with a grunt followed by silence.

Her face streaked with sand, Meredith was shaken but alive. Fury combined with fear etched her features as she tried to stand, swaying on her feet. Archer made a move towards her, but she held up a palm to stop him. Her eyes flashed with recognition and then widened, her gaze swinging from his toward the copse of trees. "He has another one . . . a pistol. . . ." she said on a ragged breath, pointing towards the tree where her assailant lay tangled in his robes with a weapon still clenched in his hand, his arm raised.

Archer shook his head, anger flushing through him, blood

rushing past his ears. He flexed his hands, imagining them around the other man's neck. This rage was unusual for him, he thought somewhere in the back of his mind, as though witnessing the scene from a distance. He watched as the man's arm straightened, the gun steadied. His own arm followed suit, his unerring aim fixed on the target lying beneath the sycamores, coiled like a snake ready to strike.

The crack of a shot broke the silence. The man crumpled without a sound, simply folding in upon himself, the loose fabric of his robes fluttering out, settling around him like a shroud. Archer turned to Meredith, who stood stiffly in the heat, a smoking pistol in her hand and her gray eyes blazing.

"You may put away your weapon now, Lord Archer," she said in that low voice that he could not have forgotten if he'd tried. She was breathing hard but there was little else to indicate her distress. Taking a last look in the direction of the sycamores, she bent over to straighten a fallen stocking, then bundled the tumble of her hair back into its knot, all with the pistol still gripped in her hand. Unorthodox though it was, Archer had never seen a more feminine sight. Her masculine garb was unable to disguise the swell of her breasts and gentle flare of her hips, the slender ankles just below the hems of her trousers.

Her eyes met his and despite the recent events, she didn't appear pleased to see him. "Don't look at me like that, my lord," she said, tense as a feral cat, her animosity towards him seemingly unabated. "I have never killed a man before, but I refuse to dissolve into a heap now that the deed is done."

Archer inclined his head, ever so slightly. "Lady Woolcott. I wish the circumstances were different."

"Hardly," she said, "or we'd both be lying dead."

Archer smothered a grin. Lady Woolcott glanced briefly toward the ruins, her expression guarded. "Why are you here?" she asked, suspicion in her voice. "I shouldn't think that moldering ruins would hold any interest for you."

"In turn, I shouldn't think you know enough about me to judge, Lady Woolcott. Besides which, you are pale and we should return to the fort, where we may renew our acquaintance, rather than standing here . . ." He closed the distance between them, taking her by the elbow, his eyes on the horizon, which seemed to stretch towards infinity.

"Out in the open, you mean," she finished with her usual directness. Given their proximity Archer did his best to keep his gaze from locking on her mouth. He hadn't forgotten that she was so tall he would have to do no more than bend his head to kiss her, the plumpness of that full lower lip of hers beckoning him, even in the heightened circumstances in which they found themselves.

She didn't move away, but looked pointedly at his waist. "If it isn't too much to ask, I am positively parched. . . ."

Archer kept his expression neutral as he handed her the flask. Outrageous was what she was. She'd been attacked, had killed a man and now found herself alone with a near stranger in a colonial outpost. Yet she stood next to him with the assurance of a seasoned general. She tucked the pistol into her trousers before taking the flask. Her fingers brushed his, and his body tightened with anticipation, the heavy air around them thickening in the heat.

"I expect you will explain what you are doing here," she said, taking a drink. It was a demand, not a question.

"There's not much to explain," he said shortly, releasing her elbow, making a bid to mask both his annoyance and attraction. He shifted his weight to his other leg, ruthlessly ignoring the way her presence pulled at him. It was positively risible that he found himself aroused in the presence of this woman.

"Indeed," she acknowledged while taking another drink with her eyes closed. She wiped her mouth with the back of her hand, a small smile, relief perhaps, flickering across her lips. Most women of her class and background were studies in comportment, stiff and rigid or deliberately louche, every

movement designed to attract and ensnare. Meredith Woolcott was something else altogether, although Archer couldn't
decide what at the moment.

She turned and walked away from him, taking first small
steps and then longer strides, testing her resilience. Glancing
at the still body beneath the sycamores, she took another short
drink from the silver flask, then strolled back to Archer, her
shoulders straightening beneath her riding jacket. Light and
shadow played across her skin, the clean line of her collarbones and the hollow of the throat.

Archer made a mental review of all the women he'd
known over the years. He was nearing his fourth decade, yet
it had been all he could do not to make a fool of himself since
he'd first met Lady Woolcott at Montfort. He'd expected a
woman of a certain age, if not precisely a dowager, but not
this amazon, with her long legs and hair lit by fire and a gaze
that refused to look away. He'd tried to charm her at the
wedding, at least in the manner he was accustomed to using
with women, but it obviously had not worked. Flattery had
utterly failed to win her. He'd tried on numerous occasions,
in the small medieval chapel, in the banquet hall, in the library with its roaring hearth, to inveigle her in conversation.
And all to no avail. He remembered the wedding supper, an
ocean of silver and china separating them, his wineglass emp-
tying and refilling as if by magic while he tasted not one
drop. He had heard her laugh, low and throaty, drawing the
entire table's attention to her. Her dress had been plain and
unadorned gray velvet with long, tight sleeves, not designed
to call attention, unlike the woman herself. He'd narrowed
his eyes, glancing quickly down the gleaming expanse before
forcing his attention back to his dinner. And she hadn't come
near him, hadn't so much as looked his way that he could
tell. As they had passed in the long corridor to the salon for
after-dinner drinks, her eyes had met his only once and raked
him with cool disregard. He would have preferred annoyance.

Her head high, she had passed him with Julia and Rowena on each arm, her glow incandescent as she bent toward her young wards, in whom she had invested everything she had. She had nearly lost them to Faron and then won them back in a twist of fate. Archer had learned from Rushford and Rowena that the specter of loss had taken almost everything from her.

But it had also brought her here, to the desert, which now began to pulse with the oncoming darkness, the sky purpling like a bruise. Meredith pushed back the hair from her forehead, arching her neck, easing the tension from her muscles. There were far more beautiful women, Archer reminded himself, surveying the boldness of her features, the mouth that was too wide and the cheekbones too sharp, the body a juxtaposition of angles and curves. He took a breath of the rapidly cooling air, then let it out slowly, his gaze roaming over her. No, not a classic society beauty, but striking in the manner of a Greek goddess, elegant and strong, with an allure just as dangerous.

The woman made his brain misfire. All he could think of was how it would be to kiss her. To drag her back to the fortress and take her up against a wall, to engender a response to his own desire and watch it catch fire in those cool gray eyes of hers. She was, after all, hardly the spinster she played at, he thought uncharitably. *Faron's former lover.*

She took another long draught from the flask, swallowing slowly. She sighed and bit her lower lip, thinking, collecting herself. Her eyes were shadowed, almost vacant.

Breaking the silence, he said, "It's getting cooler quickly. As happens in the desert when the sun goes down."

She looked up and smiled, not so much at him but at something else, somewhere in the far distance. That curve of her lips was not for him, although it had ensnared him months ago, at Montfort, when she'd bestowed it so brilliantly upon Rowena and Rushford, paired as man and wife at the simple chapel altar. The smile was a rarity and he knew then that he would have done anything to see it again.

Her smile faded when she looked at him. "It's a welcome relief, actually, from the heat. I suppose we have no choice but to return to the fort for the night. There's no chance of our getting back to the village before nightfall." It was as though ice water ran through her veins. No vapors, no remorse, when a corpse lay cooling a few yards away from them.

"Where did you learn to manage a pistol like that?" She was a better shot than any woman had a right to be.

She raised her eyebrows. "I did what I had to do. I didn't think that a fine aim was confined to the male sex. You see, Lord Archer, I wasn't confident that you'd be quick enough."

That arrogance coming from a man would have been enough to get him killed. But Archer couldn't help being amused. There was something about the way she held herself, her low voice, the fierce intelligence that burned behind the cool gray of her eyes. She was like no other woman, unique, aloof, a splinter under the skin.

To underscore her words, she rested the pistol carefully in her hand, sure and easy, as comfortable with the weapon as most women were with a needle and thread. She blinked several times, obviously irritated by his question. "Do not expect an apology or demurrals from me. And to answer your question, I have learned to look after myself over the years. I am familiar with the sound of a pistol hammer released in the dead of night, I can tell you, and it is as reassuring as an army at my back. You may put your piece away for the time being, Lord Archer. I think the party has fled for the evening. Along with my guide, Murad," she added dryly.

"His disappearance was nothing short of miraculous. I don't think we can expect either Murad or the remaining pair back again tonight," he said, deftly sliding his pistol into his belt. "I'm an optimist, but hate to be proven wrong so let's seek shelter at the fort." Her hand came up to brush away a few remaining grains of sand on her face when his arm snagged her waist, taking her roving hand in his. "Now."

She glanced up, looking uncomfortable at his touch. "This is entirely unnecessary," she said, "and highly unsuitable, bundling me off like no more than a sack of coal. The danger, if you haven't already noticed, has long passed."

"Don't be too sure." Suddenly more impatient than he'd ever been, he strong-armed her along the rubble-strewn path leading back to the low walls of the fort, half carrying her. An unfamiliar anger built within him with every step, directed at Spencer, at Meredith and, worse still, at himself.

"We should do something about the body. . . ." she said, trying to pull away. "Lord Archer!" She planted her heels, dragging to a stop. "Please slow down."

"Never mind the body. I shall deal with it once I have you out of sight." He jerked her into motion again, using his size to force her along. "We are not slowing down and if you struggle, I shall be compelled to throw you over my shoulder."

"Don't be ridiculous," she muttered, allowing him to drag her towards the far side of the fort and behind a low wall. He placed her behind him with a firm push, smiling slightly when she yanked her arm from his grasp and stood rubbing it, watching him with her familiar arrogance.

"Please sit," he said, gesturing to the ground. "We have a long evening ahead of us." In the corner he had secreted a small bag of supplies.

Her chin shot up and her brows pinched together in displeasure. "During which you will no doubt tell me why you have been shadowing my footsteps, Lord Archer."

Archer looked her up and down. Tiny bits of sand still clung to her, littering the linen of her jacket. A few specks of blood appeared on her cheek and he fought the urge to wipe them away. Instead, he surveyed their small enclosure, gaze roving around what had once been a storeroom at the fort.

Surveying the desert sky overhead turning an inky blue, he removed the pistol from his waistband once again.

"Sit," he said. This time, she dropped to the ground, hugging her knees, suddenly like a young girl, and Archer fought the urge to pull her into his arms. "I will return shortly. Don't move." It would help if she looked even a little bit grateful, but she didn't; her lips were set in a firm line. He retraced his steps quickly, intending to bring the corpse in from the night and away from the desert's animal marauders.

His movements were efficient, hauling the body into a low dugout at the entrance of the fort. Pocketing the man's pistol, he checked briefly for additional weapons which he hoped would not prove useful in the coming hours. A pouch at the man's waist divulged several heavy coins and a cylindrical object wrapped in red silk. He shook his head with increasing incomprehension, as the soft folds of fabric revealed a child's kaleidoscope made from copper and inlaid with mother-of-pearl. Its fine markings of cherubs and angels were indisputably English, and about the last object in the world he'd expected to find on the corpse of a dead Egyptian. He ran a thumb over the detailed engravings and then held it up to one eye. A spill of changing patterns formed by colored glass pieces tumbled and fell as he turned the scope, clearly intended for the delight of a child.

Archer returned to Meredith a short time later. He needed a drink, and not water. Judging by Meredith's pallor, they both did. She did not stir from her place on the ground, watching as he reached for the leather bag of supplies and extracted another flask, this one filled with spirits.

Meredith glanced at him and silently accepted the flask held out to her. "Brandy," he said.

"I would prefer whisky." Montfort was close to the Scottish border, after all.

"That's unfortunate. This will have to do."

Without a word, she tipped back the flask, exposing the paleness of her slender neck to his gaze. She let her breath out slowly as the liquid worked its way through her, warming her from the inside out. She put one hand up to her forehead, running her fingers over her brow as if to order her thoughts.

"Did you recognize the men who were trying to assault you?" he asked, still aware of the incongruity of the child's kaleidoscope now secreted away in his satchel.

"Strange question coming from you," she replied.

"Really?" The one word came out in a growl.

"You know damn well what I mean. Let's first get to the question of your fortuitous appearance here this afternoon." She settled back against the wall, and took another drink with a hand that shook.

"I find myself with a growing interest in antiquities," he said with a straight face.

"You will have to do better, Lord Archer."

"All right then, I have always wanted to return to Egypt."

"You're a little long in the tooth for the grand tour."

Archer winced dramatically.

"When you appeared at Rowena's wedding, as Rushford's friend, I knew . . . I could tell . . ." she said frowning and then trailing off. She handed him the flask, her hand now steady.

"Tell what?"

"I prefer not to dissemble, Lord Archer," she said, fore-arms resting over her bent knees. "You appeared to me as nothing more than an adventurer, a bounder, someone who chooses to involve himself in one fiasco after another, as an amusement, like a child picking up one toy before discarding it for the next. Clearly, a man of your wealth and disinclina-tion to devote himself to his estates or Parliament finds him-self battling boredom to an unconscionable degree."

Archer sat down in the dust beside her. His gaze locked on hers as the two of them stared each other down. "Quite the character assassination on such short notice. I spent all of a day and a half with you and your wards, Julia and Rowena, at Montfort. Hardly enough time for you to come to such an astonishing conclusion. I should feel offended," he added mockingly.

Meredith let out a breath. "Don't bother. Why should my regard mean anything to you? We are but acquaintances, ships passing in the night, to use a trite phrase," she said, making it doubly clear what she thought of their association. "And I already gave you my thanks at the wedding. Both Rowena and Rushford told me of your intervention on their behalf," she said. Her voice took on an edge of formality.

He knew his old friend Rushford had told Lady Woolcott very little regarding his involvement with Whitehall and would divulge even less about Archer's own past. Lady Woolcott would have learned that he was the only living son of an illustrious family whose fortunes he largely ignored, preferring to waste his time on escapades of capriciousness and daring endeavors, including a tour in the Royal Navy, which took him away from England for months at a time. And when he did deign to make an appearance, he was known for his ability at cards, his love of sailing and his discretion in his choice of lovers.

"I do recall, vaguely," he drawled. "Your words of thanks positively warmed my heart."

"You see. This is precisely what I mean. You take nothing seriously, making a mockery of the dangerous situation in which my Rowena found herself. As a man bereft of family, I shouldn't expect much else."

"I take it you prefer men of a more serious, sober character."

"My preferences in that regard are moot, Lord Archer."

He watched Meredith speculatively, neatly categorizing all the surface details of her life. Eighteen years earlier, she had escaped France, more precisely, escaped Faron, taking two little girls with her and protecting them from the threat that had overshadowed the rest of their lives. They had been kept all but under lock and key, for reasons Meredith had chosen to keep to herself.

The silence between them lengthened. He tipped his head back to take in the night sky; the constellations were as thick as a forest of lights. A thin moonlight illuminated the fortress, limning them in a ghostly light. "Very well then. I shall attempt to keep to a sober mien and subject matter, although, I suppose you do not wish to speak of it—of sober matters," he said. "I mean of the men this afternoon. And who may have sent them."

"There is no need." She paused.

"I believe there is."

"*He is dead.*" The words had the ring of finality. She glared at him, her eyes a cloudy gray, willing the wish a reality.

Faron's unspoken name wavered between them like a noose. She had been his lover, once. It was an image that Archer could not banish, and it settled firmly in the forefront of his mind. He acknowledged that he had trouble thinking around her, his responses suddenly a foreign country to him. He had never experienced even a frisson of jealousy in his life and now he'd rather put hot pokers in his eyes than imagine Meredith Woolcott with Montagu Faron.

There was something seriously wrong. His first lover flashed in his mind, the young widow from Kent. That was the first and last time he had struggled with want, with need. In the intervening years, he had learned to control desire with the finesse of a master, long having played its strings. He studied Meredith's pure profile, the slender nose, the sharp cheekbones above the wide mouth. Touching her, he knew from experience, was inevitable, sensing that she would not turn away with false innocence. She stared at him for a moment, flushing under his intense regard, and he knew exactly what she would look like after making love. The image of her, warm and tousled, made his mind go blank. The desert night faded away beneath a vision of flesh damp with exertion and desire fulfilled.

Determined to break the mood, he reached for the leather bag. "Are you hungry?"

She shook her head. "No, thank you."

"Then perhaps you should sleep." Archer didn't need to add that he would play the sentinel.

"Impossible. I'm as tightly wound as piano wire at present." She had killed a man but looked little the worse for it.

"I'm not surprised. All the more reason you may wish to talk about it. The men who tried to attack you this afternoon. A mere coincidence, you believe?"

"Murad may have taken a bribe. And led them here."

"That's one possibility."

She leaned her chin on her forearms, staring into the night, not answering him directly. "While we are discussing coincidences, Lord Archer, what of your presence here? You have yet to answer my question," she said. "A mere coincidence?"

What could he tell her? She would not be readily mollified, despite the fact that he'd rehearsed for such an eventuality. The woman was formidably intelligent, the daughter of one of England's estimable scholars and a scholar in her own right. "I will be honest with you," he lied evenly. "Lord Rushford, knowing my penchant for travel, asked that I keep watch over you, as a favor. He assumed that you would protest if you knew in advance."

She looked at him doubtfully.

He continued regardless. "He asked that I accompany you, as a guide, if you will, on your travels. I haven't been to Egypt in some time. . . ."

"Without informing me? For protection?" Her lips thinned. "I have been looking after myself and my wards for many years now. I do not require protection, no matter how well intentioned."

"A woman traveling on her own is unusual and some might say she invites trouble."

Raising her head from her arms, she sniffed in an unladylike fashion. "Oh, please, Lord Archer. You as a chaperone? You will have to do better or not try at all. This is clearly not the kind of adventure you habitually seek, hiding out in a dusty corner of Egypt with nothing more than a flask of brandy and a spinster in your sights. Hardly up to your usual standards."

"Of which you know plenty, given your earlier assessment, or shall I say assassination, of my character." Mockery laced his tone. "Besides which, I advised Rushford that I could hardly apprise you of these plans after your rather chilly reception at Montfort. I had my doubts that you would accept my offer to accompany you on your travels. You seemed to develop an aversion to my presence."

"A response you are not accustomed to from the fairer sex, I take it."

He smiled broadly. "I never thought of it that way, Lady Woolcott." The waning moonlight stroked the dark red of her hair, engraving her lashes shades darker than her hair. He tried to convince himself that she was not the most beautiful woman he'd ever seen. It was an objective assessment, for he had seen a great many beauties in the world, and in close quarters.

"I'm sure you haven't." Her voice was brittle, dismissive. Uncoiling from her position, she stretched her legs out in front of her, the fabric of her trousers tracing the contours of her long legs. She would be beautiful naked, he decided, glancing at the defined muscles, so unlike the rounded lushness of most women of leisure.

"Choose not to believe me, then," he said with practiced ease. "You may send a telegram to Lord Rushford, if you seek proof. He will tell you that I only have your best interests at heart." Crossing one booted foot over the other, he added, "I was going to introduce myself at Shepheard's earlier this week, as a matter of fact, as I had seen you in the breakfast room, but you were a veritable flurry of activity and I didn't wish to interrupt your endeavors. You were clearly intent upon visiting every museum, curio shop and ruin within miles of Cairo."

She raised her eyebrows. "Why did you wait to make your presence known, Lord Archer? I find myself awaiting your answer with interest. The fact is that you followed me here to Rashid, clandestinely, waiting for precisely what I don't know before you felt compelled to make your presence known."

"And a good thing I did."

"Don't fancy yourself a hero, Archer. I acquitted myself ably without your intervention."

It would have been churlish of him to remind her otherwise. "My apologies then," he amended. "I should have made my presence known earlier. It was inexcusable of me."

She was addressing him coolly, clearly not eager to let go of formalities, determined to make this far harder than he'd imagined or hoped. He'd rather she railed at him. Accused him. Cursed him. Anger would give him a way in.

He thought for a moment before saying, "Lord Rushford told me of your upcoming paper to be delivered at Burlington House next month. Quite an accomplishment. Few women, or men for that matter, have the opportunity to address such an august organization. Of course, I am not a member."

Her eyes lost some of their wariness. "Thank you. It is indeed quite an honor to have been invited to give a lecture to the Society. That is one reason I chose to visit Egypt to do additional research and finalize my investigations." In the pale light, her face took on a faint glow, as she warmed to her subject.

"The title of your paper, if I might be so bold to inquire?" he asked, playing along. "It has to do with the Rosetta stone, if I'm not mistaken." It was already proven that the usual flattery would not go far with this woman. Good thing, because he hadn't a sliver of a sonnet in his repertoire.

She eyed him with suspicion. "You hardly seem the type, Archer."

"The type?"

"The scholarly type."

He placed a hand over his chest. "My dear Lady Woolcott, you wound me to the quick. My Latin and Greek tutors at Eton still sing my praises these years later."

She smiled and the effect was cataclysmic. Archer felt a tightening in his groin, wondering how he would survive the night. Sunrise was a scant five hours away, he lied to himself.

"Rushford and Rowena did warn me about your irreverence, among other things," she said, shaking her head, trying to look disapproving. "All the more reason why you don't want to hear me go on about ancient tablets carved in the Ptolemaic era."

"I shall impress you with my surprising erudition, then," he said, feigning affront, ready to squander half his fortune to see another radiant smile from Meredith Woolcott. "Where best to begin?"

"You are playing with me, Lord Archer. I know very well that you helped Rushford save the tablets from being stolen from the British Museum."

"Ahh, but you see, I know much more." He waggled his brows impressively. "I know that half a century ago Napoleon's scientists and scholars first discovered the stone on this very spot. Which brings you here today, does it not?"

"It does indeed. I needed to see the area where the stone was discovered, to ascertain for myself whether any other remnants remained. Not that I expected to uncover anything of importance," she continued. "I'm well aware that both the French and the British, not to mention numerous scholars and archeologists, have since scoured the area."

"But your investigations here give your paper a certain weight, I suspect."

"That's quite perceptive of you, Lord Archer."

"For a philistine, you mean."

She laughed outright then, the sound uninhibited and free in the night air. "I don't think you are entirely indifferent to matters of intellect, sir. Although I must confess, I think you are more comfortable on your horse or *The Brigand* than in the hushed confines of a library." Rushford and Rowena had, of course, told her of their journey on his yacht, *The Brigand*, and perhaps of his penchant for sailing. And his inability to stay in one place for more than a month.

He bowed his head mockingly. "Thank you for that small crumb at least." He reached for the leather bag and extracted a thin wool blanket. Without asking permission, he tossed it over her legs. "It gets cold in the desert at night."

Her hands stopped in midair, ready to intercept the blanket. "But what about you? Here, it's big enough that we may share it. If you will come closer . . ."

The invitation was all crisp efficiency and Archer swore silently, aware that she was not in the least discomfited by their proximity and that he was. The knowledge rankled.

"Let's not stand on ceremony." She had moved closer to him and her hands briskly made short work of distributing the blanket across both their legs.

Archer cleared his throat. "Entirely unnecessary, Lady Woolcott."

"Nonsense. I insist."

"You were telling me about the stone and the implications of its inscriptions," he pressed on. Anything to take his attention away from the slender length of her, the warmth burning beneath the blanket they now shared.

"You've seen it at the British Museum, of course."

"I believe I was dragged there at some time by a tutor," he said, suddenly inclined to let his mind wander back to the sour Mr. Athrop and his Latin declensions.

Meredith rested her hands on the top of the blanket. "You were a challenge, I don't doubt, and kept your tutors busy."

"And you were quite the opposite, I take it."

"My father was a scholar of ancient languages and it was he who first told me about the Rosetta stone. He in turn had studied philology at Cambridge and subsequently with the orientalist Jean-François Champollion, who was credited as the principal translator of the hieroglyphs."

"Fascinating," he said.

"I trust I'm not boring you," she said, challenge in her voice.

"Not at all. And what did Champollion ultimately discover? I can't recall what my tutor had to say regarding the matter."

"You were clearly not paying attention to your lessons, Archer."

"I was not the most tractable pupil."

"I can well imagine. The attention span of a flea, no doubt."

"Give me a moment," he said, putting his hands behind his head and looking up into the night sky, away from her. "Something about a tax amnesty, if I recall correctly."

"Very good," she said. "The text comprises twenty paragraphs and speaks of a tax amnesty given to the temple priests of the day, restoring the tax privileges that they had traditionally enjoyed in more ancient times." She paused. "But more importantly, the translation served as the template that allowed us to see into the minds and the culture of the ancients. Once we knew their languages, a whole world was opened to us."

For better or for worse, he wanted to say. "And your paper?"

She gave him only her profile before she continued. "Hieroglyphics remained a mystery for hundreds of years, even though many people tried to translate the language. In my paper I should like to elucidate Champollion's process, taking a closer look at the three sections of the stone with writing upon it. It is essentially one message written in three languages, hieroglyphics first, then Demotic and then Greek."

"One thing I do recall in the recesses of my memory is that

after the Roman Empire expanded into Egypt, the hiero-glyphic language was abandoned completely in favor of Greek and Latin."

Meredith looked impressed. "Sadly, yes."

"Very interesting, Lady Woolcott."

She turned to face him, her eyebrows arching. "I am too old to be mocked."

"Mocking you? Surely not," he said, angling his body toward her. "But you are hardly too old." The desert was silent, too dry to support crickets or bullfrogs. A wiser man would do nothing. He would relinquish the blanket and sleep under the stars, moving away from temptation.

"I am six and thirty, far too old," she said without a trace of vanity. "In any case, I shall desist. Enough talk of hiero-glyphics."

"Then I shall leave the choice of topic up to you, Lady Woolcott."

She paused awkwardly, as though noticing for the first time the fact of the proximity of the lower halves of their bodies. "I don't suppose we have much in common. I don't sail. I don't gamble. And until recently, have not had much opportunity to travel outside the Continent."

"My life, shallow as it is, appears an open book."

She gave a small puff of derision. He closed his eyes for a moment, wishing to prolong the moment. A stretched silence followed, replete with unspoken thoughts. Experience had taught him that silence was oftentimes more effective than a battery of questions, albeit mightily uncomfortable. He was rewarded a moment later when she asked softly, perhaps more to herself than to him, "Are you concerned?"

"About what?" He opened his eyes to see her hand stealing into her pocket to extract her pistol. She laid it carefully on her lap, atop the blanket.

"That they may return."

"I sincerely doubt it," he said, his voice a low timbre.

"They could not do much in the dark, and we have the advantage. This is the remnants of a fort, after all." He deliberately lightened his tone, watching her eyes darken.

"I trust that you are right."

"Why not sleep awhile, Lady Woolcott?"

"Meredith," she countered. "We are acquainted after all."

"Meredith," he said, watching as she handed her pistol to him. He carefully laid it against the wall with his own, then reached across to her in what he told himself was a bid to comfort. It was an ill-judged gesture because something odd happened when his skin touched hers. Time slowed and his mind worked not at all, only his senses, as he very deliberately traced the contour of her palm.

It was difficult to ascertain how long the silence lasted. They stared at each other, Meredith's color spreading from her cheeks to her throat. Her eyes darted about, searching behind him, emotion skittering across her features. She was barely breathing, lush lashes lowering over her eyes. He expected her to pull away, but instead she brought one hand up to trace his cheek, her fingers disturbingly gentle, brushing away a streak of sand.

Archer froze as her finger traced the stubble that cut across his jawline. A shadow of a beard, slightly rough on either side of his mouth, pulled at the softness of her skin. Suddenly, any attempt at humor, at lightening the situation, was doomed. The scent of lavender and lemon verbena filled his nostrils, making him want to inhale more deeply.

She still had powder streaks on her face, dusting her right cheek, almost but not quite obscuring a spray of freckles across her nose. When her finger completed its journey, she let her hand drop to rest on her lap, fingers splayed out. He exhaled audibly and brought his lips down to cover hers.

It was a simple kiss. Chaste even, their lips briefly meeting. They both broke away at the same instant, separated for a heartbeat, their breaths mingling while the sliver of the moon watched overhead. Then his mouth descended again and this time, his lips were slow and hot. And not at all what Meredith had expected. Her own desperation came over her like a clap of thunder. He tasted of the brandy they had consumed together, sweet and powerful. His hands closed about her waist and she went utterly still, savoring the moment, allowing her tongue to dart out to meet his. He teased the soft edge of the inside of her lips, the sleekness of her tongue.

She kept her mind deliberately blank, wondering what she was doing, succumbing to this urgency that was only a mask for her fear. She had loved this once, she knew. The feeling of a man's hands, the way he tasted, the hardness of his body, the heat of his mouth. But this was not real, far from real. She did not know Lord Richard Buckingham Archer, did not want to know him; didn't trust him with a fibre of her being. But at the moment, it didn't matter as long as sensation blotted out the past and the future and left her with only the present.

He caressed her throat, his lips sliding along the curve of her chin to nestle in the hollow of her collarbone. Her nipples budded, impatient against the stiff fabric of her stays and the ebony fastenings of her riding jacket. Heat pooled in her abdomen, a heavy ache that throbbed in time with her blood. She nipped at his lips, urging him on, wanting more. He slipped a hand beneath the blankets to cup her bottom, pulling her hips up hard against him, forcing her fists to tightly clutch the linen of his jacket. His arms beneath her palms were iron, as was the ridge of his erection riding against her stomach.

When they'd first been introduced at Montfort, she'd felt the thin veneer of control she'd cultivated for the last eighteen years of her life crack like a mirror. Her reflection—her understanding of herself—had shattered in that instant. He was tall, imposing, with black hair, and eyes an incongruous cornflower blue over a bold nose and hard jaw. As he stood in the great hall of the house that had been in her family for generations, she'd wished she'd been the type to give him a practiced, flirtatious smile, welcoming him to her home, but easy feminine ways had never come readily to her. That she should find him compelling was incomprehensible, this man who smelled of the outdoors, of the sea, and whose forceful masculinity caused the bottom to drop out of her stomach whenever he entered a room.

This was madness. It had to be. Breathing in his scent, a part of her said that she was simply reacting to the shock. She had killed a man. Something primal had clawed its way through her, past the rational, logical self-possession that had kept her and her loved ones safe for so long. She certainly had not been looking for rescue. And certainly not by Lord Archer, who had left Montfort without a backward glance a day after the wedding of Rowena and Rushford. As though he couldn't get away fast enough.

And yet, she burned for him. *No, that was not right.* She burned for herself, lost for nearly twenty years and brought back to life at this moment. His hand went to the ebony fastenings of her jacket, slipping one button loose. She inhaled sharply, her whole body tightening, shaking. She rested her forehead against his, keeping her arms loosely around his neck. She felt his thumb trace slow circles over her throat, comforting and arousing at the same time.

She shivered, desire flooding her limbs. With difficulty, she steadied the hands that stroked the stubble of his chin. It was too tempting to lose herself in such a moment, too easy to drown in sensation, too agonizing to resurface and contemplate her reality. A woman whose youth was well behind her and who had lived most of her years in the shadows should not be allowing this, the last sane corner of her mind, dictated. She told herself to break his hold, but her body would not comply. Her arms remained around his neck, one hand locked in the thickness of his hair, never wishing to let go.

Above their heads the moon had risen to its full height in the sky. The silence of the ancient land surrounding them was all-encompassing save for his deep breath as he raised his head from hers and moved back a fraction. Her eyes opened fully, her arms trailing reluctantly across his shoulders, down the hard wall of his chest. It was her turn to take a breath, pulling herself back under control.

"You're in shock," he murmured into her hair.

"I am not," she returned, aware that he was staring at her when all she wanted was for him to touch her again. She longed to turn and curl into him, bask in the warmth of his body, of desire and of forgetfulness. Her face flushed, testament to her mortification. Not morality. She was beyond the simple bourgeois calculations of society, her past dictating that she balance precariously on the margins of life. But the fact that she had welcomed him and had thrown herself into the moment only reminded her that she was running away once more from the past.

But she was finished with running. Only moments before she'd been secure in the knowledge that she would never hide again. She had aimed at a man who would do her harm and released the hammer of her pistol to take his life. Taking control because anything else was unthinkable. For the past few months, she had felt alive for the first time in years. Rowena and Julia had come back to her. They were safe and she would never let anyone rob her of that security again.

His warm breath fanned her cheek. "Rest," he said, and she wondered whether he was rejecting her, regretting their embrace. He smiled, confident and sure, as though he found himself in similar situations often. Which, she was sure, he had. She wondered what he'd wanted and why he'd kissed her. But she wasn't about to ask him, not just now.

Men like Archer did not find women like Meredith Wool-cott to their taste. She was too clever. Too challenging. Too old. Another reason not to trust him. With an inaudible sigh, she forced herself to look away from those penetrating eyes, the sensual curve of his mouth that promised pleasure. A sudden constriction in her chest reminded her of her folly.

Romance and intrigue did not fall within her purview. She was six and thirty, for pity's sake, ready to welcome Rowena and Julia's children, content with her studies, with her horses and with whatever travels her newfound freedom allowed.

Sir Richard Arthur was anomalous, as out of place in her life as a shooting star in a cloud-filled night. She closed her eyes, shifting away from him.

She stroked the raised ridges of skin beneath the linen sleeves of her jacket, the scars everlasting reminders seared onto the inside of her wrists. Although she knew the tissue was dead, the pleated skin burned and throbbed when she least expected. The image of Montagu Faron rose stubbornly in her mind. He was dead, but she could still remember the intimacy in his voice. She recalled looking at him with young love in her eyes, at the tall and handsome youth with the coal-black hair, his cloak slung over his arm, a loose white shirt open at the throat. It was the image that remained with her, now an image from her dreams, dark and brooding like the heroes in the novels she'd loved to read as a girl.

He had been her soul mate, their love forged by the hours spent together in his father's chateau outside Paris, scouring ancient texts in the library, exchanging heated words in heated debates. She had always felt an inexplicable premonition of a shared fate.

Meredith opened her eyes to the desert sky, the pain in her heart unbearable. Faron's men had come for her today. Looking into the dark, she wondered how her life had taken such a perverse turn and why the only man she had ever loved was now the man she would hate to her grave.

Chapter 3

"You are four minutes late," the man in the tufted chair behind the screen said, his eyes closed. He was in the midst of his toilette, shaving being the ritual that it was, and the razor did not stop in its ministrations.

"I came down from Paris the moment I could, but the roads were swamped with autumn rains, delaying my travels." The countryside had been wreathed in gloom and mist, the skeletal branches of oncoming winter wrought-iron against the gray sky.

The apology was met by silence interspersed only by the soft grating of the razor. There was an audible sigh, as the man in the chair opened one eye. His mouth turned down at the corners. "How go your pursuits?" he asked perfunctorily, looking through the gap in the screen.

Tall and slight, with spectacles perched on his nose, Mr. Hector Hamilton had an annoying way of clearing his throat. Even from a distance, the man could see the ink stains on his hands and the hesitation in his stance. Nevertheless, it wasn't Hamilton's comportment that he was interested in but rather his research, ongoing at Cambridge. *The Book of the Dead* would add quite wonderfully to the collection, he thought. Most fascinating and useful, this book of ancient Egyptian spells that were deemed necessary by the ancients to pass safely through difficult and dangerous situations in the after-life. The irony was not lost upon him.

It was his wont to keep a keen eye on the universities in England, France and Germany; their dons and professors were harbingers of knowledge that could prove of incalculable value, in the right hands. Of course, his own laboratories and library were the envy of the world. The best maps, the most accurate depictions of the planets and a veritable museum of artifacts from distant lands filled shelves groaning from floor to ceiling with labeled jars and yellowed papyrus and coiled codexes.

"Very well, thank you, monsieur." Hamilton's voice was a dull monotone, but the sharpness of his eyes behind his spectacles indicated that he was keen to see the face behind the screen. It was only a footman arriving with a tea tray for Hamilton that halted the proceedings momentarily. He himself preferred strong coffee.

He was in a surly mood. Motioning his valet aside impatiently, he took up the linen towel around his neck and daubed at what was left of the soap. The servant dutifully collected his tray and backed out the door on silent feet. Rising from the chair, he looked away from Hamilton to the French doors that framed the parterre with its plane trees and disciplined shrubs.

Hamilton was biddable enough, not daring to look beyond the screen to the man who had been paying his gambling debts these past few months. If only Hamilton's prodigiously scholarly mind were as adept at cards. He'd no doubt been mesmerized by the agile fingers that cleverly shuffled cards in parlors and dens across London.

Hamilton's game was vingt-et-un with a two-hundred-pound minimum, rich play for the younger son of a vicar. But who could divine the underbelly of human nature that had taken this man from the august lecture halls and laboratories of Cambridge to the stale smoke and sour perspiration of the gambling halls? Far stranger things had happened, in his own life most of all, he reflected.

Hamilton was in debt, *his debt* more precisely, and was indeed looking rather desperate today, his pallor marked, his thin hands twitching. The game had grown too fierce for him. The professor played deep, lost often and could not hold his liquor. A perfect constellation of character flaws that only grew in magnitude with every hundred pounds that went into and flew out of his coffers.

The man turned from the view beyond the French doors, studying the fleur-de-lis of the screen shielding him from Hamilton. The room's appointments, its gilded chairs, its rosewood banquettes and its rich tapestries had taken generations to accumulate. Even after so many years, the effect still astonished him every day.

No doubt Hamilton stood in awe as well. The man recognized that there was power in rococo splendor, the accumulated accretion of aristocratic privilege. After another interminable pause, he returned to his chair and broke the spell. "Whatever more you need, Hamilton, my factotum, George Crompton, will provide."

"That is too generous of you, monsieur."

"Indeed. Spoken like a man who has never had to earn his keep."

Need overpowered shame. "My post at Cambridge pays very little, a paltry addition to the small trust left by my father."

Ah, yes, the vicar. Who was no doubt apoplectic, even in his grave, at his disaster of a son.

"Let's be clear. You are costing me a pretty penny, Hamilton," he said.

Hamilton stiffened what little spine he had. "I do share with you the fruits of my labor."

"Small recompense."

"The latest translations from the archeological sites at

Petra and *The Book of the Dead* are of some value to you, surely."

"So you should like to imagine."

Hamilton clenched his ink-stained fingers together. "Then why is it that you asked me here? Other than to discuss my debts?"

"You mean to inquire as to the purpose of your presence here? Obviously, I wish something in return." Hamilton said nothing. He continued. "Simply give your assent."

"I must know to what I am giving my assent."

The man behind the screen chuckled. "You will find out in due course. Your agreement is a foregone conclusion."

"I shall not break any laws."

"I wouldn't dream of asking you to."

Anxiety burned in Hamilton's eyes.

"Calm yourself, Hamilton. There is nothing sinister to fear. What I ask is a simple enough task. Surely you will not demur when I request that you break off your engagement to that Westminster girl. She doesn't seem much of a prize, after all, for someone of your potential, gambling debts notwithstanding."

Hamilton's pale white hands twitched at his sides.

"Your tea is getting cold, by the way." And it would continue to grow tepid as the professor's needs warred with his conscience.

"How do you know about Miss Pettigrew?" he asked finally, his mouth slackening in a combination of disbelief and resignation. He peered at the screen, at the voice that drifted over his head. He would no doubt like to put a face and name to the threat behind the words.

"It's of no import how and where I get my information. Simply answer my question." As though the younger man had any choice.

"You will concede that it is a difficult question to answer. It would all depend . . ."

"The right answer will make all your debts disappear,

Hamilton. As well as seeing that your coffers remain reasonably full. After all, isn't that what brought you to Claire de Lune? Through the cold rains and unpassable roads?"

He spluttered, indignation battling now with contingency. "Well, then . . . monsieur . . . but I don't understand what difference it will make if I leave off with Miss Pettigrew. We have been engaged for nearly three years," he added with some desperation.

"Three years do not speak to much urgency, I should note. You appear to me a natural bachelor in any case. And your freedom would make you available for another woman I have in mind for you, Hamilton."

"Another woman? That's preposterous."

The man behind the screen turned from the well-ordered vision of the Renaissance garden. He crossed his arms over his chest, considering. "The woman I have in mind shares your interests—in ancient languages. And all I ask is that you pay her court."

The silence was deafening. Hamilton had clearly never considered himself a lothario. "Pay her court?"

"I'm not asking you to grow two heads, Hamilton. She is reasonably attractive and, since you will already be attending the meeting at Burlington House next month, you have the perfect avenue to make her acquaintance. And more importantly to further your acquaintance."

Hamilton put a hand to his head, more perplexed at the request than at the sight of a quadratic equation. " 'Her acquaintance,' " he repeated. "This is hardly the thing," he stuttered. "I am hardly . . ."

"I guarantee you will find her of interest, much more so than Miss Pettigrew. And no need to sputter on. Trust me, she will appreciate your charms, Hamilton."

Hamilton took a steadying breath. "And if I refuse?"

"You have no such option available to you, I'm afraid." The specter of his debts loomed. "I'm sure Cambridge would not like to hear of your latest escapades. Your future career would be imperiled, your post given to someone of a more studious nature."

With a shaking hand, Hamilton removed his spectacles, peering through them as though to find an escape from his predicament.

"Come now. What I propose is hardly purgatory."

Hamilton replaced his spectacles with shaking hands before asking, "May I have a few days to think over the matter?"

"No." There was no need to mention workhouses, where people of Mr. Hamilton's type would die from the thin gruel, tubercular environment and hard physical labor before ever being able to retire their debts.

Hamilton stared grimly at the trompe l'oeil ceiling featuring gamboling unicorns and hapless maidens. "And to what purpose shall I make this woman's acquaintance?" he asked at last.

"You shall be apprised more fully in the coming days. Crompton shall be your guide."

"May I ask her name?"

The man raised his head to look beyond the French doors, where the bare plane trees stood swaying in the bitter wind. "Lady Meredith Woolcott." He paused, the name acid to his tongue. "She will be presenting a paper at the upcoming meeting at Burlington House."

Hamilton's brows shot up. "A woman presenting to the Society? Highly irregular . . ."

The man nodded, more to himself than anyone else. "A highly unusual woman—as you will soon learn for yourself." The blind leading the blind. It couldn't be more perfect. "Crompton will show you out." And as if he had been waiting for the command, Crompton appeared behind Hamilton, startling both with his stealth, his square frame incongruously resplendent in a superbly tailored waistcoat and jacket. "And by the way, Crompton will be following you to London, to ensure you have everything you require, Mr. Hamilton."

Crompton moved farther into the room, his bulk at odds with the well-modulated cadence of his speech. "Mr. Hamilton, wonderful to make your acquaintance. I am certain we will meet from time to time in England as I learn more about you and your varied interests, from gaming to *The Egyptian Book of the Dead.*"

Hamilton stepped back, alarm and understanding mingling in his expression. George Crompton, whose forebears had made their living in the Rookery close to Bainbridge Street, had a way of making his presence felt. Hamilton turned to the man behind the screen. "I don't quite understand how Mr. Crompton might be of service."

Crompton answered to spare the man behind the screen the trouble. "I shall explain my role in your endeavors as we take our leave, Mr. Hamilton. Shall we?" And for the moment, Hamilton was reminded of a medieval etching he had once seen in a monastery in Italy, of a hooded executioner holding out his hand to a prisoner to guide his way to the tumbrils.

When he was finally alone, the man came out from behind the screen. He strode to the exquisite escritoire in the corner of the salon and extracted a mask of beautifully tooled leather. Montagu Faron had always been impossibly reclusive as well as powerful, both characteristics bringing with them a measure of fear. And for good reason. Faron was never without his leather mask, shielding the world from the facial tremors that overtook him with unexpected ferocity. The man was seemingly indestructible, having escaped certain death by fire at the hands of Julia Woolcott only one year earlier and from drowning at the hands of Rowena Woolcott only a few months later. Now with scars from flames all over his body, there were whispers that the great man of science and reason had made a pact with the devil.

Only his right-hand man, Giles Lowther, knew the truth.

He alone executed Faron's wishes. There was a story told that when he had been a brilliant student at the Sorbonne, Faron had saved Lowther from the gallows. And hence, the man's undying loyalty.

The mask was light in his hands, reminding him of all he had lost as well as gained over the years. He chuckled, recalling poor Jerome, the troubled second cousin, whey-faced and eternally confused. Jerome was from Bordeaux, a branch of the family that had taken aristocratic inbreeding much too far. Or perhaps it was syphilis, the sins of the father visited upon the son. Didn't matter. Long dead now. And a good thing too.

It was Jerome who had attacked Faron, leaving him permanently incapacitated. It had been simple to prey upon a diseased mind, to urge Jerome onwards.

A clock struck somewhere from deep inside the chateau. The man shook his head at his recollections. Closing the escritoire drawer, he drew the mask to his face, placing it firmly over his features. The fit was all but perfect.

Meredith jerked awake, sat bolt upright and thrashed at the blanket covering her body, as though it were suffocating the life from her. Her heart hammered, her palms sweated and the wool crumpled in her fists.

"You're awake," Lord Archer said from somewhere nearby.

She slowly set the blanket aside as consciousness seeped in, strong sunlight tracing patterns against her eyelids. This was not Montfort, nor was it Shepheard's Hotel in Cairo. She pushed her hands through her hair and blinked in the direction of the voice, her thoughts struggling to catch up with her senses. The past several hours had been populated by dreams she had hoped never to have again. She'd been back at Montfort, watching the seasons change from the windows of the drawing room, the clouds streaking against a changing sky. Dusk had hung about the salon like a heavy mantle, the ghosts of Rowena and Julia's childhood lingering, their laughter mingling with dust motes in the air. The tendrils of the dream clung, along with the horrific sensation that Rowena and Julia both lay dead, beyond her reach and her help. Even now Meredith's chest still clenched at the guilt that she had not done enough to shelter them from the evil she had had a hand in creating. But they were alive. She breathed the words with relief. And Faron was dead.

She opened her eyes to blazing sunlight. Early morning in the desert.

"We need to leave now, Meredith."

She sat up. Archer. Lord Richard Archer. His physical presence was jarring, even more so now in the glare of the desert sun. He looked as though he'd been up for hours while she'd been sleeping, wrestling with her dreams, on the floor of the abandoned fort. He was smiling faintly, his eyes watching her closely.

She pushed aside the blanket and rose too quickly, anything to avoid remembering what had transpired the night before. She felt myriad twinges everywhere in her body, and she stretched to loosen them before catching sight of the perfect imprint of two bodies on the fine sand beneath her. She blanched, mortified, then quickly shuffled her booted feet over the pattern, hoping to make the evidence disappear.

A horrifying thought crossed her mind. She glanced down quickly to determine that her riding jacket and trousers were still in place and that she had indeed slept in her clothes undisturbed. Silly woman, she thought, as though she were a maiden at risk of being ravished. There were benefits to being a certain age, a matron. The tumultuous events of the day and last evening were simply an aberration. It was best to pretend that nothing untoward had happened, save a few moments of weakness on her part. Archer would most likely be as eager to forget the incident as she was.

"Of course, we should be on our way," she said. "You might have wakened me sooner, Lord Archer."

He handed her the silver flask, which miraculously still contained some water. "Have you had your fill?" she asked.

Waving away her concerns, he reached down for his linen jacket, which she had used as a pillow during the night. The image of his placing the bundle under her head sometime in the early hours was disturbing. He paused to swiftly load her pistol and then his, tapping the powder down the barrel, pressing in the ball before returning it to his waistband. Meredith felt she was still in a dream, despite the glare of the morning sun, watching this man with whom she had spent the night loading firearms.

Smoothing her hair and tugging her sleeves over her wrists from long habit, she noted that Archer hadn't said a word in some time. She wondered how he'd passed the night. Sleeping fitfully and watching her twist and turn on the hard ground, wrestling with her dreams? Or thinking about someone in his own past, or present, a woman who was important to him?

Whom had Rowena mentioned? Of course, the young and lovely Countess of Blenheim. Meredith pictured her with soft blue eyes, tipped-up nose and rosebud mouth. She had an amenable disposition and no challenging thoughts in her blond head beyond flirtation. In short, a lovely young widow, her husband conveniently dead. Of course, Archer would find the Countess attractive. Annoyed by her wayward thoughts, Meredith glanced down at Archer's hands, large, capable and elegant at the same time, working deftly. They had touched her last night, overriding whatever little judgment she had left.

She picked up her pistol and secured it in her pocket, the familiar heft reassuring. "We are on our way then," she said, her voice still husky from sleep.

"If you are agreeable and as long as you are feeling up to it." He squinted up at another hard blue sky, and she found herself studying him again. His hair was dark brown, almost black with a few threads of silver, and it waved loosely about his temples and ears. And although his jaw was heavily shadowed with whiskers, he looked as though he'd spent the night on a four-poster bed rather than on the unforgiving ground.

"Of course," she said briskly. "Why risk our good fortune?" The yolk of the sun poured through the jagged remains of the fort. She didn't want to imagine those men returning, or think of the man she had killed.

Her thoughts were a collision of images and high emotion, far from any semblance of coherence. She'd taken a life and a short time later all but offered herself to a near stranger on the bare desert ground, and in moments had been aroused to an adolescent breathlessness. Archer's nearness in the harsh light of day was a shocking reminder of her lack of judgment. For the next minute, his boots scrabbling over the hard ground was the only sound, as he picked up the blanket, shook it out before bundling it into the leather bag. Her wandering thoughts wouldn't stop and she considered whether he'd been entirely unmoved, recalling the heat of his breath over her throat, the hardness of his arms under her hands. Examining the incident with a cooler head told her that the exchange was entirely mortifying and she hoped it would sift away like the sand beneath their feet.

The heat was already beginning to build and she shielded her eyes from the sun with her hand. They should soon be on their way back to the relative civilization of Cairo, where in the elegance of the hotel they could say cordial farewells over a glass of sherry, formalities reestablished and the unfortunate incident forever unmentioned and forgotten.

"I am ready whenever you are, Lord Archer." She glanced beyond the low wall to their left. "We have your horse, mercifully," she said.

"It will have to do for both of us. If we leave now we should arrive back in Rashid by noon."

And yet they stood there, pausing so long it seemed that Meredith had forgotten how to begin and end a sentence. She gave herself another shake, looking at him directly for the first time that morning. "After we arrive in Rashid, there is no need to accompany me further. Despite your promises to Lord Rushford."

"And despite the fact you were attacked by three men last evening." His expression tightened. "You expect me to walk away and leave you unprotected."

Meredith held her head higher and then made a noncommittal sound which won her a sideways look and an upraised brow.

"I don't require heroics, Archer."

"I'm well aware," he returned. "I simply wonder how you expect the dead man's body to disappear."

The man she'd murdered. Meredith swallowed hard. "I shall take care of it. I shall alert the British Office to send someone to collect the remains."

"And tell them what, precisely?"

"That I was attacked and I acted in self-defense. Entirely true." Misgivings formed in the back of her mind.

"They will ask questions which you know you will refuse to answer. Aren't you in the least suspicious as to why and how your guide was chosen?"

"Are you intimating that the British Office had something to do with Murad's betrayal?"

"I don't know. But I wonder if you can afford to raise the questions."

Meredith eyed him warily. "And you can make all of this go away, if I surmise correctly." She paused. "And what do you wish in return?"

"Nothing. Consider it a favor to my old friend Rushford." She responded with silence. "Why you don't trust me?" He paused. "Or is it all men?" Or one man, he might as well have asked.

A tiny flame of suspicion reignited in her chest. She leaned back against a wall, where a thin shadow shielded her from the sun and his questioning. Why was he here? Why had he followed her? She rubbed her forehead and tipped her head back against the wall, closing her eyes briefly before daring a reply. "None of this is any of your concern." Her voice hardened, and her fingers closed into a fist.

"I know you don't wish to talk of it. About Faron."

The name landed like a blow between her ribs. She was speechless. For a moment, she didn't dare breathe and could only stare back at him.

"That's the danger here, Meredith. One you shouldn't ignore."

She bounced her fists softly against her thighs. "He's dead."

Archer was still studying her, steadily, as though he was looking for a point of entry. "How can you be so certain?"

"I know," she said more evenly this time. *Because I can feel it. In my heart.*

It was as though he had read her mind, heard the unsaid words. He smiled faintly. "I wouldn't have taken you for a romantic, Lady Woolcott."

He was dangerous, Lord Richard Buckingham Archer.

"We are wasting time with this nonsense," she said evenly, although it cost her great effort. Anything to make the subject of Faron go away. "I absolve you of whatever Lord Rushford or Rowena and Julia asked of you. As a matter of fact, I shall cable them directly when I return to Shepheard's so you may go about your business with a clear conscience."

To her surprise he nodded, although it was not quite a surrender. "You are correct about one thing at least. We are wasting time. We can continue this discussion once safely back in Cairo."

The subject was closed.

They left the fort by the north entrance, going down narrow, cobbled steps in silence. Archer scanned the horizon as they passed into the remains of the fort's garden, the air heavy with heat. Only the bitter tang of creosote spiked the air, as the austere landscape loomed before them. Danger was on the horizon, Meredith thought, cutting a sidelong glance at Archer, and moving back into her life.

Her every instinct warned her to back away, to send Lord Archer on a swift return to London. This man, even in claiming to protect her, opened up possibilities she never wished to contemplate again. His mount waited, tucked into the coolness of an alcove. The terrain became more uneven, steepening. Archer moved ahead of her, then turned quickly to slide his hand around her waist.

"I can manage, surely—"

Too late. He lifted her easily while her hands grabbed instinctively at his shoulders, their bodies once more entirely too close, her fingers curling into the linen of his jacket. They were face-to-face, his implausibly blue eyes inches from hers, her pulse hammering a staccato beat. It was only a moment before he lowered her down his length. But the ground was suddenly unsteady beneath her feet and she reminded herself to remove her hands from his broad shoulders. Archer still grasped her waist, his heavy palms warming her skin through the fine wool of her trousers. She remained there, looking up at him until his horse neighed, rending the silence.

He released her waist. And she lowered her hands. Perversely, her pulse did not slow and his warm masculine scent lingered in a cloud. Meredith was agonizingly aware of Archer as a man. She would have to share a saddle with him, traverse the desert in a cocoon of heat and wind, even though she knew that he was not for her, with his lean hard face and those penetrating eyes that promised more danger than help.

It was worse than Meredith expected, a struggle to hold her body away from his as they rode along the same path which she'd traversed just twenty-four hours previously, with Murad at her side. She sat back in the saddle, her hands held tightly against her waist. The air was like cotton, soaking up her thoughts, and after an hour's ride, the wind picked up, and the shifting sand made a deafening roar around her head, pummeling her ears and making it impossible to keep her thoughts straight. Archer appeared oblivious, urging the mount beneath them to keep a steady pace.

They passed some scraggly brush, leaning so far over it looked as though it would be torn up by the roots and blown into the horizon. Clouds of red shimmered in the distance, causing the sun to take on a copper hue in the haze. Meredith pulled her bonnet low over her eyes as the sting of grit bit into any exposed skin. The horse began to struggle against the onslaught, ears pinned back. Archer said something over his shoulder, his words swallowed by the roar of wind and sand. Around them the desert shimmered, a flatly undulating expanse offering no shelter from the gathering sandstorm. It was among nature's most violent and unpredictable phenomena, unleashing a turbulent, suffocating cloud of particles into the air and reducing visibility to almost nothing in a matter of moments.

Archer urged his horse off the narrow road, toward a low sand dune in the near distance. It made sense to seek higher ground and in moments they both slipped from the saddle. "This is the best we can do until the worst is over," Archer said, motioning to the leeward side of the dune. "At least we will not be struck by flying debris." Reaching quickly into the saddle bags, he procured a bandana, moistened it from his flask, and slipped it over the horse's mouth and eyes. Then the blanket reappeared.

Meredith found herself slipping to the ground, the blanket quickly settling over both of them, a makeshift cocoon. It was stifling and yet a reprieve from the assaulting dust. "How long do you think this will last?" Her voice was barely a croak, the dust having settled to the back of her throat. They were so close that their shoulders touched.

"Haven't any idea. Dust storms vary both in size and duration. Most are quite small and last only a few minutes."

"You are trying to reassure me."

He didn't glance at her, but kept holding the blanket over their heads to allow for a modicum of airflow. "You don't appear to need reassurance. So you won't blame me for being honest. I might also add that the largest storms can extend hundreds of miles and tower more than a mile into the sky, lasting several days."

As though confirming his words, the wind's muffled fury whirled about them, the blanket becoming heavy with sand. Meredith struggled to remain calm. "I have also heard it said," she said, licking her parched lips, "that the winds can pick up huge amounts of sand very quickly and one could find oneself buried alive."

"While we are comparing possible disasters," he said, his voice rising over the groan of the wind, "at least we are not in a ditch. Flash flooding can occur even if no rain is falling."

"It appears as though this situation does not disturb you in the least. I take it that you've experienced something similar."

He shrugged philosophically. "Unfortunately I have been in the eye of the storm once before. In the actual dust cloud, I've learned the hard way, rain generally dries up before it reaches the ground, but it may be raining nearby and quickly flood low-lying areas." He turned to look directly at her, their breaths mingling in the excruciatingly close quarters.

At the moment, sitting quietly against him in the semi-darkness, Meredith did indeed look like the woman who had outmaneuvered Montagu Faron. She sat up straight, no terror in her eyes, stoically waiting out the effects of the sudden blow, as though she'd done it many times before, breathing through the shock, convincing herself that it would ease. If she remained strong.

Archer thought of what he'd read in Whitehall's dossier and what had been hidden between the lines. Both Rushford and Rowena had been reticent to reveal what they knew about Meredith's involvement with Faron, believing the danger past and wishing to give her privacy and time to recover.

Archer felt restless with his partial knowledge of the woman now sitting by his side. He thought of the small cylinder in his saddlebags, and struggled against the impulse to push her into telling him what he needed to know. Both for his own satisfaction and Whitehall's, he reminded himself.

As though following the trend of his thoughts, Meredith turned her head toward him. "We cannot be that far from the village," she said.

The enforced proximity obviously rankled her, much more than her fear of nature's fury. "As long as this storm continues, we might as well be on the other side of the earth," he said.

She tipped her head to the side, thinking. "I suppose all we can do is wait." She paused. "Unlike you, this storm is a novel experience for me."

"You are managing remarkably well." Archer wondered what else, and most likely far worse, might lie in Meredith's past. "What's a little dust storm," he said with a smile, "given the challenges you've confronted in your life?" It was as close to a personal question as he dared, expecting her to shut him down with her customary crisp, one-word replies. He sensed she wouldn't welcome anyone prying into her life, having lived so long in a cocoon of isolation to protect everyone she'd loved best in the world.

Meredith hesitated so long he thought he had overshot the mark, which would do nothing but ensure continuing silence between them. But apparently, she was taking the time to respond and her voice was soft when she spoke. "We all face challenges, Lord Archer. Some more difficult to bear than others."

A gust of wind came and the blanket shook overhead, nature's discordant symphony. He trod carefully. "Rushford told me some of what happened." But not everything. How had she escaped from France, taking the two children with her? And why the need to flee?

She seemed to hold her body very still, as though her posture could deflect any further questions. He realized that he wanted to know her entire story, least of all because of

Whitehall's directives. They saw Meredith Woolcott as a means to an end. Nothing more. The waters were muddied indeed because he found the pull toward her irresistible, an undertow that urged him to entangle himself in her life, although to what purpose? Hours ago, he had found himself touching her, tasting her, but he had pulled away at the last moment, recognizing that she was clinging to him from need that had little to do with him, and everything to do with her past. His pride still smarted.

"There is nothing important left to tell," she said simply. "It all feels like a very long time ago."

Archer couldn't help pressing on. "Perhaps if you tell me more, we can lay to rest what happened yesterday, at St. Julien."

One of her hands slowly curled into a fist against her thigh. He knew that she wished to turn away from him, to be alone. Yet the sands whirling around them outside their small haven prevented her from fleeing. "What difference would it make?" she asked softly.

"We don't know unless you tell me." Perhaps he would start somewhere different. "Have you any other family, besides Rowena and Julia?" It was an innocent enough question.

"A few distant cousins, but after my father died, I entirely lost touch." She added fiercely, "Rowena and Julia are my family. I have raised them since they were still in the nursery, at Montfort." Love and protectiveness radiated from her. She was alone in her sense of responsibility and guilt. That much Archer detected. He shifted his shoulder restlessly to accommodate his unease. Familial relationships were never smooth. He thought of his mother, remarried when he was at Eton and spending most of her time in Italy, and as distant from him as the moon.

"You inherited Montfort from your father, I take it," he prodded gently.

She sighed before responding, as though the information

was being wrenched from her. "My mother died shortly after I was born and my father left England for France when I was ten."

"He never returned."

She added abruptly, "He died in a fire, along with his young wife." Perspiration glinted on her forehead. "Dear God, it's hot. Have I answered enough of your questions, Archer?"

Something in the rigidity of her spine warned him to desist. Fire. The secret behind the conflagration was hers to keep. "Of course," he said, humoring her, accustomed already to her reticence. The wind moaned around them, their makeshift shelter a thin shield against nature's fury. Other women would dissolve into tears, or into his arms, or keep up a constant chatter to keep hysteria at bay. It was then the realization struck him that Meredith had earned her strength and no longer knew how to be weak. Her father and Faron and later, Rowena and Julia, had never allowed her the opportunity.

There was a silence during which the wind continued to roar for what seemed like hours but was in reality merely minutes. Despite the suffocating heat, Meredith huddled into her riding jacket, her face smudged with streaks of sand and perspiration. He tried not to stare at her, but it was difficult at the best of times, and now he was so close he could wipe the fatigue and smudges from her skin if he chose. Her singular beauty arrested him as always, etched at this moment with love, grief and intelligence.

He wiped the sweat from his brow with the back of his elbow, an arm still supporting the blanket overhead. Despite her frosty reception of him, Meredith Woolcott was a sensual woman, a fact he had recognized from the first moment he saw her silhouetted against the stone entranceway of Montfort. She had all but capitulated last evening, and there was every reason for him to tempt her into doing it again. Danger, he knew, was a peculiar aphrodisiac and it would be nothing for him to tip her head back into his palm and take her lips with his own for another sweet taste of her mouth. He recalled the silky skin of her throat and the suppleness of her body which he could now ease to the ground, pushing down her ridiculous trousers and looking into her gray eyes while he fitted his own body between her legs.

White heat pulsed through his veins and he closed his eyes. How long had it been since he'd had a woman? He tried to conjure Camille, but he couldn't. He took a steadying breath.

"Sometimes minutes can seem like hours," she said, her low voice interrupting his thoughts. His shoulder brushed hers and she suddenly felt as fragile as spun glass. "Am I permitted a few questions of my own? It would be only fair."

He opened his eyes. The blanket overhead was heavy with sand. He jabbed it with an elbow to lighten the load before answering. "There's not much to know."

She looked askance at him. "I sincerely doubt that."

He wanted to inch away from her but couldn't. Even their shoulders touching seemed too much. "I promise you that the story may very well put you to sleep," he said evenly. "I am an only child, served several years in Her Majesty's Royal Navy, do not allow the moss to grow under my feet and spend far too little time in London or my estate in Essex, according to my solicitor." He rested one hand on his knee, the other still supporting the blanket that formed a canopy over their heads. "I probably drink and gamble too much. Love to sail. And that's about all that's interesting about me, Meredith. All of which you already know."

Stiff from sitting so long in one position, she rolled her shoulders, looking at him speculatively. "Never married?"

He went still and stared at her a moment, feigning affront. "Why is that always the first question women ask?"

She bristled. "It is your duty to marry and produce an heir."

"So I am shirking my duties? When I have a passel of cousins who have produced the next Lord Buckingham?"

Her lips curved into a smile. She cocked her head, clearly amused. "Heaven forbid should you be occupied with something serious." A small laugh and then she coughed, patting her chest. "Obviously, you don't miss family," she said when she'd cleared her throat, rubbing her face carelessly to remove some of the sand and perspiration.

"I did not have a particularly close relationship with either parent, not entirely unusual, judging by the experiences of my peers. What is there to miss?"

Her expression changed. "How very sad. Whereas my life would hardly be worth living without Rowena and Julia."

"And yet you have more in your life than your wards. You are dedicated to your scholarly work."

She shrugged. "It all came rather naturally. My bookishness and eccentric interests did not recommend me to the wider world, but I was nonetheless encouraged heartily by my father. My unusual education allowed me to realize that I had a purpose in life."

"You are implying that my life lacks purpose."

"I said no such thing. Only that my work is important to me."

"Your work," he echoed. "Quite unusual for a woman of your background, *working.*"

"Why?" she asked sharply. "Outside the rarified world which you clearly occupy, Lord Archer, the vast majority of women in the world work—in factories, in fields, in shops, to name just several examples, whether we are speaking of London or Cairo. And although the choices for women are rather limited, I was fortunate in that my father was open-minded and had the foresight to allow me an education."

Wiping the sweat from his forehead with the back of one arm, he added, "Many women of your rank and means would be content with hearth and home. Although, trust me, I have seen much of the world and woman's role in it."

Meredith bit back a flash of temper. "You do not believe a

woman capable?" she asked with deceptive softness. "Is that your meaning?"

"Hardly. Although you seem quite sensitive to the matter. I was merely referring to your undoubted dedication to your wards."

"I don't see the two pursuits as incompatible. As a matter of fact, both my wards were encouraged in their intellectual activities. Throughout their lives, they had the benefit of the best tutors and materials. You saw the library at Montfort."

He nodded. Her profile, her slender nose and full lips, were lovely in the semidarkness.

"Julia has pursued photography, and has most recently helped her husband, Lord Strathmore, with his explorations in North Africa, capturing the local flora and fauna in a monograph which she hopes soon to publish." Meredith warmed to her subject, delight in her eyes. "And of course, you are better acquainted with Rowena, who, I must tell you, was a veritable hoyden when she was a child, not that I ever discouraged her excesses." She clasped her hands together over her knees. "She is an expert equestrienne, absolutely fearless, and courageously outspoken."

"It would seem your wards reflect their guardian admirably."

She shook her head. "They are entirely individuals, which has little enough to do with me, other than providing them with the environment in which to flourish."

"They certainly have much of which to be proud. Their guardian is to present a paper at Burlington House."

"That may be so," she said modestly. "I always impressed upon them that academics are important—too many females these days come to the sciences and humanities as mere fawning spectators." She looked disapproving. "Although about a third of the audience at these Royal Society lectures is typically comprised of women, they tend to perceive scholarly pursuits as fashionable, like the latest millinery styles or fabric patterns."

"Indeed, the numbers of women who speak at sectional meetings are vanishingly small."

"I'm surprised you noticed, Lord Archer," she said with a smile.

I notice a lot of things, he wanted to say, but didn't. The wind had calmed to a low moan. And then she turned her head slowly to him, her soft smile fading. He wondered what she was thinking as she glanced over at him, whether a flutter of awareness was causing her stomach to clench, whether her lips tingled with the memory of his. Their eyes met and Archer felt it again, the chafing of his blood, the compelling desire to cradle her cheek in his hand and lean still closer toward her. Instead, he inhaled sharply, ignoring it, battling the inclination by turning his head away from her.

They sat quietly for a few moments longer, listening to the high pitch of the wind, its fury lessened. The storm had all but vented its anger. He had a captive Meredith Woolcott but a few seconds longer. "I wish to help you," he said abruptly. "Why is it that you do not believe me?"

She jerked her head away from him, recoiling from the question.

"I shall manage the incident. . . ." They both knew that he was referring to the dead Arab.

Meredith raised one brow and stared him down, eager to defuse whatever confrontation he had in mind. "I did not ask you to. I can approach the British Office on my own." A short pause. "I believe the wind has died down."

He was reminded suddenly of the predawn light that had eased through the fort earlier in the morning, waking him from a half slumber. He had kept watch over Meredith all night, absorbing her every twitch as she slept, with an ear cocked for any unwelcome visitors. He could imagine the kinds of dreams that vexed her. Had he slept at all by her side, he might have reached for her and she would have surrendered. It had almost happened—

Archer was convinced that she was thinking the same

thing, her gray eyes darkening, the pupils indistinguishable. The silence was deafening. "I think we should talk about what happened earlier."

"No." The one-word answer was abrupt. She knew he was not referring to the dead Arab this time.

She remained forbiddingly silent, glancing at him briefly before giving the canopy overhead a decisive pat.

Archer spread his arms and pulled the blanket to the side, causing a small but harmless avalanche of sand. Miraculously, a blue sky and cutting sun poured over them. Their mount nickered softly, unharmed save for a thin sheen of grit covering his coat. Archer sucked in a great gust of air, watching Meredith do the same. "I can breathe again," she said, spreading her arms out and turning in a half circle. Archer couldn't resist. He spun her about, pinned between his arms.

"Don't," she began.

"It doesn't always have to be *don't*," Archer said softly and he pulled her hips hard against him. "Don't frown at me. We have survived a sandstorm." He whispered this time and when his hands went up to her face, her arms closed around his waist, palms flattened against the hard muscles of his back. His knuckles smoothed her cheeks, still smooth as silk under a fine coating of sand. She closed her eyes because his were too probing, sensing behind her great strength, her greatest weakness.

His fingers feathered across her ears, pushing down her jacket collar to stroke along her throat, gritty with sand, and the nape of her neck. Tipping her head, he cradled it before touching his lips softly to the pulse in her throat.

"Why are we doing this? It makes no sense." The words were balanced on a sigh.

"Sense has nothing to do with it," he said, his voice low. Then he dragged his lips softly from the arc of her throat to her lips, which were parted ever so slightly. Their lips brushed and then nipped softly, and he whispered nonsense against her mouth, although she was not offering a protest, only a sigh of pleasure. Meredith's hands slid up to his shoulders, pulling him closer before her lips fell open beneath his. His tongue marauded gently at first, warm, velvet, finding and twining with hers. He lifted his lips away from hers to look into her eyes, which were closed, far from giving him any insight into the woman he held in his arms.

It seemed to work better this way. No words. He took her lips again, more decisively this time. She responded with her arms sliding up to coil around his neck as he pulled her into his body, his iron arousal pressing against her abdomen. He drove the kiss deeper and she met him, their tongues touching and tangling in a primal rhythm. She moaned softly, the sound causing him to bite her bottom lip gently.

Her eyes opened, her breath coming hot and swiftly. The gray of her eyes revealed nothing save blatant desire. She clung to him a moment longer, then her arms loosened about him. Looking as though she was considering whether to speak, she simply shook her head.

Archer took his thumb and gently brushed away the sand from her cheeks. "You think too much," he said softly.

She stared at him. "Nothing has changed," she said thickly after a moment. "The intensity of the past day is in part responsible for this. . . ."

"In part? You really don't exert any charm, do you, Lady Woolcott?"

Brushing her hands down her arms and legs, she shook her head with irritation, the smoky desire fading from her eyes. "Arrogant man."

Instead of being insulted, for some perverse reason, her dismissal made him smile and blunted the edge of his anger and frustration. It was a matter of fatigue and fury, he rationalized, that had tempted him to take her in his arms. He had wanted to gain her trust. God knew that it had worked many times before with other women in his orbit. Then again, Lady Woolcott was hardly typical.

The horse nickered again and the seamlessly clear horizon

beckoned. "We should go," she said for the second time that day. "Rashid cannot be more than an hour from here." Folding the blanket into a neat triangle, she held his gaze. In the harsh light, the skin beneath her eyes was mauve and her hair was coming loose, a narrow strand bright against the paleness of her jaw. "And in Cairo, we shall part ways, Lord Archer. I insist."

Archer did not reply, aware that perhaps for the first time in his life, things were not falling into place as easily as they might. He refused to consider the paucity of information he'd gleaned of Lady Woolcott and her past. The questions were beginning to gnaw at him, the child's kaleidoscope in his saddlebags a potent reminder of everything he didn't know.

They returned to Rashid wordlessly, meeting the barque there before making their way back to Cairo.

Shepheard's Hotel, facing the Ezbekieh Gardens, had expanded only in the past year, taking over the adjacent palace which had once been Napoleon's private quarters. Perfectly reasonable—as many believed that in no hotel in the world could one find such an assembly of people of rank and fashion sitting down to the table d'hôte. As the place to reside whilst in Egypt, many travelers simply checked in for the social life and saw less of Egypt than they would have if they had remained in London to visit the Egyptian Department in the British Museum. From the vantage point of the hotel's terrace and tearoom, where waiters glided about wearing fezzes and inscrutable expressions, anyone who was anyone could be observed.

"My dear Lady Woolcott. You gave us such a turn." Lady Tattersall smiled at Meredith with a brightness that was almost certainly feigned. Like a crow looking for a scrap of glitter, Lady Tattersall sensed something entirely untoward about the woman sitting across from her, balancing a cup of tea in her hand. The subdued mauve of her shirtwaist was expertly pressed, her high lace collar impeccable and her hair smoothed into a luxurious chignon. Quite the transformation. She had appeared the previous afternoon in the lobby of Shepheard's Hotel looking positively disheveled and with that handsome devil, Lord Archer, in tow.

Lady Tattersall had espied them from her perch in the conservatory, cooled by thick fronds of green palm and bright bougainvillea. Most intriguing, she had thought, glancing over her glass of sherry, watching as a fez-capped servant had immediately appeared to whisk them to their rooms. Shepheard's was her fiefdom, through which the caravan of her world flowed, its bustling atmosphere not to everyone's taste. Perhaps a trifle too proletarian, thought Lady Tattersall, catching up the jetsam and flotsam of life by the Nile like one big net. Of course, there were those like Lady Woolcott who were in Cairo to visit the city's antiquities museum and nearby ancient sites, often heard described as the world's largest open-air museum.

Lady Tattersall leaned intently forward. "All went well with your endeavors at Rashid. I am so happy to hear it," she trilled, freshening her cup of tea, the ostrich feather in her hair quivering. "You are positively amazing, my dear, what with your unorthodox pursuits. I can't imagine what it must be like traipsing over ruins and whatnot. Positively tedious. Not to mention dangerous." The wife of a diplomat in the British Office, Lady Tattersall had long resigned herself to the intricacies of expatriate life in Cairo, excavating for fiendishly tasty tidbits of gossip that could shorten the long, hot days.

It had been anything but tedious. Meredith held her counsel, relieved that they were surrounded by the hushed din of well-modulated chatter. Tables adorned with epergnes piled high with tiny sandwiches and sweets punctuated the conservatory, a veritable merry-go-round of pastel colors. None of it piqued her appetite; her stomach had been in a perpetual knot since her return from Fort Julien.

"And how fortuitous that Lord Archer was inclined to

visit the site at the same time. Positively serendipitous." Lady Tattersall picked up her tea, the cup clattering on the saucer in her excitement. They sat together at her table in the conservatory, reserved for diplomats and their wives. "Who knows what might have occurred without the accompaniment of a man. An Englishman, I might add." Her eyes widened, hinting at a hundred dastardly deeds. "Should you not have returned in time, delayed by that horrific sandstorm, you might have missed your packet tomorrow. Indeed, I should love to keep you here longer, as I should have liked to further our acquaintance. Nonetheless, you insist on leaving and I could not let you go without saying good-bye, dear girl."

She hadn't been a girl in years. Meredith forced a smile. "Your concern and invitation to tea was very kind." She had thought it was better to accept the summons, to smooth the water, lest Lady Tattersall's feverish imagination run away with her. "My time in Rashid was most rewarding, Lady Tattersall. So much so that I have all I need to return to London tomorrow via the steamship *Longoria*."

"What a shame. Are you certain you cannot delay your departure?" Lady Tattersall took a bite of her watercress sandwich.

"I have work to undertake so I must hasten my return."

The notion of work was as foreign to Lady Tattersall as snow on the terrace of her Cairo town house. She frowned. "Work?"

"A lecture at Burlington House."

"A lecture? My dear, I exhort you not to overburden yourself with intellectual pursuits. Not at all good for one's health, or so my physician tells me. As a matter of fact, he advised my nieces only recently to confine their reading to no more than a novel each month, and the more soporific and calming the subject, the better."

"My health is excellent, ma'am."

Lady Tattersall's eyes narrowed, not entirely convinced.

"Now what is it that you do again? Indulge me, if you please. Something about ancient translations and whatnot. How extraordinary. And I have trouble enough with my French." She sighed extravagantly.

"It has been an interest of mine for many years."

The older woman regarded her over the rim of her teacup. "You look no worse for wear, I must say. Now do not regale me with details that I won't understand and that will only bring on a nasty headache." She crisply ordered, "Instead, tell me something much more invigorating regarding your recent adventure, perhaps a little more about Lord Archer. Quite the striking figure of a man. I have a vague notion of his people. One hears so little gossip when one is far away from London, after all."

"We share a tenuous family connection."

Lady Tattersall's eyes widened. "How wonderful for you both, although I must say that from what little I've heard, Lord Archer has never shown even the slightest inclination toward domesticity."

Meredith managed a smile. "But then neither have I, Lady Tattersall."

The older woman's eyes danced with appreciation. "It is never too late."

Dear God, this was the last thing she'd wanted. Meredith held her gaze unflinchingly. "I am long past the age when a woman should be married, Lady Tattersall."

Lady Tattersall's brows drew together. "Nonsense, my dear girl." She leaned forward conspiratorially. "Dare I say, the way Lord Archer looked at you yesterday afternoon, with such intensity and concern, saving you from the hideous sandstorm . . . I don't know what I should have done in such an instance." She shivered dramatically and then returned to her train of thought. "And then he interceded upon your behalf at the British Office . . . or so I hear. Not that I shall be telling tales out of school, you understand. The Colonel, my husband, would so disapprove."

Meredith folded her hands neatly in her lap, all too aware that Archer had taken care of the matter of her attacker. How and with what explanation? The knot in her stomach tightened, but she focused instead on the trill of feminine laughter at the next table. "Entirely your imagination, Lady Tattersall," she said lightly. "I'm certain Lord Archer only met with the British Office to finalize his own travel details."

"How modest you are, Lady Woolcott." The older woman's hand fluttered to the fine lace fichu at her breast, before she lowered her voice to a stage whisper. "I'm certain he behaved the perfect gentleman during your time together. Although I might add that there is something rather unusual about the man. Dare I say he's not typical of the drawing room sort. Of course, he comes from a good family and"— she winked conspiratorially—"with a handsome fortune. So one might be convinced to overlook that rather overtly masculine quality that just might be difficult to control. . . ." She trailed off, shivering slightly.

Meredith winced inwardly, her appetite for tea and Lady Tattersall diminishing further. Eager to steer her to another subject, she endeavored to light upon a topic that might be of interest to the older woman. With desperation, and an eye on the quivering ostrich feathers in the unnaturally bright hair of her companion, she began talking about the latest London fashions, of which, in truth, she knew little.

Lady Tattersall warmed immediately to the matter of crinoline widths and the merits of jet beading over lace. "It takes such a long time for news to reach us here in the colonies, my dear girl. I can't remember the last time I saw my modiste with anything remotely fashionable in hand. Why the patterns are at least two years behind by the time they arrive by packet post." Her hand hovered over the creamer. "I do not know myself whether I prefer Mr. Worth or Mr. Manning's designs," she mused. "And you?"

"Mr. Worth," Meredith said automatically and with little thought, although suddenly aware that the relative drabness of her afternoon gown with its mauve piping did not say much about her sartorial choices. The trunk that awaited her in her rooms was filled with serviceable dresses and shoes in the earthen tones that had become a familiar and reassuring staple. There was little need for frills and furbelows in her life and she had never paid the least attention to the vagaries of fashion.

Lady Tattersall chatted on. "I do so agree," she admitted, the feathers in her hair bouncing as she began expounding upon her favorite elements in his most recent designs. "I prefer his subtle use of fabrication and his extraordinary skill with the needle. But do tell me, are his portrait bodices still all the rage?"

The very devil if she knew.

Lady Tattersall made a moue of surprise, looking away from the canapé on her plate toward the small maelstrom that had occurred at the entrance to the conservatory. All thoughts of Worth and beading fled her mind in an instant. "Why how extraordinary, Lady Woolcott. It's Lord Archer," she pronounced unnecessarily as the man in question stood framed in the doorway before beginning to approach their table. He looked out of place in the fussiness of the room and it seemed as though every female head had turned in his direction.

Meredith tried to suppress the jolt of excitement racing through her senses. But the startling width of his shoulders was too near, the taut breadth of his back too familiar and the hard muscles of his torso and arms too graphically memorable. In self-defense, she put down her teacup and drew herself up an inch. "Lord Archer," she said evenly as he reached their table, her voice neutral to bolster her resolve.

Lady Tattersall's eyes narrowed with appreciation. "Lord Archer," she echoed, but more slowly. "What brings you to tea this afternoon, or do I need to inquire?" She turned to study Meredith, her eyes widening dramatically as if she held the secrets of the universe.

"Lady Tattersall. Lady Woolcott." He bowed in turn, daz-zlingly resplendent in tan jodphurs, a white shirt and gray jacket. Clean shaven, the starkness of his features was even more pronounced, his thick hair barely tamed.

The older woman tapped him lightly on the arm with a flirtatious smile. "You are incorrigible for interrupting us, Lord Archer. Lady Woolcott and I were just debating the merits of Mr. Worth's designs over Mr. Manning's."

He said in perfect seriousness, "A splendid question for Lady Woolcott." He turned toward Meredith. "Do satisfy Lady Tattersall's curiosity."

"I shall try," Meredith returned with a tight smile.

"Will you not join us?"

"I'm afraid not, Lady Tattersall. Although the invitation is much appreciated."

Shaking her head, the ostrich feather in her hair positively quaking, Lady Tattersall affected great disappointment. "I am shattered, heartbroken, my dear man, that you do not join us. I should adore learning more about your adventure in Rashid with Lady Woolcott. She has told me little enough. Although I see by your expression that my hopes are dashed." She sighed ostentatiously. "Oh, but do take her away, sir, as I see that you are quite determined. I shall simply have to finish tea on my own."

"I'm certain you will not find yourself without company for very long, a woman of your charm," Rushford said. Lady Tattersall beamed. "Thank you for your understanding. We have some unfinished business. Before Lady Woolcott sets sail tomorrow."

"Business? How positively tedious. Do tell me that you have more enjoyable subjects to discuss. Surely you can do better, Lord Archer," she entreated. "And of course, I shan't send out a search party if you do not return to the conservatory and keep me company, you rogue."

Reluctant to cause a scene, Meredith rose to take Archer's proffered arm. "Your understanding is much appreciated,

Lady Tattersall. And thank you so much for the invitation to tea."

"So whom do you prefer, Worth or Manning?" Archer asked a moment later, as they made their way from the conservatory under the raised lorgnettes of at least thirty pairs of eyes. Meredith smiled over her shoulder for the benefit of their audience.

"Neither. And you well know it." She gritted her teeth.

The hum of conversation dissipated as they rounded the corner through Shepheard's lobby, a paen to hushed red velvet opulence where even the servants melted into the extravagant detail. Traversing the space, Archer steered them down a narrow corridor. The heavy pile beneath their feet turned to a shining expanse of gumwood parquet.

When she was sure they were quite alone, Meredith said, "I thought I had lost you in the desert and yet you persist in reappearing like a bad penny."

"Have I ever remarked upon your persistent lack of charm, Lady Woolcott?"

"What is the purpose of this encounter? Tell me now and you may save us both some time." She was all false bravado, almost afraid to hear his answer, but in response his eyes flashed with some inscrutable emotion as he propelled her onward.

"Forgive me for my presumption," he said. "Perhaps I simply wished to see you again. Is that so impossible for you to believe?"

"Ah, of course," she said softly, aware of the hardness of the muscles beneath her hand. "Do not mock me, sir."

"A constant and erroneous accusation."

He was looking for privacy and the notion disquieted her. The library beckoned, its wide doors open and flanked by two magisterial bronze lions. The shelves of books and heavy mahogany appointments were an homage to all that was British. Rich brocade drapes shut out the heat of the afternoon, but a pair of sconces burned just beyond the doors.

Archer pulled her into the room and shut the doors behind them.

She took her hand from his arm. "Please say what you wish, but I would appreciate brevity. I have little time at hand and must prepare for tomorrow's departure."

He ignored her, moving over to the sconces to turn the lights higher.

"What are you doing? I do not intend to stay. We are not here to peruse the latest issues of *Punch*."

"No, we are not. We have unfinished business. Pertaining to the matter at the fort. " He seemed in no hurry, strolling in leisurely fashion around the room, pausing to examine a letter opener on a side table before picking it up.

"I am in your debt, I realize." In repeating the words, she hoped to hasten an end to the proceedings.

He shook his head, tapping the opener against his palm. "Is that what you believe?"

"You made the body of the man I killed disappear today. The debt is mine to repay."

"You need not worry. The matter has been resolved."

"What did you tell them?"

He shrugged. "Does it matter?"

"To me it does." Meredith turned away, pretending to examine a shelf of books, their gilded titles demanding her attention as she tried to keep the anxiety from her eyes. "I should present myself to the British Office. Should there be a subsequent inquiry, I may answer their questions."

"There will be no inquiry." He said the words as though he ruled the world by fiat. Not for the first time, Meredith wondered what truly lay behind Archer's deliberately laconic façade. She turned back to face him.

"The man in question is a wanted felon with a long list of heinous crimes to his sorry credit. Besides which"—he paused for a moment, looking down at the ornate handle of the opener, before raising his eyes to hers—"I told them I was responsible. For the shot that killed him."

Meredith's breath caught in her throat. "You did what?"

"Of course, you and I know otherwise. And we also realize that there was another purpose behind the attack which you refuse to acknowledge."

"Why do you persist in taking off in that direction? You have no proof. Those men were simply after easy gold. You say yourself that my attacker has a long list of heinous crimes to his credit."

"What of your guide, Murad?"

"He would have been rewarded with a portion of the spoils."

Archer shook his head. "You are too intelligent to believe that theory. Murad is a civil servant. He would not risk his employment and his good name unless the inducement was rich indeed."

For an instant, she railed against his logic. "That is merely an assumption on your part."

He set her hands on her shoulders and she flinched. "I did not come here to argue with you. Only to tell you that the matter of the attack at Rashid is resolved."

"For which I am to thank you," she said, her eyes hard. "You would like that, would you not? To keep me in your debt."

His hands tightened on her arms. "Your interpretation, not mine. Do not put words in my mouth. I don't recall having asked for anything in exchange."

A long, uncertain moment passed. "So you say."

"Have I asked anything of you?"

The image of the two of them together on the desert floor and then in the sandstorm rose in her mind. She thrust it away. "No, you have not," she conceded with brutal honesty. "But I must ask something of you. And I have asked twice before." He waited for her to continue. "I insist that you not accompany me back to London. I appreciate your efforts on my behalf and acknowledge that Lord Rushford and Rowena are concerned. . . ." Her voice was raw. "I have already sent a cable, as promised."

Archer stood before her, like a desert mirage hovering just beyond her reach. Something inside her chest twisted and she suddenly wished that she had no past, that she was seventeen again with her life before her. Yet her weakness angered her and, ruthlessly, she shoved the thoughts away.

"What are you so afraid of, Meredith? That I will do you harm?" He took a step closer. "Or are you frightened that I can't help you?"

"I don't require help," she said, her eyes hardening. "Those years are gone when I lived with Rowena and Julia at Montfort, startled by every shadow, every missive that crossed my doorstep, a stranger's footstep. I refuse to go back."

"And if you have no choice?"

"I have every choice," she gritted out. "And it's precisely why I pulled the trigger. I refuse to live in fear any longer. When I believed Julia and Rowena dead—" She stopped unable to go on, closing her eyes.

Suddenly Lady Meredith Woolcott was as fragile as spun glass. Archer held back, the hiss of the gaslight the only sound in the room. He didn't know what he wanted. He wanted her to believe him, wanted her to trust him, even though he didn't trust himself with this woman. Frustration and lust spiked through him. She stepped back, her eyes blazing, fragility falling away. "I don't know what you wish of me, Lord Archer," she said, "when all I wish is to say goodbye."

"You have a strange way of showing it." His own breath came roughly. "Your response is not indifferent."

A flush ran up her throat. "You are all too full of yourself. My response is merely physical, and a reaction to recent, rather volatile events," she said in her low voice. "And it has absolutely no bearing on our situation."

"You are certain?" His voice had lowered to a hot whisper.

Meredith's lips parted. "All too certain. After tomorrow, I do not believe we have any reason to see one another again. You are under no obligation to me or to Lord Rushford."

Archer watched to see if the mask would fall again. She backed away from him, alone in her defiance and strength.

"If that is what you wish," he said finally. Such simple words. Words that smacked of defeat.

She clasped her hands before her and nodded. "That is what I wish." There was a weariness in the set of her shoulders. "I appreciate all you have done, Lord Archer, truly. But I have come to depend upon myself over the years. And in these past several months, my circumstances have been transformed. I truly believe that. I refuse to return to living in a state of fear."

"Despite recent events—"

Meredith threw up her hands in frustration. "Please let me travel to London and put this regrettable incident behind me. I do not need reminders, Lord Archer, and I assure you that I am no longer in a perilous situation. And please do not pretend you feel anything for me beyond duty and obligation. Find your next adventure elsewhere."

He dragged a hand through his hair. "Do not ignore the danger you are in, Meredith. Nor discount other events that have transpired. Between us."

"Don't do this, Archer. I will think better of you for it." She lowered her eyelids as if hiding some emotion. "We are both too old and experienced for such drama. And all over nothing."

He shook his head. "You are making a mistake by hardening yourself against those who seek to help you."

"Is that what I've become?" she asked softly. "Hardened? Well, perhaps that is what happens when the two people you love most in the world, whom you've sworn to protect, are ripped away from you."

Her honesty was brutal. And cut him to the core, reminding him of how good he'd become at dissembling. He no longer knew if what he was feeling was genuine or feigned. He was deeply confounded, and he was not sure why. It was the same undeniable frustration he had felt on the night he had first met Meredith Woolcott at Montfort. He wondered whether it was some buried sense of chivalry, an awareness that this woman needed rescuing when, in truth, he'd learned that it was the last gesture she wanted from him.

He should be brutally honest with himself, and now was the time. Spencer had asked him to undertake the assignment to ascertain whether Faron was still among the living, using Lady Meredith Woolcott as the temptation to lure the Frenchman from his lair. And Archer had said yes, out of a familiar combination of boredom, intrigue and admittedly from a desire to get closer to one of the most challenging and maddening women he'd ever encountered.

Though he had not spoken in some minutes, Meredith had made no effort to step back. Caught in the moment, he lifted his hand and stroked the back of his knuckles along her cheek. The thick lashes lowered, hiding her response from him.

"If this is what you call drama," he finally said, "then I find myself wanting it. Despite my advanced age."

She opened her eyes, unblinking. "We both know this is ridiculous and unsustainable, Archer. No more than a reaction to a tumult of events."

He lifted his hands to cradle her face, then stroked his thumb over her full lower lip. Leaning forward, he skimmed his mouth along the velvet of her cheek. "A reaction."

"A simple effect of recent upsets." Her voice lowered.

"The distress." He drew back and smoothed his thumb across her cheekbone.

"Exactly," she breathed when he slowly lowered his mouth to hers. He needed to savor each moment, tucking it away in the recesses of his memory, hiding it away for a time when he would not have the pleasure of Meredith Woolcott in his arms.

He molded his mouth softly to hers and, after a second's hesitation, Meredith was kissing him back, opening beneath him as he swept into the warmth of her mouth. Her hands came up to hold his face and she kept him there, their tongues twining together, her breath coming more urgently with every moment. He wanted her. She wanted him. And if it was a reaction to the tumult of events, so be it. He simply desired this woman with an intensity that cut him to the quick.

Playing at lust was what he did best, and this was merely more of the same, he told himself. She moaned softly, the sound of it vibrating in his chest. He withdrew his tongue to bite her bottom lip gently and then took her mouth again. She took as much as he did. She tasted sweet and dark, leading him down a path that had only one end. With long-learned discipline, he lifted his head, watching the flickering light play over the elegant bones of her face. Her hands remained on his shoulders, restless and urgent. He kissed her again, long and deep, experienced enough to know the precariousness of the situation. He'd had a lifetime of having sex in the wrong places, was adept at moonlit assignations and boudoir trysts, with women he knew too well and others he scarcely knew at all. Gently, he slipped a hand between her shoulder blades, freed the marching row of hooks at the back of her shirtwaist.

Meredith did not protest when the crisp poplin shuddered down her shoulders. Nor when he turned his attention to the surprising swell of her breasts beneath the fine batiste camisole. It came as no shock that there was no corset hindering his exploration. Her hands skated up the warmth of his back as she arched away from him. His mouth skimmed down her throat; then his lips brushed the swell of her breast as his hand weighed it.

He felt her hesitation; she pushed halfheartedly at his

shoulders with the heels of her hands. But her mouth and her soft lips did not hesitate when he claimed them once again, delving into her softness. And when she twisted her mouth from his, it was as sudden as a clap of thunder. Archer spread his fingers into the hair at her nape and slipped his hand from her waist.

Meredith turned her face away even as he stroked his lips over her ear, along her jaw and down the perfect length of her throat. "Meredith," he whispered. "You wish this as much as I do."

He dropped his hand along the length of her back, the indentations of her spine like a strand of pearls. A part of his mind told him that they were in the library of the Shepheard's Hotel, a public place, and only an instant away from discovery by an errant houseboy or, worse still, Lady Tattersall looking for her parasol.

"I don't want this," she whispered, lowering her lashes in a sweep. "And right now I can't think straight." All the while her hands roamed down his shoulders, stroking his biceps, then sliding around his waist and down the small of his back.

A door slammed somewhere in the corridor. They both stiffened and he became aware of the heat of her body searing his, the swell of her breasts and the taut muscles of her long thighs. In the gaslight, her breath came fast and urgent, almost drowning out a clatter in the hall, a drinks trolley perhaps or tray borne by a servant. The sound sliced through the thick air, returning Archer to the present. Reluctantly, he drew his mouth across her lips one last time and then lifted his face from hers.

First the chemise and then the shirtwaist were quickly patted back in place. Without saying a word, she turned her back to him, offering the row of buttons marching from her waist to the soft nape of her neck. He couldn't resist and dropped a kiss to the silken crook of her naked shoulder, his whiskers rasping at her delicate skin, his breath hot and swift. Her body melted into his and he heard her whisper. "Just a kiss."

Archer didn't trust himself to speak until their breathing slowed. His fastened up her shirtwaist swiftly, fearing that he could not trust himself. Then she turned around, looking into his eyes, her lips parted.

"Do you really wish me to forget any of this happened, Meredith? I will if you tell me so."

The question surprised her so completely that she did not have time to disguise the truth that blossomed on her face. He cursed himself for asking.

He brushed his palm along the side of her cheek.

She stared at him and then nodded. "I'm sorry," she said thickly after a moment.

His smile was bitter, knowing that she was right.

Chapter 4

London, six weeks later

It was another late night at Crockford's, or early morning depending upon one's point of view. A private club on St. James, luxurious and discreet, it played host to those with a robust appetite for deep play and a careless disregard not only for morality but also for good sense. The scent of brandy and fine cigars thickened the air, swirling about the six men who gathered round one of the club's mahogany tables.

The nimble fingers of Rugston, one of Crockford's world-weary dealers, shuffled the cards. His gauntness and pallor recalled those of an undertaker. With eyes that were both jaded and studiously neutral, he noted the face of each card as he dealt it and registered with preternatural precision the reaction of each of the men deep in their cups and even deeper in play. The game was vingt-et-un with a one-hundred-pound minimum and at least one of the players, noted Rugston, was in over his head.

Pale and perspiring, Mr. Hector Hamilton fingered the last of his chips like a child at his wooden playing blocks. The others had already retreated, leaving only the bespectacled man and Sir Chauncy Hunt in the game, the former having just shot Rugston a desperate glance for the last card. Hamilton had the unfortunate tendency never to hesitate, not even when a cooler head should have prevailed. The man bet wildly, lost reliably and seemed to produce a steady supply of notes to make up for his headlong rush toward disaster. His suit rumpled and his cravat stained, Hamilton looked all the more out of place in a club habituated by the aristocracy and plutocrats with their easy elegance and mantle of confidence that confirmed those to the manor born.

The cards dealt and the last bets placed, the two men each chose to draw. Hamilton won a short reprieve as he exposed his card, the jack of hearts.

"You had to win sometime, Hamilton, I suppose," Sir Chauncy Hunt murmured good-naturedly. "Will keep you in the game at least. Must have offered up your prayers to old Rugston."

Rugston pretended not to hear, as impartial a god as there ever was to importuning and petitions.

"My fortune has turned," Hamilton said, a slight slur to his voice. He could hold his liquor no better than his cards. "One more time, Rugston, but make certain you shuffle the pack."

Hunt admired the neat pyramid of winnings on his right, his pale hand fingering the chips lovingly. He narrowed his eyes, wondering along with the rest of the room's occupants, if the evening's end would be unpleasant. A man could lose his birthright, and many had within the confines of Crockford's, but never his head. No overt signs of excessive emotion were tolerated. It wasn't the done thing.

After a cursory glance at the dealer, Hunt half turned in his chair before saying, "No need to go on, Hamilton. You've finished your hand. Time to return home."

Eyes bleary behind his spectacles, Hamilton turned up his palms in protest. "My luck has changed, I am confident of it, supremely so," he managed. "Let's play another hand. Tell me that you're game, Chauncy," he wheedled. Lord Hunt threw his head back in exasperation before inclining his chin and a moment later Rugston sent the cards skidding across the table.

The march toward morning continued as the play deepened and Hamilton grew ever more reckless. A few of the watchers shrugged with the insouciance of the very wealthy and returned to their clubs, their mistresses or, less likely, wives, casually wondering how a nonentity such as Hamilton, the son of a vicar and a don at Cambridge, was filling his coffers. He should have been on the precipice of insolvency not once but at least a dozen times, but it seemed that nothing stayed his hand. Inhaling brandy, he was soon down three thousand pounds, but with optimism to spare. Brandishing a packet of banknotes, he waved to the footman to refill his glass.

He was betting as though Providence itself was behind his every hand. Tipping up the corner of his card, he showed two eights to Hunt's two tens. The card faceup on the table between them was the two of hearts. Even Rugston, face still impassive, wondered if Hamilton was on the road to ruin.

"It appears as though your good fortune is on the wane, my man," Hunt said generously. "It is close to four in the morning."

Hamilton slurred contemptuously. "Lady Fortune shines upon me. *Contra felicem vix deus vires habet.*"

Hunt pushed back his chair and stood. "Bloody annoying. Latin at this hour."

Hamilton looked down the table, bleariness in his eyes. " 'Against a lucky man a god scarcely has power.' "

"Perhaps your pockets are not as deep as the gods suggest," Hunt said while a footman held out his freshly brushed jacket. Rugston had stepped away from the table, as silent as a monk, his hands behind his back.

Hamilton's hackles went up. He stumbled to his feet. "I wish to continue." The few occupants left in the room shook their heads with the discomfiture of knowing that an exceedingly unwelcome confrontation would result. Rugston motioned to the footman, who laid a heavy hand on Hamilton's shoulder. The drunk's only response was to shove a pile of banknotes toward the center of the table.

"I wish to play," he slurred, nearly collapsing on the mahogany. "*I need to play*. Do you realize," he said to no one in particular, "what I was asked to do, indeed, what I did, not a fortnight ago?" The last few occupants of the room tensed in a paroxysm of mortification, steeling themselves against Hamilton's next words. The very least he could do was redeem himself with a tale of pistols at dawn. "My lady love," he continued. "The beauteous Cressida Pettigrew."

There was a collective groan around the room. Dear God, not this. "Go home," said Hunt for the benefit of Crockford's reputation, despite the fact that he was already halfway out the door.

"I was given no choice," Hamilton said, voice trembling. "I am affianced . . . was affianced. Broke off our engagement. And for what?" He pulled himself up on the edge of the table. "For filthy lucre," he spat, nearly collapsing again.

From the depths of the room, a deep voice emerged. "I shall see Mr. Hamilton to a hansom." Lord Richard Buckingham Archer moved out of the shadows, a study in nonchalance, the picture of boredom, his expression of amused disregard familiar to the habitués of Crockford's. He had removed himself from the game hours ago but had lingered in the room watching the drama play out. Hector Hamilton remained in his crosshairs.

"You're a better fellow than I am, Archer," Hunt murmured over his shoulder as he departed with a shrug.

Hamilton cocked a bleary eye, coming to life like a desiccated plant after the rain. "I don't require your assistance, Lord . . . whatever your name is . . . I forget, although we were introduced earlier, if I recall."

The footman backed away and Archer tried to hide his annoyance, unfortunately sober enough to find the current situation bloody irritating. "Let's not make this more complicated than it need be, Hamilton."

"You delay the game," Hamilton said, looking genuinely confused, watching as the footman and Rugston departed, leaving him alone with a formidable-looking man, several inches taller and broader than was reasonable. Wreathed in the swirls of lingering cigar smoke, Lord Archer appeared a messenger from the abyss.

"I need another drink. Allow me that at least."

"Not entirely wise." Archer stilled Hamilton's flailing arms. He patted his cravat back in place. "It may dull your pain now, but will do nothing for you in the morning. Which," he said, gesturing to the sashed windows, which hinted at the start of day, "has already arrived."

Hamilton looked at the heavy velveteen curtains which blocked out the nascent sun, genuinely confused. He collapsed back into his seat. "I cannot believe what I've done."

Leaning a hip against the table, Archer cut Hamilton a sidelong glance. "Confession is good for the soul."

"And won't help me now. What's done is done."

"But worthwhile, in certain instances, one must suppose."

Hamilton sprawled hopelessly in his chair before lifting his gaze. "My darling Cressida. I should have left this game early on and met the scoundrel at dawn to clear my name and my conscience." There was little indication that he was any better at pistols than he was at the gaming table. Besides which, the last duel had taken place in London over two decades ago. Rubbing a hand over his rumpled waistcoat, Hamilton stared into the smoky air as though looking for redemption that would never come.

"Cressida—your fiancée. That we know. And who might the scoundrel be? Do tell." Archer crossed his arms over his chest. Patience, he counseled himself, seized by the sudden impulse to simply leave Hamilton in a crumpled heap and walk out. With a cursory glance at the cards left on the table, he let his gaze drift around the shadowy depths of the room, more familiar to him than the corridors of his own London town house, which he had endeavored to avoid these past several years. Ever since his return from Egypt, his constant companion, ennui, was laced with an extra uncharacteristic restlessness, causing him to pace the floors of the vast, empty place until his unease would send him into the world again.

The crystal decanter beckoned and he studied its brandied depths. He had intended to shut the door on Egypt only to find that London had become once again his prison, but this time his jailer was none other than a woman. He could easily have let Lady Meredith Woolcott go, he told himself, should have let her go, save for the unremitting demands of Whitehall and an infuriating disinclination to admit defeat. There was no reason that it should be so. Willing women were everywhere, he'd learned long ago. Adventurous widows and bored wives, they had filled his days and nights for decades.

Since his return from Cairo, he had not even bothered to visit Camille. The lighthearted blonde with the quick wit and generous spirit had been the perfect casual companion these past few years. Temperate, easy and available, Countess Blenheim had been left unfashionably bereft, a widow who mourned her husband as only Archer could understand. Theirs was a comfortable alliance, simultaneously as empty and filling as an overly sweet meringue. The appetite had waned and somehow Camille's lilting laugh and her easy physicality no longer held appeal. There would be no awkward moments, no scenes, since they had both kept the stakes deliberately low. Archer mentally prepared to have his secretary send the countess a choker in the emeralds she preferred.

Perhaps old Spencer was correct—life came too easily to him. He had never really belonged anywhere, reluctant to put down roots, either in London or at the estate. Nor did he long for the brace of heirs, the appropriate consort, to make his life complete. He had stopped wondering at the source of his indifference long ago. It had been years since importuning matrons pushed their plump princesses in front of his gaze, having learned the hard way that his insistent bachelorhood was an impregnable fortress. Better still, his cousins had done him the unbelievable favor of producing several perfectly serviceable heirs to continue the family name without inconveniencing him in the least.

Resisting the urge to fill his glass, he forced himself to refocus on the man before him who was endeavoring to drown the devils that chased him. Not an unfamiliar sight, in his experience. Hamilton appeared no closer to leaving, his spectacles fogged with the fumes of spirit and despair. Well, it was high time to break through the gloom, Archer calculated. Little patience remained.

"Who is providing you with the means that allow you such extended play here at Crockford's, Mr. Hamilton?" He recalled the last dozen hands in which the play had risen to a fevered pitch, Hamilton playing like a madman, running a desperate finger around his collar as though it was about to choke him. In response to the question, Hamilton belched and glanced down at his hands sprawled on the table.

"Perhaps I can help you," Archer prodded, amazed at the hours he'd lost watching Hector Hamilton from the sidelines. All for a cause, he supposed, although he wondered why he had made it his. He considered not for the first time whether Whitehall and Lord Spencer had gotten it wrong. Spencer's canny gaze had never wavered when he'd relayed the information in the hushed confines of his offices in Whitehall, just a week after Archer's return from Egypt. Almost as though he relished the turn of events, damn the man. It was bloody near impossible to believe that Hamilton was the person chosen to inveigle Meredith back into Faron's path.

"I shall never be able to return to Cambridge. . . ."

"Where you are a don? Is that not correct?" No, not precisely. Hamilton was a professor of ancient languages, a piece of knowledge that Spencer had relayed with his usual coolness.

"Bugger all," Hamilton sputtered, resolve, if not sobriety, washing over him.

"Bugger whom?"

"I'm not sure. That is the rub." He swallowed hard. "And why are you so interested, Lord . . ."

So he did not know who was making him dance like a marionette controlled by strings. Archer sat down and braced both hands on the table, leaning into them. "Hamilton. If you are looking for an out, I may be of assistance."

Hamilton looked startled. "Assistance? Why would you assist me, Lord . . . when I cannot even hang on to your name?"

"I can lend you funds, if you require," Archer said, glancing back over his shoulder to ensure no one should overhear. A remaining servant had slipped into the room to refresh the drinks, but was waved off by Archer's upraised hand. The footman retreated, yanked open the door and disappeared. "Your next wager, with me, will prove undeniably tempting."

Hamilton's eyes flared wide. "Are you quite mad? Do you know whom you cross?"

"Why don't you tell me?" Archer's expression shifted.

"I don't know if I should," Hamilton said, suddenly deflated, pushing away his brandy.

"You should," Archer said lightly. "Hear what I offer, Hamilton." He was all business now. "You have three thousand pounds on the table."

"What of it?"

"You wish to play. I will match that amount. If you win, you shall double your money. If you lose, you tell me of your travails."

Hamilton rallied, sitting up straight for the first time in three hours. "Why would you do that?" he countered.

"I'm bored, Hamilton. Like everyone else in this place. I will do anything to pass the time." The words were not entirely false. Hamilton looked back and forth between Archer and the stain on the faded wallpaper across from him. He was not an unintelligent man, sensing that something was amiss, or hidden at least. Archer pasted a benign smile on his face, although he truly wanted to walk out, tell Hamilton to go bugger himself. And Spencer too.

And yet he was loath to leave. Because he knew Hamilton's drunken bacchanal had everything to do with Meredith Woolcott. Damn his memories, so recent that they flayed his very flesh. He was fleetingly drawn to the memory of the smoky gray pools of Meredith Woolcott's eyes, so vulnerable and proud at the same. She had swept from the library at Shepheard's as if she knew what lay ahead and meant to soldier through it. With her shoulders set stiffly back, she had walked through the library doors and without a backward glance had left him standing alone, with his cock practically in hand. All of which had necessitated several lies—to himself.

A chill ran through him. Unfamiliar and disturbing. When it came to Meredith Woolcott, he was a stranger to himself. Good God, he was no hero. Never had been. Why was he pursuing this travesty? Why had he returned to report to Spencer, ready to pursue the cause of Meredith Woolcott at all? He'd turned his back on Whitehall before. He chose his exploits for sheer amusement, for challenge, for the bloody hell of it, to pass the time. If there was another reason, it cut deep and several ways. He cursed Hamilton under his breath.

"Let's make this interesting, then," he said gruffly, sweeping up the previous hands in one smooth motion round the table.

Hamilton narrowed his eyes. "Will we now?"

"In return for what you know," Archer said smoothly, convinced that Hamilton knew very little indeed.

"I have money on the table."

"You need not repay it."

Hamilton sank lower into his chair, glowering. "You know me well and yet know me not at all, Lord Archer," he said, finally remembering the name.

"Very few of us are original." Archer paused. "May I?" He didn't wait for an answer but began shuffling the deck.

Hamilton nodded desultorily, scooping up his hand and then tipping the corner of his cards. In that instant, Archer made his move, aware that he was taking full advantage.

"Do you stand, Hamilton?" he asked perfunctorily.

There was nothing but silence and then Hamilton tapped the table with his knuckle and Archer slid him one more card. Archer then turned and said, "Will you draw?"

"Yes."

Archer mentally shook his head. Then, with one flick of his fingertip, he turned his cards faceup. "Look what we have here," he said into the quiet of the room. "Vingt-et-un."

If he could have turned paler than he already was, Hamilton would have blanched. Instead, he dropped his head forward on the mahogany table. His words were muffled. "I can't tell you whom," he moaned in a defeated voice.

No surprise there. "Then tell me what it is you have been asked to do," said Archer helpfully, recalling the last time he had been part of an interrogation, in Marseille, with a man much more robust than Mr. Hamilton. "Trust me. I can help. You have already cut the ties that bind. With Miss Cressida," he added helpfully.

Hamilton raised his head, fists supporting his drooping jaw. "You are right. All is lost and I am a fool if I do not follow through with this," he said on a shaking breath, as though coming to a decision. "Tomorrow I am to make the acquaintance of a lady."

Archer paused. "Hardly earth-shattering."

Hamilton was endeavoring to be coherent for the first time that evening. "I am not adept at such things. You understand, Miss Cressida has been the only woman I have ever courted. And now she is lost to me." His head thumped against the tabletop, upsetting his tumbler of brandy. The brown liquid spilled over his fists.

"So you have been telling us all evening, Hamilton." The sun was leaking through the velveteen drapes, only serving to bring into sharp relief the scratches in the table, the stains on the wallpaper and the fingerprints on the abandoned brandy tumblers. Crockford's was not meant for the light of day.

"Who might this lady be? And why is she important to the scoundrel who has put you in such a position?" There was only so much time before even Hamilton would sober up. With any luck, he would not remember enough of the conversation to make sense of it.

"Some old, crabbed creature. I'm certain of it," he mumbled into the new brandy that Archer thrust in his hand. He took a deep draught. "What else could she be, spending her time with her head in books, difficult translations, no place for a lady." He rambled on, disconsolate. "And I am to pay her court . . . the old wizened thing. What kind of female could she be? Giving a paper at Burlington House in two days. I didn't even know that sort of thing was permitted."

Archer smiled tightly, then walked over to the window, thrust back the curtains and opened the sash. Cold morning air rushed into the fetid warmth of the room.

The game was afoot. Spencer and Whitehall had been right. Archer swore under his breath as he looked out into the cold morning light of winter. Meredith Woolcott had addled his brains for the last time.

Having seen Hamilton bundled into a hansom cab as promised, Archer walked down to Mayfair, ignoring one of Crockford's footmen who insisted that he take a conveyance. Pushing a fistful of coins into the man's hand, he took the side exit, two stairs at a time, inhaling the frost-tinged morning air. The last place he wanted to go was home, only to silence and the specter of Lady Meredith Woolcott and her fate which, increasingly, he held in his hands.

Contrary to the footman's grim exhortations, the walk through Soho did not put him in the way of footpads or cut-throats but merely his own bleak thoughts. A lucid clarity had settled around him, the effect of having spent thirty-six hours without sleep, hardly a first in his experience. Days and nights had blurred oftentimes enough on *The Brigand*, courtesy of inhospitable seas, unrelenting in their demand for attention. It wasn't a bad plan to keep in practice. The last time he'd stayed up four days in succession was in the port of Alexandria, while he and Rushford lay in wait to head off an ambush set up by the Emir Damietta. Archer allowed himself the ghost of a smile. Whitehall had been pleased when they'd pulled that rabbit out of a hat.

Whitehall—and its insatiable appetite for information. He recalled Spencer's self-satisfied mien, when he'd learned about the attack on Meredith in Rashid. More evidence that Faron still lived and would not relent until he had Lady Woolcott in his grasp. His gut tightened at what he'd read in the second dossier that Spencer had readily supplied. And at the scene on *The Brigand* that Rushford had recalled.

Meredith Woolcott was my first love. And I hers.

It was impossible. Repulsive. Archer felt his stomach twist.

I do not wear this mask without reason. . . . There are wounds that go far beyond the superficialities of the skin and inward to the mind and spirit.

Faron's words. And his confession that he had set fire to the nursery in which Rowena and Julia had slept as mere babes. Archer recalled the copper cylinder, the child's kalei-doscope he had recovered from the dead Arab. More proof, if they were looking for it, that Faron still lived. Who else would have kept and sent such a horrific memento?

Archer kept walking, pulling up his collar against a rising wind. What was their story, he wondered, and how had it created the evil that followed in their wake still? It had been difficult to read the dossier, to envision Meredith as a young girl, the daughter of a scholar, the second son of a minor English baron who had been sent out to make his own way in the world. The young Christian Woolcott had found himself a position in France, at Claire de Lune, the august chateau of one of the oldest, most powerful families in France. His daughter and the young Comte Montagu had studied together, laughed together, grown up together, exploring the lush green of the countryside as their young love blossomed.

Archer wanted nothing more than to stanch the bleeding images that unspooled in his mind. Calm clarity had just dissolved into a hot burning tide. His muscles were tense, his pulse pounding, a deep dissatisfaction welling from his core. He turned down the narrow lane to find himself passing the West London Boxing Club, where in a few hours those who had not found surfeit in the clubs such as Crockford's or White's would find their satisfaction in the arena. He himself preferred *The Brigand* and a few weeks at sea. There was no better way to clear a man's blood of ill humors. *The Brigand* was currently moored at his country estate on the Channel, its constrained living quarters far more hospitable to his bleak mood than the baronial pile up the hill that had been in his family for centuries. For a moment, he considered abandoning it all, riding to the coast and disappearing into the horizon for a few months. Spencer would be disappointed but not surprised.

He couldn't do it. Simply disappear. Despite the fact that he felt a stranger in his own skin, beset by the images of a tall, red-haired woman with shadowed gray eyes. How this had happened he would never know. Bloody, bloody inconvenient. He rolled his shoulders, trying to restore a measure of familiar calm, to narrow his options and focus his anger. He stopped mid-stride. If Faron would be flushed from whatever sinkhole or grave he now made his own, he would be there waiting for him. Archer unclenched his fists, suddenly at ease with his decision.

London suited his mood in all its winter pallor, the bare branches of the hedges interchangeable with the wrought-iron fences that cordoned off handsome town houses on the main square of Mayfair. They looked down their noses at passersby, tall and proud, dominating one of the most exclusive areas of the city. Turning down one of the mews, Archer walked another hundred paces before turning into the kitchen entrance of a town house. Letting himself in with a key, he moved silently through the servants' entrance, its inhabitants still slumbering. Copper pans danced overhead as he moved with easy familiarity through the house. He stopped at the entrance of the breakfast room, an apple-green confection of watered silk wallpaper and velvet curtains as dainty as the woman who sat, her golden curls catching a shaft of morning sun, on a chaise longue, book on her lap and a cup of coffee at her elbow. The Countess Blenheim was considered by the *ton* to be a remarkably pretty widow, Archer knew.

Looking up, Camille was startled and then made as if to throw her book at him. "Good lord, Richard. You have given me a start! I will never understand how you move so silently. You're not the smallest man in Christendom, after all. You know you might have used the front door."

He strode into the room to drop a kiss upon her head. The familiar aroma of vanilla and roses enveloped him.

"It's been a while," she murmured, looping her arms around his neck, the book falling to the floor.

"My apologies," he said, gently removing her hands from his shoulders. "I have been awash in business since Cairo. As for the front entrance, I know that you'd prefer I did not alert your butler." He crossed the room, shrugged out of his jacket with long familiarity, and sat down.

Camille made a moue of disappointment. "I have missed

you sorely. Your discretion least of all." She took the sting from the reproof by smiling, showing her small, pearly teeth.

"I find that difficult to believe," Archer returned with a grin, a measure of his customary good humor returning in her presence. "When have men not beaten down your door for a moment of your company?"

"You flatterer," she said, drawing the chiffon wisp of a dressing gown more closely around her body. She watched him cast about for a servant. "You are looking for coffee, no doubt." Turning to ring a bell at her side, she moved with the confident knowledge that her household was as well run as a ship in Her Majesty's Navy. Short moments later a maid in a mobcap appeared with the requisite urn.

It was a moment's reprieve, when the truth took a back-seat to less pressing concerns. Their conversation then took a desultory turn, Camille exclaiming over the demands of the social season, the ongoing renovations to the east wing of her country estate and any other subject that neatly avoided the true reason for Archer's long-delayed visit.

Archer listened to her lilting voice, asking few questions, merely enjoying her easy presence as fatigue finally settled into his bones. He leaned forward in his chair, a steaming cup of coffee in his hand, and interrupted the flow of words. "It's wonderful to see you again, Camille, but enough of this chat-ter. I'm really more interested in learning how you fare." He noticed for the first time that she looked tired this morning, faint purple shadows under her soft blue eyes. It never oc-curred to him that she missed him; that was not the nature of their affaire. He thought of the women who had populated his world over the years with a twinge of guilt. They had all been easy and undemanding of him. Mere afterthoughts in his life. As he preferred.

The golden-haired widow fell silent, then swung her legs, her feet encased in dainty silk slippers, from the chaise to sit facing him. "I should know by now that you are not one for small talk. And yet what have I been doing this past hour?"

Ordinarily, he would have swept her in his arms without a word, satisfying both their carnal appetites as only he could. They had made love in every room of her Mayfair town house over the past two years, a welcome shock after the studiously genteel affections of Camille's late husband. A generous lover, inventive, inexhaustible and unselfish, Archer had been a revelation and, as such, would be sorely missed in her life. Camille was nothing if not intuitive and she realized that something had changed.

"So tell me of this Cairo business, if you can," she said lightly, sensing that it was not business he wanted to discuss. It never was with Archer. He skimmed the surface of life as lightly as his much vaunted yacht, never cutting too deeply.

"There's not much I can say. The weather was overly warm. The sights inspiring."

"I know what a lover of antiquities you are." The tone was ironic.

"Rocks and more rocks."

They had never been at a loss for words before, their silences amicable and comfortable. But this morning, an unfamiliar tension pervaded the salon. It would not do to examine her feelings too closely, Camille thought, her mouth already dry with loss.

"No need to prevaricate, Richard," she interjected, wondering at her courage. "I know what you have really come to say." She stopped to pour herself another cup of coffee, focusing on the spouting liquid as she spoke. "I am not entirely surprised. It is for the best."

If her confession surprised him, he didn't show it. Instead, he reached over to touch her hand, hovering over the urn. "You are a beautiful, understanding woman, Camille."

She smiled pensively, pushing his hand away lightly. "We have had a good run, Richard. You and I. I could not have survived those first years after Matthew's death without you."

He made a dismissive sound. "Of course, you could have," he said leaning back into his chair. "But I could not have found another who is so understanding about my absences and peripatetic ways."

"I won't scold but sometimes women deserve a little more than they ask for." She frowned. "And I am not speaking of jewels and trinkets." Smoothing down the folds of her dressing gown, she looked perplexed. "I can tell something is bothering you, darling. I know that you prefer to keep things light between us but now that there is no risk . . ."

Archer sipped his coffee. "Risk?" His brows shot up.

"Of course. You avoid any real topic of worth for fear of getting too close to a woman. You use humor and distance and, lest I could ever forget, a veritable cache of amorous technique."

"I've never heard you complain before."

She smiled. "And I'm not complaining now. Merely telling you that now's your chance, darling. You have nothing to lose. And dare I say it, nothing to fear. It's over between us and yet I think I know you better than most. So why not tell me what's troubling you?"

His coffee cup half raised, Archer smiled. "Nothing is troubling me."

Camille shook her blond curls. "Sometimes you are a bloody damned idiot," she said, her voice low and a little angry. "You helped me when I needed someone and now you reject the help I offer you. Do not hurt me this way."

Archer set down his coffee. "I would never hurt you, Camille." The honesty in her eyes pained him as little else could. The ice beneath his feet was thin and he feared breaking through; he realized that he had made his way through London's early morning in search of something he could scarcely name.

"Then let me help you. Talk to me." Camille's expression softened. "What happened in Cairo? And I don't mean whatever it was you got up to. Tell me what really happened. What has changed?" What has changed you, she really wanted to say.

The coffee was suddenly bitter. "Nothing happened, Camille," he lied, but he could not continue the lie in its entirety. "But you are quite right when you say that you know me better than many others. So perhaps you can tell me . . ." He paused, taking another sip of his coffee, leaving the sentence unfinished.

Camille put a hand to her forehead. "Tell you what? What you wish to hear or what you need to hear?"

"You deserve the opportunity at the very least."

"Because you have decided that we are to part company? You believe that I should like to twist the knife a little bit, in revenge?" She shook her head, acknowledging that he did not realize she loved him. "I'd hoped you'd know me better, Richard." Lord, he was a gorgeous man. Rumpled, tired, larger than life, sitting in her morning room, oozing that masculinity that she'd found irresistible from the start. Suddenly, she wanted nothing more than to stop the flow of words, to turn back the clock, saunter over to his chair and fall into his arms. She gave herself an inward shake. She'd known from the beginning that Lord Archer was not for her to keep. She'd realized it from the start, the moment she'd seen him from across the room at her best friend's Lady Dorrington's recital, those blue eyes in that rugged face . . . dear God. She took a breath. "There is no easy way for me to say it."

He arched a brow. "Then say it straight out."

"It's simply that you run away. . . . Oh, dear," she said watching his face. "I don't mean in the literal sense."

"I've never been accused of cowardice." He smiled.

"That's not what I meant, Richard."

"Then what do you mean? Please go on. I need to hear this. And from you, a woman I respect deeply."

Camille held up both hands, palms out. "I appreciate your trust."

"And respect."

She took a deep breath. "Bluntly put, this rootlessness that you seem to prefer . . . I do not quite understand it. But you cannot keep running away from people, from places, from those about whom you begin to care. You are nearly forty years of age, Richard. It is time."

"You make it sound as though I have a foot in the grave. That I should find myself some young miss and saddle her with a half-dozen babes."

She jerked out of the chaise, frustration marking her brow. "There you go. Deflecting the seriousness of the moment with some ridiculous attempt at humor."

He shrugged helplessly. "Very well then. I shall be perfectly serious. Time for what, precisely, Camille?"

Taking another deep breath, she said, "To confront what you fear most. It's that simple, my dear friend." She had almost said dear *lover*. She took a sip of her now tepid coffee, looking away.

Shoving a hand through his hair, Archer stared darkly at Camille. Unbidden, the image of Meredith shimmered before his mind's eye. *Fear*. Abruptly, he shoved back his chair. "I should go," he said, his voice gruff. "I have imposed upon you long enough. In every sense." He picked up his jacket.

The countess placed her cup carefully on the table and then stood, drawing herself up to her full, if diminutive height. She barely reached his shoulder. "I hope I have not offended you. That was not my intent."

"You could never offend me, Camille."

"We shall always be friends, I trust."

"Always."

Camille forced herself to meet his gaze. "Where will you go?" She knew how much he loathed the emptiness of his London town house.

"That's never a problem."

He thrust a hand through his hair. He'd a sudden fancy for a bottle of brandy and a biddable woman who would fuck him blind.

Chapter 5

The hansom cab rocked to a stop in front of Meredith's hired town house off Belgravia Square. She shivered as the door opened and cold air flooded the interior, lashing the tip of her nose with an icy breeze. London in early December was a world away from Egypt.

A footman materialized on the steps to hand her from the coach. A flurry of wet drops, almost snow, swirled about them, sticking to her lashes. She suddenly missed Montfort with a pang that took her breath away as she remembered how when she was chilled to the bone, a hot brick would instantly appear to warm her feet, courtesy of the small staff of loyal servants that had seen to her care over the years.

She clutched her leather-gloved hands together to warm them. Nostalgia would do her little good. What she needed was a ride in Hyde Park, to simply hire a mount for the afternoon and exercise until her nervous energy had been burned to a crisp, banishing the cold that had settled in the pit of her stomach since that afternoon in Rashid. Even now, her shoulder blades twitched and she glanced up and down the street. Despising the sensation of being watched, she tamped down the flame of fear that flickered to life. Before the incident at the abandoned fort, she had put the ever-present sense of heightened awareness behind her, but today she couldn't escape or ignore it. Trepidation stalked her, and she forced herself to walk, not run up the steps of the town house.

Once inside, Meredith took a deep breath. What a liar she was. Lying to herself and lying to Lord Richard Buckingham Archer. In her heart, she knew that those men at St. Julien had been sent by someone, a truth too bitter for her to swallow, and one she could not yet make herself digest. She had not been able to shake the ominous feeling that had come over her when she'd faced the third man in the group of Arabs that had descended upon her. There had been something wrong about the way he'd been looking at her. The dark emotions were made worse by the fact that she had killed him, an unholy secret she now shared with a man she could not permit herself to trust.

Archer. Her stomach tightened. Her independence was what had kept Rowena and Julia safe; the last thing she needed or wanted was Lord Richard Archer sniffing about. His presence in her life was entirely suspect, causing her to wonder what his real interest in an aging spinster might be. Most humiliating, he had slipped away the self-protective blanket of numbness she'd enveloped herself in these past years, reawakening in her an appetite she had long ago forsworn. It had been many years since she'd had a man in her bed, and she would do anything to keep it that way; she would maintain a distance between them. Her response to him had been entirely inadvisable, the result of a highly tumultuous situation. Nothing more.

Having left Cairo, she had returned to London to throw herself into her work, reviewing the knowledge she had collected whilst in Egypt, collating her notes, consulting her dictionaries and reference books to refine her lecture. A few forays to the Victoria and Albert and the British Museum had been her only excursions. Meredith now looked around the front hallway of the town house, slowing her thoughts by breathing in the calming aroma of beeswax and lemon oil.

Leased by her London solicitor on her behalf, the Belgravia town house was of respectable size, made of creamy stone, its narrow rooms accompanied by a suitably aloof butler and staff, the former in the habit of regarding her with a mask of well-practiced hauteur. Broton was accustomed to serving a much more demanding and fashionable master and made his disaffection known. How entirely different he was from the perennially irascible Angus McLean, Montfort's grounds-keeper and the closest thing to a butler Meredith had ever known. If a superior butler were her only problem, Meredith thought dryly, turning to the side table to quickly sort through her mail. She rifled through a small hillock of invitations, and set them to one side. There were several letters from various friends at Montfort, but none from Rowena or Julia, who, she knew despite a small fret of concern, were deliriously in love with their new husbands and traveling the Continent. All was well. There was no need for the anxiety burning in her throat.

Halfway through removing her leather gloves, she realized she did not wish to be shut up in her study for the evening with little more than her rampant imagination and a dinner tray before the fire for company. Having spent most of the morning and afternoon at the British Library, finalizing the last words of her lecture to be delivered tomorrow evening at Burlington House, there was little left to do. She would not be able to settle anything, other than making a few desultory notes about what she might do to add to her lecture. It was truly too late for anything more.

Throwing her wrap over the balustrade, she checked her watch, fiddling with the chain, which had developed a small kink. She should go riding instead to soothe her jangled nerves. Cowering in the confines of this tall, narrow house would do her little good.

One hour later, Meredith folded up the collar of her great-coat, pleased that she had remembered to pack it in her trunk when she'd traveled south from Montfort. At the entrance to Rotten Row, deserted now because of the weather, the mist was beginning to turn to snow once again. Flakes melted against her skin, sending icy rivers down her neck. Nodding to the groom from the Bathurst Stables who held out the stirrup for her, she swung up into the saddle and took a firm grip on the reins.

The gelding danced across the stones, iron-shod hooves sinking into the softening earth. Reveling in the bite of the weather, Meredith snapped the reins, focusing on the horse that pranced and cross-stepped with high energy beneath her. She smiled behind her collar, grateful for the distraction as the sleet flew past her in flurries. It stuck to her coat, soaked into the exposed wool of her riding skirt and numbed her toes.

Urging the gelding forward into a trot and then into a canter, she soon left the groom behind. Time passed in perfect rhythm, the distinct jangle of harness the only sound on the deserted path, abandoned by fashionable London because of the inclement weather. Meredith gave herself over to simple, physical exertion, the perfect tonic to days spent indoors and at the library completing her work. The tension that had enveloped her like a shroud was beginning to dissipate, along with the memories of Archer that had haunted her every day since her return.

Mercifully, he had remained true to his word, and had delayed his departure from Cairo, allowing her the peace and privacy she required on her return to London. Quite deliberately, she had exorcised any trace of Archer from her thoughts and emotions, focusing instead on the challenge that lay ahead of her.

Mentally recalling the focus of her lecture, she reviewed her notes in her mind, envisioning the three parallel inscriptions on the stone. The major breakthrough had come from a British physicist, a friend of her father's who had advanced the idea that hieroglyphic characters could have phonetic value. It had been commonly believed that in hieroglyphic writing, elliptical figures called cartouches represented royal names. It was only later that Champollion had concluded that the ancient Egyptian language had three forms. Using only fourteen incomplete lines on the Rosetta stone, he had deciphered the alphabet of ancient Egypt.

She was suddenly reminded of a night long ago, in one of the six libraries at Claire de Lune. In front of them sat the sketches of Dominique Vivan Denon, who had rendered everything he had seen as a scholar with Napoleon's army, marching past the coastline and up the Nile River. The Faron family with its unimaginable riches had purchased the drawings like so many glittering baubles. The smell of vellum, leather and paper mingled with the scent of lavender oil and the snap and sizzle of the coal in the great fireplace.

The young Faron had smiled at her, pulling the silk scarf from around his neck with one swift tug and tossing it on a chair. "Exciting, isn't it? That we have these in our possession to study, Meredith?" He walked over to her and bent to kiss her gently on the cheek. "These must have been astonishing remnants of the Egyptian culture with thousands of mysterious symbols that nobody could understand, but only dream about." His breath was warm at her cheek, his voice simultaneously teasing and exciting her. Straightening, he looked down at her with a boyish grin.

"You are making it difficult to concentrate." Meredith smiled up at him.

Faron's glance was cheerful as he took a few steps back to lounge on a corner of the desk, one long leg swaying idly. "Perhaps that is the idea, *ma chère.*"

Meredith's raised eyebrows brought forth a laugh. "There is too much for us to work through," she demurred in the suggestive tone she knew he adored. Gesturing to the notes littering the parquet floor, she was the picture of consternation.

"I think we can take our respite with a bottle of champagne in front of a roaring fire," Faron proposed. And then he pushed himself away from the desk to hold her tight, tossing her notes in the air until they showered down upon them like snowflakes.

The December snow of London now scalded Meredith's cheeks. Memories always caught her off guard, as unexpected as a knife twisting between her ribs. They were no longer clear as they once were, the words and images having slipped away, hushed by a thousand exhortations in her mind. Only the scars remained, the physical reality of their time together, pulsing on the skin beneath the long sleeves of her garments.

She urged her mount forward, riding into the fog at a smart trot, lost in her thoughts as much as the fog. Startled, she suddenly noticed a lone rider rounding the corner and materializing in the mist, coming toward her.

He slowed at her approach, clearly waiting for her, and she drew up short, cursing herself for having left her groom behind. Her mount's breath mingled with the cold as it stamped impatiently, shaking its head. She straightened in her saddle, gripping her small pistol in the confines of her greatcoat, her crop in the other hand. The horse snorted and raised its head, ears cocked attentively. Meredith tensed beneath her coat, hands and feet cold but every nerve alive. She glanced down the track to see it was utterly deserted. There was not so much as the distant tread of another rider to indicate that they weren't entirely alone.

Heart fluttering in her throat, she clenched the pistol. Across from her, the shadow of a man and horse danced in front of her, blocking her way. She could dart into the bushes lining the path, but sensed the rider would only follow her into the underbrush where they would be totally out of sight. The moment seemed an eternity as Meredith struggled to see beyond the hat pulled low over the rider's eyes.

"Let me pass." Her voice was low but her intention firm. The man who sat across from her was in for a gruesome surprise if he did not move. Anger bubbled up, cutting off reason and fear. She was prepared to take aim and fire, to inhale the familiar scent of sulfur layering the air. There would be no hesitation. Rowena and Julia—the names were all she needed, drawing upon all the years when her life was filled with just one issue—protecting her two wards. She envisioned the man pinned beneath her horse's hooves, either dead or limp with terror.

Wrath welled up within her, filling her to her fingertips, as perversely reassuring as a battalion at her back. The horseman sat straighter, still as a statue, seeming to stare through her, daring her to what? Her mind whirled with possibilities, one more ghastly than the next. Her finger curled around the trigger of her pistol, the sound of her movement muffled even in the dead quiet of the late afternoon, severed only by the unmistakable tempo of another rider coming her way.

This could be good or bad, she told herself, swallowing hard. Suddenly, the rider blocking her path spun his horse round and sped past her, greatcoat flapping behind him. A gust of cold wind kicked up, its dance gathering the dried twigs and leaves of autumn in its wake.

"Are you quite all right, madam?" a pleasant but concerned voice inquired. A man in a brown wool muffler, blond hair plastered to his head from the damp, reined in his mount.

Meredith released the hammer of her pistol. Dear God, had she imagined it all? Danger where none existed? "Yes, quite all right, sir. Thank you." Her voice surprised her with its steadiness when she felt as though she was slowly going mad. "Nothing untoward has occurred," she reassured him, forcing her pulse to slow.

"My intent was not to interfere, and if I did, my heartfelt apologies." Drawing up before her, he extended his hand. A smile lit the eyes in a thin, ascetic face. "Allow me the pleasure of an introduction. Hector Hamilton, humbly at your service."

"Lady Woolcott." Meredith took his hand. "How kind you are, Mr. Hamilton, to have stopped to ensure that all was well."

Behind his spectacles, his eyes were uneasy, looking up the path where the rider had disappeared. "Absolutely no thanks necessary. A pleasure, Lady Woolcott. But to be out on an afternoon such as this. You are an intrepid equestrian, to be sure."

"As are you, Mr. Hamilton," Meredith said unsteadily as she pushed back her hood to give it a good shake, sending small rivers of moisture to the ground.

Mr. Hamilton's thin cheeks flushed. "Certainly not. I must confess my pursuits rarely take me out of doors. I merely sought to clear my head, having been imprisoned far too long in my study." When she looked enquiringly, he added, "I am down from Cambridge, you see, but alas never far from my work."

"Cambridge—my father's alma mater. A professor, then. So what brings you to London, sir?" she asked. "The museums and such?" The sleet had ceased for a time and overhead the heavy gray clouds thinned to allow a thin, watery light. Meredith forced herself to concentrate on the normalcy of their conversation.

"Your father attended Cambridge. How splendid, Lady Woolcott. And you are quite right. The city of London has much to offer and although I confess I seldom tire of my rustications in the countryside, it does one well to venture beyond the confines of one's modest existence from time to time." Looking up at the sky, he opened his arms in an expansive gesture. "A reprieve, Lady Woolcott, it would seem."

The tension easing from her body, Meredith loosened her hold on the reins.

"If I might be so bold, might I accompany you farther, Lady Woolcott?" he asked.

Detecting nothing but kindness in his voice and manner, Meredith studied the gentleman, in truth looking less for company than escape from the dangerous and unstable nature of her thoughts. "But of course, Mr. Hamilton," she forced herself to respond brightly. "I would be pleased to have you accompany me. Perhaps you may tell me of your studies."

"Excellent," he said, offering a small bow from atop his horse. "In return, perhaps you can give me a tour of Rotten Row whilst we meander."

Meredith found herself spending the next hour with Hector Hamilton, who was an amiable and diverting companion. Despite his self-effacing appearance, he was passionate in describing his work. As they ambled slowly on their mounts through the cool afternoon, he told her of his recent appointment as don and his work at the Fitzwilliam Museum. Meredith had never visited Cambridge, but had heard of the Fitzwilliam with its collection of ancient manuscripts, coins, medals and antiquities from Egypt, Greece, Rome and Cyprus. Mr. Hamilton spoke about the extraordinarily fine series of papyrus with decoration from *The Egyptian Book of the Dead*, explaining every detail of each panel's history. His enthusiasm for his subject was contagious and for the first time in over a fortnight, Meredith felt herself begin to relax.

" 'I did no evil in that land in the Hall of the two truths, because I know the names of the gods who exist there. . . . I am pure. . . . My purity is the purification of the phoenix.' " Mr. Hector translated fluidly. "You understand, Lady Woolcott, that Inpehufnakht is dead. But the words that surround him and those contained within the shrine emerge from a series of spells designed to assist the soul of the deceased through the underworld, toward a paradiselike end."

"I am assuming that the papyrus containing these words would have been placed in or near the coffin of Inpehufnakht, along with other objects intended to ease his soul's passage into the life beyond."

Mr. Hamilton stared at her admiringly from behind his spectacles. "Indeed, Lady Woolcott. You obviously have some knowledge of the subject." Their mounts walked in perfect tandem. "I am certain that you would be eager to see the papyrus of which I speak. You would see Amun-Re, king of the gods, as he raises his hands toward a shrine with an open door."

"Where a ribbon and a perfume cone decorate his head," Meredith finished smoothly, her grip light on the reins. She was familiar with the different spells from the Ptolemic *Book of the Dead* published by a German scholar some ten years earlier.

Looking at her sharply, his brows leaping in surprise, Hamilton interrupted her. "You have seen the papyrus!"

Ahead the Marble Arch was visible, the white Carrara marble monument based on the triumphal arch of Constantine of Rome. Meredith shook her head. "I have not. But my late father had, as a student at the university many decades ago now."

"Why, of course." Mr. Hamilton nodded vigorously and then adjusted his scarf against the damp. "Then you will indulge me while I tell you what happens next—unless, of course, you already know."

"I should like to hear more," she said with a smile, pausing to lean forward and pat the neck of her mount, who snorted approvingly.

"You are indeed accommodating, Lady Woolcott," Hamilton acceded, responding with a smile of his own. "In the next section of the spell, the deceased addresses each of the deities in turn, denying any wrongdoing in his life. 'I have done no falsehood. O, Fire-Embracer, who came forth from Kheraha,

I have not robbed. O, Dangerous One, who came forth from Rosetjau, I have not killed men. . . .' "

The watery sun was beginning to lose what little strength it had, dipping behind the clouds and ushering in early evening. Suddenly cold, Meredith shuddered within her coat. "The soul is being asked to be judged righteous," she said, "whereas the corrupt soul faces utter annihilation."

"Indeed, the demon Ammut is often shown lurking by the scales, a cross between a lion, a crocodile and a hippopotamus, prepared to devour the soul of the wicked." Mr. Hamilton looked at her sharply. "I am boring you, I fear."

"Not at all, Mr. Hamilton." Abruptly, she forced a smile, well aware that it would never occur to a man that a woman might have scholarly knowledge to call her own. "I have some slight interest in the subject. One of the most intriguing scrolls to my knowledge is the one containing a scene showing the heart of a dead person being weighed against divine order, and a recitation of his sins."

"But of course." His smile lit his serious face. "You studied at your father's knee."

"And for a lifetime afterwards." She smoothed the leather of her gloves, her hands tightening instinctively on the reins. "I speak five languages fluently, as well as having a knowledge of Greek, Latin, Arabic and Coptic. And as my own scholarly interests encompass ancient languages, I have a peripheral understanding of *The Book of the Dead.*"

Hamilton's eyebrows arched again in apparent surprise. "Well done! Astounding. You have my admiration, Lady Woolcott." He brought his palms together in a show of appreciation, and then slowed his mount to a halt.

Suddenly embarrassed, Meredith followed suit, reining in the gelding, wishing to return to Belgravia Square and the warmth of a roaring fire. She proffered her hand across the pommel of her saddle. "Sir, I thank you for your entertaining company. It was a pleasure to meet you."

"You are cold. And here I've been keeping you." Hamilton took her hand and then, oddly, pressed his other hand atop hers. "Lady Woolcott . . ." he said, a bit unsteadily. "I thank you for your company."

The late afternoon had once again turned cloudy and a chilly wind sailed up from the Serpentine River. Meredith pulled her hand away, ostensibly to draw her hood over her head, taken aback by his gesture and the odd intensity of his expression. Suddenly, she found their proximity disconcerting. But how ridiculously fanciful, again. She was allowing her nerves to vex her when Mr. Hamilton was merely making overtures to further their acquaintance, after learning of their common interests. Briskly rubbing her hands together, Meredith forced herself to feel generously disposed toward the entreaty in his tone. "It is I who should thank you for coming to my aid, ensuring that all was well, Mr. Hamilton."

The wind seemed to change direction, whistling with renewed vigor. For a moment, neither of them spoke, until at last, Mr. Hamilton shifted away, his horse taking several steps back. "A nasty day, inclement weather and a chance encounter," he said rather wistfully, his eyes drifting over a low stone wall.

Meredith managed a weak smile. "And a wonderful conversation," she murmured. He returned her gaze, staring at her openly, his eyes behind the spectacles sincere, his smile warm. "And now I must return home having made your acquaintance, Mr. Hamilton. Perhaps our paths will cross once more."

"I know my words are precipitous. . . ." His tone dropped to a solemn whisper.

Meredith felt as though she should respond and opened her mouth, but she must have hesitated a moment too long. Mr. Hamilton's tone was edged with concern. "We seem to have much in common, Lady Woolcott. And so I might hope . . . although I trust I was not overly presumptuous regaling you with the details of my work at Cambridge," he rambled. "Then again, a woman of your unusual erudition must find herself exceedingly in demand."

The gelding twitched beneath her. "By no means is your company tiresome. Quite the opposite," she answered, willing the uncertainty from her voice. They did have much in common and it would be churlish of her not to respond to the poor man who had stopped to come to her aid. "Mr. Hamilton," she said spontaneously, "I am delivering a lecture tomorrow night. At Burlington House. And I should very much like it if you would come as my guest."

Mr. Hamilton's face lit up first in surprise and then at the prospect. "A paper! Burlington House—why I am a Fellow." He adjusted his spectacles, which had slipped down his nose. "I should be positively delighted to attend. As a matter of fact, I had been intending to go in any case." His fine hair whipped back from his coat collar in the breeze as he leaned across the saddle toward her. "And why am I not surprised that a woman of your obvious intelligence and interests has been asked to deliver a lecture at such an august institution? Well done, Lady Woolcott! Might I inquire as to the subject of your address?"

Chapter 6

Lord Richard Archer walked up the steps of Burlington House just before seven. He handed his coat and hat over to a footman, gave his name, which was already on the list, and made his way to the main salon off the center hall. The first floor was a sequence of interiors suitable for grand social occasions with twenty-four-carat gold leaf throughout adorning walls lined with silk damask. A ballroom with a coved, compartmented ceiling was linked to a state dining room on the south side of the building, the two yoked by an enfilade of five south-facing rooms.

The evening was not yet under way, but the agenda had been distributed in a handsome brown binding, which most of the members had folded neatly under their arms. About a hundred or so men were standing in groups of three or more and Archer found himself introduced to a rather squat older gentleman with muttonchops and a ruddy complexion, who proceeded to regale him with the most recent investigations published in the Linnaean Society journal. Resigned to his fate, Archer pretended to listen, casting his eyes about the hall.

No sign of Lady Woolcott. For some reason he did not wish to examine, Archer was in a rare temper. He had been since he'd met with the odious Hamilton and then shared his subsequently foul mood with the Countess of Blenheim. Her assessment of his situation frankly rankled and he had left Mayfair only to find himself pacing his town house, his unheralded appearance startling his butler and staff. The more he thought about Meredith's cavalier and quite frankly dangerous behavior, the angrier he had become. He recalled Camille's words, but it was anger, not fear, as she'd suggested, that drove him. Worse still, anger had not been found in his repertoire before the advent of Meredith Woolcott in his life. He couldn't remember the last time he'd been in a temper as, quite frankly, he didn't care enough about anything to set his blood boiling. Yet he'd thought of little else during the past few days. He was not given to conjecture, but he now agreed with Lord Spencer that the noose was tightening around Lady Meredith Woolcott's slender neck, although she was loath to admit it. First the attack at Rashid and now Hector Hamilton. . . .

This mood was untenable. He thought of the copper kaleidoscope wrapped in silk and stuffed incongruously in the stuffed squabs of his carriage. A spectacularly cruel reminder for Meredith Woolcott, with special import. He had read the second dossier Spencer had assembled, assimilated the facts, all the while well aware that what he was about to do would only bring Meredith's searingly painful past back to her.

Still no sign of her. He made his excuses to the mutton-chopped gentleman and wound his way to one of the seats arranged in a half-moon to face the raised dais. He tried to envision Meredith giving her paper, precise and prim and yet passionate all at the same time. *Passion.* Suddenly he saw her lying naked in a tousled bed, a secret smile illuminating her face, her hand reaching out to draw him down to her, her long limbs gilded by firelight.

With great difficulty, and a darkly muttered curse, he returned his attention to the dais behind which Lord George Cavendish, whose outrageously wealthy uncle had bequeathed

Burlington House to the Learned Societies of London a decade earlier, rose from his chair and began to speak. The audience settled into chairs.

"Gentlemen, first, allow me to welcome everyone to this month's meeting of the Learned Societies. I am certain I speak for all of us when I say that I'm pleased so many of our Fellows could be in attendance this evening." Cavendish was a barrel-chested man balanced precariously on two spindly legs. He was carefully and somberly dressed in a jacket and waistcoat that barely closed around his paunch, straining the mother-of-pearl buttons on his waistcoat. He wore thick spectacles, a seemingly unacknowledged prerequisite for membership in the Learned Societies, Archer thought uncharitably. Polite applause rippled around the hall accordingly. Cavendish droned on about important business and then gave a short dissertation on the society's newest acquisition, a series of drawings by the sixteenth-century architect Andrea Palladio.

Archer's thoughts drifted elsewhere. The salon was magnificent, an incongruous backdrop to the balding heads and spectacles bathed in the light of an astounding crystal chandelier. Around him came the drift of hushed concentration, allowing him to survey the room from his seat. Hector Hamilton would be certain to make an appearance, sobriety and necessity cruel taskmasters. He would recall little of their conversation at Crockford's or what he had unwittingly revealed, and confirmed. Archer counted upon it.

In the interim, another gentleman had approached the dais, having been introduced as a gifted mathematician and an exceptional experimentalist. Michael Faraday, with a white mane of hair and brusque manner, brandished a magnet in his hand before launching into the phenomena of electricity and magnetism and explaining how a moving magnet could induce an electric current in a wire.

"If changing magnetic fields may induce a current," he told the audience, "what is the effect of changing gravitational fields? If you believe that, at the deepest level, all forces have some common cause—as *I* do—then what shall we find?"

Twenty minutes passed. A whispered conversation began to Archer's far right. He would not have thought Hector Hamilton a latecomer, but he drifted near the back doors before sliding into a seat. Faraday had just finished his dissertation, gathering his papers before Cavendish took his place behind the dais. With hands clasped behind his back, straining his waistcoat further, he waited for the attendant applause to dissipate before clearing his throat portentously.

"I should like to introduce the last of our lecturers this evening." The room fell into a deeper hush. "Our history is a long and distinguished one. From the establishment in 1788 of the Linnaean Society to the Royal and Geological Societies founded in 1807, our intent has always been to give a stronger impulse and a more systematic direction to scientific and scholarly inquiry, to promote the intercourse of those who cultivate learning in far-flung regions of the British Empire and indeed, with foreign philosophers, to obtain attention for the objects of scholarly inquiry and to remove any disadvantages which impede its progress." Cavendish looked meaningfully at his audience. "However, it behooves us to preface this presentation by addressing the question—the female question—if I might be so audacious, to which learned societies such as ours are increasingly being asked to entertain." There was a rumble in the audience, which Cavendish endeavored to still with raised palms. "It's a highly contentious issue, the entry of women to learned societies." A few well-timed guffaws reached the podium. "It is of course, out of the question," he said with confident assurance. "However, we cannot dismiss the increasing number of ladies, eminent as travelers and scholars, as contributors to the stock of our knowledge. There is evidence brought forward of a desire to enjoy the practical privileges conferred by our Fellowship here."

Cavendish stepped out from behind the dais. "Which

brings us to our next lecturer, a woman whose father, you may recall, was one of the foremost philologists in the ancient languages, the late Lord Christian Woolcott." His tone dripped condescension. "It would appear that Lady Woolcott, his daughter, inherited in some modest way her father's talents and prodigious intellectual interests. As a result, she is here this evening to deliver her paper, based on recent excursions to Egypt, regarding the Rosetta stone and the intriguing questions it continues to pose. I should like to introduce Lady Meredith Woolcott."

A smattering of applause, faint praise indeed, as Meredith appeared. Her head held high, she acknowledged the room briefly. Archer had the sense that she was searching for something, grappling with a notion she could not fully understand, standing before an audience who did not welcome her. Her garments for the evening were well chosen, a high-necked blouse with lace marching up to her chin, an emerald-green jacket and a narrow skirt that displayed a modest bustle. Save for the green jacket, which complemented her hair, the ensemble was deliberately chosen not to draw attention.

The strategy did not work for Archer. Images looped through his mind and speared directly to his groin. To see her, touch her, taste her. It had been close to two months since he'd been able to do any of those things. An eternity that engendered a kind of thirst that he couldn't hope to explain, to himself or anyone else, much less to Camille, whose insights had touched an open nerve. Meredith stared down at the audience for a moment, her mouth set in a firm, almost disapproving line, her color high, cheeks flushed a faint pink. Her eyes widened when she saw him and he could see her consider turning about and marching off the podium. Pride prevailed and she raised her chin and stared him down for a moment before turning her attention decisively to the neat collection of papers in her hand.

Her low voice, like honey, poured through the salon. She thanked Lord Cavendish and her reluctant audience with a hint of irony in her tone. "To find myself in such august company is indeed a rare distinction, one to which I should never have imagined to aspire." Holding the disgruntled spectators with the directness of her gaze, seemingly unaware and unconcerned about being the sole female in the company, she continued. "The Rosetta stone unlocked one of the world's great mysteries by providing a key to the meaning of Egyptian hieroglyphics. However, I, among other philologists, still relish the remaining mysteries of this large fragment of stela, originally placed in a temple of Ptolemy. I should add that the decoding of the Egyptian script is not a single event that occurred in 1822 when we deciphered the enigma, but a continuous process that is repeated at every reading of the artifact. Such study," she continued coolly, "I would argue, is the closest one can come to speaking with civilizations long past. And like any act of reading, it is a process of dialogue. It is therefore my contention that the deciphering of the stone and of ancient Egypt is an engagement that has scarcely begun."

Archer found himself mesmerized. Several strands of her hair fell forward over her shoulder, only to be pushed impatiently back again. Shifting uncomfortably in his chair, he was acutely aware of the sudden constriction of his breeches, despite the arid and lofty subject. He realized with no embarrassment that he'd spent half the night thinking about Meredith, sunk in the inadvisable imaginings that came all too readily to him of late. Sleek, naked limbs, a cloud of auburn hair and her cries echoing into the darkness. He scrubbed a hand down his face, wondering yet again when last he'd had a woman. He couldn't remember, that was the problem. There was something about the way she held herself, there on the podium, with her low voice, and that fierce intelligence that seemed equally passionate and defiant. This was a woman who had battled fire, isolation and fear. And bested a madman. Meredith Woolcott was extraordinary to the point of distraction.

In the end, he decided, with another spurt of anger, he would have to bed her. Perhaps fucking her would be enough to cure him. As it was, he didn't want to give further thought to Lord Spencer's dictates and whether he had the bollocks to see them through.

Archer paused, waiting as Meredith finished glancing at her notes. She wielded a formidable intelligence without restraint. As her gaze swept the audience, Cavendish hovered indecisively behind her.

"Interesting indeed, Lady Woolcott," he said, damning with faint praise once more. "Now I see we appear to have a query—yes—Sir Beauchamps." A flurry of questions ensued, all of which were answered with measured tones, testament to her confidence in her subject matter: questions about her father's work, the nuances of Champollion's translations and mysteries yet to be uncovered.

"Many still question, Lady Woolcott, whether the inscription was written first in Egyptian or in Greek. Do you have an opinion upon the matter?"

Meredith graciously nodded, stepping away from the dais. "I should think that it was composed simultaneously during a fractious meeting between courtiers and priests," she answered definitively, following with evidence from her impressive command of previous translations by Thomas Young and Jean-François Champollion. Several questions followed while Archer wrestled with the entirely unfamiliar urge to swoop her away from this veritable swarm of men. He wished to drag her off, even though half of London would bear witness to his outrageousness.

Another question was asked, which Archer half heard, only paying attention to Meredith's response. "Indeed, traces of pink pigment were found recently on the stone. We cannot determine whether the pigment is ancient or used by the

French scholars who first worked on the stone. We also do not know exactly where the stela was placed in the temple, although during my recent visit to the remnants of the fort of St. Julien in Rashid"—she paused to take a short breath—"I discovered indications that it was placed against a mud wall in the outer part of the building." Archer recalled Meredith leaning into the shadows, Murad holding the lantern higher. And then she'd scribbled something into her notebook.

"The significance of the question has to do with who was intended to read the stone," she continued. "An elite group which had access to the inner temple or a wider audience. If the pigment proves to be ancient, that also would support the notion the stone was inside the temple, because the pigment would make the inscription visible in low light."

Behind Archer, several rows to the rear, came a familiar voice. Hamilton blinked owlishly back and forth from Cavendish to Meredith. He raised a hand to speak. "Lady Woolcott, I simply wish to thank you for the extraordinarily insightful and erudite paper you delivered this evening. I can only speak for myself when I say that you have given us an unprecedented look into one of the world's great mysteries. . . ." Archer gritted his teeth, suppressing the urge to roll his eyes while Hamilton continued for several minutes applying his unctuous praise.

When he could bear it no longer and without waiting for Cavendish's nod, Archer rose from his chair, and without ceremony, abruptly interrupted Hamilton. "Lady Woolcott," he said. His voice was like a thunderclap, commanding absolute silence in the salon. Even Cavendish, hovering like a hesitant chaperone behind the dais, did not intervene. Archer inclined his head ever so slightly. Meredith returned his gaze, her expression guarded. "If I might be permitted to ask you about your recent visit to Fort St. Julien," he asked. "Perhaps you might share with us the highlights of your investigations there."

Her expression remained passive, but he knew that she

was raining curses upon his head, realizing precisely to what he referred. She met his gaze squarely. "I don't believe we have time to spare for such discussion, sir, and it would in all likelihood have little bearing upon the significance of the stone." Her tone was brittle and dismissive.

"I should like to disagree, respectfully, of course."

"Perhaps it is your ignorance of the subject matter that causes you to disagree." A rumble of disapproval rolled through the salon as throats were cleared and chairs pushed back. And with a curt nod to Lord Cavendish and a frown for Archer, Lady Woolcott gathered up her papers and left the dais. Despite their overtly hostile exchange, it was not possible to shock her audience to any greater degree than her presence already had. Moments later, the proceedings having come to their official conclusion, Hector Hamilton was leading Lady Woolcott like a prize on his arm, through the salon to the main hall, where roving gentlemen were making their way from group to group. Meredith's narrow hooped skirts bounced slightly with each step, rhythmic, suggestive and, for Archer, impossible to ignore.

Archer stood in the wide doorway for an instant, then stepped forward as Meredith looked up from the men who were gathered around her.

"Lord Archer." She raised one brow, trying not to allow her simmering anger to take over good sense, but she refused to stand down. "It appears as though you intend to continue your inquisition." Here he was, larger than life. And in the most obvious, forward way imaginable, making an appearance at Burlington House. She had been adamant about his not seeking her out, to no avail. Torn between the desire to rain fists upon his arrogant head and simply walk away, she took a steadying breath. She would be calm, cool and aloof. That was the proper response to maintain control of herself and the situation. Instead of giving in to irrational impulse, she turned to Mr. Hamilton, who was eyeing Archer with an inexplicable combination of hesitation and dread.

"Lord Archer, Mr. Hamilton." She began the introductions, but not a moment later both men had indicated that they had already met.

"In other, somewhat more trying circumstances," Hamilton explained to her, with what could only be called an importuning glance at Archer.

"Which are best forgotten," Archer returned smoothly. He gestured toward Meredith. "As for my acquaintance with Lady Woolcott . . ."

"Also best forgotten," Meredith said, taking Hamilton's arm. "We are the slightest of acquaintances, actually. Through marriage."

Hamilton began to ask more about their acquaintance. Meredith must have stiffened, and Hamilton paused before completing his query. "Should we continue our way through the crush, Mr. Hamilton?" Meredith interrupted. "I do believe that Lord Lyttleton had several questions he wished to discuss with me."

"And small wonder," Hamilton proclaimed. "You have set them all agog with interest."

Archer's jaw hardened at the familiar tone with which she addressed the man clinging to her side like a limpet. "I should not wish you to delay on my account, Lady Woolcott, but"—he turned to Hamilton—"we have some family matters to discuss, if you would excuse us, Mr. Hamilton?"

"I do believe this can wait, Lord Archer." Arrogant and foolhardy man. Meredith's eyes narrowed with displeasure, attempting to shut out his presence, admittedly overwhelming in a sea of spindly-legged scholars and pretentious sages. If only she did not wish to be alone with him, she fumed inwardly, agonizingly aware of the blue of his eyes so at odds with the spare planes of his face.

Perhaps a good fight was exactly what she needed, and the opportunity to remind Archer of his promise to her. Blood pounded in her ears. She was both exhilarated and relieved that she had delivered her paper with a modicum of success, despite the constrained response of the audience, due to her gender and the intractable belief that women had no place in the halls of higher learning. And now to have Archer interfere with what should have been a triumph for her . . .

Hamilton cleared his throat. "Lady Woolcott is in great demand this evening. And I, too, should like to take the opportunity to learn more about her exciting endeavors. My questions are endless."

Meredith's expression softened, and she lightly pressed Hamilton's hand. "You flatter me unduly." Her escort smiled back warmly and squeezed her hand in return. Archer's jaw clenched. "Mr. Hamilton has invited me to Cambridge." Her eyes sparkled while Hamilton almost absently retained her hand in a light clasp.

"Is that so?" Archer asked, his tone grimmer than expected.

Hamilton chuckled and replied that he was entirely at Meredith's disposal. "But for now I believe we should take ourselves off to find Lyttleton lest he, or anyone else for that matter, accuse me of monopolizing your company. And taking advantage of your graciousness." He adjusted his spectacles, pulling her infinitesimally closer to him at the same time.

"You are hardly taking advantage. However, I will concede that perhaps we should attend to Lyttleton." She tipped her head to look over the knots of people in the hall, deliberately ignoring Archer. Yet she was all too aware of his eyes boring into her. He shouldn't be so compelling and she shouldn't allow that magnetism to influence her as it did. She knew the feeling uncoiling within her and she didn't want any part of it.

Several men drifted over to their tight circle. For the next half hour, Meredith tried to follow the conversation while struggling with her growing unease. Beauchamps, his jowls trembling, needled her about the final comments in her lecture while Lyttleton, having found them at last, proffered an interesting interpretation of one of the stela. Her lips dry and her shoulders aching from the strain, she vaguely listened while Grenville articulated a hypothesis with enervating detail. All the while her mind was simply churning to find a way to escape them all.

Yawning discreetly behind her hand, she was aware of Hamilton at her side and his hesitant offer, whispered in her ear, to escort her home. Her pulse leapt as Archer cast her a sharp glance. She grimaced back at him.

A moment later, Sir Staunton claimed her hand and bent over it with a flourish. Meredith greeted him and several other men as they filtered by her, refusing to surrender to exhaustion when all she could really feel was the hollow and insistent ache of desire. Archer stood back watching, but when she swayed on her feet, he shoved both hands in the pockets of his trousers and said, "I've waited long enough, Lady Woolcott." The low growl of his voice cut right through her, vibrating inside her chest.

He wouldn't let her go and for some reason the thought rankled. *That she should be so weak around the man.* "Ah, yes," she said. "I had almost forgotten about you, Lord Archer."

"So it would appear," he said, the words close to a threat. She flicked her gaze over him and his eyes met hers. Meredith removed her arm from Hamilton's and stepped from the circle. "Judging by your tone, it cannot wait any longer."

"No, it can't."

Hamilton's open mouth gaped like a fish's, before he attempted to splutter a question.

"Then if you would excuse us, Mr. Hamilton," she said. "Gentlemen," she added for the benefit of Staunton and Lyttleton. Surprising even herself, she brazenly placed a hand on Archer's arm, her knees nearly buckling as a wave of desire racked her. It didn't matter that she was still angry. She found herself wishing to be alone with him in a way that did not bode well. "We shan't be long."

She smiled over her shoulder, allowing Archer to lead her from the hall. "So good of you to be acquiescent for a change," he ground out. "It only took an hour." All around them the salon and its occupants seemed to recede into the background. Nothing else existed except the heightened emotion between them, a heady mix of fury, desire and pent-up frustration.

Meredith slid her hand over the tense muscles of his arm, tugging him toward the center of the room, a part of her wishing to delay the moment alone with him. "I truly should not make myself scarce."

"I think I'd rather have you join me for a brandy." He tucked her hand decisively into the crook of his arm and led her toward one of the rooms off the hall.

"To discuss this family matter," she said with a raised brow. As they pushed past the throngs of debating men that had spilled into the ballroom, she found herself led into one of the alcoves that opened off it. The door closed behind them decisively.

It was empty, save for two brocade-covered benches and an enormous canvas by Boucher depicting Diana after the hunt. The flesh-toned scene was overtly sensual and Meredith backed away until her bustle hit the back of one of the divans. "The refreshment salon is the other way," she said tartly. "I don't see a drinks table anywhere nearby."

"You've found me out," he said, cupping her chin with his hand. His thumb swept over her cheek. His touch was a shock, but a welcome one. Meredith rallied the remnants of her anger.

"I asked you to leave me alone."

He gave a dismissive snort. "You owe me, Lady Woolcott, lest you forget." He pressed closer, so large he seemed to fill the small space. "I should have never let you go, but forced you to listen to reason."

For the first time since they'd met, he was angry. She wanted to push him away, but somehow her body refused to obey, her senses filled with the scent and heat of him. It was like a thirst. She was parched, drinking him in. "You are ridiculously high-handed. And we had agreed to leave what happened in Rashid behind us. And yet here you are this evening, in the audience, asking your ridiculous questions."

"You were magnificent, by the way." He ran his thumb over her lower lip. "Brave, bold and brilliant."

Her skirts began to rise on one side of the bench as he bunched them up with a hand, making short work of the bustle, irritatingly familiar with the working of feminine garments. "You believe that I will be swayed by simple flattery, Archer. You could not be more wrong." She said the words but knew she was lost, felled by how much she wanted him to touch her, by how much she'd missed him in the weeks since Egypt.

His hand slid up her stockinged thigh. "I should also have added beautiful."

Talk between them was useless. She was lost. His other hand strayed up her hips, palm hot on her flesh, burning through the thin silk of her chemise. How had he managed her petticoats? She looked over his shoulder at Diana lounging nakedly and in total abandonment in the woods, feeling her own face flushed with pure desire. It didn't matter that she was close to hating him. "Can we at least attempt a conversation? After which I will reiterate that you are to leave me alone." She trembled, having lost any shred of rationality, terrified of what might happen, that she might acquiesce. More than acquiesce.

His warm breath teased the sensitive skin behind her ear, stirring her hair, a hand slipping between her thighs. Her spirits were unnaturally high, she told herself, the result of the evening, her lecture. Much like the night in Rashid, she was not herself, vulnerable in a way she would not ordinarily allow herself to be. "I am not myself," she uttered on a released breath.

"You are absolutely yourself," he said, "and this just

proves it." He ran a finger over the inside of her thigh, the thin muslin of her drawers the only barrier. Her hips rocked in response and she desperately wished to reach down, free him from his trousers, and let him take her here, upon the divan. Her palm slid down his chest against the crisp cotton of his shirt, seemingly of its own will, and suddenly he was pulling away, hand out from under her skirts, tugging the narrow skirt down, over her petticoats, to cover her.

"What are you doing?" Her words shamed her. She wanted him so badly she shook from the force of her need and yet he stood, two inches away from her, as calm and collected as a rector at Sunday service.

"I need you to listen to me."

"You have a peculiar way of making yourself heard."

"It seems as though it is the only way to get your attention."

And then it struck her. He was simply taking advantage of her neediness, her wretched vulnerability. The spinster who would lap up any crumb that was thrown her way. "You insufferable, arrogant bastard." She shoved at his chest until he stepped back, growing even more enraged that he permitted her to do so. Bigger, stronger and certainly more physically adept, Archer believed that he had her cornered. "Keep your hands and your caresses to yourself. I told you, I neither need your help nor do I trust you."

"You don't know what you're doing, Meredith."

"How dare you! I know exactly what I'm doing. I have been taking care of myself and Rowena and Julia for almost twenty years." Mortified, she felt her eyes fill with unshed tears. "And then you come along and begin interfering with my life, the moment I have a semblance of freedom. I asked you to leave me alone and what happens? One of the most important evenings of my life and whom do I see in the audience? Lord Archer, who doesn't give a fig about anything more than his next exploit, who last cracked open a book or visited a museum or library when he was in the schoolroom.

Desperately trying to keep a handle on her thoughts, she tamped down her disappointment. Archer's strategem—and it was a strategem—had left her in a state of acute distress. The ache of unfulfilled desire pulsed through her. She felt trapped in this small room as he stood rigidly across from her, his jaw clenched so tight that she expected to hear bone shatter.

Chin raised, she stared back at him appraisingly, refusing to give ground. He took one step closer, a booted foot pushing between her own. Then another step that forced her back against the cushions of the divan. His lips covered hers before she could think; her feet tangled among her skirts and the divan's curved wooden legs. The room, no bigger than an alcove really, left her nowhere to go. Archer leaned in, his hands dropping to either side of her waist, deepening the kiss. His tongue stroked enticingly, pushing her toward surrender. Humiliation battled with desire.

Then, just as suddenly as he had begun, he raised his head, leaning back while his body still held her captive. He was not even breathing heavily, whereas each exhalation shuddered out of her.

She pushed her arms between them so that her hands rested on his chest. "I never want to see you again. I cannot make my wishes any clearer."

"Impossible." His mouth was right by her ear, his breath burning her skin. His hands tightened, palms pressing into her ribs.

"Let me go." She thrust her hands out, pushing past him, hoping to leave him behind forever. She stormed back into the main hall, pausing just outside the salon. Smoothing back her hair, she straightened her skirts and adjusted her jacket. Damn him! Why was Archer pursuing her this way? How dare he storm into her world when it had just righted itself? She had been given a reprieve, but the freedom to live her life as she chose, without the punishing anxiety that had stalked her for close to twenty years was all too short-lived.

She pushed an errant pin into her hair, welcoming the pain. The problem was that she'd kissed him back, and for the moment, it was all she could think about. Annoyed with herself, she moved with what she hoped was an elegant pace into the salon, glancing about, taking in the dwindling numbers. All she wanted was to go home, settle in front of the fireplace and review her triumphant evening, lest she forget. She had delivered a paper on the Rosetta stone at Burlington House.

Muffled steps by the salon door made her stiffen. Hector Hamilton hovered on the threshold, his concerned expression slackening into relief.

"I have been looking everywhere for you, Lady Woolcott." He came to stand beside her. "You disappeared with Lord Archer for quite some time—I was anxious."

"Lady Woolcott was safe with me." Archer was steps behind her, his gaze locked on Hamilton as the two of them stared each other down. Hamilton looked away first. Meredith let out the breath she hadn't realized she'd been holding. *Go away, Archer. Just go away,* she mouthed silently.

Without acknowledging Archer, she said to Hamilton, "I believe I am ready to return home. It has been a rather long, albeit gratifying, evening."

"And I am most eager to escort you, if I might be so permitted."

"Not necessary, Hamilton."

Meredith glared over her shoulder at Archer, overriding his objection. "I would much appreciate your finding my wrap, Mr. Hamilton." The snow of the previous week had given way to a warm spell.

Hamilton blinked twice before casting about for a passing footman. She had made up her mind. She would leave at once, without Archer.

"If you don't believe what I have to say, I have something to show you," Archer said. "Something that may make a difference to you."

She looked over her shoulder and met his gaze briefly, before swallowing hard. It seemed as though ten pairs of eyes watched them expectantly. Her pulse raced and she repressed the urge to flee. Nothing he could show her would make a difference. She did not say the words, her expression telling him everything he needed to know. Her hands clenched into fists, the raised ridges on her forearms were scalding, and she thrust them into her skirts. Archer reached for her, but then obviously thought better of it, letting his arm fall back to his side.

Cavendish appeared alongside Hamilton. Pasting a smile on her face, Meredith accepted his praise with a nod of her head, even though she knew that the man disapproved heartily of her and her interests. His commendation somehow managed to belittle her at the same time. Hamilton hovered behind Cavendish, her wrap draped over his arm. Meredith allowed him to drop the cashmere over her shoulders.

When she looked up, Archer was already ahead of her, calling for his coat. Meredith watched him leave, anger and desire nearly choking her.

"Shall we?" Hamilton asked tentatively. Meredith nodded, welcoming the assault of the damp London air as the wide doors of Burlington House yawned open. Attuned to her mood, Hamilton followed her silently down the wide staircase and onto the arcade, his arm raised to call a hansom cab. Then he seemed to change his mind. "Perhaps a brisk stroll might be in order? You seem to be in need of some air."

Leaving the arcade, they walked toward Old Bond Street, now shrouded in a yellow fog. Meredith felt the urge to agree with Hamilton, a wave of heat coating her cheeks. "Wonderful idea. Walk with me?" she asked, moving a little faster ahead of him, the rain-slick cobblestones not hindering their progress. A clattering racket startled her, but it was only a carriage pulling away from the entrance of Burlington House.

"Why, of course."

Taking longer strides, she kept ahead of him, dreading the questions that were sure to follow. He could not have helped noticing the tension emanating from Archer. He would wonder at the source of it. *A family matter.* Despairing of herself, she could still feel the hollow ache. Desire denied, simple as that. It did not matter that Archer knew exactly where to touch her, how to touch her. He was obviously an experienced lover. She gripped the edge of her reticule.

A tall man in a cap appeared out of a mews, and Meredith tensed unconsciously, waiting for him to pass. After he did, she looked back over her shoulder until he was well away.

"Something that may make a difference to you." The words echoed in her head as Hamilton fell in step beside her. She'd hoped never to see Archer again, at least that was what she believed when she was not beset with this madness. She had believed herself to be free from the ties that had bound her for too long. Archer's presence threatened her freedom with his repeated insistence that she was somehow in danger. From Faron.

"The fresh air does one good at times." Hamilton gave a rueful laugh and suddenly the night did not seem quite so gray or the rain so cold. Carriages lined Stratford Street, the horses standing wearily in the damp. "We shall make the best of it, although the rain's not ceasing. I could dash back to Burlington House and arrange for a hansom. Or use my umbrella." Hamilton peered down the street. "We may find ourselves out of luck if we go much farther."

"Just a few more moments' walk. I feel the need for air. I suppose with all the excitement . . ." Hamilton nodded, his eyes behind his spectacles concerned, and Meredith sensed that he was somehow uneasy. She looked to her left, where the wide alley of Albermarle Street stretched to the north toward the Thames. She pictured the river with its sluggish, dark water carrying odd bits of debris. She shivered, remembering how she'd thought they'd lost Rowena forever to the currents of the Irthing. The wind moaned through the gaps between the bridge's balustrades, the pale stone gaze of the Southbank Lion just out of sight. Puddles marred the street, dimpled under the light rain. A familiar prickle skittered down her spine, the awareness of being followed or watched, bringing with it a world of horrendous possibilities: a blow to the head, someone strangling her from behind, a watery grave in the Thames. She shivered in the dampness.

It had been ever thus, looking over her shoulder. Until the moment that Rushford and Rowena had told her Faron lay dead, drowned in the swirling tides of the Channel. Her heart had twisted, shocking her with the ferocity of the pain. A man she had once loved and who had tormented her for too many years was now gone.

Hamilton was saying something, but Meredith heard very little. Each step she took carried her deeper into her thoughts. She knew that she was neither a weak nor emotional woman and had done her best for her wards for many years. Inheriting Montfort upon her father's death, after he'd been predeceased by an older brother, she had come into the means that allowed her to shelter her young charges from the evil she had had a hand in creating. When she'd thought Julia missing and Rowena dead, she had spent what seemed like days scanning the expansive grounds of Montfort, expecting to see Rowena on her horse Dragon, or Julia setting up her photographic apparatus by the gazebo. Desperate to have the girls returned to her, hoping for a miraculous gift, she only saw a horizon that was an unforgiving gunmetal gray. They could not be taken away from her, her conscious mind had cried, even though cruel logic had dictated that she must give up hope and give in to her grief.

Then the gift came. Her girls brought back to life. Back to Montfort.

The tightness in Meredith's chest eased. Barlow Place stretched out before her, the cobblestone road slick with damp, reflecting the dull glow of gaslight. There was nothing left to fear. Meredith turned to Hamilton, whom she'd all but forgotten. He kept pace with her long strides, respectful of her need for silence. "Thank you, dear Mr. Hamilton, for your company," she blurted out, suddenly, unaccountably grateful. The man demanded nothing of her save her presence.

He gripped his umbrella more tightly beneath his arm. "For what, my dear Lady Woolcott?" he asked. "This has been a most enjoyable evening." He took stock of her weariness. "Although you must be both entirely exhausted and exhilarated so I shall insist that we stop here. I shall see to our getting a hansom."

Without waiting for her agreement, he pulled her back to the corner where Charles Street intersected with a narrow alley. They both looked reflexively up and down the road, willing a conveyance to make an appearance. Instead, out of the mist, two men approached, the first with an unkempt beard, and a few yards behind him, a taller man wearing a top hat. Meredith tensed, watching the bearded man walk by without acknowledging their presence. She glanced over her shoulder as he passed. When she turned back, the man in the top hat stood before her, his right arm raised, and sharp, polished nickel gleaming in the rain.

Meredith made a sound low in her throat, but before the cry faded, Hamilton had placed himself in front of her. A sickeningly soft sound rent the air and Hamilton fell back, propelling them both to the ground. The world tilted, the cobblestones biting into the back of her head. Instinctively, Meredith thrust an elbow into a rib cage, hearing a howl of agony. The arm holding her went limp for an instant. Then came the sound of running feet, fading in the distance.

Breathing heavily, Meredith struggled to rise, Hamilton atop her, far heavier than he seemed. Every bone in her body protesting, she turned onto her stomach, propping herself on her elbows. A few feet away sat Hamilton's discarded umbrella. Stretching out an arm, she gripped the handle, using it to push herself up from beneath him. On her knees, swallowing nausea, she looked up and down the deserted alley before her gaze returned to Hamilton. He lay on his back, eyes open and fixed on the sky.

"Dear God." The words came out on a sob. The subtle rise and fall of his chest told her he was breathing. She would get help. But before she could rise, Hamilton had grabbed her wrist in a surprisingly strong grip. "Don't leave me . . . please."

She shook her head, hair tumbling around her. "I won't leave you." She smoothed a palm over his brow, righting his spectacles, which remained miraculously in one piece. Desperately, she surveyed his body. The gaslight illuminated the dark glisten of blood on his right thigh. It appeared to be a knife wound. Realization swept over her—he had protected her from attack, possibly saving her life.

"I won't leave you," she repeated, all the while wondering how she would get help or the attention of a hansom. Biting her lip, she gently put Hamilton's head on her lap, realizing that he had yet to release her wrist. "Can you sit up?" she asked gently. "When you're ready."

Gradually, with a hand supporting his back, he raised his torso, swaying like a puppet for a moment, before taking a steadying breath. "I think it's simply a gash in my leg," he said, turning a bilious green underneath the glare of the gaslight.

It began raining in earnest and it seemed an eternity that they remained splayed on the cobblestones like two abandoned creatures. Finally a charwoman, returning from her evening duties, came muttering to herself down the alley toward them. Meredith handed her most of the contents of her reticule, promising her the remainder if she procured a conveyance.

An hour later, they were in her Belgravia town house. Hastily discarding her sodden cashmere wrap on the pristine parquet floor, she watched Broton support a limping Hamilton into the library, where a fire burned brightly. She stayed back in the hall to compose herself, studying her too pale face in the oval mirror, mud on one cheek and hair in disarray, before sinking into an occasional chair. Slowly, she bent forward, lowering her forehead onto her arm, forcing herself to draw in deep draughts of air. The hall was blessedly cool, unlike the library, and the blood slowly returned to her head.

Bitterness closed her throat as a warm tear slid down her nose. Shamed by her lack of control, Meredith jerked up her head to dash away the tear. There was no time for useless ruminations and dark speculations. She stood, shook out her skirts, and returned to the library, where she saw Broton arranging Hamilton on the divan. Recognizing what needed to be done, she quietly asked him to summon a doctor and rouse the housekeeper from her sleep to procure linens and salve. Sniffing his disapproval, Broton obeyed, his silence remonstration for having to witness such irregularity.

"We will have you set to rights in no time," Meredith said brightly to Hamilton, whose color was returning. Anxiety and guilt tinged her words, born of a reluctance to examine too closely what had occurred. What should have been a triumphant evening had become a nightmare. Her hands trembled slightly as she picked up the silk throw and bundled it around Hamilton.

He smiled wanly. "All this fussing is entirely unnecessary, Lady Woolcott. There is very little blood, simply a minor injury. I could have returned to my rooms and summoned the doctor in the morning."

"Nonsense." She dropped to her knees on the rug, beside Hamilton's legs. "I shall let you roll up your trouser so I may have a look."

Hamilton froze when Meredith slowly tipped her head back. "Let's have a look. We do not wish the wound to fester." She felt guilty enough as it was. "When Rowena and Julia were in the schoolroom, they were forever coming to me with their scrapes and bruises. Rowena adored climbing things, the gazebo or the lofts in the stables, with predictable results. So there's nothing I haven't seen before," she said, welcoming the task at hand as a means to banish dark thoughts. When Hamilton still didn't move, looking rather like a child hiding under a blanket, she placed a hand gently upon his pant leg. He tensed against her touch. "Once we have this resolved, I promise I shall put you in a hansom to return to your rooms. Please—it is the least I can do."

"None of this is your fault, Meredith," Hamilton began, but when he met her steely gaze, he shifted on the divan, his hands diving beneath the throw. Meredith waited, not wishing to embarrass him further. Hamilton inhaled, then sighed out a breath, rolling his trouser leg up to his lower thigh. Reluctantly, he extended his leg to her and she expertly tugged until the boot released its hold. He sat stiffly and stared at the watercolor over the mantel, a flush high on his pale face.

Keeping up a low chatter about the evening that had just passed, Lord Lyttleton's questions about the positioning of the stela, Cavendish's chilly reception, and Faraday's revelations regarding magnetization, she rolled his stocking down with impersonal efficiency. Thin ankles emerged with barely thicker calves covered by a fine down of hair. The door to the library opened quietly as Broton, unsuccessful in rousing the housekeeper, placed a tray of arnica salve and strips of linen on the floor at her side.

The butler arranged a decanter of brandy and two glasses by the divan before straightening. "Shall I stay, madam?" The tone of his voice told her it was the last thing he wanted to do.

"You may go. As long as the doctor is on his way."

"Indeed, madam. I asked him to proceed immediately to Mr. Hamilton's rooms at Watlings near Charing Cross."

Hamilton looked down at her guiltily. "I made the request of Broton, although he wished to defer to your wishes."

"You may go, Broton," Meredith said wearily, without looking up. In moments, the library door clicked quietly behind him.

Hector was appraising her with concern in his eyes. His expression told her that he'd expected her to faint, perhaps, or at least reach for her smelling salts, not that she had any at hand. "I have asked far too much of you, Lady Woolcott. You, too, have had quite a shock. And all you have been doing is looking after me, whilst I should have inquired about your well-being earlier."

Meredith smiled, forcing her quaking nerves to quiet. "I've taken worse spills from a horse, Mr. Hamilton. This was merely a tumble thanks to your blessed intervention. In return, the least I can do is make quick work of this wound so you may be on your way safely to meet the doctor at your rooms."

Pulling the top from the tin of arnica, she focused on the small gash in an attempt to spare Hamilton any more embarrassment. Her fingers were steady as she dipped into the salve. He made a sharp sound through his teeth when the ointment touched his skin.

She clenched her jaw. "So sorry this hurts. But the salve will help until the doctor can see to the stitching." And with the other hand, she fished out a snowy square of linen, spreading it open. He remained utterly still, only his breathing betraying his tension. His skin was hot beneath her touch as she continued to coat the wound, which had stopped bleeding. Glancing up, she was surprised to find his eyes closed, his spectacles in his right hand. The flush still on his pale cheeks, he gripped the spectacles as though hanging on for dear life.

The situation was awkward, not that she ever gave a thought to appearances. Hamilton was a veritable stranger, in her house in the dead of night. However, she was a woman of independent means, of a certain age, who did as she wished. Continuing to apply the salve, she listened to Hamilton's uneven breathing, wondering briefly what he was thinking about, perhaps imagining another woman laying her hands upon him. It made her aware of how little she knew about the man, other than their fortuitous meeting in Hyde Park and his scholarly pursuits at Cambridge. The fact remained that he had intervened twice in her life, saving her from what exactly? The dark thoughts threatened to return, and she steadied her hand. The danger that afternoon on Rotten Row with the unknown rider was nothing but a product of her feverish imaginings, to be sure, and this evening they had found themselves the victims of footpads, nothing more. Regardless, she thought, she owed the man a debt of gratitude.

Too many debts in her life, of late. She pushed the image of Lord Archer from her mind, taking hold of a strip of linen and wrapping it around Hamilton's thigh softly, then tightening the ends securely.

He let out a breath of relief, donning his spectacles. Before she could protest, he leaned forward to roll down the trouser leg. "You have done enough, truly," he said, a flush of embarrassment on his pale cheeks. "I thank you." He sounded subdued and tired, but there was a questioning in his eyes as he looked down at her, kneeling on the floor.

"It is I who should thank you. Had you not placed yourself in front of me to deflect the knife—" she began, rocking forward on her knees.

"I wasn't thinking at all. In truth, it all occurred so quickly that it was the only response that came readily to mind. So I cannot take credit for any heroics." The flush had left his thin cheeks, but the taut line of his mouth indicated tension. It seemed as though a combination of shame and guilt held him in its grip. "None of this would have happened had I not suggested that we walk. A hansom would have been much wiser," he concluded with some bitterness.

Meredith admitted lightly. "I am equally responsible, if not more so, Mr. Hamilton. Clearly, neither of us is accustomed to the dangers of London. I had just read in the broadsheets this morning about the terrible poverty in certain sections of the city, no doubt giving rise to thieves, pickpockets and worse. When people are desperate, they are driven to desperate measures." She replaced the lid on the arnica salve. "We were simply in the wrong place at the wrong time," she added, trying to convince herself of the fact. The two men seemingly waiting for them not far from Burlington House had nothing to do with her situation, nothing at all. She was allowing that damned Archer's baseless warnings to eat away at her nerves and fuel her anxious imaginings. "Rest awhile and no more talk of guilt. These types of encounters are random, nothing more." She glanced up at him. "Your normal color is returning. I will have Broton call a carriage to take you to your rooms at Charing Cross."

Hamilton appeared doubtful, smoothing the fine silk of the throw over his lap. "I still feel responsible, terribly responsible. I promised to take you safely home and I failed in my responsibilities."

"There is nothing you could have done differently. I beg you to stop punishing yourself when, in reality, you acquitted yourself admirably. I would not be here before you, unharmed, had you not put yourself before me. Both literally and figuratively."

"Even still."

Waving away his apologies, she rose from her knees. "Entirely unnecessary." She sat opposite him in a wing-backed chair, oblivious to the stains her soiled jacket would leave on the brocade. Broton would not be pleased, she thought dryly, summoning the butler with the bellpull. She had offered earlier, but felt the need to fill the awkward silence, and gestured to the brandy and glasses. "Are you certain I can't find you some refreshment?"

He seemed not to hear her. "I do not wish to see you harmed, Lady Woolcott," he said suddenly, uttering the non sequitur out of the blue. And quietly, as though he thought it necessary to say the words aloud. She answered with silence, twisting a piece of linen between her hands.

"It is the last thing that I should wish." His voice had acquired a plaintive tone.

"Of course," she murmured. It was shock speaking. The man was injured, had lost blood. "You will feel much better once the doctor does his work. Perhaps he will give you a tincture to help with your discomfort." Broton appeared at the doorway, interpreting her nod with a glance before disappearing to summon the hansom.

"It is a small gash, hardly fatal. I am not at all concerned. But there is another matter which has been preying upon my mind." He cleared his throat. "May I ask a question, of a personal nature?"

A flicker of pressure lit in her chest. "It depends, of course."

"I do not wish to pry. . . ." Then don't, thought Meredith, tensing.

"Lord Archer," he began tentatively.

Meredith dropped the linen strip, hands up to ward off questions. "I believe I mentioned a tenuous familial connection. That is all. Lord Archer is no more than an acquaintance."

He persisted. "I am relieved to hear of it. There is something rather alarming about the man."

"Alarming?"

"If you might permit me to say, there is an intensity about him that strikes one as rather unseemly." He paused delicately. "When he is around you in particular, Lady Woolcott."

Meredith smoothed the linen on her lap. "I appreciate your concern, Mr. Hamilton, but Lord Archer is merely rather forward. Regrettable behavior perhaps, but hardly sinister." She could not believe that she was defending the man.

"Of course, I understand and I do not wish to pry, but I do

admire you immensely, Lady Woolcott, and should not wish to see you in any way . . . compromised . . ." He trailed off, unable to complete the sentence. "As I indicated to you earlier this evening at Burlington House, Lord Archer and I have met before. Briefly."

Suddenly, Meredith was bone tired, the last of her reserves draining from her body. She did not wish to think about Lord Archer, ever again. And she didn't want Hector Hamilton to think that Lord Archer had any role in her life at all.

"And in that brief meeting, I came away with the impression that Lord Archer could be . . . dangerous to have as an acquaintance." He shook his head in disbelief. "There now. I have said it."

"Dangerous," she said lightly. "I think that is a trifle melodramatic."

"It is not my place, of course, to pass judgment," he relented. In front of her was a man who had saved her from footpads this evening. The least she could do was listen to his concerns. Even if it meant bringing the specter of Lord Archer to life in her library. Hamilton paused for a further moment, giving her a chance to ask him to desist or to leave. Which she couldn't. Instead, she sat back in the chair and waited.

"I know very little about the man, and should hate to cast aspersions." His fingers twitched as they were wont to do when he was hesitating over a matter. But then his conscience must have dictated that he complete his confession, and he added abruptly, "We met in a gambling den."

Meredith swallowed a small laugh. That was it? Hardly an earth-shattering revelation. "Not unusual for Lord Archer from what I'm led to understand. But for you, sir?" She kept her tone casually disapproving, hoping to change the direction of the conversation.

His brows knit together. "You sound exactly like my Cressida—" He stopped in mid-sentence, and cleared his throat again. "Has Broton summoned a carriage as yet?"

Fatigue and pain had obviously eaten away at Hamilton's sense of decorum. The corner of Meredith's mouth curved at the mention of a woman's name, glad the conversation had drifted away from Lord Archer. "And who is Cressida? She must be someone close to you to voice her concern about such matters." A sister, an aunt, a wife? Hector Hamilton appeared a comfortable bachelor, but for the second time that evening, Meredith was struck by how little she actually knew of the man now sitting in the library of her town house as the clock on the mantel ticked past midnight.

Hamilton looked guilty and crestfallen simultaneously. He nervously swept the throw from his knees and thrust it aside. "Cressida Pettigrew and I were affianced," he said shortly.

"I see." Meredith sensed that she trod on delicate ground.

Hamilton hesitated briefly before starting again. "Cressida is . . . was the woman I intended to marry, ever since I can remember. We grew up together in Hampshire."

"A youthful love, then?"

Hamilton looked pleased with her description, but then his frown returned. "Yes, a youthful love. However, now well in the past, behind me." The words seemed to lack conviction.

Meredith listened with a certain detachment. She lifted her head, her eyes distant. It seemed that once again, she and Hamilton had more in common than they realized. "Life does not always proceed as one has planned."

"Indeed," he said carefully. "We had a falling-out, you see." Meredith wondered why he was telling her all this. A sense of forced intimacy invaded the room, settling over them like a heavy mantle. "Our parting was final and irreparable," he added with downcast eyes.

Meredith made the appropriate noises before rising from her chair, wary of what she was hearing. She hoped that it was the blood loss talking, slight though it was. Hamilton could not possibly be hoping to *court* her, of all things. It was as though he was telling her of his prospects, assuring her that he was indeed free of romantic entanglements. Groaning inwardly, she clasped her hands in front of her, and moved diplomatically toward the door. "Perhaps one day you shall see yourself together again with Miss Pettigrew," she said. Then looking in the direction of the hallway, she added awkwardly, "However, I do believe the hansom is here. I shall confirm with Broton."

She strode to the door only to see Hamilton rise and feel his hand upon her elbow—looking for balance or staying her exit, she wasn't sure. "I did not intend to make you uncomfortable. It is the last thing I should wish to do. I seem to be apologizing again." His smile was sad.

"You have nothing for which to apologize, Mr. Hamilton." Her heart wrenched. He favored his leg slightly. The dying embers of the fire were reflected in his spectacles.

"I wish you only the very best, Lady Woolcott. And my counsel regarding Lord Archer was not intended as interference but rather a reflection of my high regard for you."

"No need to explain. Neither of us is at his best. We have both had enough adventure for one evening, I fear."

Hamilton leaned upon the doorjamb. "I do so hope the events of this evening have not led you to change your mind about Cambridge, Lady Woolcott. Unless the doctor indicates otherwise, I intend to return within a few days and should delight in having you visit. At your convenience, of course."

"As promised, Mr. Hamilton, I shall give your kind invitation some thought."

"My colleagues would be delighted to meet with you to discuss the Rosetta stone," he added with a shy smile, "and, of course, I should be pleased to show you the papyri of *The Book of the Dead.*"

Meredith insisted upon escorting him into the cold night where the hansom was waiting. She looked up and down the street, expecting Lord only knew what to leap from the neatly trimmed hedges. She refused to go back to living this way, she told herself, helping Hamilton to clamber into the carriage, a footman on either side of her.

"I wish this had never happened, Lady Woolcott," he repeated again, wincing. "And I beg of you not to think poorly of me regarding my comments pertaining to Lord Archer."

"I value your opinion, Mr. Hamilton, I can assure you. As for the attack, for the last time, it was not your fault. Now let's not hear any more of this nonsense. Return to your rooms and let the doctor do his work." The door closed decisively on his protestations. The footman gave instructions to the driver before the conveyance clattered down the empty street.

A scant twenty minutes later, Meredith curled into a ball, tucked into the large armchair in her bedroom. She shut her eyes, inexpressibly fatigued and anxious at once. She had wanted to wash the whole night away, climb into a tub of steaming water and scrub until her skin was raw. But it had been too late and she did not wish to disturb Broton again or the staff. It had been a robbery, nothing more, an attempted robbery, she told herself, the phrase unspooling in her mind. Unsavory sorts were a common hazard in London and it was her own stupidity—and her hot anger with Archer—that had led both her and Hamilton to linger on a dark and wet London night.

Dry eyed, she stared at nothing, recalling Hamilton's words of warning about Archer. Her mind seethed with the implications. It was peculiar, she thought, since meeting with Archer, there had been two attempted attacks on her person, not including the strange encounter on Rotten Row. A flicker of doubt curled to life. She'd somehow sensed it, but the confirmation, here in the depths of her consciousness, shook her more deeply than she could ever have believed it would. Meredith took a deep, slow breath and stood up. The house was silent and there was a disturbing quality to the stillness. The ormolu clock on the mantel chimed three o'clock.

Perhaps Hector Hamilton was right. Lord Richard Buckingham Archer was somehow behind the recent attacks upon her person. And if not, she was simply going mad.

Archer's jaw tightened.

He waited alone in the mews, by the town house off Belgravia Square, his blood running cold.

Meredith had looked like the slightest breeze could knock her over. Pale, disheveled, as though she'd been to hell and back. He had dissolved into the shadows of the hedges and watched her walk back up the steps to the front door of the town house, the cold wind ruffling the hem of her skirts. She had cast a quick look over her shoulder at Hamilton's receding carriage.

An attack? What in bloody hell had she been talking about? Hamilton had obviously been injured. Archer swore again under his breath, unable to account for the surge of adrenaline coursing through his veins. He should never have let her flounce away from him at Burlington House, and with that milquetoast Hamilton yet. Even from a dozen steps away he had heard Hamilton's plaintive tone. It was an indulgent, possessive sound that made him want to strangle the conniving wastrel.

When he was done here, he vowed, she was going to damn well talk to him if he had to drag her kicking and screaming from London. Getting into the house would be simple, despite the burly footmen and the sour butler he'd spied. The kitchen entrance was usually best, he thought, moments later casting about the back of the town house, noting that the windows were locked against the cold night air. He extracted a thin blade from his boot, a souvenir from a sojourn in Harar, and jammed the lock twice before it snicked open. His exploits had rendered the servants' quarters of London townhomes all too familiar to him, the location of the granary, the larder and the entrance to the cold cellar, where a man of even his size could go unnoticed behind sacks of flour.

There was a rustling sound. His senses came alert. Someone or something was rummaging about in the kitchen. He saw no candle. Ducking into the corner by the pantry, he lifted his head, eyes trying to penetrate the darkness. Framed in the doorway leading to the front of the house, a figure loomed, feet shuffling along in the dark. In the gloom, he could scarcely make out the slender outline of someone who clearly wished to slip through the house unnoticed.

A faint scent of lemon verbena. Archer lunged, grabbing Meredith Woolcott around the waist in the narrow space between the pantry and the kitchen doorway. Something metallic clattered across the floor as they tumbled down. She strangely made no sound. Instead, she was quick and deadly silent. Kicking and flailing viciously, she gave Archer an elbow to his ribs in a blind, backward jerk.

"It's Archer," he whispered, a hand clasped around her mouth. Instead of holding still, she twisted fiercely against him, their arms and legs entwined, her elbows flying. Archer cursed softly, and caught Meredith just before she could land a sharp jab to his throat. Another grunt, and she almost squirmed away. He'd had about enough and hauled her up ruthlessly before slinging a leg over her body to weigh her down.

She did her best to squirm from beneath him, attempting to knee him in the groin. He tried to grab her around the waist again, but Meredith twisted violently, splayed against his body, panting for breath. Her body was slender and warm beneath his, and while he didn't know what had just happened, he had no intention of letting her go.

"Bloody, bloody hell, Archer," she whispered in the dark. "What the devil are you doing breaking into my home?"

Archer snapped, "And why are you attacking me like a she-wolf?"

Meredith twisted impotently. "Let me go this instant. Or I shall . . ."

"I don't believe I will. You're not the screaming type. We've established that already," he said, thinking back to St. Julien and the cool gray eyes framed above the smoking pistol. Archer peered at her in the dimness. Her hair was drawn back tightly, and he fisted his hand in a thick coil and forced her face closer to his. "Who attacked you tonight? And when were you going to tell me?"

"How do you know about what happened after we left Burlington House?" Her body tensed beneath his. "And for the hundredth time, why are you following me?"

"How I know doesn't matter. What does is that you are in danger and refuse to believe me."

"I owe you absolutely no explanation. What makes you believe that I have to account to you?" But Archer had ceased to hear her. His mind had seemingly disengaged, an uncharacteristic and totally unfamiliar mixture of anger, fear and desire pulsing through him. He heard only her breath in the darkness, felt only the tautness of her body.

She tried to jerk free.

"Don't even try. If this is the only way to have you listen to me, I'll hold you forever," he said, pressing his lips to her ear. "We've unfinished business, you and I. I'd prefer not to have to say it again."

Meredith Woolcott maddened him. He had never in his life felt so on edge, unbalanced, thinking of nothing but thrusting a hand beneath her buttocks and lifting her hips against his suddenly raging erection. She squirmed desperately, unwisely. Anger and lust swept through him, his hands determining that she wore very little save a narrow skirt and only a thin layer of petticoats. He wanted nothing more than to touch her, jerk her skirts free until her flesh lay bare, soft and inviting.

But Meredith Woolcott was anything but soft and inviting. The pelisse over her shoulders told him that she was intent on going out into the night. To do what exactly? A jolt of possessiveness shot through him: *Hamilton.*

"Where are you going in the middle of the night?"

"Let me go." Each word was a chip of ice.

He gritted his teeth, wishing for his usual calm. He dropped his arms and lifted his body off hers. Meredith moved away from his grasp, rubbing her arms, watching him with eyes that could freeze a rushing river in summer. "I have nothing—"

"To say to me, I'm sure. But I have several things to say to you and all I am asking is for some semblance of cooperation."

Her eyes narrowed and she brushed past him. Archer followed, his temper straining on its leash. She paused at the kitchen entrance. "I do not wish to alert the household, so we can conclude our business here."

Extracting a flint, she expertly lit a small lamp on the wood block table. A teapot and bits of crockery, cups and saucers, sat abandoned. Archer looked her up and down. "Tell me that you are not slipping out to see Hamilton."

Her breaths were coming more evenly now. "How dare you even inquire! You are the most insufferable, high-handed—"

"I get the idea. But before this goes any further, tell me exactly what happened. And I don't mean your tête-à-tête with the professor. Explain to me who attacked you this night."

To infuriate him further, she waved him away, turning instead to pour the last of the dregs of tea into one of the china cups at her elbow. She took a sip, taking her bloody time before answering him. He leaned heavily against the doorjamb.

"Exactly what will it take to convince you that someone is trying to harm you? I said that I have proof that will convince you." *And cause you pain.* The child's kaleidoscope, a toy belonging to a long-gone nursery, burned in his jacket pocket.

Meredith let her breath out slowly as the tepid tea worked

its way through her. She put one hand up to her forehead, as though to keep her raging thoughts from spilling over. Yet she refused to answer him.

"I heard you outside this very house not an hour ago speaking about an attack by footpads to that damned wastrel Hamilton." Archer's voice came out in a growl.

"He's not a wastrel. Mr. Hamilton is a respected scholar. . . ." Putting down her teacup with a clatter, she continued, "And what were you doing skulking around my home without making your presence known? Truly, I despair, Archer."

"Don't change the subject. You know damn well what I'm asking."

"Furthermore, Mr. Hamilton acquitted himself admirably this evening, coming to my assistance, and in the course of such honorable actions, he suffered an injury. If it had not been for him . . ."

"You should have left with me. You know absolutely nothing about Hamilton. " Archer barely recognized the possessiveness in his tone.

"Left with you?" she asked haughtily. "No doubt that would have made it all the more convenient for you."

"You are making no sense." He crossed his arms over his chest.

"I think I'm making all the sense in the world." She paused deliberately. "I am beginning to consider the facts, Lord Archer. The fact that since meeting you at Rushford and Rowena's wedding, I find myself suddenly imperiled. As you have pointed out several times, perhaps I should be concerned. And I am beginning to agree—but in a way you will not find comforting."

The stock around his neck was suddenly tight. "What are you accusing me of, Meredith? I should be careful."

"For God's sake, Archer. That's where I was going tonight. To confront you," she hissed. "And to ask you questions that so far you have been unable or unwilling to answer." She spun about and took the few steps toward the hallway lead-ing back to the main house.

But Archer was faster. He reached her side and thrust a powerful arm over her shoulder to hold the door shut. He leaned into her again, urging her body against the door, knowing that the wood was cold against her breasts. He laughed, low and dangerously, against her temple. "You were coming to see me. I'm flattered, Meredith."

"Don't be." He knew that she was too proud to ask him to let her go again. She shifted her weight, but his other arm came up to brace against the door, trapping her face against the polished wood.

"What were you going to confront me with, Meredith?" he whispered against the back of her head. "What was it that could not wait until morning?"

"You are despicable. Using your size to intimidate me."

"And I can do worse, if you are to be believed," he contin-ued. He allowed his hand to glide over her collarbone and upper arm, as if he might brush her pelisse from her shoul-ders. "So perhaps you are quite correct in your assumption which, it appears, you have yet to articulate clearly. In any case, I find myself disinclined to continue our conversation here. I have a much better idea."

Chapter 7

Meredith breathed fire into the cold wood beneath her cheek. "I'm not going anywhere with you, Archer. Let me make that clear."

She felt him move away, but not before he grasped her around the waist. "You will trust me soon enough. I know of a place where we shall remain undisturbed and where I can get you to listen to reason." He pulled her along to the back of the kitchen.

"Reason? You are the one behaving entirely irrationally." She twisted to face him, her feet rooted to the flagstones. "And don't ever attempt to physically intimidate me again."

"I don't think it's intimidation that you fear. It's desire. Don't lie to yourself or to me."

A flush suffused her cheeks. "If you are going to say something, you can say it to me here and now. Along with showing me this evidence you claim to have."

"Eventually." He guided her swiftly toward the door. "If I dare believe it, you were sneaking out of your own house to confront me. So let us have that confrontation, Lady Woolcott, but not here."

She opened her mouth to speak several times before finding her voice, and then decided on a different approach. "If your residence is the venue of choice, then so be it."

He shook his head, not letting go of her waist. "Not my town house."

"Then where are we going? You must tell me." She glared at him in the dimly lit room. "I somehow cannot shake the feeling that this is all fitting neatly into some scheme of yours. Mr. Hamilton may be right in his suspicions."

Archer grimaced. "Hamilton is the last man you should trust."

"I find that assertion strange coming from you." Yet she found herself offering little resistance when he pulled open the door. He drew her into the chill air, toward the coach that materialized from the early morning mist, awaiting them at the corner of the mews. Pulling the pelisse more closely around her shoulders, she shook off his offer to hand her into the coach. He followed behind, settling beside her on the tufted seat.

The coach lurched forward as Meredith pressed herself deep into the corner of the upholstery in a vain attempt to create a whisper of distance between them. He was right. Desire, not fear, washed over her. Damn the man, and his ability to set off a ricochet of unwelcome sensations that she had thought exorcised many years ago. The banquette was too small and Archer too big, his long legs and broad shoulders filling the space.

The sudden turn of events did not fit with her plans at all. She spared a sharp glance at his fierce profile, the lines etched around his mouth, the furrow between his brows, the thick hair with the threads of silver that defied taming. Unease uncoiled within her. Her past would not let her go and the depth of her loss, so many years ago, could not be erased. It was through loving that her life had collapsed, that she had brought danger to those closest to her. Love and deception and betrayal had wrought a sea change in her years ago, warning her against allowing anyone such power over her again. Not ever.

But here she was with Archer, a man who was both stripping away and building up her carefully constructed armor, forcing her to confront a past that she believed she had put behind her. She wavered between desperately wishing to trust him and being unable to do so. And yet she was riding in a coach with him, to an unknown destination.

His words startled her. "Your staring is making me uncomfortable." The customary mockery was back in his voice. Even in the dimness of the coach, she could make out the penetrating blue of his eyes, stripping away yet another layer of defense before she could snatch it back. "I don't believe I can withstand it, and we still have several miles to go."

"My staring should be the least of your concerns."

"Please enlighten me. I suppose Hamilton put all manner of doubts about me in your head."

Meredith forced a note of calm into her tone. "You dislike the man, I can tell, when there is nothing to dislike about him. He all but saved my life."

"Saved your life? At least you admit that you are in danger." His eyes narrowed and Meredith tensed, sensing a turn of his thoughts.

"I didn't say that."

With the grace of a man half his size, Archer rose and pulled her up alongside him. He watched her with the intensity of a predator, but she refused to move away from him. Instead, she gazed out the carriage window. They had left London behind them, she noticed.

"Whatever you do, do not trust Hamilton."

"You know nothing of him. Besides which, whom I choose to spend time with is none of your concern."

"You may change your mind."

She twisted away from the window, throwing him a cool glance. "So you continue to maintain. However, the only man I find it difficult to trust sits beside me at the moment." She hunched further into the seat.

"We will get to that shortly," he said. "In the interim, you are cold." Without waiting for an answer, he took off his greatcoat and drew it around her shoulders. Meredith fought the urge to melt into the warm folds and inhale the scent of sandalwood and man.

Unaccountably grateful, she held the coat close with one hand, the wool crushed in her grip. "Why do you not tell me where we're going?"

His breath stirred the soft skin of her ear. It would be quite natural, Meredith thought, to feel protected with such a man. Entirely safe, if her situation was anything resembling normality, which it wasn't. Nothing she was feeling was making any sense. And in the end which was more dangerous, the threats from the past or her own physical weakness? Even as he loomed over her, a lush heaviness freighted her body. He was not wearing a cravat and the top fastenings of his shirt were loosened. His boots brushed the hem of her gown. The impact of those small details consumed her.

For the next two hours, she sat in agonizing silence, mounting a wall between them, glancing at her reflection in the dark opaqueness of the carriage window. The road beneath the wheels became rougher, pockmarked with ruts and potholes that challenged her to maintain her rigid posture. The cold country air gave way to a hint of brine. They were close to the sea, the sound of the surf audible over the grinding of the coach wheels beneath them. A moment later, the carriage careened around a sharp curve and drew to a halt. Opening the door before the coachman had a chance, Archer grasped her hand and swept her down the stairs. A few remaining stars glittered overhead in the icy sky, the lapping of the water a quiet murmur in the stillness of early morning. Meredith eyed the elegant sweep of *The Brigand* with a sharp inhalation of breath. No other ships were tied at the mooring sheltered in a cove surrounded by rocks silvered in the dawn light.

"We are at my country estate," he said curtly.

"All I see is *The Brigand*."

"Forgive me. I prefer it to the forty-room monstrosity up the hill." He gestured to the cliffs above them.

"You must be hungry," he said without further elaboration and as though she must gird herself for the battle to come. It was winter, but the small gangplank had been cleared of ice, and Archer bundled her quickly aboard the yacht. To her surprise, a wall of heat hit her from a small coal-fired stove. Meredith's gaze took in the cabin, the floor covered with a painted canvas drugget, several paintings on the bulkheads and two chairs and a settee covered in green damask. A large mirror filled the port side, opposite a table that could seat several guests. In the corner, shadows hid a narrow alcove where she saw a bed.

Archer remained silent, gesturing to the table. There was an ease in his manner, a decided comfort that he took in his surroundings. Every line in his body declared his ownership of the yacht. She did not know the man, but it appeared as though he was at home on the elegant sloop. She bent slightly to slide into a low chair, letting his greatcoat fall from her shoulders.

"You had all this prepared in advance, didn't you?" Settling opposite her, Archer watched as she took in the platter of cold meats, cheese and wine. "I did," he said. "I didn't think I was that predictable," she murmured into the silence. "And whilst I thank you for your hospitality, I find myself not particularly hungry. Instead, I would prefer that we have that confrontation we're both so keen to enter into." She looked around the cabin. This was the ship that had sent her Rowena into danger and saved her at the same time. It did not bear thinking about, Meredith told herself.

Archer read her thoughts. "I had it refurbished since Rushford and Rowena's adventure." He did not elaborate, preferring to keep the details of the explosion that nearly took her ward's life to himself. "Now please eat. You look as though you need it."

He opened the bottle of wine at his elbow, pouring them

each a glass. With hooded eyes, he watched her hesitate and then finally pick up a fork and begin to arrange food on her plate, first some cheese and then some meat, as though by rote. After a time, she said, lifting her eyes to his, "You're not eating."

"I seem to have lost my appetite," he began, his fingers toying with his glass.

"As have I," she replied defiantly. She pulled the napkin from her lap, and placed her fork carefully on the side of her plate. "I find these circumstances exceedingly trying. You promised to show me some kind of evidence, to prove that there is real danger." She refused to be more specific, to mention Faron, to give credence to Archer's claims.

He narrowed his eyes over the rim of his glass, picking up a thread that they had lost in the carriage. "First you must promise me to stay away from Hamilton."

"The very devil, Archer. You drag me hours from London to the Channel in the depths of winter, promising me that all will be revealed, and this is the best you can do? Mr. Hamilton is my friend and I shall hear no more about him."

"You don't know anything of the man," he said enigmatically.

"And I know even less about you, if truth be told. My apologies if I don't see your point."

"You are persisting in making things difficult—for yourself, most of all."

Meredith shook her head. "You are the one who is holding something back. I sense that you can handily deceive those who lay their trust in you, Archer. And yet you expect me to believe, upon no evidence, that you are acting nobly on my behalf. In the interim, all I have experienced since our meeting is a heightened sense of peril."

The wine flamed clear to her stomach and she wondered why she should suddenly feel as though the ship's keel was moving violently beneath her. The wind was still.

"For which you blame me."

"Not entirely." She hesitated. "But I can't help thinking that you are holding something back."

"I could say much the same."

"I have had just about enough of your prevarications." Instinct tore the words from her chest. "If you are trying to spare me . . . don't." And then she felt a crushing sense of defeat, the certainty that she could not go back to the world of fear that had once held her in its thrall. The blood must have drained from her face because he anticipated her flight, trapping her forearm beneath his on the table. Reaching for the bottle of wine with his free hand, he refilled her glass and leveled at her a probing look. She strained her arm against his.

"Running away won't help. I should have thought you would know that by now." His eyes blazed with certain knowledge. "At least not anywhere that I or the truth won't catch up with you." He released her arm and settled back in his chair with a confidence that grated on her.

Meredith felt her lips curl and a tightness in her chest, the desire to flee stifled for at least a moment. "I do not know what you expect, Archer. Why would you ask me to bare my deepest soul to a man I scarcely know and hardly trust?" The scars, long healed, burned underneath the sleeves of her shirtwaist. "Why are you so desperate to learn about Montagu Faron? Particularly when he is dead."

A shadow descended between them and in the small brazier, the coals hissed and sang, reminding Meredith of another fire, long ago but never far enough away. She forced her hands to her lap.

He did not answer directly. "I do not wish to hurt you." His tone stilled her fingers, shocking her with its compassion. *Then don't*, she wanted to say. His gaze stripped away every layer of reserve she possessed. And then she knew what she was running from, not simply from her past but also from Lord Richard Archer. Her heart constricted.

"But I need you to be honest with me if I am to help," he said softly.

"You know nothing of what lies in my heart or my past," she bit out, her fingers digging into the heavy wool of her skirt, twisting. "And why should you?"

"Would you believe that I care?" His voice was little more than a growl. "Look at me, damn it!"

She was already staring at him, dry eyed, across the table. "Why will you not believe me?" he asked.

Meredith had to bite her lips to keep from screaming. They were well-chosen words, but they could mean nothing to her, could not be allowed to penetrate the scar tissue around her heart. She had felt his caress even in the angry grip that still burned on her arm. "There is no possible way I can begin to answer your question. It is a rare thing to be able to tell the truth about the past." She shook her head. "How long do you propose we stay here? On *The Brigand*? Until I change my mind, perhaps? And begin to believe and trust you?" As though the enforced proximity could make any difference.

"You came with me willingly." His features tightened. "You wished a confrontation, or so you said, and now you have it."

He spoke the truth about suspicions she could not easily lay to rest. "Very well," she said, hating the fleeting satisfaction that shot through her, almost as much as she loathed her instinct to follow his lead. "Let me put this as clearly as I can, sir. As I have already stated several times since I have met you, my life has recently been a series of mishaps." The images roiled in her mind. "First Rashid, then Rotten Row—"

He leaned over the table toward her. "Rotten Row?"

She had no choice but to answer him. "A rider whom I encountered when I was alone. It was probably nothing, but nonetheless disturbing in my present state of mind."

His voice was deadly quiet. "And you suspect me. That I am somehow behind all these encounters, including last night outside Burlington House."

The challenge tumbled from her lips. "Tell me that it doesn't make a strange kind of sense."

"Whatever reason would I have to hurt you?"

"I don't know. That's the problem." It was difficult to trust. The old wounds beneath the fine cambric of her sleeves ached.

He bit out, "You should have told me, Meredith. About Rotten Row."

She had to lower her eyes when his burned hotter than the sconces surrounding them. "Whyever should I come to you with anything, Archer? When there is nothing between us, no past, no present and no future. And most of all, when you have yet to answer any of my questions honestly."

"I have done so, repeatedly."

"Hardly to my satisfaction."

"You still don't believe that I care for you. Aside from my connection with Rushford."

She lifted her eyes to his. "That is a ludicrous claim and you well know it. We barely know one another and we couldn't be more different in temperament or interests. Further, I am hardly of an age . . ."

Archer loomed forward in his seat, forcing Meredith deeper into hers. "You are disingenuous in the extreme, as you well know. I am a man, hardly immune to your charms, much though you would like to deny them."

She waved away his statements, turning her eyes towards the glowing brazier.

He continued unabated. "Even you cannot deny that there is something between us. Your head won't let you believe it, but your body tells a different story."

Damn him. "I don't have to listen to this." She gripped the edge of the table. "I wish to return to London."

"Yes, I believe you would, because you seem intent on inviting disaster. You can only tempt fate for so long, Meredith, before it catches up with you. And yet you wish that I set aside every thought of protecting you."

She closed her eyes against his words. "For the last time, I don't require protection, least of all from you." Who was she running from? Faron? Archer? From herself? She didn't know anymore.

"Don't fear me, Meredith," he said. "I'm the only safe haven you have at the moment." His words sounded more like a threat, a last warning. He drained what remained of his wine. His large hand dwarfed the crystal, seeming to make a conscious effort not to crush it in his long fingers.

She thrust her chin up at him. "We are getting nowhere with this conversation. I don't believe your protestations of affection, which places us at an impasse."

Archer set the crystal on the table, presenting her with his strong profile. "I may have something that could help us with this impasse, much as I regret having to use it." He turned and stared at her with such intensity that she again sat back in her chair. Just as she'd feared, he had somehow maneuvered her into a corner.

"So you have threatened repeatedly. It causes one to wonder why you are so reluctant to produce whatever evidence you have that you feel certain will change my mind."

He arched a brow. "I've little doubt that it will produce the desired effect."

"Which is what precisely?" she asked.

He paused for an imperceptible moment. "Convincing you that Faron is somehow behind the attacks on your person." His voice was smooth, yet something simmered there, just beneath the surface. Something that sent a chill through Meredith.

Faron was dead. "I have nothing to say on that topic."

His eyes glittered. "Perhaps not at this moment."

Meredith's blood pounded. "Do not play with me, Archer."

"This is far from a game."

The breath became trapped in her chest. Beneath her

booted feet the floor of *The Brigand* seemed to tilt again, despite the fact that they were in port.

Archer withdrew a small bundle of red silk from the inside of his jacket and placed it on the table between them.

For a moment, it appeared like a glistening stain of blood. "What is this?" Meredith clutched a hand to her abdomen, unable to bear the impenetrable look on Archer's face.

"I did not wish to hurt you. Believe me, Meredith."

"Believe you?" she breathed, wishing to back away from the table and the blot of crimson amidst the discarded dishes.

"This might be the only way of convincing you that you are in danger. And not from me." The ship groaned and a piece of coal fell with a hiss in the hearth. With efficient movements, Archer unfolded the silk.

She had never thought to see it again. Copper, with mother-of-pearl inlay, and so innocent, it was the kaleidoscope from the nursery at Claire de Lune.

She nearly tipped her chair, rising abruptly. Tears stung hot at the backs of her eyes, and she gritted her teeth against them. In an instant, Archer was by her side, holding her so close that their chests pressed together with each breath they drew. Memories roared through her mind, a storm of images. Visions of Faron taking her in his arms, of Julia settling Rowena on their beloved rocking horse in the nursery, the fire devouring everything she held dear.

"Where did you get this?" she said into Archer's shoulder, unable to look away from the table.

"I wish none of this had been necessary," he said his eyes pinning hers.

She looked up at him, disbelieving. "I never took you for a cruel man." She choked on the bitterness that coated her tongue. His hands fell from her as if he'd been burned. She drew a step back beneath his regard, but perversely wished to feel the strength of his arms around her again.

He said with deceptive softness, "There was nothing else I could do. To convince you."

Meredith could hardly still the trembling in her hands, a nauseating combination of rage and fear burning in her chest. "Again," she said hoarsely, "you are denying me answers. For once tell me where you found . . ." She could not complete the sentence, gesturing at the table. The glowing embers of the brazier forced her to close her eyes. She so feared stirring the coals in her heart, searching for that clear spark of hatred and vengeful determination that she knew was there. For Faron, the two-headed Janus. *Odi et amo.* I love and I hate.

Fleetingly, she saw Faron's face, his passionate black eyes, his wide, humorous mouth, his hair the color of a raven's wings. And for an instant her skin remembered the feel of his hands on her body, the assured touch of a first love who had known the deepest recesses of her soul. Pain washed through her as harsh as a knife's blade, robbing her of her breath.

She was back in Archer's arms. "What is it?" he whispered into her hair. "Tell me."

She shook her head with effort, her eyes clouded. One hand came up to his chest to clutch at his waistcoat. Her fingertips hooked over the edge of the fine linen of his shirt with desperation. She struggled to form a sentence. "Please tell me where you got this."

He pulled her closer still. "The Arab. At Rashid," he said.

Meredith groaned, the sensation of her pistol back in her hand, the memory of raising it and releasing the hammer. She tilted her face up to his. "Where could they possibly have found it? From whom did they get it?" The question was laughable and she knew it before it was out of her mouth. She wondered whether Archer felt her pain in his own body, transmitted through the skin that burned beneath his hands.

"Dear God," she said, squeezing her eyes shut. "Will it never be over? I thought it was over. . . ." She repeated the words like a litany. The smoke enveloping the nursery, the rocking horse, the kaleidoscope, the crackling of the flames overtaking Julia's plaintive cries.

And even now, almost two decades later, she could still not reconcile the fact that the fire had been set by Faron, the man she had thought she loved. "Sometimes," she whispered into Archer's shirt, the words echoing in her mind, "I think his scent still lingers on my own skin, his taste on my tongue, his laughter ringing in my ears." And she needed to make him go away, drive him from her blood like a disease that had been held at bay only to come rushing back with full force. She slid her arms around Archer's neck.

He stiffened, suddenly stone beneath her hands. Nonetheless, his hands moved slowly down her body, soothingly, comfortingly, until they gripped her hips. Desire began as a low pulse, rising steadily, the urge to press her lips to his was overwhelming. She was taken by a sudden desperate need to feel his stroking tongue filling her mouth. He looked down at her and she was captured again by the blue of his eyes.

"Just this once," she said. "Just this one night." To make it all go away. She needed to be all body and no mind: she wanted the purity of physical desire and no painful memories threatening to pull her over the edge.

Archer pulled her closer to the hardness between his legs, impatient now. "I'm hardly flattered," he said, his voice low. "You do know that you're not doing this for the right reasons."

She stiffened slightly. "Are you turning me away?" Her eyes shuttered and she put one hand up to his chest and pushed him back a fraction of an inch.

"I didn't say that," he said, pressing close again, his hardness riding against her abdomen, clear proof of his inclination. His gaze was searing and she wondered what it would take to appease his pride. "Don't pretend that you don't know what it is you do to me."

"Do to you?" Her eyes flashed.

"I know exactly what you're doing. And I should feel offended." He cupped her jaw, ran his thumb along her cheek, savoring the softness of her skin. He dropped an open-mouthed kiss on the skin just below her ear. "You are using me, Lady Woolcott."

She shivered when he bit her softly on the neck, teeth grazing flesh. It was true. And there was little she could do about it. "Forgive me," she said weakly, breath shuddering out of her, along with the memories. All was blotted out save for the hard muscles under her hands and the skylit blue of Archer's eyes burning into hers. He brushed her chin with his before tonguing her earlobe and then moving on to her mouth. "I need this," she breathed against his lips.

Archer just smiled and kissed her lightly, knowing she had nothing more to offer than her desperation, first proffered not so long ago under a desert sky and on the hard ground in Rashid. "My pride smarts, madam. So I surely can ask for a fair trade." He pulled back slightly, just enough for the cooler air of the room to rush between them and rob her of his warmth. "Remain with me here for twenty-four hours," he said brusquely.

Her hand locked on to his lapel. "That is patently unfair to ask." She was desperate with need, and she wanted to drown in the blue of his eyes. There was something in the depths that she couldn't read, something of an intensity at odds with the lightness of his tone that sent renewed chills over her skin. But it was simple passion that she wanted, anything to override the legacy of memories that threatened to engulf her.

"Fair or not fair. It's what I demand," he replied with a challenging glint in his eyes. He pushed her farther away from the table toward the brazier that lent a dull glow to the room. A single candle burned on a gleaming shelf. He put one hand out to her, beckoning, and pulled her toward the alcove hidden in the shadows. His eyes never left hers, confident of her response.

The bed was mounded with pillows and a fur rug. The room suddenly seemed too still, too quiet. Wrenching her gaze from his, she began removing her pelisse, still fully clothed, and watching him. In their movement, her skirt had ridden up, revealing her stockinged calves, and outlining a slender thigh that glowed in the dim light. She had not worn stays, but even her camisole felt suddenly too tight beneath the high-necked lace of her shirtwaist.

Archer watched as she watched him. He slipped the buttons free at the neck of his shirt, pulled it over his head and threw it onto the floor. Then he pulled her over to the bed, and began with her heavy skirt, undoing the tapes until it slid to the floor. Tugging at the tie at her waist, he unwound the long strings from her rib cage. She slid her dress down her arms and abruptly stopped.

"We will go slowly," Archer said. He couldn't remember exactly how he'd rid himself of his coat or what had become of her pelisse. She tried to steady her breathing and that only served to make him all too aware of the rise and fall of her breasts, of her slender arms still wrapped in the sleeves of her dress. She was even more beautiful than he'd imagined. Slender, with high breasts, and long legs encased by cotton stockings.

Stroking her arm, he kissed her, one hand cupping her breast, his palm filled with warm flesh. "Are you cold?" he asked, drawing the crisply pressed sleeves over her elbows and wrists. His hands caressed her skin and she gasped, letting her breath out in a hiss as his fingers lightly brushed the inside of her arm, up and down its length. He let his hands roam, reveling in her reactions to his softest touch. A nail traced lazily along her collarbone and she was shaking. She seemed to still, not even daring to breathe, each time he touched her.

He gently pushed her onto the bed, rolling her onto her back, placing a string of kisses along her neck, blazing a trail to the soft spot where her neck met her collarbones, biting down lightly, savoring the way her head fell back when he did, and the way she said his name in a small gasp. Moving lower, he laved her nipples through her chemise, making her twitch, running his tongue down the valley between her breasts.

Her arms were still imprisoned between them and she didn't seem to notice as he kissed his way down the soft skin, pulling the cambric along with his palms. A long pucker ran across the inside of each wrist, a perfect match, a silver slice marring the perfection of her skin. He had seen enough scars in his lifetime not to be shocked, and had earned a few in his own right. But suddenly he wanted to know, *would know*, who had done this to Meredith Woolcott.

Now was not the time. A shudder ran through her as he carefully ran his tongue down the inside of her wrist. Such a small action to provoke such a response. He studied her face, her beautiful face, taking note of what caused her to close her eyes and what brought her to trembling attention. She had wanted this escape, and he was going to give it to her, leave her wrecked and boneless with nothing in her head or her heart save for excruciating pleasure. She lay resplendent on the fur, eyes closed, clad only in her chemise and her pantalettes, as he leaned forward to run his tongue along the beautifully defined line of her hip. She clenched, the muscles in her stomach tightening. His hardness twitched and thickened, demanding attention.

But he wouldn't let her go that easily. His mouth slid up her leg, from the stocking covering her knee to the bare flesh above it. He licked the fine skin at the top of her thigh and she groaned, turning her face further into the soft fur. Knowing that she wouldn't protest, he slid his tongue up the valley between her thighs, parting and exploring. His hand came to rest against the skin of her abdomen, keeping her on her back as his mouth locked over the sensitive peak just covered by the fine silk of her drawers. Her fingers wound themselves in his, palms turned upwards as she writhed, trying halfheartedly to dislodge him.

No escape. Not now. Archer smiled to himself and flicked

his tongue over her, first slowly and then faster, pressing in against the sensitized flesh. His mind stopped working, shutting out the realization that he'd wanted to taste her like that since the first time he'd met her. He would have done anything to get his mouth on her like this. She writhed beneath his ministrations, her panting mixed with groans, her body tensing beneath him. Her feet pressed against him, a knee pushing hard against his shoulder. He wrapped his hands around her hips and held her down while she made a series of protests, incoherent with need.

Archer's stomach clenched while his erection swelled more inside his breeches. Working under her drawers, he slid two fingers into her lavish wetness, locked his mouth over her, and took her to the precipice. Instinctively, her long legs wrapped around his shoulders, squeezing with a panting release that seemed to go on forever.

Her knees finally relaxed, legs splayed open, she lay silently taking great gusts of air. Unwilling to mar the occasion with talk or protestations, Archer stood, opened his breeches, and pulled her towards him, pushing her pantalettes down her legs and onto the floor. Her eyes widened, still dusky with desire, as his hands slid over her exposed bottom and gripped her hips. He leaned onto the bed, the head of his erection finding entrance to her body.

Meredith closed her eyes, her hands fisting in the fur. With excruciating slowness, he moved in a fraction of the way, then out again, repeating the disciplined motions with infinite patience. She was tight, tighter than he'd expected, the slickness of her warmth inviting him in. And then she surprised him as, without preamble, she arched up, rising to meet him, stockinged feet digging into the bed. With a shudder, she took all of him, encasing him in tight, hot flesh.

They found their rhythm, ridiculously, outrageously well matched. Fast, then hard, then exquisitely slowly, they lost themselves in the sensation of body meeting body, nothing else. When Meredith had been reduced to writhing sensation,

Archer leaned forward, using his weight to hold her in place, running his hands up her torso. There was nothing but a layer of fine cambric between them. She twisted, the muscles of her back and waist alive under his hands. She moaned as he counted to ten somewhere in the wide universe. Giving in to the sensation, to the hot wetness, he was past coherence. He vaguely felt her nails digging into his back, her whispers in his ear. He changed the angle of his thrust and suddenly she was crying out beneath him, clenching around him as she found her release again. The muscles climaxing around him were all he needed. He shut his eyes, and with a few more rocking thrusts he came, pulling out of her in time as his own breath came in ragged gasps.

The sun hung low in the sky, turning the red roses at the cottage door to fire. Fluttering muslin curtains wafted gently in the summer breeze. It was a book-lined room, papers scattered on the polished wood floor. The center was dominated by an opulent bed, high and fitted with the finest sheets and damask coverlets, where two naked figures slept entwined, their bodies heavy with fulfillment. The woman lay on her back, her red hair fanned across the pillow, one arm falling loosely around the back of her partner. His dark head was pillowed next to hers, a leg flung possessively over her thighs, trapping her in the sumptuous feather mattress.

A small sigh escaped her lips, a muted sound of remembered desire that faded into a contented breath. Meredith felt the familiar body by her side, in tune with hers after long hours of passion. She kept her eyes closed and a smile on her lips, breathing in the scent of the summer breeze finding its way through the open door of the cottage.

Then the scene shifted. She dozed beside a sickbed, awakened by a rustle, like the sounds of a creature scurrying in the underbrush. It played at the fringes of her senses, getting louder, gaining momentum. She pulled herself straighter and took a quick glance at the bed. There was no one in it.

The noise was louder now, a building crescendo invading the room. A curl of smoke insinuated its way between the spaces of the open doors, curling toward the bed. Her stunned gaze took in the coiled plume of gray that expanded suddenly into every corner, clogging her throat, stinging her eyes.

She lifted her stunned gaze to find a figure wreathed in smoke, coming from the nursery next door. Only the blank stare of eyes behind a leather mask was visible, his arms raising a truncheon. She opened her mouth to scream, but no sound emerged. And then he was gone, enveloped in the choking smoke. In the chamber of her mind, her scream continued as if her breath was infinite, the piercing cry matched by the clanging of a fire bell and the violent barking of hounds.

Meredith awakened drenched in sweat, shivering, her heart pounding and her throat hoarse. The sheets beneath her were damp with perspiration, her eyes wide with terror. Another man was at her side, one with broader shoulders, thicker muscles, the intense scrutiny of his blue eyes calling out to her. Not Faron.

Archer took up the coverlet beneath the fur rug and draped it around her shoulders, covering her nakedness. He said nothing, simply gathered her into his arms. He took her chin between finger and thumb and brought her face around. Immediately, she closed her eyes to hide her pain. "You're safe. You're fine," he said, softly insistent. Her eyes opened reluctantly and they were shiny with unshed tears. She did not wish to weep, for Faron and the love she thought they'd had. Her pulse still raged in confusion and terror, afraid that somehow she was beginning to feel deeply for the man with whom she had just made love.

Archer stroked her back, bending his head to press his lips to the curve of her neck as his hand smoothed over her shoulders in a caress that gave warmth and reassurance. It was as though he understood her nightmare, absorbing the terrible confusion of emotions that had left her shaking. Harsh winter daylight poured through the unshuttered portholes.

He asked nothing of her, simply rocking her in his arms. She tried not to notice how broad and hard his forearms were or how his heavy, dark hair fell across his strong brow. His vital presence soothed her senses, drawing her away from her nightmare. She had not given a thought to how she would feel about doing with Archer what she had only done many years ago with Faron. When Archer had covered her body in kisses, she remembered other lips skimming the softness of her skin. When he moved his clever hands over her breasts and thighs, setting her aflame, she experienced a languid pleasure only vaguely reminiscent of a response long ago.

She was not ready for this. What had she done? She tensed at the hand on her back, and she turned her head aside, to the portholes letting in the daylight. They lay silently, her back spooned into his body for an eternity, the gentle lap of the water the only sound intruding upon their self-imposed silence. Meredith fell asleep first, her head pillowed in the crook of his arm, his arm folded across her waist. Archer felt her irregular breaths ease as he lay awake listening to the familiar sounds of his yacht, adjusting to the ebb and flow of the water.

Chapter 8

Hector Hamilton woke to the din of the coal man making his weekly delivery at the Watling Inn. An inauspicious hostelery in Charing Cross, it was all he could afford, what with his gaming debts. His leg pounded with every beat of his heart, with every moan of the creaking floorboards overhead and with the hoarse cry of the fishmonger seemingly right outside his window. He slowly rolled over, trying not to move his leg too quickly.

He blinked in the dimness of the weak morning light. The lumpy mattress protested every move he made and he suddenly wished to be back home in Cambridge, in his own bed, at his venerable college, waiting for the housekeeper to prepare his morning tea. He ran his tongue over his teeth. His mouth was chalky and bitter. He had a vague recollection of the previous night, Burlington House, the footpads, Meredith Woolcott's ministrations and then the physician, Dr. Codger.

He'd never felt worse in his life. Not even when Cressida's tears began to flow, her rosy little hands coming up to cover her pale cheeks, when he'd told her that he no longer wished to make her his wife. Hamilton stared across at the cold grate and considered whether he was suffering from a fever, given his fit of tremors. The wound must be kept clean, the doctor had cautioned, to avoid sepsis. An unpleasant taste lingered in his mouth, the result in part of the bitter medicine the doctor insisted he take and the remnants of outrage that he had sunk so low. . . .

Lady Meredith Woolcott was nothing like he'd imagined. Truth be told, she was something of a temptress and he blushed at the thought of her vibrant hair and that full mouth spouting ideas that were absolutely brazen coming from a woman. Her lecture at Burlington House was outstanding and, if she were a man, she would definitely take her place beside scholars at Cambridge or Oxford. She was a woman totally outside his ken, so different from Cressida Pettigrew that she might be another species entirely. He burrowed under the covers, cursing himself for having the weakness that had caused him to hurt two innocent women who, he had to admit, had a hold on his conscience and his plummeting self-regard.

The gambling curse. It was the only reason he finally clambered out of bed, his head swimming. He would wager his last one hundred pounds for coffee and a piece of dry toast to still the rumbling in his stomach. He dissolved back into the thin pillows, draped an arm over his thigh and imagined the scent of coffee wafting into the room.

His leg throbbed, a reminder of his humbling weakness, a devouring beast that demanded to be fed. Unbelievable that he, shy and retiring Hector Hamilton, son of a rector, was willing to risk life and limb, not to mention self-regard and pride, in order to feed the beast. He covered his head with a pillow when he heard a knock that seemed to make the whole room shake. Head pounding, he removed the pillow just as he heard the doorknob turn.

"What in hell's damnation went wrong last night?"

"Wrong?" Hamilton sat bolt upright. The pain in his leg was staggering. The man standing at the foot of his bed was almost as startling.

"You damn fool."

Dear God, no. Crompton, short, wide and aggressive, stared

down at him. "Meredith Woolcott was the one who should have incurred injury. Not you." Crompton's dark eyes narrowed with irritation under his low brow.

Hamilton clenched his teeth and counted the brass buttons on Crompton's coat. He was a henchman made to order, delighting in carrying out his directives to the letter, despite his unsuccessful attempt at adopting the affectations of a gentleman. Hamilton tried to straighten, aware of the pitiful figure he must make in his nightshirt.

He attempted to explain. "When I received the message to rendezvous at Charles Street with Lady Woolcott, I had no idea that you were planning to do her physical harm. You had arranged our first meeting on Rotten Row and I expected more of the same. Merely a scare, not—"

Crompton scratched his scalp, visible through his closely cropped gray hair. "What did you think, Hamilton, that we were inclined to meet you both for tea?" Crompton sputtered to an end, unable to find words excoriating enough to make his point. A vein popped out on his forehead.

Hamilton pressed his lips together to keep both his nausea and outrage in check.

Crompton was just gathering a head of steam. "There is nothing I can do to make your marching orders any clearer, but I see that I must," he said, addressing Hamilton like a dog called to heel. "Yours is not to wonder why, Hamilton. But if you must know, your throwing yourself in front of the Woolcott woman only served to get yourself in the way of a knife."

"You never intended to injure Lady Woolcott?"

"Don't get softer on me than you already are." Crompton's gaze was contemptuous. "The idea was to frighten her and have you come to the rescue. Instead, and truly, it comes as no surprise, she saved your lamentable hide. The woman has more bollocks than you."

"The end result is the same," Hamilton persisted weakly. "She is now indebted to me."

"Right. You took a knife wound to your person on her be-half." Crompton sneered. "The reason for my visit, if you haven't determined it already, was to help you see your way out of this tangle. I trust that she is still eager to visit with you in Cambridge. And that your injury does not keep you from returning to the university, sooner rather than later."

But to what purpose? The pain in his leg seemed to sharpen his mind. "Lady Woolcott has expressed an interest in journeying to Cambridge, but given the circumstances, and our short acquaintance, we require more time to solidify our relations."

"For a scholar, you can be terribly thick." Crompton's eyes shot daggers. "We do not have time at our disposal. At this point, the woman probably pities you, so I should sug-gest you find a way to work that to your advantage. You ap-pear as though you require a nursemaid at your side."

Crompton raged on. Hamilton let the tirade wash over him, his vision blurring. Arguing was pointless as the man at the foot of his bed was accustomed to having his own way. Better to allow him to wear himself out, if such a thing were possible.

"Tell her it's a country weekend, at Warthaven Park, your uncle's residence."

"Uncle's residence?" Hamilton blinked. Clearly, he'd missed something.

"Don't you recall? George Crompton, your uncle, at your service." Hamilton's mouth slackened in disbelief. "You can-not expect to entertain the lady in your humble rooms at your college. I trust that you will make a proper show of courting her, acquaint her with your work at the Fitzwilliam Museum, a sure way to a bluestocking's heart." Crompton grunted an afterthought. "*The Book of the Dead* and all, what with her interest in Egyptian hieroglyphics. Make sure of it."

Chapter 9

After several hours of deep sleep, the lanyards awakened Meredith. When she opened her eyes, she was alone in the bed, only the soft fur rug for company. The tendrils of the nightmare still troubled her, but she closed off the memory, another kind of panic filling her. She needed Archer, sensed that he was not far away, and she needed to remind herself that the past was dead and gone. Slipping out of the bed, she picked up a crisp shirt that lay at the foot and pulled it on. Walking from the alcove on bare feet, she looked into the open galley where Archer glanced up from his seat before the brazier. His expression was neutral, as she stood dumbly just inside the room. He closed the book in his hands with deliberate precision. As he stood, the daylight slanting through the portholes cast his profile in shadow. She jolted, coming to her toes, when he touched her. Sandalwood flooded her senses, making her long to bury her nose in his shoulder. His hands slid over her, arms wrapping around her waist, locking her against him. As though he knew.

This time she didn't have to ask. His mouth came down on hers, his lips like coming home. He pulled her to him, palms sliding around her, down her back, around her ribs. Her whole body was shaking, with need, with desire, with fear that he didn't want this as badly as she did. He moved her back until she came to rest against the teak wainscoting.

Archer leaned in to her and allowed his palms to part the neckline of the hastily commandeered shirt. Her eyes stared up into his, her gaze locked upon him as clearly as the proof of his desire pressed against her hips. He watched her warily, head slanted back and away from her.

This time, she knew that she must take the lead. Her hands went to the front of his trousers and loosened the belt, pushing the fabric down his narrow hips and muscled legs to pool at his feet. He was suddenly naked in the harsh light of day, hers to do with as she wished. Meredith slid her arms around his strong neck, and drew him to her. Hands slid into the thickness of his hair and dragged his mouth to hers. She played with his lips, and then her mouth roamed down his neck, hot and wet. Without letting go of her, he danced them back to the bed, sprawling them both onto the decadence of the fur rug.

She kissed him hungrily, tongue playing with his. One leg crossing her hips to hold her in place, he slid one hand underneath her shirt. He rolled off her slightly, leaned back on one elbow, and efficiently undid the buttons. Pushing the garment open, he was distracted by the pull of her lips, the slow dance of her tongue, sending jolts through his body and lengthening his erection. She was hungry for this and suddenly wanted nothing more than to have the last layer between them gone. Her nipples peaked and the cleft at the apex of her thighs ached. Never taking his eyes from hers, he ran his long, strong fingers from her collarbone to the valley between her breasts, ending with the slight indentation at her belly. He pulled the shirt from her body, his eyes darkening as he took in her form, naked beside him. He straddled her then, making sure she could see the raging state of his erection, undeniable evidence of his need for her. Leaning down to kiss her again, he pressed himself into her belly. As a reward, her hands slid across his shoulders and circled to the small of his back.

Responding to her hitched breaths, his hands traced her

curves as he roamed, mouth following his palms, down her neck, along the pulse at her collarbone, across her chest to her breasts, where he lingered to suckle and nip. He paid homage to her belly, the elegant slope of her hips, licking the secret place behind her knee before working his way up her thigh. She groaned as he parted her thighs and lightly kissed the inside of her leg.

Meredith gasped as Archer pressed his mouth to her, parting her with his lips and tongue. She arched against his lips, and her hands clutched at his head as he worked his way achingly slowly to her throbbing peak near the top of her cleft, laving the swollen flesh before taking it into his mouth. She seemed to stop breathing, writhing under his devilish incursion, her hands straining against the thickness of his hair.

Unwilling to cede any ground, Archer brought an arm back around her body, palm across her abdomen as he flicked his tongue over her, pushing with his hands and mouth, a potent reminder of what was to come. The sensitive skin between her thighs burned from the roughness of his beard, but she welcomed the pain that seemed only to heighten the pleasure. Clenching one hand in his hair, she gripped the fur with the other, every ounce of her flesh concentrated on the spirals of sensation pushing her higher. She took a deep shuddering breath as her release swept over her, her cry echoing in the room, the light behind her closed lids bright.

When she took another breath, it was to feel him slackening his grip, lazily retracing his steps with his lips, skimming her body from her thighs to her belly, to her sensitized breasts until she drew him up for a soft kiss. Meredith ran her hands down his back, reveling in the hard muscles, exulting in the pleasure/pain that nipped at her earlobe, as he teased her with his lips, teeth and tongue. She moved her hips against him, feeling his hard length between them. Languid and desperate to feel him inside her at the same time, she brought her knees up slightly so that he was pressed against her slick folds. She was wet and waiting.

The inviting nudge of her hips and her low moan as he kissed her neck were all the encouragement he needed. With a skill that was nearly her undoing, he slid into her with one long, devastatingly hard thrust, stifling her gasp with a deeper kiss. Meredith extended her legs and locked her feet behind him.

How did he know? How did he know exactly how to fill her, how to leave her gasping, how to thrust and withdraw until she was wracked with pleasure? He gave an extra push at the end of each thrust, grinding into her. And she wondered, bodily sensation taking over her traitorous mind, if she could simply stay in bed with him for the rest of her life, would the past be kept forever in abeyance?

He whispered hotly into her ear, the words darkly passionate, urging her on. He angled his thrust and suddenly the world unhinged and she was crying out beneath him. She held him tightly against her, her legs wrapped around his hips, her heels pressing into his buttocks as a throbbing climax gripped them both. He pulled out and rolled away from her, leaving her with her arms thrown back and her legs flung wide in wordless fulfillment.

It was dusk when they awoke again. Meredith's eyes snapped open and Archer could see the exact moment when she remembered where she was and what they had done. He'd been sleepless for hours, watching her in the afternoon light. He'd studied her as she slumbered, itemizing the faint freckles that dusted her nose and the high curve of her cheekbones. Asleep, she appeared soft, like a young girl, the fine lines around her eyes diminished, her features relaxed. What was she, really? He still needed to determine the answer to that question but, at the moment, some of the urgency left him, seeming less important than it had a day ago.

Their coupling had been intense, explosive and yet he knew nothing more about her than the deepest intimacies of her body, which she had given up with the same lack of reservation she did everything else. Bold, courageous yet intensely private, Meredith had welcomed the sensual excesses of the night with a fervor that was alien to his wide breadth of experience. And that was a first, he thought.

He glanced beyond the alcove. He had removed the copper cylinder from the table hours ago. The last thing he wanted to do now was to disturb the fragile détente between them. She gave him a small frown. "It's not morning is it?" Placing her palms over her eyes, she grimaced. "More like late afternoon." She seemed unaware of the sinuous scars on the inside of her arms, as much a part of her as the creaminess of her skin.

"Time for some food, in any case," he said abruptly. Pulling the blankets and fur aside, he stood and ran his hands through his tousled hair, arms upraised, looking at her in an assessing way. "You must be hungry," he said softly.

"You are forever trying to feed me, it seems." There was a translucent pallor to her cheeks, evidence of a vulnerable, deeply private woman whose sleep was filled with nightmares. "I sense that you've done this sort of thing before," she said dryly, very deliberately putting distance between them. This was a woman who had single-handedly kept her wards safe from the hands of a madman, killed an assailant in cold blood and now was intent on displaying the kind of sangfroid more typical of courtesans and rogues.

"Never. You're the first," he said in a partial lie. He had never before brought a woman aboard *The Brigand*.

His reply clearly startled her. "You'll forgive me if I don't believe you," she said tartly, sliding to a seated position, carefully tucking the fur around her shoulders. He watched the rapid pulse beat under the fine skin of her throat, remembering how it felt to kiss the pale flesh. Turning away abruptly, he pulled on the trousers that lay discarded on the floor and shrugged on his shirt. He picked up her clothes and flung them toward the bed. Meredith snatched them from the air with her instinctive grace and Archer couldn't help take in the supple play of her body as she turned her back to him before bending to pull on her stockings. "There is a pitcher of water in the wardrobe," he said, and then deliberately looked away.

He made quick work of assembling a breakfast of bread, butter and cheese, the small stove quickly providing an urn of strong coffee. The brazier warmed the small interior despite the traces of frost on the portholes. The housekeeper at his estate kept the larder stocked for all contingencies as it wasn't unusual for Lord Archer to make surprise visits to his yacht with little notice. He wondered absently when was the last time he'd visited the seventeenth-century pile just up the hill beyond the mooring.

Meredith sat down at the table after a quick glance to determine that the kaleidoscope had disappeared. Despite her determined air, a residue of stark pain remained in the depths of her gray eyes. Completely dressed, every looped button seen to, she smoothed the wool of her skirts with her palms.

He pulled out a chair across from her. "I suppose that you don't wish to talk about it." The nightmare that had sucked the air from her lungs.

"No."

"The dream must have been disturbing to leave you in such a state."

She tested the hastily configured chignon with a steady hand, assuming a neutral expression. "It was nothing, truly." Archer heard the beginning of resignation in her tone.

"Nothing you wish to disclose in any case." Impatience, never far beneath the surface when he was dealing with Lady Woolcott, warred with compassion.

Meredith straightened. "We are all entitled to our privacy. Just because we . . ." She hesitated briefly before resuming, "Just because we . . ." And stopped again.

Archer knew very well what she was trying to say. "Just because we spent hours together in that bed, you mean?" he asked quietly with only the gentle lap of waves disturbing the stillness.

Meredith cupped her hands around the mug of coffee, inhaling the pungent steam gratefully. "It was a moment's weakness, as I'm sure you're aware," she said. "A moment's respite."

With a tinge of his customary mockery in his eyes, he said, "I've never been described quite like that before. A moment's respite." Smiling at her in perfect comprehension, he added, "No need to apologize. My pride shall recover."

"Your pride has nothing to worry about," she said bluntly. "You are a stupendous lover. As you well know." They had shared a bed but she would not hide behind hypocrisy. The pragmatic voice of reason prevailed. "However, it would demonstrate your chivalrous nature should you allow a discussion of more pedestrian subjects. Please leave me a modicum of self-respect."

He raised a brow. "Self-respect? That sounds somewhat dire. I thought you might be rather more broad-minded, given all your diverse and unorthodox interests, Meredith."

She waved his comments away with a small laugh. "For once would you indulge me, Lord Archer?"

"If I recall correctly, that's what we were doing."

"You are incorrigible."

He took a sip of his own coffee. "All right then. What would you like to talk about, Lady Woolcott?"

She raised her eyes to him over the lip of her mug, gaze appraising. "Let us turn the tables for a change and instead of mining the life of Lady Meredith Woolcot, let's discuss the life and times of Sir Richard Buckingham Archer. At this point, I only have the bare bones of a story that you are prepared to reveal."

He shrugged and allowed a flicker of boredom to tinge his words. "A woefully dull life until this point."

She shook her head impatiently. "So you say. Although entirely discreet, Rushford led me to believe otherwise. What with your peripatetic ways and taste for adventure. You've traveled all five continents, so I understand."

"The Royal Navy."

"And afterwards? Your thirst for travel remained unslaked?"

"I think we already determined that fact in Rashid. You were the one who correctly suggested that I was a difficult child and an even more difficult young man. With the 'attention span of a flea,' I believe were your words."

She did not spare him the directness of her gaze or a small smile. "There must be more than that to a man like you."

Archer threw his hands wide. "Ask any question you like, and I shall try to be honest and forthcoming in my replies." And so the inquiries began. Where he was born, the years at Eton where he'd first met Rushford, the death of his father in a hunting accident. The details were rushed over lightly. His mother's indifference and remarriage told with a desultory shrug.

Meredith turned away from him for a moment and stared into the brazier, as though tucking away the information for future reflection. "Rushford maintains you never stay in London or at your estates very long." It was a statement, but it was clearly intended as a question.

"I get bored very easily. Perhaps the years away in the Royal Navy gave me a taste of the wider world. London can be hopelessly provincial."

"You love *The Brigand*," she said abruptly. "I can tell that you feel yourself to be at home here." She smiled lightly over the rim of her mug. She cast her eyes around the polished teak interior, beautifully honed but modest nonetheless for a man of his rank and wealth.

"Yes," he said shortly, uncomfortable suddenly.

"You prefer these humble surroundings when you could be cosseted by the finest comforts the world has to offer. It does give one cause to wonder why." She paused to take a breath. "And to make one's own breakfast, a peer of the realm? Amazing."

He shrugged. "There is beauty in simplicity."

"Ah, yes, and yet that simplicity is not enough. Boredom stalks you at every turn."

"Rushford talks too much," he grunted.

"Rushford doesn't say nearly enough," she said. Her smile broadened. "It's all right, Archer, to give up a little sliver of your soul. Particularly when you are so demanding that I give up mine," she added with the customary glimmer in her eye.

Archer shook his head in rueful acceptance. "So I've been told." Camille's words came back to haunt him.

"Perhaps by someone who cares for you and for whom you care?" she asked, intuition on full alert.

He shook his head in brusque dismissal, but she continued carefully, "Rowena mentioned the Countess of Blenheim."

Archer leaned back in his chair, his gaze raking her face. Her expression was calm and inquiring, the gray eyes returning his scrutiny with candor. "Don't look at me like that. You ask me about my past with alarming regularity, if you'll recall."

He continued to regard her. His relations with women were open and honest, a rarity among his peers and their set. He knew from a young age that women often followed him with their eyes and that his past, although somewhat of a mystery, communicated a hard resilience that women seemed unlikely to resist. He simply gave pleasure and wished not much more in return. "I didn't think you cared," he said, deliberately casual.

"I don't," she replied. "No worries there. I am simply endeavoring to maintain some kind of balance between us. Rushford and Rowena mentioned the countess and I thought you might wish to elaborate. Although you need not worry.

This *incident*"—she emphasized the word carefully—"will remain between us only, I trust."

"You're not the jealous sort, I take it."

She nearly sputtered a mouthful of coffee. "Don't be ridiculous."

"Then for the record, the countess was once a lover and is now a very dear friend."

Meredith reached for a piece of bread, savoring the tang of butter. She added another splash of coffee to her mug. "I appreciate your candor." Calm and cool, she was as damn frosty as the weather outside.

"I take it that I've satisfied your curiosity, then," he said abruptly, not caring at all for her answer. Rising from his chair, he moved toward her, taking the mug from her hands. "The weather overnight and today has been unseasonably cold. I know of a pond nearby that is frozen solid and I suggest we conclude our conversation and take advantage of it."

Meredith was only too eager to agree, wishing to escape from the dangerous confines of *The Brigand* and into the harsh cold of the outdoors. Unresisting as Archer threw his greatcoat over her pelisse, she allowed him to pull her down the icy gangway and over the low hills in the near distance. The sea was somnolent because of the unusually frigid weather, the masts of the sloop covered in a sheen of ice, like a thousand diamonds sparkling in the low sun.

The pond was in a small copse of trees, a short scramble from the yacht. Miraculously, Archer produced two pairs of skates, helping her strap them on over her boots. Since Montfort enjoyed colder winters than most of England, she waltzed onto the ice with ease. It was difficult to count the number of times she'd skated on the river with the girls when they were young, Rowena sleek as an otter on the slick surface, Julia with round cheeks and rosy nose hanging on to Meredith's skirts. Content for the moment with the memories, Meredith skated in lazy figure eights around the pond, the wool of Archer's coat tickling her cheek as he skated beside her. The breeze raised a flurry of snowflakes lingering on the surrounding trees. Although only a hoarfrost covered the ground, the effect was of a crystalline fairy tale.

They didn't exchange any words, the tension between them as finely honed as a razor's edge. The memories of the girls retreated as reality intruded, forcing her to contemplate the fresh disaster she had wrought in the past hours. She pushed the thoughts aside, but they stealthily stole back into her consciousness, sharper than before. She had believed the world of passion was closed to her forever. Even now, she reveled in the memory of Archer's heated words and languorous touch. She closed her eyes and relived how he'd told her in intoxicating detail what he was going to do to her and how she'd feel and where he would touch her. It was an escape, an enchantment long thought forever out of her reach. But right now, even with the cold biting into her skin, she knew she would never forget how Archer had kissed her, his mouth trailing down her throat, helping her push away the past and the future, allowing her to obliterate the clouds on the horizon. He had given her oblivion, even though she knew it had been madness to take advantage of it. Wasn't that what this was all about? She recalled the stabbing pleasure, the avalanche of sensation. There was no comparison with any other days or nights of her life.

The sky above them turned a bruised purple, lit by a half-moon so unlike the one they had shared on the other side of the earth two months earlier. An owl hooted somewhere in the trees, a plaintive counterpoint to the melancholy mood. They skated around one another, an atonal duet, careful not to touch, the simmering undercurrent between the two of them ready to explode into something more. She set her expression in a rigid mask to hide her growing realization that their uneasy alliance was far from over.

Archer was down at the other end of the pond, skating in swift, sure circles as though chasing some frigid demons around the ice. Meredith forced herself to quit watching him until his shout caused her to look up from the patterns made by her blades.

"Care for a game of tag?" he shouted across to her. And before she could answer, he raced toward her, hurtling past her in a moment, catching her greatcoat in his hands, which sent her flailing across the ice and onto the ground at the pond's edge. Archer's calling her name drowned out everything else as she floundered to sit up between gusts of laughter. Her petticoats were hiked up, displaying most of her legs from the knees down. Her stockings were askew, her skirts in a shambles around her, leading Archer's gaze directly where it was wont to go. Lust and annoyance pulsed through her, as she followed his eyes with hers.

When he held out his hand, she wondered whether she should accept his help. Putting her gloved hand in his, she felt his fingers brushing her palm as her hand curled around his. Her gaze met his, and she was unable to bank the spark of desire in it. Bracing on the edge of his skates, he pulled her up as though she were a piece of down. She found her footing easily, mesmerized by the hard blue of his eyes, the disorderly riot of hair that he pushed absentmindedly back from his forehead. He smiled at her in the waning light and she knew it was insanity to feel this heat blossoming inside her, intemperate to allow this irresistible impulse to melt into his body.

He was a man like no other, she was forced to admit. He reached out and softly touched her cheek with his gloved fingertips, then her mouth. With delicacy he brushed downward until his palm caressed the skin at her throat left bare by the opening of her pelisse.

"I thought we needed a little fun. Are you cold?"

Warm, pulsing rapture throbbed undiminished through her senses. She shook her head. His low voice sent a shiver down her spine that had nothing to do with the weather and all her plans blurred. It took a full moment for cooler reason to prevail. With the lengthening silence between them, her mind whirled, backing away from the harsh reality that would soon intervene. It was going to be a living hell. Because nothing had changed in the real world, the one outside the charmed circle that seemed to close around her when Archer held her.

The lines around his eyes deepened with his rueful smile. "I'm like a boy. You affect me that way." He placed his hands solidly on her shoulders. "The last thing I'd ever thought to confess at this stage." He grimaced.

Meredith couldn't answer in a way that would please him because she knew that they were together here for the wrong reasons, despite the fact, at that moment, she wanted only him. Sliding her hand out from under her coat, she held it out to Archer, and in the short seconds before he took it in his, it seemed as though they'd never touched before. As though the passion were achingly fresh. "I will confess, it is the same for me," she whispered, her eyes taking in his broad shoulders, strong arms and wide chest. "And because of that, I'm definitely not cold," she murmured. Her body seemed heated from within. She had forgotten how desire could fill her with a fierceness that was staggering. Archer's gloved fingertips touched hers and then slid down, interlacing smoothly until their hands touched, palm against palm, his long fingers curled around hers.

His grip tightened on her hand and the smile in his voice was tinged with suggestion. "Nevertheless, we should absolutely make sure that you aren't cold."

"You have a suggestion?"

"I do, indeed," he said before he drew her gloved hand to his mouth and pressed her palm to his lips. And it all came hurtling back in a rush, searing memories of their hours together, the unguarded pleasure that together they could create. Archer's mouth hovered above hers and he smiled. "The suggestion is waiting back at *The Brigand*," he said in a quiet, intense voice, "guaranteed to sweep away any chill."

The following hour was both extravagant and excessive, culminating in a copper tub that had been miraculously produced and filled with steaming water. Meredith lay with her head back against a small cushion, considering herself fortunate and blissfully satiated, the world outside the confines of the sleek yacht locked out.

Archer sat on the edge of the tub. "You are no longer cold."

"I never claimed to be," she murmured.

"Then I've kept you warm."

Her eyes opened, half-lidded. "A job well done, Lord Archer," she assured him, sinking deeper beneath the thin film of bubbles. She was tender in places that did not bear thinking about. She was content to wallow, feeling the ache leave her muscles.

"Good," he replied blandly, watching as she arched her neck like a cat, pleasure enveloping her. Her dark red hair clung silkily to her shoulders. It was clear that he enjoyed the sight of her long slender limbs and slick breasts in the candlelight. "Although, I should think the water must be getting cold."

"I suppose there is no calling a maid," she said.

"I could get someone from the estate, I suppose. They were kind enough to provide the tub in the first place."

"The water would be far too cool by then. So I suppose you are the only one at hand."

"Of course," he said, half beneath his breath. He had hastily donned his shirt and had not bothered to button it. "On one condition," he supplied casually, undeterred by her commanding tones.

"And what might that be?"

"That I join you first in your sybaritic pleasures in the tub."

A sudden flare of excitement raced through her. It was like a flood after a decade's long drought. Archer's hands on her body, his mouth on hers, the exquisite pleasure when their bodies joined. For the moment, it filled her world. She tried for levity. "I don't suppose I could dissuade you."

"Only with a pistol," he said lightly. "I've seen the accuracy of your aim. But alas, it's out of reach, at the moment."

"You make a good point."

"So is what I have in mind." His voice lowered.

She sat up, splashing him in response, but it was too late as he had already shrugged out of his breeches and shirt and climbed in beside her. The water sloshed onto the teak floor, but neither of them seemed to care.

A good time later, she said, "You did this on purpose." Her tone was mocking.

"I do everything with purpose." He arched a wicked brow. He stood up and held out his hand. She stood thigh-deep in the water next to him, as he wrapped a towel around her. Her long legs, slick with water, gleamed in the firelight. In one motion, he scooped her into his arms and moved toward the bed, her body pressed warm and damp against his chest. Although they had just made love, he would have given his soul to slide his fingers into the knotted towel and peel it from her skin.

The urge was clearly not his alone. Meredith's fingers clutched at his shoulders as though she needed to keep him there, hovering over her. He looked for no further encouragement, as he lay down beside her.

"How is this possible?" she murmured against his neck. "That I want you again?"

It was a question he couldn't answer. Instead, he rested his forehead lightly against hers. His lips brushed her skin. "Perhaps," he tried carefully, "we should endeavor to speak of other subjects."

Her eyes spoke rueful appeal as she looked up at him. His expression was encouraging. "What are you looking at?" she whispered when the tension of their silence became unbearable.

"You," he replied simply. Against the furs she looked as decadent as an odalisque, making it nearly impossible for him to think clearly. The silvery marks on the inside of her arms reminded him of his folly. He was quiet for a long time, his arms loosened around her. He lifted his head up, looked down into her eyes. He appeared as if he was considering whether to speak.

"What happened, Meredith?" he asked finally. He took his thumb and gently brushed it over the inside of one arm and then the other.

She stared at him. "They are the price I paid rescuing Julia and Rowena," she said thickly after a moment.

He nodded, continuing with his stroking. "How?"

"It was the nursery fire," she said, staring at the ceiling. "I had awakened to the sound of flames as my bedroom was adjacent to the nursery. They were little more than babes." She took a deep breath. "I didn't think but simply plunged through the smoke. Julia was standing by the rocking horse while Rowena was in her crib. When I reached in to gather her into my arms, the heat of the crib's metal spindles singed my flesh."

Archer was silent, his rhythmic caress continuing.

"It was well worth it," she said fiercely. "These are scars that I welcome because they saved the lives of two innocents who would otherwise have perished."

"As your father did."

She nodded.

"And the kaleidoscope?" he asked softly.

She kept her eyes on the ceiling. "First belonged to Julia and then to Rowena. It was most often found in the nursery."

There was much he wanted to say but couldn't.

"I know what you're thinking. And what you would like to ask." She turned into his arms. Her eyes were wide and filled with truth. "Faron set fire to the nursery." She said the words too quickly, too breathlessly, and he stared at her intently.

"That is what Rushford told me," he said gravely. Then he asked, "Why would he do something like that?"

She shuddered in his arms. "Revenge. Madness. But it was my fault."

"I don't believe it."

And as if it were yesterday, Meredith saw Faron standing in the light of the summer afternoon inside a simple cottage. "It happened in a little cottage outside Blois," she said, her eyes looking into the distance, almost able to smell the roses that scented the air around the place. "Of course, Father knew we were falling in love. Faron's parents were always in Paris and thought their son's dalliance with his tutor's daughter was something they could simply ignore, in the assumption that he would grow out of it." She paused. "He surprised me one day by taking me there," she said softly.

"You fill my heart, mon amour. I would give you all the world as a bouquet." Their eyes had met, and the magic that existed for them alone filled his gaze. It seemed like yesterday, despite the years that flashed by and the memories that threatened to engulf her. Her eyes had shone with tears of love at the sight of Faron, his arms overflowing with red roses he'd gathered from the bush outside. He was across the room at her side before the first tear spilled, dropping the flowers and sweeping her up into his arms. "Don't cry," he whispered into her hair, cradling her against his chest. "Think of the happiness we share and all the years ahead of us." They walked to the cottage door and she stilled in his arms, gazing out at the sunset, and the gentle forest beyond. The radiant summer sun lit up the young couple looking into the promise of a shared future.

"You are my life and my love," he murmured, his dark eyes turning toward her. "My best friend. My intellectual equal, lest I forget, and also," he whispered, lightly brushing her cheek with his lips, "my passion."

She smiled at him tremulously. "And your chess partner."

"And a colleague whose interests match my own. I could never have translated that last stanza of *The Bacchae* without you," he said, love in his voice and eyes. "Although I should add that you also cause my heart rate to accelerate when I see you in that beautiful gown you wore at the Comte de Polignac's dinner a fortnight ago."

Lifting her head from his shoulder, Meredith dropped a quick kiss on his mouth. "Enough of this flattery. Father is convinced that it will go to my head and I shall lose my focus on my studies."

Faron shook his head, taking her pale hand and placing it against his chest. "Impossible. You have both—blazing beauty and intellect. And I am the most fortunate man in the world to have you by my side. Will you marry me?" he asked her with a brilliant smile that she knew she would never tire of for as long as she lived.

Beside her on the bed, Archer pushed the hair back from her face, his expression shuttered. "You said yes, of course."

"I never had the chance."

"His parents wouldn't allow it. The daughter of a tutor who was only a minor English nobleman."

She shook her head. "I literally never had the chance." Then she told him. After they had made love, Faron had left the cottage, in the early evening. On his way back to the chateau, he was viciously attacked by his cousin Jerome, a deeply disturbed young man who had always been bitterly jealous of Faron. He was left for dead, with a grievous wound to his head. He barely survived and the injury left him with a lifetime of seizures and a diminished intellect. Jerome committed suicide, but not before leaving a note, swearing that Meredith was the cause of his jealousy and the reason for his heinous act.

"The young man I knew was not the same," Meredith continued. "Plagued with wild mood swings which he hid behind a leather mask, as his formerly handsome features were beset with wild tremors beyond his control."

"He blamed you."

She shrugged helplessly, recalling the weeks he had spent recovering in the northeast wing of the chateau. The act of opening his eyes had been torture, the pounding in his head like an anvil. Meredith had sat by his bed, memorizing the fleur-de-lis patterns on the rich silk hanging, the heavy mahogany furniture, the bed curtains pulled back. A tapestry hung on the wall, its unicorn and frolicking maidens all distantly familiar. For weeks, she had watched as he broke out into cold sweats, the first of a series of convulsions racking his body. He had drifted in and out of his fevered state of alternating pain and awareness.

"He was never the same," she repeated. "And poisoned against me. He believed that because of me, he was left a carapace of a man, imprisoned behind a leather mask, with scarred flesh and a scarred mind. I had no choice but to flee after the fire with Rowena and Julia."

She remembered the last time she'd seen Faron. She was on a stolen horse, galloping like the wind, her cloak flowing behind her, her hair escaping from her hood. Faron had somehow known where she was, and intercepted her on the road outside Blois where she had managed to secrete the children. He drew rein and pivoted his mount to stop her. Her horse, whipped to a frenzy only moments before, tossed its mane and danced impatiently, poised to disappear over the horizon. She met his gaze for what would be the last time, his eyes obsidian behind the mask. At that moment, he was still everything that she had ever loved him for in the beginning. Then her heart closed forever, before it could shatter.

"Do you see why I am so concerned for you?" Archer held

her closer, breaking through the memory. "Say that you understand."

He could tell that it took all her strength to keep her tears from spilling over. "You are the one who needs to understand, Archer. I have said it once before. I know in my heart that he is dead, as Rushford and Rowena attest. There is no possible way that the toy from the nursery came from Faron."

She moved from his arms and sat up, pulling the fur rug around her shoulders.

Fascinating choice of words, Archer thought, startled by the bitterness of his thoughts. "You are a woman of intellect and you pride yourself on your logic. Your *feelings* about the matter should not signify."

She rose from the bed, pulling a sheet around her, although it was far too late for modesty. "I do not have to explain everything. Surely I have explained enough." She was exhausted, enervated, but becoming increasingly out of temper at Archer's damnable presumption. Marching from the alcove, she threw herself on a chair by a porthole, drumming her fingers restlessly on the chair arms, looking out into the black night.

When he joined her moments later, she looked away, trying to visualize where their strange alliance would lead next, cursing herself for having revealed more than she should have in a moment's weakness. It had begun to rain, she noticed distractedly, more sleet than rain, really. When the small clock on the mantel chimed some time later, she looked away from the porthole and was startled to see how late the hour had become. How long had she been here with Lord Richard Archer, in this hothouse fantasy of desire and excess?

Why, she thought indignantly, was she sitting here like some fearful child? She was a grown woman, long since able to face reality and its demands. "I believe it is time that I leave," she began, finally turning her head in the dimly lit interior, her gaze drawn to Archer's powerful form seated across from her. He was whipcord lean, full of constrained energy; the strong, stark lines of his face did not bode well.

"Of course, you're free to go. But I should advise waiting until morning. The roads to London will be more hospitable." His intense scrutiny belied his casual sprawl; his feet bare, he was clad only in his breeches. "Before you leave, tell me at least that you will not resume your relationship with Hamilton."

"Good Lord, Archer. Not that again! I don't believe you have any right to dictate with whom I spend my time," she snapped.

"I think we have determined that you are in danger," he said quietly.

"I shall not have him threatened," she said heatedly, incensed by the way he commanded the space with his presence. "He is a lovely man who has only shown himself to be a loyal friend. It would behoove you not to forget how he came to my assistance, not once but twice."

"Precisely." His voice was flat, his response simple. "I have not forgotten. And there's the rub."

"Why do you not like Hamilton?" she asked, angrily, then reconsidered his neutral expression. "What do you know that you are not telling me?" she asked in a hushed, hesitant voice, her nerves on edge.

"Just call it instinct." Rubbing his head with both hands, he raked his fingers through the thickness of his hair to smooth the disheveled roughness.

"That's no reason to ask me to avoid a man. You can't do this," Meredith declared, "every time I make a new acquaintance."

Leaning back in the carved chair, Archer rested his head wearily against the teak wainscoting. "I realize that," he murmured with a faint grimace. A moment later, he rose from the chair, pushing it aside with a harsh gesture. He strode away from her to look into the blackness of the port-hole.

"I should leave now," she said quietly. Before the situation deteriorated.

He shrugged, his powerful shoulders in his hastily donned shirt outlined against the dark glass. "Not until I have your word that you will not visit with Hamilton in Cambridge. At least not without me at your side." He stood motionless be-fore the porthole, looking out as though there was something to see beyond the pitch black.

"At my side. Are you mad? I don't understand you at all. What is it that you want?" Meredith rested her hands on the arms of the chair, hoping to steady them. Her heart was beat-ing rapidly, like the young girl she no longer was.

"Clearly what I can't have," he muttered into the black night. Turning, he faced her, in shadow still, his expression shuttered. He took a step forward and the glow of the brazier fire threw into sharp relief the stamp of weariness on his face. There was a flat silence and then he said softly, "It frightens me."

"My situation frightens you." It was a startling admission.

"What else can I say to convince you?" For the first time the words were without arrogance.

"I have given you every chance to explain yourself, to prove to me that you are not somehow behind the events that have been befalling me with alarming regularity. The kaleido-scope is disturbing. But it does not definitively point to Faron's hand."

"After what you told me tonight, how can you say that? Who else could possibly know the import of such a highly personal article that you last saw in your wards' childish hands?"

"I can't explain it."

"Everyone else who would have known of its import is

gone, no?" he continued undeterred. "Your father, Jerome. Faron's parents, we know, passed away shortly after you left France. Frankly, that leaves you and Faron."

Meredith took a deep breath and eyed him speculatively. "You are so passionate about this entire affair, Archer, and I have to wonder why. It makes one suspicious. You have given me so little to go on." She paused, fingers at her throat. "And neither of us is a romantic fool, so don't let us make too much of what happened these past hours. There is something else that you are reluctant to reveal."

His smile was cynical. "You will have to take it on blind faith."

She looked up at him, a world of weariness in her eyes. "I have given you the truth. Perhaps you could do me the same courtesy. We have shared incredible physical intimacy, my lord, but I still am no closer to learning the truth from you than I was at the outset of our meeting a day and a half ago. And I sense that is not about to change. So either you send for a carriage, or I shall make my way in the dark up to the main house and secure one for myself. And don't believe for a moment that I will not make good upon my word. Remember who I am, sir, and what I have done."

"I don't think so," he said, a muscle clenching in his jaw. "You will stay the night here, or if you choose, remain at the main house until morning." His voice was low and perfectly level.

Meredith's heart stopped at the finality of his statement, as though there was no other alternative than to respond as calmly as he'd spoken. She was desperately tired and confused. How could someone so open, so gloriously profligate in his desire and responsive to her needs, be dangerous? And how could she lose all sense of that danger when he was inside her, when she was part of him and he of her? With sheer willpower, she kept her voice from rising. "Very well, Lord Archer. Until morning, then. But I shall sleep in this chair. You may take the bed."

She turned away from him, the light from the candles flickering across the portholes. This interlude had gone on long enough. Faron had been the one great love of her life, a doomed love that did not bear repeating. What she'd had with Lord Richard Archer was passion, lust, escape—or perhaps far worse.

Chapter 10

"I don't fully understand." The man behind the screen paced in the library at Claire de Lune, a perturbed frown disturbing his expression. "Lady Woolcott is with Lord Archer. How did that happen without my knowing?"

"I'm not sure," said Crompton, with more than his usual patience. He was leaning against the mantelshelf, awareness in his small eyes as he sensed the man's agitation. It was never comfortable to have one's judgment questioned, particularly by a powerful superior.

"Are they lovers? I have a suspicious mind, Crompton. Entirely useful, I've found. I advise you to cultivate the same."

"It appears that Archer swept her away after the incident outside Burlington House," Crompton said, with a brusque gesture that set the amber liquid in his crystal glass sloshing against his wrist. He had never quite mastered the manners of a gentleman.

The man behind the screen sighed extravagantly. "Not what I'd intended. The goal, as you will recall, was to have Lady Woolcott find herself enamored of Hamilton." He raised an eyebrow in reproach.

Crompton stared, incredulous. "You've met the man. Hardly a charmer." He drained his glass in one gulp and thumped it on the table, reaching for the ornate snuffbox. It was an affectation he wished to cultivate.

The man behind the screen said nothing, watching as Crompton took a hefty pinch of snuff only to succumb to a fit of sneezing and coughing. When the spasms had subsided, the man said calmly, "It is never a good idea to rise too far beyond one's station. You would do well to remember that."

Crompton blew his nose vigorously, patting his embroidered vest in vain for an extra handkerchief. The admonition was hardly welcome. Eager to restore confidence in his usefulness, he said, "If we're smart, we may be able to use Archer."

"You mean the way you were able to use Rushford?" the man asked, derision in his voice. "Archer is a man to be reckoned with, if you'll recall. I believe you found yourself roundly beaten to a bloody pulp outside the British Museum. If you're fortunate, he won't recognize your face when he sees you next."

"It was bloody dark down in the damned crypt."

"It was not a damned crypt. It was the bloody museum."

"We were close, so very close. If it had not been for the baron . . ."

The man's lips thinned. "The baron is dead. He has paid for his folly. Clearly, close was not good enough. So I would ask you to reassure me that the plans for the trip to Cambridge are proceeding apace. Have we the proper reconnaissance at the Fitzwilliam?"

"We do indeed."

"You know what I want. And how I wish it to be delivered."

Crompton grinned reluctantly. "Ingenious on your part, if I might say so."

"I didn't ask for your opinion." The acerbity in the voice behind the screen made it clear his employer bristled at the familiarity in Crompton's tone. *Well, sod him.* Crompton reveled in the secret knowledge that he was not the only one who sought a station that just might have exceeded his grasp. He leaned over to refill his glass from the decanter on the side table and then sat back, cradling the goblet between his hands.

"I suppose you are looking for a new addition to your collection."

"Your job is not to wonder why, Crompton. Only assure me that all will be well and go according to plan."

Of course, the man was right. Every precaution was essential. They could not afford a repeat of the British Museum debacle.

It was an exhaustive session, but the two men parted company in the early hours of the morning, Crompton having satisfied his superior that he had covered every contingency. He was confident that Archer was theirs to use, particularly if he was already sniffing the fine skirts of the Woolcott woman. All that remained was to fling open the doors of Warthaven Park and assume the mantle of Hamilton's uncle, welcoming the scholar and his lady friend to his estate in the countryside outside Cambridge.

He was rather looking forward to it, playing the role of country squire. For a man who hailed from the bitterest London stews, breathing in the fragrance of fresh lime blossoms on the grounds of a venerable French estate was quite a change. It was not long ago that he had inhaled the smells of garbage and damp stone from the Thames flowing sluggishly through his East End neighborhood.

How quickly things changed.

Lord Hubert Spencer was thinking much the same, as his horses drew to a halt in front of an imposing mansion off Montrose Place. He disembarked, looking up at the double-fronted façade of the Earl of Covington's London home. Not that he expected to find Archer in residence, but even he did not dare to visit him at his country estate on the Channel. That pile of stones, as Archer referred to it, had been part of Essex county for close to four hundred years.

The door opened before he reached it and a dour butler

bowed and swept him within. Spencer relinquished his hat and noted the highly polished banister, the gleaming marble beneath his feet, the sparkling chandelier. A few moments later, he was ushered into the library behind an enormous gilt-edged door.

With a frown, Archer looked up from his desk, a snow-drift of papers spread before him. "To what do I owe the pleasure this time, Lord Spencer?" he asked without pream-ble.

"I apologize for arriving unannounced. Truth be told, I did not expect you to be in residence."

Archer waved away the platitudes impatiently. Spencer unclasped his hands behind his back before taking a chair. "I realize that we don't stand upon ceremony," he said conver-sationally, his gray hair agleam in the cold-blue afternoon sunlight, "so you won't take offense when I tell you that you look like the devil himself. Actually worse than after the three weeks you'd spent on that Spanish island, the guest of Col-onel Estavez."

"He was not the most hospitable host, as I recall." Archer did not elaborate for they both knew the unwelcome sojourn had netted Whitehall the information they needed to make inroads with negotiations with the Spanish. Never an easy lot to deal with, Spencer thought, but Archer had survived hand-ily. Spencer was an avid student of human nature, as was cus-tomary in his line of endeavor, and as such he discerned that something was amiss with the earl. He had known Archer to possess an impenetrable shell of reserve, even in the most po-tentially explosive situations. He hid ably behind a laconic façade, a patina of boredom that obscured what lay beneath. But a thin crack had suddenly appeared on the smooth sur-face.

"I take it that you did not appear at my doorstep to make observations regarding my health."

"One can't blame a man for being concerned." Spencer glanced absently at the carpet beneath his feet.

"I'm touched, Spencer," Archer said dryly. "So what is this latest disaster you no doubt wish to regale me with?"

Spencer lifted his gaze to Archer, eager to introduce the matter at hand, which they both knew to be urgent. "I should rather ask that question of you, my lord," he countered with exaggerated formality.

Archer let out an exasperated grunt. "Well?"

"The Woolcott woman," Spencer said, though he felt there should be no need to remind him.

"What of her?"

"I was expecting a report at the very least."

"There is nothing to report."

"I see," Spencer said carefully, eyes neutrally surveying several portraits of estimable ancestors gracing the walls. "I had rather hoped differently," he continued with delicacy, not wishing to allude directly to the fact that he had ascertained from his people that Archer and Lady Woolcott had disappeared for thirty-six hours to his estate in Essex.

Archer rose to stand by the side of his desk, examining his mud-splattered boots. He was still wearing a riding coat and jodphurs. He came to the point with customary lack of ceremony. "There is nothing that I can tell you that you don't know already, Spencer," he said grimly. "As predicted, she is off to Cambridge with Hamilton. As soon as the bounder rises from his sickbed."

Spencer digested the news before turning to the sideboard. "May I?" he asked. A few moments later, he turned to Archer, a cut-glass decanter in hand. "Drink?"

Archer took a glass. "It is what you wanted, is it not? Hamilton, as you pointed out during our last meeting, is indebted to Faron's people, and as a result, is forced to do their bidding, including courting the fair Lady Woolcott. To what end I'd wager he doesn't even know himself." Having finishing his tightly wound delivery, he drank deeply of his brandy.

Spencer leaned back in the wing chair and thoughtfully sipped from his own glass. "And you let her go, I take it."

Archer nodded, his eyes sharp with attention. "I believe we must run this thread to the ground. Lady Woolcott does not believe herself to be in danger from Faron. She believes him to be dead. Worse still, she believes I might have something to do with the events that have recently befallen her."

Spencer permitted himself a satisfied smile. "Of course, you haven't told her the nature of your role in this situation."

Archer stood up and went to refill his glass. "I have not. But Lady Woolcott is far too intelligent and suspicious to think that my only interest in her is personal. She's an unusual woman, clever, with wit and courage."

"No doubt," Spencer murmured. "All the more reason you might wish to keep close to her and to Hamilton. This is far from over, I'm afraid."

Archer looked skeptical.

Spencer leaned forward and kicked a fallen log back into the grate, adding absently, "I'm not accustomed to seeing you so indecisive, Archer. Dare I say you are not certain as to your next step?"

He looked across at his now-silent companion.

"Whatever gave you that idea?"

"You appear uncharacteristically morose. One can't help but wonder."

Raising his glass, Archer said. "This obsession of yours regarding my good humor or lack thereof is getting us nowhere." He asked pointedly, "Any news regarding Giles Lowther? I thought you would have had your henchman run him down like the fox he is by now. I reviewed the dossier you sent over a fortnight ago. Interesting that he and Faron are almost of an age."

"Lowther has lived at Claire de Lune, alongside the Frenchman and his disciples, since the tender age of eighteen. He was quick to learn, formidably intelligent, which Faron has always appreciated and exploited. As discussed previously, he has been willing to undertake just about anything on Faron's behalf, the more dastardly, it would appear, the better." He paused. "What are you thinking?"

"Nothing important."

Spencer examined Archer shrewdly. "Out with it."

Archer examined the inch of liquid left in his glass. "Just wondering if Lowther was at the chateau when Lady Woolcott and Montagu Faron were lovers." The dates in the dossier, they both realized, answered the question. Neither could resist logic and fact.

Spencer sat back, crossing his ankles, his eyes narrowing. "Does it matter?"

"Everything matters in a case such as this." Archer got to his feet again. "Although damned if I can put my finger on it."

"Your instincts are keen." Spencer inclined his head. "You know your business best."

"When it comes to Lady Woolcott, believe me I do," Archer said curtly, putting down his glass. He gestured to the snowdrift of papers on his desk. "To that end I have been studying Hamilton's obsession, *The Egyptian Book of the Dead*. One thing we do know about Faron, living or dead, he was an avid collector, or should I say thief, of antiquities. Egyptian in particular. *The Book of the Dead* is a composite of ancient Egypt's oldest and most important religious texts, magic spells, hymns and rituals, written by the priests of Egypt over its long history."

"Astounding actually," Spencer murmured. "Four thousand years old at the time of Christ."

"My understanding is that the scribes filled the papyrus rolls with spells for protection as well as instructions on how to render the body workable in the next world. In other words, how to protect the body in the tomb, how to make the journey to the netherworld, how to pass the judgment of the gods and how to exist in the next world, after having been accepted by the gods."

"You have done your homework."

"Why is Faron interested is the question. How does this relate to the Rosetta stone? To this point I've gleaned that the two hundred or so different spells or chapters that appear in *The Book of the Dead* do not appear in a fixed order. The actual title might be translated as the 'going forth by day,' which might refer to the deceased going forth to the netherworld. The Egyptians were fearful of the night and it would have been considered advantageous to make the journey during the day." He frowned. "I'm going round and round."

"Have you thought to ask Lady Woolcott?"

Archer sat back down behind his desk, rifling through the papers on his blotter. "Didn't believe that wise. The less she knows, the less danger she's in. Although it is rather obvious, isn't it?"

"What is?" Spencer asked, trying to keep up.

"It's about a translation somehow. Lady Woolcott possibly has the key." He threw his booted feet upon the desk. "It can't be a coincidence that Hamilton, ridiculously pathetic bastard that he is, was chosen. It must have been specifically for his entrée at the Fitzwilliam."

Spencer was disinclined to interrupt a second time, realizing that Archer had set the wheels in motion whether he liked it or not. In his experience, he had never seen the man quite so at loose ends, his usually relaxed demeanor nowhere in evidence. Suddenly ill at ease with the transformation, he was compelled to interrupt. "It would be unwise, Archer, to become overly invested in the outcome."

Blue eyes shot daggers from across the desk. "What are you implying, Spencer? That my usual cool head is somehow compromised when it comes to Lady Woolcott?"

Spencer held up his palms in a gesture of contrition. "No offense intended." Archer scowled at the rolls of documents covering his desk. "What is it that you intend to do next, then?" Spencer asked with all the innocence he could muster, staring at the dregs of brandy in his glass.

"Sod it," Archer said mildly. "You know how much I

loathe interference from Whitehall. I shall proceed however I please."

It had worked in the past, Spencer thought silently, his face brightening. He had received the report he needed, albeit by a circuitous route. "I shouldn't expect otherwise," he said with a satisfied smile.

Chapter 11

Meredith stared down at her breakfast with a marked lack of interest. The porridge and kippers, and even the artful scones with their flaky crust that she had taken from the sideboard, held no appeal. With little appetite since having returned from *The Brigand* two days earlier, she pushed the dishes aside and proceeded to do nothing more than brood in her room and the library for the rest of the day, listening to the unrelenting sleet on the windowpanes and the coal fire in the grate. The unseasonably cold London weather resulted in her drinking pots of tea and pacing about in her dressing gown.

Most of all, she thought of the girls, missing them with an ache that was physical, a part deep down inside always afraid for them. Throughout the town house, there were deliberate reminders of her wards, mementos she had brought with her from Montfort. Her eyes fell upon Julia's favorite daguerreotype of the three of them, taken in front of the south garden of Montfort when it was in full bloom. Rowena appeared lit from within, careless and carefree, no doubt having just returned from a ride. Then Julia, her beautiful eyes shadowed and all too aware for a young girl. And finally, Meredith, her arms around both of them, protective, watchful.

Meredith looked away and continued her pacing in the

small salon at the front of the town house. Her eyes shifted to the elegant side table, where her hand strayed to Rowena's pen, a gift for her thirteenth birthday, nestled in its ebony box, sitting alongside a copy of Wordsworth's poems. Sentimental fool, she told herself, knowing that she also kept the girls' baby slippers somewhere in a trunk upstairs. The girls were women now, married, happy and safe. She wiped her eyes with her hand, pulling herself up straighter and gathering her cashmere scarf more closely over her shoulders.

This was no time to let down her guard, no time for vulnerability. She had been managing on her own for years and it was only recent events that caused her to call her decisions into question. The child's kaleidoscope rose in her mind's eye. She had taken it with her upon her departure from *The Brigand*, a painful reminder burning beneath her pelisse, but one she could not leave behind. Standing at the window overlooking Belgravia Square, she tried to cope with the implications of that time spent with Archer.

She blew out a breath and shut her eyes for a moment, drawing upon what sliver of good sense remained to her. It was entirely unhelpful remembering awakening in the bed they'd shared only to find him watching her, an inscrutable expression on his face. She knew that look. And distrusted it. What had she done? She had never envisioned being with a man again. It was not the specter of fire and brimstone or bromides concerning chastity that had ensured she did not seek out masculine company. Her fall from grace the first time had been enough to shut down the stirrings of her body and her heart. Until Archer.

Determinedly, she pulled the brocade curtain closed, obliterating the gray outlines of the street below wreathed in cold winter weather. What did she wish for most desperately in her life? A sense of normalcy, a return to a quiet, undisturbed existence where she could pursue her studies and revel in the satisfaction that Rowena and Julia were safe at last. The past was better left dead and buried—if only she could. Damn

Archer and the toy from the nursery at Claire de Lune, so innocent and yet so vile a reminder of that which was better left undisturbed. Lord Archer seemed to have that effect upon her, exacerbating her moments of vulnerability with catastrophic results. It was her fault entirely, her failing and her panicked need that had led them to cross a boundary from which she desperately hoped she could return. She wasn't going to open herself up to the possibility of love again. Not after Faron. The path from love to corrosive hatred was not a journey she would risk again.

She huddled into the richness of the cashmere around her shoulders, convinced that she could put both Archer and the temptation he represented behind her. She had fallen asleep in the chair on *The Brigand*, as promised, but had awakened in the bed, alone, with Archer nowhere in sight. A carriage waited for her and had taken her back to London with only the sharp cold and even sharper regrets for company. She had been dealing with the specter of danger for years—and she could do so again. Without Lord Richard Archer. It was time to resume living. It was better to be going off to Cambridge to spend a few days exploring the university town and the Fitzwilliam collection with Hamilton. That Archer had no use for the Cambridge don made the prospect all the more enticing.

Shortly after dawn the following morning, Meredith shook off her melancholy. Energized by a goodly dose of guilt, she sent Broton personally to fetch Dr. Codger from Harley Street to Mr. Hamilton's lodgings. Having forwarded a note to the inn expressing her wish to visit later that morning, she berated herself for not having inquired as to his convalescence. Stingingly aware of what she owed the man, she pulled herself together and set out for Charing Cross.

The rain and sleet had left deep puddles on the cobblestone street; the sky overhead was the color of gravel. Waiting for Dr. Codger at the entranceway as he alit from his carriage in front of the modest inn, Meredith introduced herself, reminding the doctor of their meeting several years before when Julia had had a bout with scarlet fever during their stay in London.

The doctor cocked his head and squinted at Meredith, rummaging through his recollections. "Of course, of course, my dear lady, I recall very well. Such a sweet child." After the brief exchange, they passed the taciturn innkeeper sitting behind a polished desk in the entranceway, who diffidently waved them upstairs.

The physician took his time climbing the narrow stairs to Mr. Hamilton's rooms, somewhat winded, but at last he arrived, clutching his worn leather satchel in one hand. He was close to seventy and stout, with disorderly white hair and a threadbare suit coat. Meredith stood tentatively behind him as he knocked on the door to Hamilton's rooms.

Not waiting for a reply, the doctor turned the knob with Meredith hovering on the threshold. "Mr. Hamilton," she called out, averting her eyes. "It is Lady Woolcott and Dr. Codger. So pleased that you are able to entertain us upon such short notice."

"Do please come in, Lady Woolcott. It lifted my spirits to read your earlier missive. What a welcome tonic!" Paler than his white nightshirt but clearly prepared for her visit in a green dressing gown, Hamilton was wreathed in smiles. He rose stiffly from a chair by the window of the small sitting room. A cache of books listed in the corner by a grate steadily giving off warmth. A pot of tea sat in readiness on a table covered by a worn lace cloth. Stiflingly warm with the aroma of camphor about it, the overall atmosphere was of a sickroom.

"Please do sit down," Meredith entreated, taking a step inside. Hamilton eased himself gingerly onto the bed, still favoring his leg. "I brought Dr. Codger along to ensure all is well and, quite frankly, to assuage my guilty conscience," she said lightly, aware that the physician also served as chaperone for those concerned about propriety.

Hamilton's eyes sparked behind his spectacles. "I do so wish you would do away with the apologies, my dear. Entirely unnecessary. Now come and sit here by me so I do not feel entirely unlike a gentleman."

Meredith demurred. "Not until Dr. Codger has had some time with you, Mr. Hamilton."

"May I take your coat, at the very least?"

"I can manage quite well." Meredith slipped her pelisse from her shoulders, happy to remove it in the crushing heat.

Hamilton watched as the doctor set down his tattered satchel. "Doctor, I assure you this visit is entirely unnecessary. Your earlier ministrations have done me a world of good. Although the tincture is foul tasting indeed."

"It has no potency unless it tastes foul, Mr. Hamilton." The doctor cocked his head and looked back at Meredith. "We can't be too careful, so let's have another look. Would you not agree, Lady Woolcott? Mr. Hamilton here is still favoring his leg. Shouldn't wish sepsis to set in." He threw back the buckles of his bag. "Now let me see to these dressings."

Meredith shrugged helplessly, the closeness of the room enervating. Smiling encouragingly at Hamilton, she sensed he would give in.

"Is there still pain at the site of the wound?" Codger asked.

"At times," Hamilton said, wincing when the doctor's hands hovered over his thigh. Muttering to himself, Codger turned back to his satchel to begin extracting a number of medical implements from within. Once or twice, the patient glanced at Meredith as if expecting her to excuse herself rather than hovering on the threshold. Instead, she shut the door quietly behind her, aware of Hamilton's gaze upon her.

"Not that it is any of my business," the doctor muttered,

looking into the recesses of his bag, "but are the two of you by any chance affianced?"

"I beg your pardon?" Meredith said.

"Whatever made you think that?" Hamilton echoed.

The doctor looked between them and shrugged. "It is unusual for a woman to visit a man in his sickroom unless they are relations or..." He trailed off. "Never mind. Now kindly extend your leg for me," he said to Hamilton, who was observing the doctor with a dubious eye, made clearly uncomfortable by the physician's blunt question. Nonetheless, he submitted to the doctor's ministrations. Dr. Codger spent the next quarter hour asking him all manner of questions while prodding and poking him from his neck to his chest to his abdomen and finally ending with his leg.

A gnarled hand bore Hamilton back down onto the bed as the interrogation continued. "Does it hurt when I do this? Have you experienced any fevers?"

"Truly, I am fine, Dr. Codger. Perhaps just a change of the dressing."

With a small smile, Codger turned around and motioned to Meredith. "He's a stubborn one, but then all men are when it comes to illness." He turned back to his patient and pressed his ear to Hamilton's chest. "The heart is strong," he announced, listening. He straightened and finally opened his patient's dressing gown and began unwinding the bandages while Meredith spent her time studying the dusty tower of books teetering at the edge of the doorway.

"We are quite finished now, Lady Woolcott," the physician announced some time later. When she turned around, he motioned her to a chair opposite Hamilton. He too sat down, rubbing his hands on his knees. "You will live, Mr. Hamilton," he proclaimed with a sigh, beginning to throw an assortment of instruments back into his bag.

"No fever?" Meredith inquired.

"I feel almost entirely myself," Hamilton interjected,

"with only some stiffness remaining." He managed a reassuring smile for Meredith before turning to the physician. "Well, I daresay we are finished here. I thank you for your time, doctor." The physician remained silent in his chair, as though awaiting his tea.

Meredith's shoulders fell. "There is nothing else, I trust?"

The doctor scrubbed a hand around his unshaved jaw. "Well, Lady Woolcott, to answer your question, Mr. Hamilton is taking longer than expected to heal," he said finally. "And I don't quite know why, given the slight nature of the wound."

Hamilton considered it. "My constitution has never been particularly strong."

The doctor set his hands over his knees and drummed his fingers for a moment. "Your predisposition may indeed play a role in your convalescence. Interesting, you are not putrid, feverish, or swollen about the lymph nodes." Codger waggled his head from side to side, equivocally. "I should recommend then, no strenuous activities for the next while, despite the fact that your leg appears to be on the mend. You can put your full weight on the limb, I take it?"

Hamilton gave a terse nod. "Not entirely. But almost. So you see, it is just this weakness, or perhaps I might call it a malaise."

Dr. Codger threw up his hands. "No worries. You will be entirely well as long as you do not overexert yourself, young man."

Meredith exhaled audibly, sliding forward in her chair, her fingers braced on the arms. "I shall see to it personally, Dr. Codger. I feel somewhat responsible." The doctor knew some of the story about the attack outside Burlington House.

The doctor added cheerfully, "Every man needs a nursemaid at some time in his life, certainly. Now not total bed rest, of course. Simply no vigorous activity of any kind and a bland diet—beef broth, well-cooked vegetables and the like."

"He will do as you say," Meredith said, as Hamilton looked grimly over both their heads.

"I suppose it is for the best if I am to fully recover," he added, much subdued.

"We're finished then." Codger grasped his satchel.

Hamilton rose from the bed, suddenly eager. "If you could perhaps wait for Lady Woolcott in the vestibule, just for a moment, doctor. I have something I should like to discuss with her." His concern to observe the proprieties was obvious.

Snapping his satchel closed, the doctor squinted at them both, murmuring something indistinct under his breath before shuffling his way to the door with a wave over his shoulder. "Take your time. Take your time. I shall wait for you outside, Lady Woolcott, and perhaps I can secure you a hansom when you and Mr. Hamilton have concluded your conversation." His footsteps receded as he carefully made his way out of the room and down the hallway stairs.

"I thought he would never leave," Hamilton confessed.

"Dr. Codger is thorough, no doubt." The windows were thin and Meredith could hear the throaty yell of a fishmonger on the street below. She smoothed her skirt and looked at Hamilton expectantly. "I am pleased you are well, sir," she said sincerely. Her gaze was candid.

"I cannot thank you enough for your consideration, Lady Woolcott." He blinked behind his glasses, looking suddenly boyishly handsome. He was fair and fine featured and with a smile so sincere, Meredith almost looked away. "I do so hope we can put the matter of Burlington House behind us and that you will still consider visiting Cambridge in the near future. Now that the doctor has given me leave, I believe I shall depart within the next few days. I am eager to be home."

"I am certain you are."

"I am only concerned that you do not allow the attempted attack on your person the other evening to dull your scholarly triumph, Lady Woolcott. Your paper was magnificent

and, as a matter of fact, I have just completed a series of letters to my colleagues at Cambridge detailing your intriguing
hypothesis. I am sure they would be eager to hear more
about your ideas when you visit."

He looked at her with such kindness, Meredith suddenly
felt the sting of tears behind her eyes. She tamped down the
twinge of vulnerability which came all too easily to her these
days. "What a lovely gesture, Mr. Hamilton. I should indeed
like to visit with you and your colleagues in Cambridge," she
answered honestly. Wishing to steer the conversation to safer
ground, she added, "I suggest that we journey together, in
case you should require assistance as the doctor indicated.
We can have one of my servants accompany us."

She still felt inordinate guilt. He had intervened so gal-
lantly on her behalf. She experienced an unsettling rush of
emotion. He was always so kind and gentle, not to say courageous, reminding her of all she'd never had.

He dipped his head toward her, the faded blue of his eyes
only inches away. "How very, very kind, Lady Woolcott," he
said, his placid expression like his voice, forbearing and mild.
"I should be honored to take you up on your generous offer
to accompany me to Cambridge and, if I might be so bold,
my uncle has offered to host us both at his country home on
the outskirts. Warthaven would offer you many more comforts
than staying at a rustic inn and, as well"—a faint ruddiness
tinged his pallor—"your reputation would be safeguarded."

It was a way out. More important, it was a step in the direction Meredith wished to take, away from the past and
into the future. There would be no opportunity to think
about recent events or the damned toy from the nursery at
Claire de Lune. And best of all, she would forget about
Archer, about his whispered words and heated touch. She
would not lie restless and eager in her bed each night, allowing her desires to rule her mind.

Hamilton and the Fitzwilliam were precisely what she required.

*　*　*

Cambridge University was a world onto itself. The ghosts of Sir Isaac Newton, Wordsworth and Byron passed through the great gate of Trinity College and lingered in the shadows of the Pepys Library. Everything was reached by climbing narrow stairs, or traversing tapered streets filled with the rush of students and dons, their black capes flapping in the wind. Medieval doors opened to the rivers Granta and Cam, which flowed behind the college buildings and curled about the town in the shape of a horseshoe. The town behind the colleges was called the Backs and oftentimes described as the loveliest view in England, with its pristine meadows, gardens and lines of tall trees, green and peaceful.

Poised on the riverbank, Meredith took in the willows and their branches bending gracefully toward the water. A weak sun limned the stone bridges looping across the divide and framing the colleges whose deep-colored brick or stone merged in a glimmering reflection, joining one another along the curve of the river. Meredith was entranced.

Late that morning, she and a fatigued Mr. Hamilton had arrived at Warthaven Park. Perched on the heights above the River Granta, Warthaven's crenellated silhouette had been visible from afar. It was a rambling structure added to and improved upon over the centuries, the latest Palladian wing pale against the gray winter sky. Its dark shadow cast the gentle valley below in shade. At close range, it was just as impressive, a great pile of granite set over a cobblestoned court where their carriage had come to rest before an enormous door. Their host, Octavius Blythe, Hamilton's uncle, had not been receiving when they'd arrived, but they were shown to their rooms. Meredith insisted that Hamilton rest while she eagerly finished a hasty toilette and set out to explore the university town, unable to wait until the morrow. They would meet with their host for dinner.

A curricle was put at her disposal and she spent a glorious afternoon retracing the steps her father had taken many years earlier, with a visit to Clare College. After a brief introduction to the officious secretary in a tiny office off the college's main hall, she was met by a junior don who, he informed her, had heard of her father's illustrious although short-lived career at Cambridge. With his academic gown fluttering behind him, he insisted upon giving her a tour of the library and the main hall. Martin Carlyle was a plump little man, clearly unaccustomed to speaking with a woman who was not only openly interested in the college's history but could also intelligently discuss the high points of Newton and Tennyson's tenure. They spoke at length of various books and treatises that had been recently produced by the college, many of which Meredith was familiar with. The subjects ranged far and wide until Carlyle's eyes widened when he learned of Meredith's recent presentation at Burlington House.

"You understand, the lecture is in its earliest stages," she clarified modestly. "It was the result of an extended trip to Egypt, Rashid, more specifically," she amended, her mind going back to the hot sun and the hard earth and, reluctantly, to her time with Lord Archer. She gave her head a shake and brought herself back to the present by studiously admiring the vaulted ceiling above her, the flying buttresses extending to the sky. They were simply magnificent.

"How very interesting, indeed. When you have finished your research to your satisfaction, Lady Woolcott, please allow me to pass along what will surely be transformed into a monograph to several of our professors here with an interest in antiquities."

"That is very generous of you." There was a trace of bitterness in her tone, reflective of the fact that the doors of learning had been closed to women for centuries. She took a short breath, her ambitions paling into insignificance against the backdrop of a university that pre-dated the twelfth century and had produced scholars who had changed the world. "In addition to my father's time at Clare College," she said, "I have another connection to Cambridge. An acquaintance here whom you must surely know—Mr. Hector Hamilton, who, from what I understand, is with the Fitzwilliam."

Carlyle appeared momentarily perplexed, his forehead beading. "Ah, yes, of course. Mr. Hamilton," he said, his voice echoing off the arches of the cavernous hall. "Do you know him well, Lady Woolcott?"

There was a sudden hesitation in his manner. "I only inquire as we have not seen much of Mr. Hamilton of late, since early last summer, as I recall. I believe he has taken a leave, perhaps even a sabbatical."

Her look of confusion must have deepened. Carlyle hesitated, as though girding himself for something unpleasant and wondering whether to say more. "Some unfortunate personal matter, no doubt," he said vaguely.

Perhaps the matter of Cressida Pettigrew, Meredith thought. "I can assure you that Mr. Hamilton is in good health."

Carlyle was immediately flustered, casting about for a tactful phrase. "Of course, Lady Woolcott. I should not suggest otherwise." But there was something more. She wished the rotund man would be plain. He was definitely keeping something to himself.

"From what I understand," she continued, "Mr. Hamilton is quite renowned for his work on *The Egyptian Book of the Dead*."

Carlyle's face brightened. "Quite so, quite so, Lady Woolcott, although I'm afraid ancient languages are outside my ken. I should wish otherwise, given the gems that the Fitzwilliam holds. Perhaps you would allow me to accompany you and Mr. Hamilton on a tour of the collection, once he has returned to the area."

Shifting her gaze from one of the ornate stained-glass windows, she said, "He has returned to Cambridge, but perhaps you did not know that he is staying with his uncle at Warthaven Park for a time."

Carlyle hesitated, this time pinning her with a pointed

stare. "I did not realize he had an uncle in close proximity—at Warthaven? Are you entirely certain, Lady Woolcott?"

"Absolutely. Why do you ask?"

"Warthaven has been closed for at least a decade with only a groundskeeper present. The Blythe family has been on the Continent for most of that time, or so I've been led to understand. There is not much that goes on in Cambridge and its environs that we do not know about," he answered with a rueful smile.

Meredith returned his smile resolutely, trying to make sense of the situation. "Well then, there will be quite the welcome for Lord Blythe on his recent return this evening at dinner."

"Strange," Carlye openly mused. The comment stung somehow.

Meredith studiously ignored her misgivings as she returned to Warthaven to prepare for the evening. There had been something disturbing about her conversation with Carlyle, she thought, walking down the sconce-lit corridor to her suite of rooms on the first floor, at the end of a long gallery that housed family portraits. She paused in front of the painting of Lyon Blythe and his older brother, George, the two of them with their receding chins and hairlines like peas in a pod. Neither bore any resemblance to Mr. Hamilton, she thought. The boys' parents were next in line, from whom they had inherited tawny hair, brown eyes and acquiline noses. The final portrait showed a gentleman at the summit of his power, his wig tumbling magnificently over his shoulders, his garments rich with seventeenth-century lashings of embroidery and lace. She stared at the paintings, a sudden tightness in her chest. She frowned, a hand at her mouth, discomfited by the suspicious train of her thoughts.

It had taken a full measure of reserve to politely respond to Carlyle's comments. Not for the first time, Archer's exhortations rang in her head, and she gave some consideration to

Hamilton's sojourn in London, returning to the issue of his cast-off fiancée and, more revealingly, this seemingly long-lost uncle of his. No doubt, the man would be elderly, if he was Hamilton's mother's cousin, as Hamilton had explained, and possibly dull. Reaching her room, she stood in the doorway. She would have preferred spending the evening in her rooms, reviewing several of the books she had purchased at one of Cambridge's ubiquitous bookstores. Moving to the armoire, she noted that a maid had already unpacked her trunk, but had left the silk-encased kaleidoscope untouched at the bottom of her smaller case. It had become Meredith's talisman now. Looking away from the scrap of red silk, she drew out a gown of soft crepe the color of slate, with long tight sleeves that buttoned to the wrist. A triple tier of mauve lace at her throat formed the high neckline, an appropriate ensemble for a dinner with an elderly host.

It was with some surprise when she made her way down the main stairs to Warthaven's cavernous hall that she saw a broad, stocky man leap down from a carriage to the cobblestones and stride through the same doors that had impressed Meredith upon her arrival. With short cropped hair and a thin mouth, he greeted the butler with a curt nod, oblivious to his mud-spattered boots leaving a track on the Oriental carpet.

His gaze settled upon her instantly. "You must be the lovely Lady Meredith Woolcott," he said, moving toward her, leaving a muddy trail from the entrance hall to the grand staircase. He bowed, tossing his hat to a footman, his small brown eyes assessing. "I am Lord Blythe, but you must call me Octavius. Hamilton, the scamp, did not tell me how beautiful you are, Lady Woolcott."

Mr. Hamilton's uncle was not anything like she'd expected, nowhere near the four-score that she'd anticipated. While still murmuring appropriate pleasantries, she was rushed down toward the drawing room, the earl's grip firm on her elbow.

"I believe it is time for champagne," Blythe said. "Out in the countryside most of the day in this blasted weather. Could use a drink. Now where's that milquetoast of a nephew, Hamilton?" he blustered.

"He should be with us in a few moments." Overstuffed upholstery in hunter green and a roaring fire greeted them. She watched as Blythe rummaged around the drinks table before thrusting a flute into her hands.

He turned to pour himself a drink. "No more malingering, I trust, on his part. Heard about the unfortunate business in London and so I must thank you for having accompanied my nephew to Warthaven Park. Hector does not take after the rest of the family in robustness. All this scholarly nonsense when he should be spending more time out of doors." He glanced over his shoulder at her. "Well, at least I know I will never have to serve as a second to him in some duel." He gave a bark of a laugh.

Meredith did not immediately answer, sinking into the chaise by the hearth. Blythe tipped the whiskey down his throat, put his glass back down and said to himself, "Fill it up," and blew out a breath of relief. He was anything but the refined, elderly aristocratic gentleman that Meredith had been led to expect, and resembled the relatives in the hallway portrait gallery not one whit.

Blythe dissolved into one of the chairs near the fire and proceeded to describe the state of his coverts, deer herds and hunting pack, making no mention of his long-term sojourn on the Continent. It was a tour-de-force performance, his observations rambling and without end. By the time Hamilton arrived with the book he claimed he'd been searching for most of the day, Meredith had barely gotten a word in edgewise.

"There you are, Hector. I was about to send an able-bodied footman to rip you out of your bed." Blythe glanced at him disparagingly. "You look as though a strong wind could knock you over. What have you been up to—other than squiring this beautiful woman about London?"

Hamilton appeared rather bewildered and sank down into one of the chairs farthest away from his uncle, but not before pouring himself a glass of brandy with unsteady hands. "Good to see you again, Uncle Octavius," he said with stiff formality. "And to answer your question, I have been busy with my convalescence."

"Enough of that by now, I should hope."

The barb did not miss its mark. "I am all but myself again, Uncle, so much so that I have been looking forward to our visit. Thank you again for opening Warthaven Park to us."

The fire burned briskly in the hearth, but Blythe just shook his head, one stocky leg crossed over the other, foot swinging. "A pleasure. I should hope you will show Lady Woolcott the delights of Cambridge. Including the Fitzwilliam, of course." He turned to Meredith. "Quite the bluestocking, I hear."

Hamilton cradled his glass between his hands. "Of course. Although I shouldn't expect you to accompany us, Uncle Octavius, knowing your dislike of musty libraries, museums and such."

Blythe shrugged, but not before taking a large swallow of his drink. "That's not an inaccurate way of putting it, although now that I've met the fair lady," he said with a sidelong glance at Meredith, "I just might change my mind."

Hamilton let his breath out through his teeth. "I should have thought hunting might be more to your liking." He looked thinner in his evening jacket, the shoulders hanging loosely from his frame. The familial resemblance between the two men was nowhere to be seen.

Blythe gave him a curious look, brown eyes piercing, brows raised. Firelight licked his muddy boots and sparked from the ruby in his cravat. "How perceptive of you, Hector. I do so enjoy the hunt."

An indefinable tension invaded the room like a faint scent.

Meredith placed her flute on the table by the side of her chair. "I understand you have spent quite a few years on the Continent, Lord Blythe, and that you have only recently returned to England."

The older man met her gaze, a small smile playing about his thin lips. "I've spent the last few years in France, as a matter of fact." A slight pause, to allow the fact to sink in, and then he rose. "Time for dinner." Meredith momentarily wilted in her chair before taking his hand and allowing him to escort her to the dining hall.

Lord Blythe exhibited a prodigious appetite. In short order, he had eaten his way through several servings of roast beef, a variety of vegetables and a lamb terrine, washed down by copious amounts of red wine and followed by a singularly spectacular blancmange. Throughout the whole extravagant display, seated in a dining room that could easily accommodate fifty for dinner rather than three, Meredith fought a growing unease.

Pushing his plate away with exuberance, Blythe leaned back in his chair and surveyed Hamilton and Meredith with a faint smile. "I forget what contentment is until I return to Warthaven Park." He half lifted his hand like a rector about to give his blessing. "And so pleased that you both could join me."

His plate barely touched, Hamilton smiled weakly in return. "Your warm welcome and hospitality are much appreciated," he said in the tone of a child, as though by rote.

"You needn't wait for an invitation next time."

"Well understood," Hamilton said.

"And so tomorrow we repair to the Fitzwilliam." Blythe folded his broad palms on his stomach, replete at last.

"You need not accompany us, Uncle."

"Oh, but I insist, Nephew."

Meredith folded the crisp linen napkin on her lap, suddenly finding it necessary to escape from the strange tension that had been building between the two men. Pleading a headache, she excused herself, not waiting for a footman to pull back her chair, and left the room with murmured apologies. With her skirts bunched in one hand, she made her way down the corridor until she was well away from the dining hall and leaned back against the linen fold paneling. She was only half lying when she pretended a migraine, now taking in great gulps of air in an attempt to alleviate the pounding pressure at her temples.

Just as she was feeling more composed, she saw Hamilton coming toward her, straightening his spectacles under the shimmering lights of the overhead chandelier. She experienced an unsettling rush of emotion. As he reached her, he took note of her pallor and her attempt at a smile, clearing his throat awkwardly. "You left so suddenly. I had no choice but to excuse myself and come to see if you required anything, my dear Lady Woolcott. Headaches can be the very devil."

"I'm feeling better, truly. I simply needed some air."

He took note of her distress. "My uncle can oftentimes be somewhat overwhelming."

The ornate chandelier above, its multiple candles burning, threw shadows into sharp relief. The muffled sound of servants clearing away crystal and china resonated through the hall. Meredith glanced up the broad staircase, the familiar sensation of being watched prickling her skin. Would it never leave her, this heightened awareness? Forcibly, she pulled her attention back to Hamilton.

"Are you certain you are well, Lady Woolcott? Perhaps I should accompany you to your rooms."

What was this madness? she thought, her shoulder blades stiffening. Her eyes traced the darkness of the stairwell, peering into the dimness. Nothing. Ignoring her disquiet, she straightened away from the wall while at the same time Hamilton moved closer. And the next moment she stood in the circle of his arms, breathing in the scent of starched linen and dry ink. "Lady Woolcott," Hamilton murmured, clearing his throat once again, "I am here if you need me for anything—for anything at all."

The pounding at her temples increased and she knew she must get control of her emotions and seek some semblance of calm. Interpreting her agitation as invitation, Hamilton drew her nearer, holding her close, implicitly offering her his strength and understanding. He gently stroked her back, tentatively brushing her cheek with the back of his hand.

Lifting her face to his, she gave him an uncertain smile, prepared to offer the appropriate blandishments about gratitude and friendship. Despite the jumble of misgivings, the pieces of the puzzle that refused to lock into place, she told herself that Hector Hamilton was truly a sweet man. Modest, kind and courageous—so different from the previous men in her life. Her smile broadened and he mistook the gesture as an opening and dipped his head, his faded blue eyes only inches away. And then he kissed her, a gentle, tentative kiss. And for a moment, Meredith let him, overwhelmed and confused, no longer certain she wished to face the world alone. But almost as quickly as she'd given in to impulse, she regretted her rash response, recoiling from the sensation of his lips upon hers. She pulled away. "I'm sorry. Mr. Hamilton . . . please."

Stammering and flushed, Hamilton dipped his head in polite withdrawal, embarrassment tightening his fine features. "My apologies, Lady Woolcott. I should not have . . . If I have overstepped the boundaries of our friendship . . . I did not intend to cause you distress. Please forgive me." He bowed faintly, hands clenched at his sides. "I cannot begin to explain what came over me."

"It is quite all right, Mr. Hamilton. No damage done. Simply a lapse in judgment. Mine as well."

"I would do nothing in the world to harm our friendship," he stuttered, blinking rapidly. "It was simply that you appeared in need of comfort. Please do tell me that you are not upset by my boorish behavior."

"I am not upset," she said, taking a step back. "And will be delighted to tour the Fitzwilliam with you tomorrow."

It was as though she'd absolved him of all sins. He heaved a sigh of relief. "So looking forward to it, Lady Woolcott. We shall put this unfortunate incident behind us." Meredith smiled her agreement, watching as Hamilton backed down the corridor away from her.

Her headache now pounding, she made her way up the grand staircase to her rooms. Lights from the sconces flickered and she could not dispel the notion that someone watched from the shadows. The portraits glowered in the half-light, observing her progress, eyes boring into her back. Once in her rooms, she gratefully shut and locked the door behind her.

The fresh scent of the outdoors and of wet wool assailed her senses. Had someone left open a window on such a bitter night? Turning around, she saw Lord Richard Buckingham Archer dripping mud and winter mist from his cape onto the Oriental rug. His unruly hair was sleek with droplets of snow, a trace of stubble shadowing his jaw. He looked as though he'd ridden hard, a dark and towering presence in her bedchamber, his gaze outrageous.

Chapter 12

Montagu Faron had always preferred summer, glorying in the nighttime scent of the lime blossoms that graced the estate of Claire de Lune. Now the aroma was but a memory lingering in the cold of winter.

Giles Lowther looked away from the secured French doors and the moonlit parterre with its plane trees and disciplined shrubs and instead paced the length of one of the chateau's many laboratories, the tang of formaldehyde warring with nature's perfume. Two rectangular tables lined the generous space, topped by rows of microscopes, the instruments now covered with dust. There were ghosts in the room, of a youthful Faron and Meredith Woolcott.

Lowther stared at a desiccated butterfly, its wings pinned back under glass, framed on the altar of Faron's vaulting ambition. The bright yellows and blues were faded now, though the colors had once been brilliant against the cold glass upon which they rested.

He knew firsthand of Faron's agony, the ongoing torment of loss, relentless torture that had invaded both his waking and sleeping hours. His life had been a palimpsest, layers of bitterness and regret that had fueled his appetite for revenge against those who were closest to Meredith's heart—Rowena, the rebellious one, and the more subdued sister, Julia, both of whom had brought Faron to the portal of death.

As with Faron, Lowther did not believe in fate or God but only his own driving thirst for knowledge and revenge. The first had brought him alongside one of the greatest minds of Europe and then offered him the opportunity to take what was in his grasp. Jerome and Meredith were the sacrificial lambs. Lowther ran his hand along the finely wrought leather mask covering his face. Now whose was the greater intellect—his or Faron's?

He smiled behind the mask and looked out the French doors to the ordered park outside which had been designed by Le Notre, esteemed landscaper to Louis the Sun King himself. The roots of the Faron family in France ran deep, their association with the Renaissance and the Enlightenment forged in blood and wealth. The numerous libraries at Claire de Lune held ancient texts. Egyptian artifacts like the Rosetta stone and *The Book of the Dead* belonged to the Farons by right of fiat, or so they believed.

How the mighty had fallen. And at the hands of a guttersnipe, an English one at that, raised to unimaginable heights by wit and stratagem alone. He had assumed the mantle of Faron's wealth and power with the ease of slipping on a mask. No one believed him truly dead. He chuckled at the thought. There was little else standing in his way, thanks to the Woolcotts, whose every move had seemed to doom Faron to failure and finally death. Now was the time to dispatch Meredith Woolcott like the specimens in the room that no longer served any use. That she and her wards had slipped through his grasp, not once but twice, was unforgivable.

Hector Hamilton was a worry and Lowther despised weakness of any sort. Of course, Crompton was now at the helm. He had nearly beaten Lord Rushford to death, not an easy task. Lowther's eyes lit briefly on the butterfly pinned to its crucifix, before walking to the French doors to see the skeleton of winter outlined in the bareness of the trees. Just a few more days, and the circle would be complete. He would welcome Lady Meredith Woolcott to Claire de Lune himself—where she would finish what she and Faron had begun almost twenty years before.

"Have you gone entirely mad?" Meredith hissed. "This time I truly intend to scream!" She jerked away from the door and put an escritoire between them, taking no chances.

"Truth be told, I was not expecting a warm reception," Archer said coolly, scrubbing a gloved hand down his wet face. "Especially with your attentions already taken by Mr. Hamilton."

"It was you. You were spying from the staircase," she whispered, circling from behind the table. "You are despicable, unconscionable, sir."

He looked at her in some surprise, surprise which quickly shifted to something else. He stalked closer, so close that she could drown in the blue sea of his eyes. "I felt no need to interrupt, Lady Woolcott. As you well know, if it had been me with you downstairs, I'd have had your drawers round your ankles in minutes."

Meredith fumed, pushing a hand through her hair in frustration. "You have no right to interfere. I demanded that you stay away from me and here you are again, having broken in to a home and invaded my rooms."

"Perhaps I find you irresistible. I cannot help myself."

"Oh, please. I suppose you have been overcome with lust for my erudition. Or is it the fact that my advanced age is a welcome change from the parade of young women whose mamas no doubt keep you on your toes?"

"Actually," he drawled, "it was your mouth. Ripe and sensuous. And that's when you're not talking."

Insulted beyond belief, she felt her color heighten. "I see," she whispered. "You are mocking me, but for the last time. Leave right now." She pointed to the window. "Using the same entrance by which you came."

Archer lifted one brow at her command. "Forgive me, Lady Woolcott, but your protestations are wearing thin. Or perhaps I was confused, as the last time you were more than willing to use that luscious mouth—"

Meredith drew back her hand to strike him. Like quicksilver, Archer's hand snared her wrist, dragging her against him, the drops of mist quickly soaking her gown. "For all your learning, you do seem to have a propensity to violence. Had I not seen you with a pistol not so long ago, I should never have been forewarned."

"Well, I shall warn you once again, Lord Archer, and I don't require a pistol with which to do it. I have the right to kiss whomever I choose. And that includes Mr. Hamilton."

His eyes dark, his mouth hard, he whispered hotly against her ear, "You are a very poor liar, Meredith."

"And you are a poor excuse for a gentleman," she hissed.

He drew back, his gaze running over her face. "I never claimed to be one." Challenge fired his eyes. He jerked her fully against him, catching her by both wrists and forcing them against the escritoire, pinning her with his body. The evidence of his desire was hard and unequivocal. For an instant their gazes locked.

"Why do you always fight me?"

Her breath, too, was short. "I don't want you here."

His grip did not loosen, his lips moving toward hers again, and she felt her eyes grow heavy with surrender. His voice was silk. "Such a liar."

Fighting him physically would be useless. Damn, damn, damn the man, she thought, taking in the splendor of his tall, muscled form. It was impossible to forget his raw virility or repress the heat turning liquid between her thighs. More angry with herself than with him, she took a deep breath. "Archer, listen to me. We must be rational about this." Even as the words left her lips, her body was intent on defying logic, heat coursing through her veins.

"I'm pleased that you finally agree with me."

Meredith waited for him to do something other than gaze at her. He still held her wrists, his face so close to her own, his eyes narrowed with a predatory gleam that she hadn't seen before. "What are you looking at?" she whispered when the tension of their silence became unbearable.

"You," he said. But still he made no further move. "We don't seem to do at all well with words." Without releasing her hands, he brought his mouth to hers. His hand rose to her throat as she kissed him back, the other pressing her abdomen into the hard shaft of his erection. Finding her wrists suddenly released, she moved her hands down his back, down to his buttocks, her fingers biting into the hard muscles, expressing a need and demand that matched his own.

It was Archer who drew back. His hand on her throat seemed to be imprinted on her skin. "This solves nothing," she said, her voice strange, as if emerging through a fog. "You cannot protect me."

"Yes, I can and yes, I will," he said. His hands went to the opening of her gown and the delicate fabric parted as he made swift work of the hooks and laces until it puddled at her feet, the gray silvered in the moonlight falling through the window. The cold air brushed her body and her nipples hardened. She reached up to touch his lips, moaning softly in infinite satisfaction as he touched her, drawing a finger down her throat, between her breasts, to her navel and slipping between her thighs. Her feet shifted as a questing finger probed and found what it sought, all the while his eyes held hers, watching and measuring her every pant and breath, mastering her body. He held her tightly and the cold damp of his coat rubbed her nipples, the leather of his britches smooth against her belly and thighs, which were covered only in thin batiste. Then he kissed her again, his mouth hard and possessive, his tongue driving deep until her head fell back under the pressure of his ravaging mouth. Her body arched against his hands in the small of her back when she peaked, panting her pleasure into his mouth.

Without removing his lips from hers, he carried her to the bed. Her skin was sensitized, every nerve ending close to the surface, the rich brocade coverlet rough against her naked back. Kneeling astride her, he ran his hands over her breasts, circling the nipples with his fingers. He looked up and met her gaze and suddenly, Meredith knew what she wanted. "Come closer," she whispered, angered somehow with the cool detachment in his gaze, as though she were something that had to be tamed and understood. She didn't wish to think, not now, when her fingers pushed the wet wool from his shoulders and quickly unfastened his waistband. She moved her hand to enclose him.

Inching down the bed, she took him in her mouth, her hands resting on his hips as she pleasured him. She knew he watched his erection move in and out of her mouth, its length swelling even more with each slide of her lips and tongue. She gloried in the power she held over him. Wanton, ravenous, she took him deeper, feeling his hands play over her buttocks and her inner thighs.

Just before he was about to explode, he jerked away. Hair a glorious tumble around her face, her nudity covered in the sheerest batiste, she slid her way up his body, rubbing her breasts against his chest.

"You want me. And I want you. Nothing is simpler or truer than that," he said, his voice rough with desire. He pulled her up against the pillows and she spread her legs; her gray eyes were clouded with passion.

"Say it," he demanded, as he touched the fluid of desire gleaming between her thighs. "Say it." More harshly this time.

She smiled and the curve of her lips was enough to unman him. They never had any luck with words. "Hush, darling," she murmured, quickly straddling him, urging him into her body, removing her drawers; widening her passage until he impaled her. She arched up and then down in desperation to meet him. Her hips writhed and pumped, drawing him deeper and deeper, her need for consummation verging on the precipice of frenzy. Finally, after she had peaked once again, he pulled her beneath him, entering her body with one long, slow thrust that penetrated her core. Meredith cried out, curling her legs around his hips. His mouth covered hers, suppressing her pants of pleasure before they broke from her lips. He rode her with a ferocity and force that ended in his own spine-wrenching orgasm, which he spilled on the softness of her abdomen. His breathing was as rough and shallow as though he'd run ten miles.

Meredith couldn't move, nor find the breath to fill her lungs. The fire crackled in the hearth, their labored breathing a counterpoint to the soft tap of snow against the windowpanes.

"I still want you to leave," she said.

His head lifted from the mattress. "Don't say that."

She measured his critical gaze for a moment and then softly exhaled. "How does this"—she gestured weakly—"change anything?"

He rolled away, reaching for the sheet. "Does your meeting with Hamilton not make you suspicious in the least? A man whose interests serendipitously align with yours—the Rosetta stone and *The Book of the Dead*?"

She rolled her eyes, flinging an arm over her forehead. "Not this again," she moaned.

He growled deep in his throat, a contemptuous sound, and glared at her for a second. "And what about the child's toy from the nursery at Claire de Lune? How have you reconciled that bit of evidence?"

"Do not let's begin again," she muttered. "I don't wish to hear it. So please leave."

"I'm not leaving without you."

Sitting up, she pulled a portion of the sheet around her shoulders. The silence was oppressive. At once pleased and disappointed that she'd locked the door to the room, she pushed a hand through the tumble of her hair. "Will you not give me some credit, Archer? Do you really believe that I would give over my independence for whatever it is you are offering?"

He looked at her, his expression swept clear of all emotion. "You hide behind these bluestocking notions, Meredith, when truly, they do not exist for you. You are a beautiful, passionate woman, and there's no use denying it. Your father and Faron have much to answer for in terms of your unorthodox notions."

She began to rise from the bed.

"Not just yet," he murmured, grasping her wrist.

"Release me." Her voice was cold.

"Because you are afraid to hear the truth."

She was rigid, her gaze filled with rage. "Do not dare judge me or my past." Each word was a chip of ice.

He raised a brow. "And why would I? You spend enough time there as it is."

She seethed. "Did you ever think that I might be able to piece a few things together myself? Of course not, that would be too much to expect from even a bluestocking." She edged closer to him on the bed, fearless now. "I know what I must do. I know the possible danger that Hamilton represents. I know better than anyone the implications of Rowena and Julia's kaleidoscope from the nursery at Claire de Lune. And further," she spat, "I know what I must do to confront my past."

His gaze turned cynical. "I don't believe you have the courage to finally leave the past behind—where it belongs."

"You have no right—"

"I have every right. Particularly, when I see you marching straight into danger."

"What do you mean?" As she rose to her knees, he hauled her back, his grip on her waist firm. The lamp at the side of the bed sputtered.

"You are going to France, to Claire de Lune, are you not?"

The sheet fell from her hands. She was not ready for this, never would be.

"Not so much to escape from danger," he said slowly, "but to discover whether you still love him. Faron."

The lamp at the bedside sputtered one last time and went out, leaving the room bathed in shadow and moonlight. It was difficult to ascertain the moment when she knew, except to note that the euphoria erupting at his touch had not dissipated and that she finally understood she'd been fooling herself. She tried to capture the memories, but like fine-grained sand, they slipped through her fingers. She could explain none of it, either to herself or to Archer. They faced each other on the bed in silence, still holding themselves away from each other, almost as if they were afraid to move closer, that one or the other would prove a phantom.

Then Archer said softly, "Come here." He pulled her across the bed toward him, slipping his hands into her silky, dark red hair, drawing it forward over her shoulders.

"I have never seen hair this rich, this beautiful." He traced her mouth with his fingers. "How can you doubt what happens when we come together?"

She tried to disguise the huskiness in her voice. "I don't doubt it," she said. "I'm just not sure what it means."

He shook his head. "I know what it means." He pulled his shirt over his head and tossed it aside. His nude torso was burnished by the remaining light, his virility impossible to ignore. "We have all night."

Warming to the thought, Meredith stretched luxuriously, her breasts snagging his gaze. "We have all night," she murmured, honey replacing the anger in her veins in a heartbeat.

"If you need proof"—his voice deepened to a gravel pitch—"look at what you're doing to me." His erection surged higher. There was a stomach-wrenching jolt when he touched her and she knew that she'd made the right decision. His scent flooded her senses as his hands slid over her shoulders, arms wrapped around her, locking her tightly against him. His mouth came down on hers. Without letting go of each other, they fell back into the enormous bed.

Meredith kissed him hungrily, tongue twining with his. He slid one hand under the batiste of her chemise and rolled it off her with an impatient tug. And then she reacted as he knew she would, helpless to do otherwise. They wanted each other again, there and then. From the waist down she moved under his hands with slight rotations of her bottom. He fondled her everywhere, parting the shadows, viewing her, telling her how beautiful she was and how wondrous their coming together had been. He teased and taunted her with memories, the memories that they had made together, driving them both further down the road toward momentary oblivion. He knew how to set her aflame, how to hold back to increase the pleasure. He thrust swiftly, deeply and after one powerful movement, Meredith placed a hand over her mouth to stifle her moans, abandoning the world as she rode out her orgasm.

He stayed with her, never stopping the careening pleasure, continuing until she crested again, slowing only when they came together. When he finally withdrew for the last time, his hands still on her slender hips, he pulled her into his arms. Neither of them moved.

"I won't let you go. You know that, don't you?" he finally said as the pale light of morning leaked into the bedchamber.

She turned her head toward the pillow. "I know," she said softly. "But I must resolve this, as only I can."

"With me by your side," he growled, temper and passion rising within him.

"There is no need to be so high-handed, Archer." Her fists clenched in the sheets.

"Trust me. I'm not usually like this. Only with you. I don't seem to have any other way of expressing my feelings."

"I do trust you. In every way," Meredith said, forcing a calm into her voice she didn't feel.

Archer loomed over her in the bed and took her head between his hands, his fingers in her hair. "You don't know how long I've waited to hear those words," he said savagely.

"I trust you," she repeated, the notion entirely foreign. "But on my own terms."

His fingers tightened in her hair with passionate intensity, his eyes darkening. "I will be there, at the Fitzwilliam," he said darkly. He brought his mouth to hers and the instant before their lips touched, Meredith knew she was truly lost.

Chapter 13

The Fitzwilliam Museum was hard to ignore, a looming neoclassical building with an aggressive portico on Trumpington Street. It was decked out in full Corinthian style, unparalleled in a university town that was accustomed to architectural marvels. The entrance to the museum was suitably impressive, approached by two flights of ascending stairs.

The collections of the department of antiquities offered superlative galleries displaying Egyptian artifacts, ranging from stone and wooden coffins to painted pottery, marble portraits, figurines and cuneiform tablets. The treasures had grown over the centuries through the vagaries of archeological explorations and imperial theft, the upheavals of war and the passage of history.

Lord Archer had arrived early, his anxiety deepening with each passing moment. He still felt the weight of it, here in the museum's atrium, just as he had when he'd slipped with heavy reluctance out of Meredith's bedchamber earlier that morning. Upon her terms, as she'd dictated, and against his better judgment.

He felt like a rutting schoolboy, as though last night and a million more would never be enough. All the previous affairs, all the entanglements in his life, had simply fallen away. He only remembered Meredith Woolcott as his lover, remembered the sensation of her long legs clenched around him, her face buried in his shoulder, the unmistakable sighs of a well-satisfied woman. He'd nuzzled the soft skin of her neck when she'd curled up against him, pillowed her head on his chest, a hand lazily circling his ribs. And then she kissed him again, lingeringly, before settling into his arms and seeming to immediately fall asleep. He lay there for what felt like hours, watching her, his head swimming with plans before he finally moved from beneath the covers, pulled on his clothes and slipped through the window from which he'd come.

A light crowd now circled the atrium, perusing guide-books, brandishing umbrellas and wearing studious expressions. Although taller than most men, Archer knew how to lose himself in a crowd, fading into insignificance, edging himself close to the porter's office, his eyes scanning the expanse of marble and stone. He shoved a hand through his hair and kneaded the muscles bunched at the base of his neck. Lack of sleep sent an exhilarating rush through his bloodstream. Meredith had finally let him in, allowed him his victory. The intensity of her response attested to the transformation of their relationship. From the first instant he'd set eyes upon her in the drafty entrance hall of Montfort, he'd sensed that she was like no other woman. But now, months later, he understood how it had all begun, understood her passion, her intellect and her courage. Difficulties aside, including her pride, her stubbornness and her acute need for privacy, he had little intention of leaving her vulnerable to Faron's ghost, particularly now that the pursuit had taken a distinctly aggressive turn.

Archer had not wanted to learn in the eleventh hour that Crompton was part of the chase. Brutal beneath a thin veneer of civility, Lowther's henchman had just raised the stakes. Archer's gut tightened.

He had never counted upon finding himself entirely consumed by an unfathomable contempt for what he'd done, what he had promised to do. Accusing Meredith of clinging to the past was rich when he himself refused to admit what was right before his eyes. No matter that he'd never experienced such consuming desire or incomprehensible pleasure as when he was with Lady Meredith Woolcott, the fact remained—this woman was the first weakness he'd ever known.

In the old days, once he was seated behind his desk delving into mounds of briefs or at the helm of *The Brigand*, a singular woman would be forgotten in the amount of time it took to wash her perfume from his skin. Unbidden, he remembered Camille's words. And he smiled, aware that he was no longer running away.

Ignoring consequences was what he did best, usually as a gambit to keep boredom at bay. But this was entirely different. He knew only that he would protect Meredith Woolcott from the specter of Faron—and Crompton—with his last breath. To hell with carefully laid plans created solely for the sake of preserving Whitehall's flow of information. To hell with safeguarding the ancient artifacts whose provenance was murky at best. And to hell with anyone like Hamilton or Crompton that got in his way. A buoyancy suffused his being, as if the shackles he'd borne for years had fallen from his shoulders and limbs.

A few moments later, he glanced at the open doors of the museum. A coach emerged onto the square, a light mist enveloping it with an eerie sheen. Several other coaches clogged the boulevard, along with growing crowds hurrying to take in the exhibits. Five men in top hats and afternoon suits slipped from one of the conveyances and mingled with the crush now spilling through the Fitzwilliam's doors. Archer heard Crompton's voice before he saw him, the man's booming tones reminiscent of a night not long ago in the belly of the British Museum. Elocution lessons could not quite change the long vowels bequeathed by an East London childhood. Short but stockily built, Crompton moved through the doors and into the crowd brandishing a walking stick, the superb tailoring of his suit coat sitting awkwardly on his shoulders. He looked like the pugilist he once was.

And then he saw her, with Hamilton. The dark red hair, the full lips, under a small cloche bonnet, hiding her expression. He swallowed thickly, lust and fear for her rushing through him, fire shooting from heart to groin. She moved like a beacon in the crowd, the dark blue of her dress standing out against the dull browns of the greatcoats surrounding her.

Archer pushed himself away from the wall, veering left into a narrow passage that led to the rear of the building and closer to the Egyptian antiquities. His eyes never stopped tracking her, though she moved in the opposite direction.

Something jabbed into Archer's ribs. "I would advise you to let Lady Woolcott go about her business, Lord Archer." Archer glanced at a man who shared his height but was at least two stone heavier. It would take nothing to disarm him, but he was not quite ready to do so. Instead, he poked the bear with a stick. "I'll make that decision," he said coolly. His response elicited a deeper jab of the pistol into his ribs. Archer sensed the eagerness in the man's heavy finger as it slipped over the pistol's trigger.

On his other side, another man, with a ginger beard, appeared and it was clear that he had a weapon tucked within his greatcoat. Yet they looked, by all outward appearances, like any of the other gentlemen in attendance, ready to partake of great cultural offerings.

"Wonderful day for a stroll," Archer said, as they turned into a corridor leading to a flight of stairs. They had been ready for him, but not prepared well enough. When they entered the coolness of the stairwell, he decided he'd had quite enough. With sudden violence, he thrust himself at both men, simultaneously twisting the pistol from one grip while deftly extracting the other from the ginger-haired man's waistband. The larger of the two retreated a step, but not soon enough.

In a series of rapid blows, they crumpled at his feet. With careful calibration, Archer had ensured the injuries were minor; both men were still able to speak.

"Now," Archer said, pocketing one pistol, his breath even, "let's review our options again." He aimed the second pistol with enviable nonchalance. "You may begin by telling me what Crompton is doing masquerading as the Earl of Warthaven?"

A voice came from behind him. "Why don't you ask me yourself?" Crompton hovered on the landing above, a pistol shoved against the back of Archer's head.

"We meet again," Archer said.

"It seems like only yesterday," Crompton concurred, his elocution overly precise, his vowels smooth. "The British Museum, am I correct? Your colleague Rushford displayed a particular penchant for punishment, if I recall. And I assume you, Lord Archer, were along for a lark."

The stairwell was narrow, voices bouncing off the elongated space. "Good thing I came along," he continued, motioning for the two men at Archer's feet to rise. "I suppose some assignments must be accomplished on one's own. I don't much care for the mess you made of my men, Lord Archer."

Archer shrugged, heedless of the snub nose of a pistol at his head. "You might think to choose better next time."

Crompton nodded contemplatively. "I shall take that under advisement. Thank you. In the interim, please keep your hands precisely where they are." He gestured for his men to reclaim their weapons, which they did with haste.

"Why are you at Warthaven?"

A flicker rose in Crompton's small brown eyes. "Useless question. You will not live long enough for the answer to make a difference."

"Has Faron promised you an English castle of your own? Or perhaps a packet of sovereigns is all it takes to buy your loyalty?"

Crompton pursed his lips, leaning against the balustrade. "While you are asking useless questions, I am considering whether you will take your last breath here in this narrow, mean corridor, or whether I will have my men throw you into the Thames. Perhaps I should leave the choice up to you."

Archer crossed his arms over his chest, the innocent movement causing the two men, still wiping trickles of blood from their faces, to startle. "You're certainly taking your time."

"My prerogative," Crompton tossed off.

"And what has all this to do with Lady Woolcott?"

Crompton puffed in derision. "As though you have to ask, Lord Archer." He continued genially, "You know how *difficult* the Woolcott women are. And yet in the case of Lady Woolcott, useful at long last."

Archer's eyes flicked toward his. "In terms of her expertise."

"Lord Archer," Crompton reminded him, still deceptively gentle, "it is quite apparent that Lady Woolcott presents us with a host of possibilities, none of which I choose to discuss with you at the moment. Or ever, for that matter."

Under the glass, the papyrus glowed, a four-thousand-year-old testament once placed in the tomb of a deceased nobleman to keep him company on his perilous journey through the netherworld of the afterlife. Suddenly finding themselves alone, Meredith and Hamilton lingered over the magical inscription. It was breathtaking, the hieroglyphics dancing across time and space, their secrets unfolding before their eyes.

"I can see here that this hymn of praise to Osiris mentions two important features of the deceased," Meredith murmured.

"Indeed, the Egyptians believed a person was comprised of five different elements, all of them coming into separate existence only after death," Hamilton said, hands clasped behind his back.

Their two heads were bowed over the case. "My understanding is that they were almost encyclopedic in their concern with various parts of the body," Meredith said, "catalogued by priests who drew up lists of every body part that would be needed in the next world and then created a spell to protect it." Her gloved hand hovered over the glass. "I suppose that's hardly surprising given that *The Book of the Dead* was considered essential to anyone seeking immortality. This belief continued well into the period of Greek occupation of Egypt."

"The texts themselves remained virtually unchanged for more than a thousand years."

The silence in the room was that of a cathedral. As though aware for the first time that they were alone, Hamilton looked over his shoulder before returning his gaze to the glass case in front of them. He extracted a key from his vest pocket and before Meredith knew what he was doing, had lifted the glass cover, exposing the papyrus directly to her gaze.

"Do not look startled, Lady Woolcott. It's quite all right. I have access to the collection because of my position here at the Fitzwilliam."

"Dear God, it's impossibly delicate," Meredith breathed.

When she looked up at Hamilton, she saw him not focused on the artifact exposed to the air but studying her with a look of almost sadness in his eyes. Flushing under his gaze, she blocked out the memory of their chaste kiss, regretting her impulse, along with the suspicion that all was not well. There was something amiss, something she could no longer deny, as she had confessed to herself and to Archer late last evening. She could still see him, standing in her bedchamber, large, powerful, so handsome in her eyes, his dark hair damp with melting snow. And he'd melted her.

For now it was enough. She had struck the bargain that she would sever the ties that bound her to the past, take heed of Archer's warnings. But it was something she would do on her own, ending what she had started by fleeing Claire de Lune so many years ago. It was the only way, not to hide or to cower, but to take action as she had that afternoon in Rashid, aiming her pistol, putting the past in her crosshairs once and for all. It was an affirmation, taking Archer into her bed, allowing herself to feel once again the stabbing pleasure and mutual, unrestricted giving that had returned her from the netherworld and placed her once more among the living.

She returned her focus to the open case, noticing that Hamilton was still regarding her with that peculiar sadness in his eyes. He caught her glance and cleared his throat. "Lady Woolcott—I am keen to have my uncle see this wonderful artifact and yet he has somehow left us behind. Probably bored already, but one can only hope that the opportunity to cast his eyes upon such a marvel might just help win him over to the delights of history," he said with a small smile. "Might I ask you to step outside in the hall and see if you can find him?"

It was a peculiar request, but one Meredith found herself unwilling to refuse. In short order and with a quick backward glance at Hamilton still standing by the opened case, she found herself in the large atrium, where knots of visitors milled about the great expanse. The museum housed over one hundred paintings and a hundred and thirty medieval manuscripts, none of which would appeal to Lord Blythe, Meredith thought. Blythe had expressed a love of cigars last evening and it would not be surprising to find him smoking in some corner of the building. Skirting the perimeter of the atrium, she tried to deny her growing sense of unease, a knot expanding in her chest. It seemed that every step she took was somehow preordained.

She heard the sound of muffled voices, at the end of what appeared to be a corridor. Meredith stopped, looking around to ensure she remained unobserved, her head tilting toward the barely audible words.

"Although it would seem that you have an interest of your

own, having feigned a tendresse for the woman. Marvelous piece of acting, which causes one to wonder the reason behind the drama."

Meredith tensed, moving closer to the opening, recognizing Lord Blythe's voice.

"I'm amazed at your perceptiveness." It was Archer, his tone lethally soft.

"Lady Woolcott was more than eager for your blandishments." Blythe's appreciative chuckle. "But why the subterfuge, Lord Archer? Perhaps Whitehall is as interested in Lady Woolcott's expertise, as you put it, as we are."

Abruptly, the conversation stopped, only a thin piece of wood separating Meredith from an abyss. Whitehall? A fault line ran through her mind, a jarring and ugly reality hurtling to the surface.

"I suppose you'd like to know the answer to your question before you put a bullet in my head," Archer said quietly.

"Now I'm the one amazed at your perceptiveness," Blythe said.

Meredith froze. Dread sliced through her.

"Whitehall will stop at nothing to get to Faron," Blythe continued. "He has been a thorn in their side for years, as you well know. And Lady Woolcott just happens to be the ideal conduit, as you also understand."

Pain was replaced with a cold clarity of purpose, more ruthless and infinitely more dangerous than the previous hot surge of rage. Tucking a gloved hand that was surprisingly steady in the pocket of the jacket under her pelisse, Meredith took a deep breath. Every muscle suddenly jolting, she lunged forward, turning the corner and rushing to the end of the corridor to reach a stairwell.

"Good afternoon, gentlemen," she said coolly, her pistol nestling into Lord Blythe's well-padded back. "You should be more careful as to where you decide to hide. You never know who might come looking for you."

Archer, Blythe and two unidentified men stood paralyzed

by her sudden appearance. "Now, anyone moving without my express request will cause my finger to release the trigger of my pistol. Lord Blythe here, or whatever his name happens to be, will be dead in an instant. Because I never miss, as Lord Archer can attest, and certainly not at such close range."

Blythe's normally ruddy complexion paled, and the two men standing on the lower level of the stairwell let their mouths gape open.

"Lady Woolcott," Archer said quietly. Meredith ignored him, unable to trust herself to meet his eyes. Each breath she took was a dagger in her throat when she thought of how he had used her.

"Now, Blythe," she continued, "throw your pistol onto the floor. And I suggest your men do the same. I shall count to three." She tried to look disdainful as her eyes swept over the outraged men glowering at her.

"You are making a mistake, Lady Woolcott. Betting on the wrong man." But Blythe slowly lowered his pistol from Archer's head and threw it on the floor. The two men followed suit. He added lightly, "Faron will not be pleased."

Meredith managed to keep hold of the pistol, riding it up along Blythe's spine. "I intend to confront Faron at Claire de Lune myself, and I suggest you do not worry yourself on that score." Dots danced before her eyes at the prospect and a dull nausea settled into the pit of her stomach.

Blythe kept his hands raised. "Perhaps you might like to hear what Lord Archer has to say about the matter."

Archer's glance was dark and chill with open contempt. "Give me the pistol, Meredith. And we shall discuss this later."

Her voice was a cold whisper, driven by a sickening desire to hear what Blythe had to say. "Remain silent, Lord Archer. I shan't ask again."

Blythe cocked his head over his shoulder, his gaze assessing. "Do you not wonder at the reason behind his interest in you, Lady Woolcott? Of course, you do, I can see it in your eyes. Lord Richard Buckingham Archer is not what he seems. And I would dare guess that his ambitions are directly allied with Whitehall's. As you are no doubt aware, Whitehall has had a long-standing disagreement, if that is not too strong a word, with Faron's territorial possessiveness. Perhaps you care to elaborate, Lord Archer."

"I shouldn't bother, Lord Archer, as I don't care in the least," she said, warning in her voice.

"Then why are you hesitating? After the matter at Fort St. Julien, I know you have the courage, Lady Woolcott. Shoot me," Blythe prodded. "Perhaps you hesitate because you realize that I tell the truth, which you will see for yourself once you cross the Channel to reunite with your one true love"— his voice was mocking—"who awaits you at Claire de Lune after all these years."

With the slowness of a nightmare, Meredith raised her eyes over Blythe's stocky shoulders, her gaze finally meeting Archer's fearlessly. She refused to look away at the new intelligence staring out through his eyes, knowing, cold and fierce. And then before she could fire her pistol, Archer had the two men standing at his side doubling over, a series of blows to the backs of their necks causing them to wilt to the floor.

In the next instant, Archer wrenched the pistol from her grip. As Meredith watched, heart pounding and heat blasting through her veins, Blythe was caught in the chest with a crashing fist. His eyes rolled into the back of his head as he crumpled to the ground.

Meredith felt her face go white as she looked from Blythe to the men and back again. She tried to back out the door, but Archer caught her elbow, their bodies just inches apart. "For the last time, you're going nowhere without me."

Her expression froze. "I don't intend to ever speak to you again." Her coldness was like a slap in the face. On a stab of anger, Archer yanked her hard against him. "You believe Blythe's lies?" His boot rested by the man's still body.

Meredith tried to wrench away, but he tightened his grip. "Would you have killed me if you had the chance?" The question was a whisper. His hand tightened on her elbow.

"I still may have the chance," she said, her voice strong.

His hard smile taunted her. "It all meant nothing to you, didn't it? All those protestations of trust last night, blown to the winds, and on the basis of a few words from a man whose true name and identity you don't even know."

Meredith's eyes glittered dangerously. "I dare you to deny those words, Lord Archer, or your involvement on behalf of Whitehall." She turned her face from his. "I don't know how I could have ignored the obvious." Shame coursed through her. "Please just go, do what you bloody well need to do but finally, leave me alone."

"The least you can do is hear me out, damn it!" He seized her chin and jerked her eyes back to his. She wrenched herself from his grasp, but before she could back out the door, he overtook her and scooped her up into his arms.

Her eyes flared. "You have gone too far, you bastard. You can't abduct me."

"For an intelligent woman, you can be amazingly obtuse."

She wanted to slap him so hard that he would feel the blow all the way down his spine, but she feared it would only make her appear all the more vulnerable, further out of control. Descending the stairs, he took two steps at a time. "Damn you, for the last time, put me down." She opened her mouth to scream, only to find her cry stifled as a hand came down over her lips. Reaching another stairwell and a door, he leaned into it before pushing it open. Suddenly arching her back, she kicked out violently, trying to break free. Ignoring her struggles, he simply gripped her more firmly and opened the door. A blast of cold air swept over them.

Anticipating the need of a quick escape, Archer had left a

horse with a groom in the adjacent courtyard. He broke into a run, his hand still over Meredith's mouth, convinced that for the first time in her life, she was actually going to scream. As arranged, the groom and his mount were rounding the corner. In short order, he was quickly mounted, settling Meredith on his lap with only minor difficulty, while throwing the stable boy sufficient coins to assure his cooperation and indifference to the fact that he'd held a struggling woman in his arms. Wrapping his greatcoat around her, he pinned her arms to her sides as he spurred his horse forward. Resisting the urge to launch into a full gallop, he kept his hand over her mouth, guiding his mount toward the back of the museum in a bid to avoid Trumpington Street. He nodded at the guards at the back of the arcade, taking the precaution of holding Meredith's face hard against his shoulder. It was only when they reached Huffington Road and an open stretch that he urged his mount into a gallop and relaxed his hold. She had ceased her struggles, but he did not trust her. His mount stretched out into a pounding gallop, its huge strides lengthening, gathering speed. Traveling east, the journey to *The Brigand* and the Channel would not be long.

Even once they'd arrived on the yacht, she refused to speak to him, struggling in his arms, threatening to escape with every movement she made. Archer held his breath on a wild surge of fury that for a moment knew no bounds. What the hell did she think she was doing—accusing him of betrayal when all he could think of was how she had so easily thrown away her trust in him with both hands?

"I will not hesitate to use constraints if you continue this way," he threatened, afraid to let her go. She struggled violently, as he pulled her onto the bench in the corner of the stateroom. She twisted her body, trying to get leverage with one hip to throw him off. He threw a leg across her thighs, her feet drumming on the floor. It didn't seem to matter that she knew it was Archer who held her, that she should believe in her soul that he wouldn't hurt her. She continued to fight with a primal panic and with a horrifying awareness of her own weakness.

"It is December and the Channel crossing will be challenging," he said. "I have no choice." She opened her mouth on a sobbing breath, a moment before she was pressed to the floor, her hands jerked behind her, her wrists bound with swift efficiency. It was only a matter of seconds before she sat trussed on the hard bench. Her eyes flashed awareness, recognizing the strength in his frame, the dark competency of his movements, the ruthlessness of it all.

"I do not know who you are, Lord Archer," she said, hoarsely. "And I never did." She had made an unforgivable mistake, forgetting a particular reality in an onslaught of passion that was nothing more than a terrible weakness.

Archer looked down at her. "Of course, you know who I am, although you refuse to admit it," he said with soft ferocity. His expression was less than encouraging, his blue eyes hard stones.

"What I refused to admit," she said as harshly as before, watching as he stood with hands on hips, "is what I sensed from the beginning, from that first afternoon at Fort St. Julien. You were not following me on behalf of Rushford, you were following me on behalf of your own masters at Whitehall." She yearned to run the back of her hand over her dry lips, and tried to moisten them with her tongue. She sat up even straighter, refusing to be intimidated by his arrogance.

"Why?" he demanded. "Why do you believe Blythe and not me?"

"Because I wanted you and was willing to overlook the obvious." Meredith spoke the truth because there was no lie that would be as convincing. "And I believed that you wanted me too. How feeble an explanation is that? There is no other reason for our relationship except your own hidden agenda. And that is why I believe Blythe or whatever his name is." She shook her head, berating herself. "I should have known. *I did know*. But I refused to admit it to myself." Her anger seemed to have exhausted itself and the reality of the grimness of the situation was made plain. Her pelisse had fallen back from her shoulders, and her hair had escaped from its chignon. "What about Hamilton?" she asked tonelessly.

"Gambling debts," he said briefly. "Someone was filling his coffers and in return he was asked to pursue you."

Poor Cressida, Meredith thought. "Do we know by whom? And why?"

He crossed his arms over his chest and she hated herself anew. She could still feel the heat of his hands on her body as she'd fought him, the hardness of his muscles, the smell of soap on his skin. He excited her in a way she wished she didn't understand. His eyes held hers. "Faron's people."

"Meeting him in Hyde Park was no accident," she murmured, nor was the invitation to Cambridge and the Fitzwilliam.

There was a soft knock on the stateroom door. Impatiently, Archer went to the threshold and after a brief exchange of words, returned with a small package in his hand. Recoiling on instinct, Meredith watched in horror as a scrap of red silk drifted to the ground and he withdrew the kaleidoscope.

Archer cursed darkly. "Another warning, delivered anonymously."

Faron's people knew where she was and, worse still, where she was going. Fighting the nausea rising in her throat, Meredith tensed her shoulders. She could not bear to see the reminder of the nursery at Claire de Lune. "Put it away, please," she whispered. She watched him lift the lid of a trunk at the end of the bed in the alcove. The bed, where they had spent so many blindly blissful hours. She looked away.

He pushed a hand through his hair, disheveled as always. "I warned you about Hamilton."

"The Rosetta stone and *The Book of the Dead*—even I determined there was a connection," she said wearily. The image of Hamilton, standing by the open glass case holding the papyrus, rose in her mind. "I stand defeated, Archer."

"Turn around." She obeyed, and to her inexpressible relief he unfastened the belt that bound her wrists. "You still wish to return to France?"

She rubbed her hands together, the circulation returning. The kaleidoscope. It was a message somehow. "I must. I should have done it years ago."

"And yet you believe Faron is dead."

She repeated the same words to him that she'd shared that long-ago day at Fort St. Julien. "I know he is gone." She raised her eyes and looked at him, her expression swept clear of all emotion. There were no other explanations or excuses, and Meredith would not offer them.

"Very well," he said. Meredith shivered as though unable to absorb the warmth glowing from the small brazier. Despite the bleakness in his eyes, there was a recognition that matched her own, that all was at an end between them. "Dead or alive, do you still love him?" The question was stark. "You owe me that answer at least."

"Owe you?"

"You don't understand, do you?"

She shrugged helplessly.

"I deserve to know if you still love another man."

She shook her head. "Why?"

"Because," he said quietly, his expression bleak, "I love you."

For as long as she lived, Archer's words would merge with the most horrendous Channel crossing of Meredith's life. The winter winds were at gale force, the waves so high that death by drowning was a very real possibility. Each time the craft climbed a tower, an avalanche of water threatened to sink it to the bottom of the Channel. The wind howled and mast-high waves washed over the decks, the wood beneath their feet pitching and sinking, leaving Archer no choice but to take over the wheel from his small crew and fight to keep the vessel afloat. Punished by wind and pelting rain, he tied himself to the wheel and battled the storm as though taking on his own inner demons. Nature's fury would not survive his silent, pitiless rage. The harsh winds scalded his skin, robbed him of breath, but no more so than Meredith Woolcott had done. And for the first time, he had a shadow of understanding of what Montagu Faron must have experienced when he thought he'd lost her forever.

The reprieve, when it came, was short lived, the howling of the wind slowing only enough to coat the decks with ice. He handed over the wheel at the sight of Meredith at the deck rail, wrapped in oilskin, insulated against the weather and Archer. "I do not wish to turn back," she said resolutely, anticipating his question when he came to stand beside her.

"I wouldn't ask you to."

She paused for a moment. "Thank you for doing this." Her eyes held a lifetime of pain. "You must be cold, wet and exhausted."

"Doesn't matter." He stared moodily over the rail at the dark, heaving mass of the sea.

Her eyes followed his. It was easier this way, to pretend that they were gazing out into a starless night with no more worries than whether the sun was going to rise in the morning. She was aware of his damp clothing, the hair clinging to his forehead from the sea spray. "You love this in a way, don't you?"

He turned to look at her, and that piercing, troubling intensity was in his gaze again. "I do. And I know that you somehow understand, despite everything."

"Thank you for that," she said. "I believe that I do understand." There was no anger in her voice or his.

Archer pulled himself up sharply. He shook his head, passing a hand over his eyes. "As do you. We are a fine pair, as it turns out."

She burrowed into her borrowed oilskin. "When did you know, Archer?"

He didn't pretend that he didn't understand. "After the wedding at Montfort, I was contacted by Whitehall," he said briefly. "But when I saw you again at Rashid, I knew where my loyalties lay."

"I don't see what you mean."

"Perhaps you do not wish to," Archer said thoughtfully. "At this point, I have no reason to lie. Yes, at the beginning I was working at the behest of Whitehall in their attempt to flush Faron out. But shortly after our meeting, I knew that whether I liked it or not, the nature of the assignment had changed."

Meredith gave a bitter laugh. She did not look impressed with his choice of words. "'The nature of the assignment.' So I was always an assignment to you. Even when we . . ." she trailed off. The wind resumed its high-pitched howl. "I think I shall go below."

It was best to sit on the floor of the cabin with its swinging lantern and bolted-down furnishings. Meredith noted with a faint grimace that her stomach was in an upheaval, her head swimming with the rhythm of the yacht. Archer sat down beside her and put his arm around her and she was reminded of the sandstorm that they had survived, just outside Fort St. Julien. "First sand and now water," she joked feebly, sensing that he was remembering also. They sat in silence for half an hour when the motion of the boat changed dramatically. Meredith's stomach dipped and she staggered to her feet, reaching the stairwell just in time. Her clothes were wet from both rain and spray and she lurched as the boat pitched violently, barely holding on to the contents of her stomach. Heedless of the wind and spray, she sucked in gulps of cold, night air.

The light was graying with the approach of a December dawn and she huddled gratefully on the leeside railing. It had been only a twelve-hour crossing, perhaps fourteen with the horrendous weather.

"Meredith." Archer stood beside her, a small flask in hand. He took her shoulders gently and turned her toward him. "Drink some of this. Brandy," he added with a smile. "Although I know you prefer whisky."

This time she gave him no argument, sipping the fiery liquid, which burned its way down her throat and calmed her stomach. "Only a few more hours, I hope," she said.

"Have more. It will help," he said, watching as color returned to her cheeks. He ran his hands through her tangled hair, pushing it back from her face, and she didn't pull away. "We are almost at Calais. You are cold and wet. Come below and change your clothes." He reached to pull her up and she staggered against him. The contact was both reassuring and magnetic, the sexual current running between them undiminished despite the violent sea and a bout of retching.

Meredith stumbled her way into the main stateroom and swayed toward the bed in the alcove. Holding on to the mattress, she stripped off her wet clothing, aware through the haze of her exhaustion that Archer watched her rummaging through his chest for a fresh shirt. Wearing only her drawers and chemise, she was conscious of his gaze, and her body stirred. It was impossible that he should have this effect on her, even in the grimmest of circumstances when the world pitched and sawed and threatened to come undone, as though offering a fitting end to their tumultuous relationship.

"I shall be at the wheel," he said abruptly, watching Meredith shake out her skirt and place it in front of the brazier. "We should be landing in an hour or so. There's a secluded cove behind a small island that we can negotiate safely." His tone told her that he had done this, and other, more dangerous landings, many times before. She looked out the porthole and spied the ripple of water that marked the opening to a narrow inlet. Unwillingly, she blinked back tears as the cliffs of the Normandy coastline rose into view, gray and forbidding in the winter light. But a bittersweet sight, nonetheless.

An hour later, Meredith was back on deck, her clothes reasonably dry, breathing fresh, restorative air as she considered the approaching coastline. The boat tacked gracefully toward the mouth of the cove. Meredith looked up to see Archer swing the helm, monitor the sail, skillfully pulling the mainsheet to catch the wind at the perfect moment. The yacht obeyed as the wind filled the sail and danced over the line. Meredith caught her breath as she waited for the keel to scrape over jagged rock but the yacht glided silently onward and into the calm safety of the cove.

She stood with feet braced on the now gently moving deck, the wind whipping back her hair, her face lifted to the weak sun. French soil—for the first time in close to twenty years. The leather saddlebag clutched at her side held the gold coins from her reticule and the silk-wrapped kaleidoscope. She held her resolve to her just as tightly.

After disembarking, Archer, in surprisingly fluent French, made quick work of sending a boy to a hostelery, where they secured two horses. They rode hard for the next seven hours to Honfleur and onwards in the direction of Berney, stopping finally in the small village of Orchaise, a few miles outside Blois. Archer helped her down from her horse in front of a small inn, his hands lingering on her waist for an extra moment, and just long enough for her to fight the urge to lean into him. It was important to keep a tight rein on her emotions; the beauty of the French countryside threatened to unleash a tide of memories. She had spent seven years of her life here, and as the soft hills sped by, it seemed as though her life was moving backwards. Her father still lived, Rowena and Julia were mere babes and she was a young woman in love with learning and with a young man who would be hers forever.

The small inn was tidy and warm, with a welcoming scent of red wine and freshly baked bread. Meredith noted how smoothly Archer explained that he and his wife would be requiring a room and simple dinner, all of which the innkeeper, a man with sharp eyes and a neat moustache, was keen to provide.

Dinner was a wonderful pot-au-feu served on a small table in front of a roaring fire in their room, their glasses filled with a rich burgundy. A strange calm had descended over both of them; the stormy seas and the revelations of the past day had stripped both of them of any defenses. He watched her, his eyes taking in her shirtwaist, now open at the neck, her dishabille born of a recklessness that was somehow more daring than anything he'd ever seen in the most decadent gaming dens or perfumed boudoirs. They both shifted uncomfortably in the inn's hard chairs, their awareness of their mutual vulnerability inescapable.

For the first time in his life, Archer could not keep his thoughts straight, could not form a strategy for the days ahead. He simply sat across from Meredith at the table, trying to come up with reasons that would keep them both in this small French inn forever. If he could stop time, he would, because at the moment, he wanted to forget that the world existed outside their room. Nothing mattered anymore.

"You must be exhausted," she said, her own gray eyes heavy with fatigue.

"I don't think I could sleep."

She took another sip of her wine. "We could talk."

He smiled grimly. "I think we've established it does not do us much good."

"Perhaps we should give it another try." She looked at him with her beautiful eyes, and the vulnerability he saw shocked him.

"There is something I must say," she began. "I think I understand now that what's happened between us cannot be distilled to simple black and white. I have been unfair in thinking otherwise." She stared at the glass of wine in her hand before meeting his gaze, reading great hurt and bitterness there. "Please forgive me, Archer."

He shrugged. "We've both made mistakes. We didn't trust each other enough and maybe with cause, on my part at least," he added honestly. "Trust only comes with knowing the truth and it's taken us some time to get to it."

"I was wrong about you."

"No, you weren't," he said abruptly. "At least not at first."

She shook her head. "And I think you were wrong about yourself, hiding behind that laconic façade when really, Archer, you care very much. About your friends, about loyalty and doing what's right. You are far from the rootless adventurer you pretend to be. That's why you are here right now, beside me, having risked a perilous Channel crossing and so much more."

Archer was silent for a long moment. "Why the change of heart?" His voice was hard, armor against further pain.

Her eyes softened. "I do recognize love when I see and feel it," she continued, her gaze never wavering from his, showing courage to the end. "I think I loved you from the moment I saw you standing in the entrance at Montfort," she confessed. "You were so tall, so large and so damnably distant despite your easy charm. And here I was, a woman well into her fourth decade, and you made me stop and catch my breath like a young girl." She stopped. "No, not like a young girl because that pales in comparison to what I felt, what I feel . . ."

He sat unmoving, and for a moment she thought he hadn't heard her.

Her fingers playing with the stem of her wineglass, she continued carefully. "You were right. I was married to a past that was keeping me from living, hanging on to a ghostly love that was never right, even in the beginning. I know that now. If Montagu"—she paused, "if Faron had truly loved me, he would never have believed his cousin Jerome's lies about me, despite his grievous injuries. Nor would he have done those sick, heinous . . ." She stopped, placing a hand over her lips.

When she recovered, he was at her side, and her sorrow made his heart clench. He pulled her into his arms, raising a hand to brush a curl away from her eyes. He swept it back, fingers tracing the curve of her ear, trailing down her neck. "I love you and nothing else matters." There was triumph and assurance in his voice.

"And I love you," she whispered fiercely. "If you need further proof, when I heard Blythe's voice in the stairwell at the Fitzwilliam, all I could think about was the danger you were in. I knew then that I would risk anything to save your life."

He kissed her tenderly, as though for the first time, his hands stroking her hair. "No wonder I love you," he said, his breath warm on her lips. "My courageous, beautiful, brilliant Meredith."

She pulled back and laid a finger over his mouth. "You are the courageous one, getting involved with me and my complicated life. The attack in Rashid, the sandstorm and then all the business with Whitehall. And then the night I came to you, using you . . ."

He smiled. "The least of my complaints, my love." He cupped her jaw, ran his thumb along her cheek, savoring the softness of her skin and the tremble of her body in response to his touch. He leaned in, setting a hot kiss on the delicate skin just below her ear.

The breath shuddered out of her. "We do well in that regard," she said, her voice low.

"Yes, we do," he said with a slow grin. "Why do you think I never gave up on you?"

"You are a cad after all," she said, but with a responding

smile before a shadow crossed her face once more. "I just wish it were over."

"It is over," he said with typical arrogance. "Tomorrow we will go to Claire de Lune and discover who is behind these events, root him out once and for all." He kept his suspicions to himself, relieved that the painful intensity in her voice had dissipated.

She stiffened slightly, her eyes shuttered. She placed one hand upon his chest and pushed him back a fraction of an inch. "In my heart I wish nothing more than for us to return to England together, rather than traveling on to Blois. And I feel guilty having you by my side, risking you as I have risked the lives of Julia and Rowena, for too long. And yet, I know this is necessary, to end things that should have ended years ago. It is something I must do." By myself, she wanted to add, but didn't.

A small lie on her part, but before she could continue, he stopped the words with his mouth on hers, his hands sliding around her body to cup her buttocks, pressing her hard against him until he felt the playful resistance leave her. Her lips were soft and yielding, her body moving on his. He raised his head, his familiar, wicked smile back in place. In response, she grabbed hold of his hand, her grip confident and sure, and pulled him toward the bed in the center of the small room, never taking her eyes from his.

Chapter 14

Meredith waited until well after midnight before she carefully slid out of bed, murmuring to Archer, who slumbered beside her, something about using the privy down the inn's narrow hallway. Her escape was simple, slipping into her clothes and out the door, her saddlebag gripped in one hand. Taking the servants' stairway down, she edged out the kitchen door. No cook or proprietor was to be seen.

The cold was a slap in her face, the night clear with a full moon. A groom slumped in the corner of the stables unaware that she led her horse from its stall. She waited to saddle it and tie on the saddlebag until she was a few yards from the stables. She led the horse in silence only moments as the road to Blois appeared

Archer would awaken and encounter cool sheets instead of the warmth of her body. She wasn't certain that he knew the location of Claire de Lune and desperately hoped that he would understand and not follow her. A hastily scribbled note was all that she had left as explanation. This was the final battle and one that she would fight—at last burying Montagu Faron and the shadow he had cast over her life and those she loved for far too long.

Riding through the night and early morning, she was alone with only her thoughts, a dangerous place to be. She recognized firsthand now that the workings of the mind were as dangerous as those of the heart. Thoughts of Archer intruded, were pushed aside, suppressed. Then they insistently stole back into her mind, more relentless than before. She loved him with the zealousness of the converted, and the acknowledgment did nothing to dispel the hurt of leaving him behind at the inn. Her chest ached with the pain of it and with every mile she came closer to Claire de Lune without him. Even if he managed to follow her to the chateau, he would not know the location of her true destination.

The road was suddenly heart-stoppingly familiar. Claire de Lune rose in the distance, a fortress built in the sixteenth century by Charles I, its four sides centered around a courtyard with a back wall, later destroyed to obtain a better view of the Loire River below. With its hundred rooms, its turrets, graceful arches and mullioned windows, it seemed conjured from a Renaissance fairy tale. But Meredith knew that fairy tales were for children, best outgrown and left behind like toys in the nursery.

Instead of following the curved road to the chateau framed by plane trees arrayed like a regiment of soldiers, Meredith urged her mount onwards. The sun was cresting the horizon, burning off the frost on the pastoral landscape. Here was a moderate climate long beloved of kings, queens and the powerful. Years fell away as she found the narrow roadway outside Blois where the little cottage waited. The trees were bare now yet still graceful, the bowers of shrubs and roses waiting for spring. Even in December, she recalled the smell of blossoms, the delicate scent setting off a small explosion of memories.

She stopped before she could see the cottage. The rosebush was still there, and she dismounted. The ground at her feet was crisp with frosted leaves and the imagined scent of blossoms disappeared. The air was acrid with burning vegetation, a gardener's bonfire, she reminded herself, starting at the scent. She gathered her pelisse closer, despite the warming sun marching its way across the blue sky above the river.

It was time to go. She walked her mount along the narrow path, kicking away leaves in her way, surprised that she was no longer beset by memories. Like the dusty mementos in an attic, the yellowed portraits, the forgotten toys and love letters tied with ribbon, they were the detritus of a squandered life. That was the reason she had come today to exorcise the past, without which she could not go forward into the future with Archer. She owed it not only to herself, but even more to him, Julia and Rowena.

The small cottage had changed very little from her dreams and nightmares. And why should it? It had been built three hundred years before and would last another three. Tying up her horse behind it, she approached the door and peered through the window.

Where there had once been a book-lined wall, there was emptiness, and the bed that had once dominated the main room was gone, along with its rumpled silk sheets and damask coverlets. She opened the door and closed her eyes.

Muslin curtains wafted gently in a summer's breeze. It was a book-lined room, papers scattered on the polished wood floor, a single candle burning low in its holder. The center was dominated by an opulent bed, fitted with the finest sheets and damask coverlets where two naked figures slept entwined, their bodies heavy with fulfillment. The girl lay on her back, her red hair fanned across the pillow, one arm falling loosely around the back of her partner. His dark head was pillowed next to hers, a leg flung possessively over her thighs, trapping her into the sumptuous feather mattress.

A small sigh escaped her lips, a muted sound of remembered desire that faded into a contented breath. Meredith felt the familiar body by her side, in tune with hers after long hours of passion. She kept her eyes closed and a smile on her lips, breathing in the scent of the summer breeze finding its way through the open door.

*   *   *

Meredith opened her eyes to an empty room, with wood floors covered in dust. The empty bookshelves mocked her save for one object glowing in the slant of sunshine. It beckoned, a finely tooled leather mask, calling her closer. She took a step, then another, the distance seemingly insurmountable. Her hands shook, hovering over the mask.

"It has been a long time indeed." A familiar voice came from behind her. "Welcome home, Meredith Woolcott."

With the slowness of nightmares, she tried to turn around just as her feet flew out from under her, spilling her to the floor. A blinding pain split the back of her head, and the room blurred, faded and then returned, before the light contracted to a pinpoint and finally disappeared.

Each time Meredith tried to move her limbs, she felt her whole torso resist. She wanted to open her eyes, but she feared what she would see, preferring to stay in the protectiveness of deep sleep. She slipped away again, the surface under her hard and unrelenting. Gradually the darkness coalesced into a series of shapes and densities of gray. The silence was profound, deeper than anything that she had ever experienced and yet she sensed with sickening dread that she wasn't alone.

The warmth of an afternoon sun pouring through glass coaxed her eyes open. Her head pounded from a bruise at the base of her neck. She pulled herself upright against a wall. A man was sitting by the open door, his face obscured by shadows, the wings of the chair seeming to envelop him, cutting him off from the rest of the empty room.

He held the mask in his hands. Meredith's throat went dry, the pounding of her temples keeping time with the rising swell of bile in her throat. The man awaiting her was not Faron. She knew simply by the way he held himself and, when he turned his head away from the shadows, the way his lips thinned over his teeth.

Giles Lowther. He slowly raised the mask and placed it

over his face. Meredith struggled with nausea, swaying to a seated position on the floor, her hands and ankles bound. Her first attempt to speak was a rasp, inarticulate and cut short.

"I never did think you were that intelligent." The words hissed through the slit in the mask. "And this ridiculous denouement only proves it."

Meredith could not have reached for her pistol in the folds of her skirt. In any case, it would be gone.

"For once, you don't know what to say," Lowther said, admonishing her with an upraised finger. He sat up straighter, and as though looking in a mirror, made a minute adjustment of the mask.

There was nothing to say. She understood now, the pieces of the puzzle sliding into a horrifying whole. He was looking at her expectantly, forcing her silence into another kind of submission. "You were always jealous of Montagu," she finally said, trying to control her voice. "It was never Jerome, was it? It was you who was behind the attack that changed everything."

Lowther ignored her, flicking a hand over the mask. "Nor for that matter, did I ever believe that Faron was so bloody brilliant." His voice rose, echoing in the emptiness of the room. "I was the brilliant one. I was the one who came from nothing, the gutters of East London to the gallows of Paris where he found me. And a good thing he did. Because I was the mastermind behind every success Faron ever had."

Meredith's mind flashed back in time, and saw the hazy outlines of Giles Lowther shadowing Montagu Faron, a mere silhouette that she could scarcely remember.

He laughed softly, as though at a private joke. "Oh, yes, I recognize that you were barely aware of my existence. The two of you." His lips curled in disdain. "I was the one who plotted to ensure we would get the maps that Lord Strathmore led us to, with your half-sister Julia used as bait. Don't look so shocked. How long did you believe you could keep that a secret? That the two children you plucked from the nursery fire were your father's daughters, his bastard children, the pathetic result of his affair with a village slut? The daughter of a priest who met her end in the nursery fire. Well deserved, if you believe in God and retribution." He shook his head. "It was only Faron's maudlin sentimentality, and the fact that you held him in thrall, that prompted him to allow those children at the chateau."

Meredith closed her eyes against the tears, but they came anyway. When she opened them, his eyes locked upon hers. "And Lord Rushford and your beloved Rowena—I was the one who strategized the theft of the Rosetta stone so Faron could add it to his bloody collection." His pale eyes glowed behind the mask. "I did not attend the Sorbonne. I did not have the benefit of tutors, such as your well-respected father, the Cambridge don. But what I did have was the ambition and the sheer intellect to absorb knowledge as it came my way. As castoffs, as discards."

A moment ago, she had felt grief. But now something harder quickened her blood, a desire to know, to understand.

"You attacked Faron that night after we met here. And later, you set fire to the nursery." It was a test.

Lowther took a deep breath, inflating his barrel chest. His eyes settled upon her, trying to gauge the depth of her knowledge. He smiled behind the mask, shaking his head slowly. "I didn't have to, you fool. Jerome was easily led, the half-wit, the product of generations of aristocratic inbreeding." He sneered. "And amazingly, after the accident, Faron was putty in my hands, eager to believe every last poisoned seed I planted in his mind." He glanced at her slyly. "I even told him that you had rutted with his cousin Jerome. Urging him to set fire to the nursery was child's play after that. Please forgive the figure of speech."

Lowther had stopped talking, but his voice continued to

echo in her head. The pounding at her temples turned to a ringing in her ears. She twisted her wrists against the leather bindings, the scars on her forearms burning.

"I watched him die, you know, my dear Meredith." His tone had turned to a ragged whisper, whistling from the slit in the mask. "The first attempt at the hands of your half-sister Julia—immolation. And the second at the hands of your half-sister Rowena—drowning. And Faron did drown, I assure you, in the cold waters of the Channel." His voice was hoarse with triumph. "I made sure he died once I no longer had need of him."

Meredith clenched her fists, the nails drawing blood. The physical pain sharpened her senses, giving her a window of clarity as she forced herself to her knees. The door tilted and the walls rippled.

Remaining seated, the mask still in place, Lowther watched. "You feel unwell," he said at length.

Another wave of nausea rolled through her.

"There's nothing to fear. Don't fight it." He sighed and then smiled behind the mask with something like compassion. "If I'm feeling generous, I shall ensure that the smoke kills you before the flames do." And then he looked past her, through the glass wall of the French doors as though the cottage was already nothing more than smoke and ashes.

A surge of anger spiked through her, straightening her spine, conserving her strength. If there was only a weapon, a wine bottle, a vase that she could use. Her eyes settled on her saddlebag sagging next to Lowther's chair. Her stomach clenched.

Lowther caught the direction of her gaze. "Of course, of course," he said like a remiss host. "Thank you so much for reminding me. I might have forgotten. . . ." He leaned over and opened the bag, extracting the copper cylinder, still wrapped in red silk. "You were most helpful, Meredith, even more so than your wards, in bringing me precisely what I wanted. Now can you guess what this kaleidoscope, this innocent child's toy, holds? Other than a few glass beads that so delighted Julia and Rowena when still in the nursery at Claire de Lune?"

Meredith forced herself not to wince when he smashed the glass opening on one side. With careful fingers, he coaxed out what at first appeared to be a piece of vellum. It was the papyrus, the spell from *The Book of the Dead* that she and Hamilton had admired at the Fitzwilliam. Awareness slammed into her like a fist.

"He stole it. Hamilton."

Lowther shook his head. "Not quite. *You stole it*, and returned to France, as you longed to do, what with your questionable past and eccentric interests, so distasteful in a woman," he explained as though to a small child who could not quite grasp the whole truth. "A fact to which Mr. Hamilton will attest, with perhaps the aid of some small coercion."

A strange smile lit his eyes. "And think of the poor dears, Julia and Rowena, when they hear the truth, believing that you've deserted them and returned to the arms of the man who has plagued them for so long."

And Archer. What about Archer? The question drummed in her mind. Would he believe that she had reunited with Faron?

Lowther rose from the chair with deceptive nonchalance. "If only I'd left the door open, you would be able to savor the rich aroma of burning wood. The fire should be well along now, so with absolutely no reluctance after such a short reunion, I will bid you farewell, Meredith."

He walked a few paces toward her, his hand raised in mock salute. "You were ever the challenging opponent, albeit unwittingly, I'll give you that."

If she listened hard, she thought she could already hear the crackling of the fire coming toward her. The noise would grow louder, a building crescendo, insinuating its way, curling toward her. The mask leered and she closed her eyes, only to hear a shattering cacophony like a thousand mirrors breaking.

There was a swift movement of air, and she opened her eyes. Lord Richard Buckingham Archer moved quietly for a large man, his arm around Lowther's throat, exerting pressure from behind. Meredith's heart hammered as a combination of relief and horror cut into her belly. Archer towered over her so close that she could smell the fury emanating from him. The impact was of power and a deep rage that was capable of crushing anything or anyone in his path. She drank in the strong features, the lined face and piercing blue eyes of the man she loved with a conviction that seared her soul.

Epilogue

Two months later

"Your beautiful nose has been buried in that book far too long for my liking."

"I always noted that you were hardly the scholarly type." Meredith pretended to continue scribbling her notes, sitting cross-legged on the bed beside her resplendently nude husband, whose physical pull was nearly impossible to ignore.

He sighed, one hand coming to rest on her knee covered in a wisp of silk. "How quickly the honeymoon fades." Claire de Lune was now a distant memory, the remains of Giles Lowther buried in its ashes, Meredith's past finally laid to rest. And then the future—they had spent the past four weeks first locked in her apartments at Montfort, after which they had reunited with Rowena, Rushford, Julia and Strathmore at Archer's London town house, which suddenly no longer echoed with silence but was filled with laughter, friendship and love.

The warmth of Archer's hand burned through the thin silk draping Meredith's leg. "I should like to finish this article detailing the latest discoveries at an archeological site just outside Alexandria. The translation, as far as I can glean, is nowhere near complete." They had returned to Montfort three days ago and had hardly left the large bedchamber with its monstrous fireplace and large mullioned windows for more than a brisk ride over the rolling hills of the estate. Spring was coming, and a tender, nascent green enveloped the countryside.

Archer's hand crept along the inside of her thigh. Meredith snapped the book closed. Smiling, she turned to him, touching his mouth with a fingertip. "I wish I knew what it was about you that I find irresistible, Lord Archer, because you really are the most impatient man."

He caught her wrist, his fingers circling the bones, feeling the rhythm of her pulse. He placed a lingering kiss on the inside of each forearm, soothing the scars. "There must be something, madam." There was a contentment in his voice that came with the realization he would no longer need to look for his next adventure—because Meredith was by his side.

"I can think of a few things, but with great difficulty," she said teasingly. She put her head on one side as though giving the question real consideration. "Lust, I think, might be one."

Archer smiled. "Finally, you admit to it." His mouth curved beneath her caressing finger. From the first, Meredith had ignited his response, seeming to have no fear of his limits or hers. She was not an ordinary woman who would be satisfied with a circumscribed life and he would make sure that she never had to. A sizable donation to Burlington House and its Learned Societies was the first step in ensuring they would eventually open their doors to women. It was only a matter of time.

She was a challenge, the most exciting he'd ever met, and he could no more resist her than keep the sun from rising every day. Catching both her wrists in one hand, he pulled her against his body. "Time to prove your assertion, Meredith," he challenged. She laughed beneath his mouth, her breath mingling with his. Her teeth nipped his lower lip, the sensual sting sending his blood racing.

"With pleasure," she said, her body melting into his.

Did you miss the other books in Caroline's fabulous series?

The Deadliest Sin

Dark Dreams

They had haunted Julia Woolcott all her life, but the strangest of all began with an invitation to a scandalous house party, and a game more dangerously arousing than any she'd ever imagined.

Unbound Desires

Driven by his ruthless ambition, Alexander Strathmore would do anything to come face-to-face with the mystery man who'd challenged him to first decauch Julia, then destroy her.

Deadly Sins

A wild shot . . . a frantic carriage ride through the night . . . a forbidden seduction. Rakehell adventurer and sheltered spinster, Alexander and Julia will break every rule of propriety to chase down their nemesis and consummate their unlikely passion.

The air was like a heavy linen sheet pressed against Julia's face, yet a cold sweat plastered her chemise and dress to her body. It was peculiar, the ability to retreat into herself, away from the pain numbing her leg and away from the threat that lay outside that suffocating room.

A few moments, an hour, or a day passed. She found herself seated, her limbs trembling from the effort. Guilt choked her, a tide of nausea threatening to sweep away the tattered edges of her self-regard. Why had she ignored Meredith's warnings and accepted Wadsworth's invitation to photograph his country estate? Flexing her stiff fingers, Julia felt for the ground beneath her. A film of dust gathered under her nails. If she could push herself higher, lean against a wall, allow the blood to flow . . .

The pain in her leg was a strange solace, as were thoughts of Montfort—her refuge and the splendid seclusion where her life with her sister and her aunt had begun. She could remember nothing else; her early childhood was an empty canvas, bleached of memories. Lady Meredith Woolcott had offered a universe unto itself. Protected, guarded, secure—for a reason.

Julia's mouth was dry. She longed for water to wash away her remorse. New images crowded her thoughts, taking over the darkness in bright bursts of recognition. Meredith and

Rowena waving to her from the green expanse of lawn at Montfort. The sun dancing on the tranquil pond in the east gardens. Meredith's eyes, clouded with worry, that last afternoon in the library. Warnings that were meant to be heeded. Secrets that were meant to be kept. Wise counsel from her aunt that Julia had chosen, in her defiance, to ignore.

She ran a shaking hand through the shambles of her hair, her bonnet long discarded somewhere in the dark. She pieced together her shattered thoughts. When had she arrived? Last evening or days ago? A picture began to form. Her carriage had clattered up to a house with a daunting silhouette, all crenellations and peaks. Chandeliers glittered coldly into the gathering dusk. The entryway had been brightly lit, the air infused with the perfume of decadence, sultry and heavy. That much she could remember before her mind clamped shut.

The world tilted and she ground her nails into the stone beneath her palms for balance. She should be sobbing but her eyes were sandpaper dry. Voices echoed in the dark, or were they footsteps? She strained her ears and craned her neck, peering into the thick darkness. She sensed vibrations more than sounds. Footsteps, actual or imagined, would do her no good.

She felt the floor around her, imagining rotted wood and broken stone. Logic told her there had to be an entranceway. Taking a deep breath, she twisted onto her left hip, arms flailing to find purchase to heave herself into a standing position. Not for the first time in her life, she cursed her heavy skirts, entangling her legs. If she could at least stand . . . She pushed herself up on her right elbow, wrestling aside her skirts with an impatient hand. The fabric tore, the sound muffled in the darkness. The white-hot pain no longer mattered, nor did the bile flooding her throat. Gathering her legs beneath her, she pushed herself up, swaying like a mad marionette without the security of strings.

She held her breath. The silence was complete. Arms outstretched, her hands clutched at air. No wall. Nothing to lean on. Just one small step, one after the other, and she would encounter a wall, a door, something. She bit back a silent plea. Hadn't Meredith taught them long ago about the uselessness of prayer?

Suddenly, her palms were halted by the sensation of solid muscle. Instinctively, she stopped, convinced that she was losing her mind. She felt the barely perceptible rise and fall of a chest beneath her opened palms.

Where there had been only black, there was a shower of stars in front of her eyes and a humming in her head. She saw him, without the benefit of light or the quick trace of her fingers, behind her unseeing eyes.

She took a step back in the darkness away from the man who wanted her dead.

The Darkest Sin

Desperate Deceptions

Lord James Rushford is the only man in London who can lead Rowena Woolcott to the villain who has been tormenting her family for years, and she will stop at nothing to enlist his help. Even if she must pretend to play a dangerously enticing role: his mistress.

Shadowed Secrets

Rushford has demons of his own—a dark past that haunts his memories. Yet the temptation that Rowena presents is more than he can resist.

Relentless Desire

Claiming to be lovers should not be so easy—or feel so achingly appealing. But as Rushford ushers Rowena through London's most elite clubs and sinister underworlds, truth and fantasy blur. And as the threat to Rowena grows near, the masquerade of passion begins to feel startlingly real . . .

R owena Woolcott was cold, so very cold.

She dreamed that she was on her horse, flying through the countryside at Montfort, a heavy rain drenching them both to the skin, hooves and mud sailing through the sodden air. Then a sudden stop, Dragon rearing in fright, before a darkness so complete that Rowena knew she had died.

When she awakened, it was to the sound of an anvil echoing in her head and the feeling of bitter fluid sliding down her throat. She kept her eyes closed, shutting out the daggered words in the background.

"Faron will not rest—"

"The Woolcott women—"

"One of his many peculiar fixations . . . they are to suffer . . . and then they are to die."

"Meredith Woolcott believed she could hide forever."

Phrases, lightly accented in French, drifted in and out of Rowena's head, at one moment near and the next far away. Time merged and coalesced, a series of bright lights followed by darkness, then the sharp retort of a pistol shot. And her sister's voice, calling out to her.

The cold permeated her limbs, pulling down her heavy skirts into watery depths. She tried to swim but her arms and legs would not obey, despite the fact that she had learned as a child in the frigid lake at Montfort. She did not sink like a stone, weighted by her corset and shift and riding boots, because it seemed as though strong hands found her and held her aloft, easing her head above the current trying to force water down her throat and into her lungs.

She dreamed of those hands, sliding her into dry, crisp sheets, enveloping her in a seductive combination of softness and strength. She tossed and turned, a fever chafing her blood, her thoughts a jumble of puzzle pieces vying for attention.

Drifting into the fog, she imagined that she heard steps, the door to a room opening, then the warmth of a body shifting beneath the sheets. She felt the heat, *his heat*, like a cauldron, a furnace toward which she turned her cold flesh. Her womb was heavy and her breasts ached as he slid into her slowly, infinitely slowly, the hugeness of him filling the void that was her center.

Was it one night or a lifetime of nights? Or an exquisite, erotic dream? Spooned with her back against his body, Rowena felt him hard and deep within her. She slid her hip against a muscular thigh, aware of him beginning to move within her once again. She savored the wicked mouth against the skin of her neck, pleasured by the slow slide of his lips. Losing herself in his deliberate caress, she reveled in his hands cupping and stroking, his fingers slipping into the shadows and downward to lightly tease her swollen, sensitized flesh.

"Stay here . . . with me," he whispered, breath hot in her ear.

And she did. For one night or a lifetime of nights, she would never know.